RUNNING STRONG

AN LCR ELITE NOVEL

BY CHRISTY REECE

Running Strong

An LCR Elite Novel

Published by Christy Reece

Cover Art by Patricia Schmitt/Pickyme

Copyright 2019 by Christy Reece

ISBN: 978-1-7337257-1-2

To obtain permission to excerpt portions of the text, please contact the author at Christy@christyreece.com.

RUNNING STRONG

When passion meets destiny, the consequences can be fatal

Having seen the worst of humanity, Raphael Sanchez has always wanted to make a difference in the world. Years ago, Last Chance Rescue saved him from certain death, and from that moment, his primary goal was to become an LCR operative. Now an Elite operative, Raphael lives his dream daily, rescuing victims from horrific circumstances.

Giselle Reddington barely remembers the life she once lived and desperately wants to forget the life she chose. She lives for only one goal, has only one focus. Last Chance Rescue is her last hope, her only hope. Though terrified of the secrets that will be revealed, she has no choice but to ask for their help.

Raphael and Giselle were once in love, but fate ripped them apart. Now they must reunite for a mission neither of them imagined. To Raphael, this is the most important rescue mission of his life. For Giselle, there is no life if the mission fails.

The forces of evil can carry deadly consequences, and innocence can be lost beneath the heavy load. But Last Chance Rescue was created for times such as these, and there's no one better to rescue the innocent and wreak havoc on the wicked.

The only thing necessary for the triumph of evil is for good men to do nothing.

~Edmund Burke

PROLOGUE

Charlottesville, Virginia

Dear Raphael, I'm so very sorry.

Ugh. That was a terrible way to start a farewell letter—even a fake one. But she was sorry, so very sorry.

Dear Raphael, by the time you read this I'll be gone.

Even worse! And she wanted to be a journalist? She could practically hear the sarcasm in Professor Sanderson's smoke-graveled voice. *Speak from the heart, Giselle, but use cool, sound logic to make your point.*

Cool, sound logic? In the face of disaster? Of heartbreak? Not possible.

Raphael, I can't be with you.

Okay, a little better. But tell him what you're really feeling.

I'm dying inside. My soul is crushed, my heart is broken. There aren't enough tears in the world to overcome this pain.

And then: *Oh, Raphael, please don't hate me!*

Giselle Reddington blew out a frustrated sigh. That might be exactly how she felt, but revealing the truth would do no one any good. She had to end things quickly, cleanly. The thought of causing Raphael pain sliced her heart open, shredding it to pieces. Doing so in a letter was a coward's way out, but she had no other choice. If she told him the truth—what she was doing and why—he wouldn't let her do it alone. It was as simple as that. He would, in fact, do everything to prevent her from leaving without him, even sacrificing himself to do so. She could not, would not, allow that. He was the love of her life. It was time to show him that love by letting him go.

A quick glance at the clock told her she was running out of time, she had to get this done. Her pen slashed across the paper, and as the words spilled out in a gush of emotion, she gave him everything.

Exhausted from pouring her heart and soul onto the pages, she folded the letter and slipped it into an envelope. Scrawling Raphael's name on the front, she slid the small packet into a cubbyhole on the desk.

And then she did the right thing, the noble thing. She wrote another letter. This one was easier. Who knew she was such a great liar? Maybe she should try her hand at fiction, since not an ounce of what she'd written was real.

She sealed the letter, wrote Raphael's name on the front, and placed it beside the thicker envelope. She would retrieve them later.

She looked at the clock again. Dread and giddy anticipation were incongruent emotions but fit this moment perfectly. He would be home soon.

Not a day went by that she didn't want to hug herself in sheer joy for being with a man like Raphael Sanchez. Honorable. Disciplined. Compassionate. Courageous. All the things she'd always wanted in a life partner were embodied in the man she loved. That would never change.

Other things were changing, though, and she'd had a decision to make. A painful one. One she'd never thought she'd have to face. If she made the choice she wanted—the selfish one—it would destroy his dreams, completely annihilate every plan he'd made for his future. If she made the choice based on love alone, she would let him go and never see him again.

Heaven help her, she didn't want to let him go.

The last year and a half had been both nightmarish and glorious. The father she had adored, had always looked up to as a man of strength and integrity, was a monster. Everything she'd thought she knew about him had been a lie. Stanford Reddington was a human trafficker, responsible for the kidnapping and selling of humans as if they were merchandise. That knowledge alone made her hate him, but she had learned so much more…much more than she thought she could bear. Her mother had been his first victim.

Sarah Reddington was the strongest, most courageous person Giselle knew. How she had been able to maintain her sanity was a miracle. The fact that she had raised four children and had done everything she could to shield them from the fiend was nothing short of phenomenal.

Justice had finally caught up with Reddington. He had stood trial and been convicted of a plethora of vile deeds. Nothing could make up for the pain he'd caused, but it was a good start—a new beginning.

Her mother was a changed person. Finally free from the monster who had raped and abused her for years, she had a new light in her eyes. No, not everything had turned out as they'd hoped. Sarah had gone back to her childhood home to find that both her parents had died years ago. At first, her grief had been inconsolable, but she had come a long way in recovery. She had been living a new life, with a bright, new future ahead of her.

And now this.

It should have been done, finished. Evil should have been conquered. Good should have triumphed.

But Giselle was coming to realize something. Evil never died. It might be suppressed for a while, diminished for a time. But then evil bloomed again, reborn into a different shape, a new way to cause destruction.

Evil continued to thrive.

Raphael had been her light in the darkness. Falling in love had always seemed like a nebulous, far-reaching goal. She, like her mother, younger brother, and sister, had been locked away on Reddington's island. Meeting anyone remotely eligible should have been impossible. If she had one thing she could thank Stanford Reddington for, it was bringing Raphael to the island. Reddington had believed Raphael wanted to learn about business from him, but Raphael had instead orchestrated the entire scenario to bring Reddington to justice.

From the moment Giselle had set eyes on Raphael, she had been entranced. Yes, he had been one of the few young men she'd ever met, but that hadn't been the reason. And yes, he was tall, broad-shouldered, and unbelievably beautiful with golden-bronzed skin, thick, ink-black hair, and eyes the color of rich, dark chocolate with just a hint of gold in their depths. His looks had drawn her to him, but his character, the man he was on the inside, made her fall in love with him. In her world, strength, courage, and gentleness were rare combinations. Raphael embodied those and so much more.

Their connection had been instantaneous. Behind his handsome face and gorgeous smile, she had recognized a kindred spirit. What had begun in deception had developed into the deepest and most heartfelt emotions she had ever experienced.

After Reddington's arrest, Raphael had been there for her. Every step of the way, he had been the hero she'd often dreamed about.

She understood so many things that were once a mystery. Love overwhelmed her, swept through her in a tidal wave of feelings and emotions she'd never known existed. Poetry now made sense. Songs that once seemed a mass of sentimental silliness now touched her heart.

Love did that, she supposed. Made the incomprehensible easy to understand. She also understood that Raphael's happiness meant more to her than her own.

She tried to console herself that the happiness she had experienced had been unexpected and therefore all the more special. She had never believed she'd be able to attend a university. To see other cities, other cultures. She had thrived, glorying in the new and different.

Thanks to Noah McCall, leader of Last Chance Rescue, she and Raphael were in college together. They were experiencing life, learning and growing. Each day was a new adventure, and they were living their best lives. Together.

And now all of that was about to end.

Headlights swept across the window, and despite all the pain of tomorrow, her heart leaped for the now. He was home.

She barely breathed as she waited. At last, the door opened and he walked inside. Spotting her by the window, he gave her *the look*—the one that melted her insides and caused her heart to pound uncontrollably. His smile…his smile reflected all the things she felt. She wanted to jump into his arms, wrap herself in his warmth, in his strength. He was everything to her. She loved her family dearly, but Raphael…Raphael was her heart.

She ground her teeth until her jaw ached. Raphael was so good to her. When her life became a tumultuous sea, he was her rock. She leaned on him, and he was her strength. Now it was time for her to be the strong one. She was coming to realize that love often meant sacrifice, and she was about to make the biggest one she could ever imagine making.

A gentle, teasing light twinkled in his eyes. "Something smells good."

"Just a little something I cooked up in between poli sci and English lit."

He grinned. "Crock-Pot?"

"Best invention ever."

Needing to be in his arms every second until she had to leave, she ran to him and threw herself into his embrace. As his arms closed around her, she breathed a sigh. This was home. She might go far away, but Raphael's arms would always be where she belonged.

For several seconds, they held each other. What they had was special. Even without having had any previous relationships, Giselle already knew that. Love didn't always have to grow through months or years. Sometimes, love was love from the very beginning.

And in just a few hours, she would have to say goodbye to that love forever.

Holding her close, Raphael blew out a silent sigh as his tense muscles relaxed. For some reason, he had been worried about her today. His concentration skills were excellent, but today he had been distracted…something hammered at his subconscious. His gut was usually right on the money, but seeing Giselle, having her in his arms, right where she belonged, erased the worry. She was here, with him. Everything was fine.

Her head on his chest, she snuggled against him. "I've missed you."

"Five hours since you've been in my arms. That's too damn long."

"Much too long," she agreed.

He frowned as he felt the faint tremble in her body. "You're shivering. Everything all right?"

"You make me shiver."

"In a good way? Yes?"

Pulling away, she smiled up at him. His Giselle, the love of his life. How had he gotten so lucky?

"A very good way." Stretching up on her toes, she gave him a quick kiss and tried to pull away.

"Uh-uh, not enough. Not nearly enough." Bringing her back to his mouth, he spoke against her lips. "Let's see if I can make you shiver even more." He kissed her then, the way he'd been dreaming about all day. The way he'd been dreaming about since the last time he'd kissed her. She tasted delicious, like strawberries, cream, and a touch of honey.

While his mouth was busy with her taste, his hands roamed over the soft, gentle curves of her body. At one time, he'd never dreamed he'd have a chance to even kiss her, and now his hands were filled with her, and his lips had kissed every luscious inch of her body. He wanted to devour, relish that he could, savoring that she wanted him as much as he wanted her.

Her body pressing into his told him she was his. Giselle gave freely, loved with all her heart. That she loved him was a miracle. His miracle.

Pulling away, he grinned down at her. "Crock-Pot meals can keep. Right?"

"Like I said, best invention ever."

Tugging on her blouse, he pulled at the buttons, all the while kissing her as if his life depended on it. Sometimes at night, when he was holding her, he felt an odd sort of desperation, as if she couldn't be real. As if this couldn't last. Nothing and no one had ever meant more to him than this one beautiful woman.

Stupid, really. This wasn't like him at all. He was sensible, pragmatic. He had a plan for his life, knew exactly where he was going and what steps he had to take to get there. There was nothing whimsical or fanciful about him, but when it came to Giselle, all of that flew out the window.

With a heart as big as the sky and a spirit as sweet as a summer breeze, Giselle had swept him off his feet. He fell hard the moment he met her and was still falling.

Need washed through every cell in his body, wiping away coherent thought. This was Giselle, his love. His future.

Keeping his mouth on hers, he pushed her toward the bedroom. She giggled softly when she accidentally stepped on his foot. Once they reached the edge of the bed, he stopped, stood back, and just looked at her. From the silky dark fall of her hair to her long, narrow feet, and everything in between, she was pure perfection. Slender, curvy, soft, luscious. He wanted to devour every inch, savor and enjoy her. At the same time, he wanted to take her quickly, the need inside him almost more than he could control.

He slid his hands beneath her shirt, almost groaning at the warm silkiness.

"Raphael?"

"Yes?"

"I love—" She swallowed, tried again. "I love how you love me."

Humbled at the adoration in her eyes, Raphael tamped down the urgency in his body. He wanted to cherish every single inch. With that thought in mind, he gently removed her clothes, tenderly kissing every inch of skin he bared. When she lay before him, beautifully nude and almost squirming with need, he slid his fingers inside her, rolling her gently into and over her first climax. Before she could recover, he quickly pulled his clothes off, hurriedly slid on a condom, and slipped into her warmth.

She wrapped her arms around him, and they moved together as one. Slowly at first, until hot need consumed them both. As she gave herself totally to him, he thought about how lucky he was. He had never believed in luck, but he couldn't deny its existence now. They were together, the way they were meant to be.

Nothing and no one could ever tear them apart.

***

The honking of geese doing a flyover above the apartment pulled him from the deepest sleep he'd had in a while. Even without looking at the clock, he knew it was late. Throwing his feet to the floor, Raphael stood and stretched. He'd overslept. The memory of why made him smile. After dinner, they'd returned to the bedroom, where they'd stayed awake most of the night—laughing, talking, making love, making plans.

Something was bothering Giselle, though. She had explained it away with the excuse of being tired. That hadn't been it. He believed he knew what it was and had every intention of fixing it soon. Neither he nor Giselle were the type of people to sleep with someone they weren't committed to long term. Even though he had told her he loved her, and she had said the same, he knew she wanted more. So did he. They hadn't talked about the future. With both of them still in college—she was a freshman and he was a sophomore—getting married wasn't the most sensible thing to do. And while he prided himself on being practical, practicality in this went out the window. This was Giselle—he loved her, body and soul. He wanted a permanent commitment. This weekend, he was going to propose. He was one hundred percent sure she would say yes.

After he graduated college, he would fulfill his dream and become an LCR operative. He and Noah had already had the discussion. That part of his future was securely mapped out.

Giselle had shown an interest in journalism right away. Maybe it was because of her upbringing. She had been denied the basic right to be informed, to know the truth of what was happening in the world. It only made sense that she would want to pursue what had previously been kept from her.

They had separate career goals, but when it came to each other, they had the same goal—they wanted to be together. Forever.

Noting Giselle's purse that she normally left on the dresser was gone, he thought about how tired she must be. She had an early class today, but could hopefully come home after it was over and take a nap. It was his turn to make dinner tonight, and he was planning to go to the grocery store before he went to his afternoon class.

After showering, he threw his clothes on from last night and headed to the kitchen. Coffee first, and then he'd—

The doorbell stopped him midstride. Detouring, he headed to the living room to open the door and was more than a little surprised to see Noah McCall standing there. The LCR leader had recently moved to Virginia with his family, but he rarely stopped by without calling first.

Raphael's quick smile of welcome dropped away immediately at Noah's solemn expression. "What's wrong?"

"Can I come in?"

"Of course...sure." Raphael backed away, his heart still at a steady beat, but a growing dread was spreading through him.

"Sarah called me yesterday."

Having Giselle's mother call Noah wasn't that unusual. They had become friends over the last couple of years. Still, Raphael could see that the call had disturbed Noah. "Is she okay?"

"Yes and no."

McCall was obviously struggling with words. Whatever it was, it couldn't be worse than what Raphael was imagining.

"Just spit it out."

"Reddington's made some threats. Sarah and the children are going into the WITSEC program."

His heart sank like a stone. Sarah's testimony had put Reddington behind bars. Her agreement with the prosecutor's office had been that if Reddington made credible threats to her or her family at any time, they would be put into witness protection.

"Why now? He's in prison...never going to get out. What's the point?"

"His last appeal was denied yesterday. He's out of options."

Understanding came quick. "All he has left is revenge."

"Exactly."

His jaw clenched with fury at what the bastard continued to put Sarah and Giselle through. Knowing there was no other option for them, he asked, "So when do we leave?"

At the look on Noah's face, an icy chill swept through Raphael.

"Noah," he said hoarsely, "where is Giselle?"

Instead of answering, Noah held out an envelope with Raphael's name on it in Giselle's handwriting.

Grabbing it from his hand, Raphael ripped it open and withdrew a single sheet of paper. Denial beat a heavy drum inside his head even while he read the words she began with:

Raphael, it's been fun.

CHAPTER ONE

Seven years later
Birchwood Sanitarium
Trenton, Vermont

Screams. Screams. They surrounded her, inside her head, outside in the darkness. Everywhere. Her hands covered her ears, tried to muffle the sounds. They wouldn't go away. Was it her? Was she the one screaming?

She touched her mouth, thankful that it was closed, that she wasn't the one making that hideous sound.

Her eyes darted left and right, the terrible dread filling her once again. They would be coming soon. With their fake smiles and devious plans. Why didn't they just kill her and get it over with? Did they expect her to take care of it for them? Do the deed herself so they would have fewer questions to answer?

She refused to give them that satisfaction.

She dropped her hands and stared down at them, almost surprised to see that they were soft, slender. A young person's hands. How could they belong to her? She felt old, ancient.

Odd that she could have these coherent thoughts now, but then when they came, with their fake smiles and little pills, her mind would go cloudy, and she would drift away once again, forget. She searched for more of that coherency, clawed through the thick, dark clouds of her mind. The answer was there. She just needed to reach out and grab hold.

When the darkness came again, as it inevitably would, when she knew nothing and no one, she would close her eyes and see a man. She couldn't describe him, but she knew his face as if he was imprinted on her heart and soul. Why couldn't her mind hold the image? All she could truly remember were his eyes. They were dark, deep, beautiful. Full of warmth and compassion. Love. Gentleness and humor often glimmered in the dark, golden depths. They were eyes you could fall into, drown, and be reborn. Who they belonged to and what this man meant to her, she had no idea. She only knew she wanted to get to him, find him, and forget this nightmare she was living.

A door slammed shut, and she jerked up on the bed, her heart thundering with awful anticipation. They would be coming soon. Another meal laced with drugs. Another pill. Another beverage tainted with something noxious. They liked to mix it up, keep her guessing, but it was all for one purpose, one reason. They wanted to destroy her. When would it end? Why didn't they just do the deed and get it over with?

No, no, no. A sob built up in her chest, and she wrestled it back down. There was someone waiting for her, someone who needed her. She didn't know who or why. She only knew she had to get out of here. Someone was depending on her, and she could not, would not, fail.

A scream like that of a banshee sounded only a few feet from her door. The cry echoed in her soul. She wanted to join in, to scream and beat her fists against the walls until they stopped, until they listened. But she wouldn't let loose. No...no. They couldn't know that she was having these odd moments of clarity. They pretended...they lied. They acted like they cared. No one did. Not even the man with the beautiful eyes. She was alone... completely alone.

Another scream sounded. Men shouted. Lights flared all around her. More screams. The madhouse had erupted!

Voices sounded outside, close-by. She shuffled as quickly as she could to the door. They rarely spoke in the hallway, but tonight they were vocal.

"What the hell's going on? Everybody's gone crazy."

"What else did you expect in a place like this?"

"Tonight's worse."

"It's the full moon."

"That's a crock of shit."

"No, it's not. I've worked here for almost a year. Happens a lot. Even though most of the crazies can't see the moon, they know it's full. It's like it calls to them."

"Sounds like you've been here too long."

"You got that right. Depressing as hell, but the pay's all right. As long as we keep 'em drugged and out of everyone's way, everybody's happy."

"Except these poor fools."

"Yeah. Well. Shit happens and all that."

Another voice, this one female and authoritative, snapped, "Hey, you two. You want to stop gossiping and actually do some work around here?"

The two men mumbled some curses and moved away from her door.

The crazies.

Was she one of them? Had she been put here because she had a mental illness? She didn't feel mentally ill. But did people with a mental illness recognize they were sick? Or did they rely on others to tell them?

If she was sick, had she agreed to come here, or had someone brought her here? No. No. They hated her. Wanted her dead. Who? Who hated her? Who wanted her dead?

Why couldn't she remember? She pulled at her hair, barely registering the pain. Looking down, she noted her clothing—soft, loose pants, a long-sleeved T-shirt, thin, white slippers on her feet. The clothes hung from her body. Were they the wrong size to start with or had she lost a lot of weight?

Her hands slid beneath her shirt. Her ribs were prominent, her stomach concave, her hipbones protruding. This wasn't right. She felt like she was touching a stranger's body.

She glanced around the room. Usually, it was so dim in here, she could barely make out her surroundings, but for some reason the lights glowed brighter tonight. A hospital bed was against one wall. Beside it was a nightstand holding a plastic cup and a water pitcher. A thin, blue robe lay on the bed. A toilet sat in the corner. There was a bookshelf with some books along the wall. She shuffled closer. Picking up the most interesting-looking one, she flipped through pages and then dropped the book, panicked. She grabbed the next one, then another. The books were fake, the pages blank. There was nothing in them. Why would she have fake books on her shelf?

Panic spiked again, and though she did everything she could, she couldn't stifle it this time. She had to get out of here!

A cacophony of noises spiraled up around her, whirled inside her brain, making her head hurt. Were they outside, or were they all in her mind? She tugged at her hair again. A shrill, ear-piercing siren ripped through the air. She slapped her hands over her ears. Too loud, too loud. It was too much.

The door to her room opened. A large man stood there. He wore white and was holding a tray. More drugs, more things to make her forget. Forget what? How could she forget what she didn't remember? She laughed…she didn't know. She laughed harder, feeling free, not caring that the sound was like the cackling of a demented witch.

"There, there," the man said in a soft, soothing tone. "Take this, and the noises in your head will disappear. Everything will be fine."

Was he right? Was all of this in her head? Would the noises stop if she did what he said?

He took her hand and placed a white pill on her palm. It was deceptively small. The power this small pill had was breathtaking, mind-blowing…mind-stealing. It would suck her soul from her body, make her disappear. Soon she would no longer exist. And they would be happy. Who? Who would be happy?

No. No. No.

A voice screeched outside the room. The man turned slightly to look behind him. She didn't think, she acted. Grabbing hold of the nightstand behind her, she swung with all her might. She heard the thud. The vibration of the impact to his head went through her body. With a small grunt, the man dropped to the floor. She hurriedly rifled through his pockets. Came up with a wallet, candy bar, and, sweet heaven, keys!

She raced to the door and into the hallway. People were everywhere. Were they the crazies or the not-crazies? Was there a difference?

She darted through the milling crowd. Some were sobbing, others screaming. A few shouted and cursed. She made eye contact with no one…just kept moving.

A door several feet away caught her attention. Something told her if she got through that door, she would be home free.

"Stop!"

She didn't turn, didn't stop. If they caught her, they would kill her.

Her legs pumped faster and faster. She had to do it, had to make it. There was someone out there for her. Someone she loved…needed to protect. Who, she didn't know. She only knew if she didn't escape tonight, she would never have another chance.

Her breath heaved as her lungs worked to full capacity. She could feel them behind her, hear their warnings. With all her remaining strength, she gave it her all and reached for the door. Jamming a key into the lock, she twisted. It wouldn't work. Swallowing a panicked sob, she tried another. Then another. They were coming toward her, yelling at her. *Please, oh please, oh please. Let the next one work.* She shoved in the key. It worked! The door swung open, and she ran. She couldn't stop. She wouldn't stop until she was in the open, away from here.

She raced down the stairway. One flight, two flights. When would it end? They were behind her. She could hear them running. Hear them shouting. Their hot breath was practically on her neck.

Her lungs ached, her endurance depleted. She fell forward and tumbled down the stairway, landing on the harsh, unforgiving tile floor. Pain was secondary to desperation. Bumps and bruises, even broken bones would not stop her.

Ugly, ungodly sounds surrounded her, and she knew they came from her. Part wailing, part rasping breaths. Her lungs felt as though they could explode any moment. Ignoring all the pain, she surged to her feet. A brief look around showed her another door with a bright red Exit sign only a few feet away. Sobbing her relief, she hobbled toward the door, pushed.

The door slammed shut behind her. Darkness surrounded her. The only light was the brightness of the moon above her. She was outside!

For the first time in she didn't know how long, she was breathing fresh air. But she couldn't stop and appreciate any of it. Just because she was outside didn't mean she was safe.

Thankful for the brightness provided by the moon, she followed a rocky trail that led into the woods. She would have to go on foot until she was far away. She had no plans after that. For right now, her only goal was to get as far away from this place as possible.

As she stumbled into the woods, she looked over her shoulder. The night was clear, and the moon was indeed full, allowing her to see what she had escaped. A building, at least ten stories high, spiraled toward the sky. Surrounded only by deep, thick woods, it was austere and isolated. Whatever the place was, it was evident that it was meant to be hidden, meant to stay hidden.

When she had time…when she was safe, she would sit down and think. She had so many questions, so many things she didn't know, couldn't remember. One question burned in her brain above all others. She fought for the answer and almost cried when she couldn't come up with one. Who was she?

CHAPTER TWO

Bucaramanga, Colombia

Raphael swatted at the biggest mosquito he'd ever seen. Damn thing had to be on steroids. The mosquito repellant he'd sprayed on a few hours ago had melted off in the stifling heat, but he wasn't sure that would have deterred these bloodsuckers. When he got back to camp, he'd be dousing his entire body with anti-itch ointment and alcohol.

He glanced over at Brennan Sinclair, one of his partners for this particular mission. Rivulets of sweat rolled down the man's face. Raphael huffed out a small laugh when Brennan growled softly as he, too, backhanded one of the giant bloodsucking insects.

Hearing his amusement, Brennan glanced over at him and grinned. Even as miserable as they were, he knew that neither one of them wanted to be anywhere else at this moment. They were about to bring down some major shit on some very bad people and rescue a truckload of kidnapped victims. Didn't get much better than that

Sinclair had come to LCR a few years back, before Raphael came on board. Brennan Sinclair was dedicated to saving lives, just as he was. Rescuing innocents no matter the cost was LCR's motto.

More than once he'd heard Sinclair say that LCR had not only saved his sanity but had brought him the love of his life. Sinclair was married to one of the world's top models, and as a former NFL player he likely didn't need to work. If there was one thing Raphael had learned, though—LCR operatives didn't do this job for money. The money was good, but there were a lot of easier ways to pay the bills.

He'd come to LCR in a different way. Once a victim…one whom LCR rescued. And from that moment, being an LCR operative had been his number one goal. Working for Last Chance Rescue in any capacity would have been an honor. To be an Elite operative was beyond his wildest imaginings.

Hadn't been easy, but as McCall had told him more than once, nothing worthwhile ever was. The man should know. The LCR founder hadn't had an easy road either, but the things he'd been able to accomplish inspired Raphael. Thanks to Noah McCall and LCR, he found a family and his destiny.

Whoever said dreams didn't come true was wrong. You just had to work your ass off to get there.

Sure, there had been some bumps along the way. Things he'd wanted that hadn't worked out the way he had thought they would. He still thought of her on occasion, the girl he'd once loved. That had been a tough time, one he wouldn't relive for all the money in the world. But that was life. You took the good with the bad.

Seven years was a long time to pine for something that hadn't been real in the first place. They'd both been young, too damn young to make life-altering decisions. They were both older now, and hopefully wiser. They likely wouldn't even look twice at each other if given another chance.

Not that he would ever see her again. She was married now, probably had a kid or two. He hadn't checked. Didn't want to know. Checking would have been a weakness, an indication that he wasn't over her. He was. Had been for years. It was done.

His life was full, he had what he needed. Family, friends, and the best damn job in the world. Someday he'd give some thought to settling down, but for right now, he was exactly where he wanted to be.

"See some activity headed your way. Looks like two vans and a couple of SUVs." The voice that came through the earbud was that of operative Jake Mallory. He and his partner, Angela Delvecchio, were parked in a truck about a quarter mile down the main road.

"About damn time." Discomfort was obvious in Aidan Thorne's growl. Raphael couldn't blame him. While he couldn't say anyone was in a comfortable position, Thorne had the worst of it physically, as he was in the trunk of an abandoned rust-bucket car just outside the compound. Good thing the guy wasn't claustrophobic.

"I agree." The soft voice of Olivia Gates revealed the tension she likely felt. While everyone outside battled mosquitoes and stifling humidity, Olivia and Elite operative Sabrina Fox were inside the compound dealing with subhuman turds. They'd definitely drawn the short end of the straw. Dealing with blood-sucking insects was a damn sight more pleasant than having to associate with the scum who kidnapped and sold people for a living. Couldn't get much lower than that.

The op was months in the making. Knowing a human trafficking ring existed and actually being able to infiltrate and bring it down took planning, coordination, and a whole lot of luck.

The first phase had begun three months ago with gathering intel. Two tech analysts had worked around the clock, digging deep to find the head of the organization. The group was both well organized and well funded—one of the largest LCR had encountered. The entire Elite team, along with LCR operative Dylan Savage, was involved in this mission.

Deep cover was Savage's forte. In the dark underworld, lives were bartered with or destroyed on a whim. It was in this world where John Wheeler, Dylan's undercover persona, existed. Dylan created the identity years ago to bring down Stanford Reddington and had maintained Wheeler's reputation of sleaze and filth for operations such as this one.

There was no one better at deep cover. Period. It was a testament to Savage's strength and fortitude that he was able to work with such garbage and still remain a decent human being. Raphael figured Jamie, Dylan's wife, had a lot to do with that. More than once, Raphael had heard the man refer to Jamie as his sunshine.

It had surprised him at first, how a hardened, take-no-prisoners man like Dylan could wax poetic like some sixteenth-century bard. Once he got to know him and the other members of LCR, he came to understand one thing—family was everything to LCR.

McCall set the tone for the organization. Though totally devoted to Last Chance Rescue and the work they did, McCall made it clear that family was the most important thing in his life.

"Listen up, boys and girls. John Wheeler just notified the house that more guests will join the party. Three more than expected."

"The head asshole?" Thorne asked.

"Not sure yet. Doubt we'll be that lucky this soon. Probably just more muscle. Likely in prep for the big kahuna coming later on. Either way, keep on your toes. Gonna be a helluva party once everyone arrives."

The calm tone of Sabrina Fox's voice made Raphael smile. She had been with a covert government agency before coming to LCR and had nerves of steel. Not only was she in charge of this op, but she and Olivia had been able to infiltrate the group, pulling out information with the precision of skilled surgeons extracting a bullet. The operation was a delicate one, but Sabrina had the chops for the job.

The plan was to lie low until the main man, referred to only as "the boss," arrived. Their intel indicated that he inspected each shipment himself at what was apparently called the "processing plant."

The evil that one person could do to others didn't surprise him…hadn't for a long time. He'd been in the midst of evil too many times. What he did know, what he knew to his soul, was that there was goodness that counteracted that evil. Sometimes it didn't seem that way. Sometimes it looked like evil would win. That all the shit in the world would take over and nothing good could survive. And that was the reason he wanted to work for Last Chance Rescue. Good did exist. It occasionally took everything you had and then some to fight for it, but it damn well existed.

Like this op. They would grab the main asshole and his scumbag employees. One more human trafficking ring shut down, dozens of innocents saved. One more win on the side of good.

"Okay, listen up." Fox's voice was as calm as before but now held a new tone of seriousness. "Looks like the boss is riding along with the shipment after all. Stay alert. Execute on my command."

Raphael shared a look of affirmation with Sinclair. Yeah, they were more than ready.

The plan was to wait until everyone was within the compound walls. Saving innocents was always their number one priority. As much as they wanted the leader and his people, they were secondary to the mission. Each operative had an assignment. His and Sinclair's was the same—over the wall, go in from the back, neutralize the threat.

They listened as trucks drove through the gate. Voices shouted, demanded. More shouting. Waiting was hard, the hardest part of the job. He wanted to run into the melee and take these bastards down. That would accomplish nothing and likely get him and maybe his teammates killed.

He waited, adrenaline spiked with determination, tempered by experience and skill.

"And we are a go," Fox said softly.

Raphael took off. Sinclair ran alongside him.

Ten yards in front of them stood a whitewashed brick wall. The alarm system had complicated things. The only time the alarm could be disarmed was by the person who controlled the system at an unknown location. Until security was shut down, no one could enter or exit without setting the thing off. However, as soon as the caravan of vehicles approached, the system would be disarmed. That gave them a window of about forty-two seconds. Raphael and Sinclair made the most of it.

Another good thing—the wall was about twelve feet high, so it was an easy up and over. Raphael threw his rappel cord over the top. Once hooked, he tugged hard, ensuring himself a good hold. He climbed quickly. Sinclair, only a few feet away, was one step ahead of him. They reached the top, secured more rope, and went down the other side just as quickly.

The stark emptiness of the backyard told them this place wasn't used for anything other than business. All trees and bushes had been ruthlessly cut down, leaving absolutely no cover. They'd need to move fast to avoid detection. They both hit the ground running.

Raphael went east, Sinclair headed west. The plan was to keep everyone outside, taking them before they could rabbit into the mansion. With thirty or so rooms, there were way too many places to hide.

Staying low, he stopped at the edge of the structure and peered around the corner. The area was large, flat, and open. An old fountain sat in the middle of the courtyard. The mother and child statue, crumbling and decayed, was the perfect imagery for what took place here. Lives were destroyed, innocence lost.

Other than the fountain, there was nothing else in the courtyard where anyone could hide. The area was designed to load and unload cargo, with no options for hiding or escaping. He didn't have to imagine the despair one would feel stepping down from the truck and seeing no hope for escape anywhere in sight. He had lived with that hopelessness.

Three SUVs and two transport trucks had rolled through the gate. The smaller vehicles parked on one side, and the large trucks carrying their human cargo parked on the other side.

Men, at least eight of them, piled out of the vehicles. One or two laughed and joked, but most of them wore the solemn look of business on their faces. They were human traffickers, and this was just another day for them.

A gleaming black Mercedes-Benz GLS came through the gate. Raphael held his breath, his eyes keenly focused on the passenger-side door. A luxurious ride like this would hold the boss man. The one who would inspect the "merchandise," approve or disapprove. Decide on the value and ultimately the destination of the stolen women and children.

Three doors opened. A slightly rotund man of medium height, dressed in khaki pants and an eye-piercing lime-green shirt, climbed out on the front passenger side. Since the other men were well-built, mercenary types, dressed in faded jeans and work shirts, Raphael had no problem picking out the head honcho.

Two of the men headed to the back of one of the trucks. Before the door could be unlocked and raised, shrill voices sounded from inside the house. Seconds later, two women stomped out into the courtyard, yelling at each other. The distraction caused every eye to focus on the women.

"You bitch, I told you to stay out of my stuff." The tall, auburn-haired woman lunged toward the slightly shorter, more delicate-looking blonde.

"I didn't touch your stuff!" the blond woman screamed.

Blows were thrown with inelegant precision, landing as sloppy, haphazard slaps. Hair was pulled and half-thrown punches barely skimmed off each other. Neither woman acted as if she'd had the least bit of fighting skill. Since he'd gone up against both of these women in one-on-one training sessions, Raphael knew that was not true. However, the slapping, pinching, and hair-pulling had mesmerized the crowd of men. Just as they'd planned. Not one of them, including the boss man himself, was immune to a good old-fashioned catfight.

No one noticed that five armed strangers dashed inside the compound just before the gates swung closed.

As the two women tried to scratch each other's eyes out, the rest of the team got into position. Thorne, Delvecchio, and Mallory stood between the two transport trucks. Justin Kelly and Riley Ingram crouched behind one of the smaller trucks, close to where the largest group of men and their boss stood. Staying low, Raphael and Sinclair ran to join them.

The two women were still pulling each other's hair, screaming obscenities now. The men continued to stand, laughing, while some called out encouragement or crude suggestions.

As if choreographed by a professional dance instructor, the two women whirled away from each other. Pulling weapons hidden at the small of their backs, they turned in unison, pointing their guns directly at the main boss.

The rest of the LCR team moved in, surrounding all the men. It took a couple seconds before the men realized what was going on. As soon as they did, guns were drawn.

Stepping out into the middle, Sabrina looked directly at the boss man. "You're outnumbered."

"Who the hell are you?"

"Doesn't matter. Only question you need to answer is, do you want to die today?"

"You stupid bitch. Do you know who I am? I can—"

"See, that's where you're wrong. You can't. Now tell your people to drop their weapons, or it's going to get bloody."

His body vibrating with insult, he snapped out an order to the man beside him. "Shoot her."

Before the man could obey or refuse, Sabrina fired at the man's feet, missing his toe by a half inch. The man jumped back, yelping.

"I missed on purpose," Sabrina said coolly. "I won't next time. Drop your weapons. All of you."

His jaw clenched with fury, the man swept his eyes over the yard. Apparently noting that he was indeed surrounded and there was no way out, he gave a grim nod to his men. "Drop your weapons. We will live to fight another day."

Soft growls and harsh curses came from the men, but they thankfully obeyed their boss and dropped their weapons. Raphael didn't let down his guard. These people were the worst of humanity. To trust that they were giving up this easily would be stupid.

Proving his point, one of the men close to the gate took off running toward the back. Raphael called out, "I got him," and loped after him.

Figuring the man would try to get inside the house from the back, Raphael kept his gun at the ready. He jerked to a stop when he spotted the man trying, unsuccessfully, to scramble up the wall.

The man made it two feet before sliding back down. With a vicious curse, the idiot went for it again. If he hadn't needed to get back to the team, Raphael would have taken a few moments to enjoy the show.

Pulling a zip tie from his pocket, he waited until the man slid down the wall again. The instant he touched the ground, Raphael pushed him flat against the wall. "Stay still," he snapped. He grabbed the man's arms, pulled them behind his back, and secured his hands. Taking the man's gun from his holster, he secured it at the small of his back and then pushed the guy forward.

"I did nothing wrong. I am a victim, too."

"Oh yeah? Why'd you have a gun?"

"They…um…" Apparently not able to come up with a good reason for that, he struggled against Raphael's hold.

They headed to the front of the house again. Just as they reached the corner, the shrill shriek of a child burst through the air.

Raphael eyed his prisoner and then mentally shrugged. Muttering a vague apology, he clipped the man's chin, knocking him unconscious. Propping him against the side of the house, he secured his hands to a drainpipe.

Gun at the ready once more, he took off toward the front of the house. The sound of distress he'd heard could have been the cry of one of the already rescued victims, but he could take no chances.

At the corner of the house, he stopped and peered around the corner. The scene was an odd one, almost as if everyone had frozen in time while staring at one horrific image. All eyes were on the man holding a little girl, maybe four or five years old, in front of him, a knife at her throat.

"I will kill her," the man snarled. "Gut her like a fish unless you do what I say."

"You do that," Sabrina said, "you've got no protection. We'll drop you where you stand. You'll be dead in an instant."

"No, I won't. You're not going to let the brat die."

He was right about that. What the asshole didn't know was that LCR practiced this very scenario numerous times. Each operative knew exactly what to do. Protecting the child was the number one priority.

Sneaking up on him slowly was not an option. The man's friends would warn him. He could, however, move fast and take him by surprise. Taking off, he was behind the asshole in seconds. Pressing his gun to the back of the guy's head, Raphael said quietly, "Let the kid go and you'll live. One scratch, just one scratch on her neck, and you're dead in an instant."

Stiff with tension, the man snarled, "You're bluffing. You won't risk the kid getting hurt."

"It's not really a risk. We have a doctor with us. He can save the child's life. You won't be as lucky. Even if you survive a bullet to the back of your skull, we'll do nothing to help you. You'll die in agony, and we'll stand here and watch. Now…drop the knife. Then, very slowly and very gently, hand the child to her mother."

Determining the mother was easy. Though there were several women standing a few yards away, one woman had the same hair color and features and was sobbing uncontrollably as she called out a name.

Several seconds passed, and Raphael was beginning to think the man was going to do something stupid. The child in his arms was whimpering, but thankfully no longer struggling. The large knife stayed at the little girl's neck. Any small movement might nick her skin.

"Don't take the chance, man," Raphael said softly. "Do what your boss told you to do. Live to fight another day. You do not want to die."

Growling curses under his breath, the man dropped the knife. Whirling around, he shoved the little girl toward Raphael. Still holding the gun on the man, Raphael took a one-armed hold of the little girl. Jake Mallory grabbed hold of the asshole, pulled his hands behind his back, and zip-tied his wrists.

Raphael would swear a collective sigh of relief went through the entire area. The little girl was crying hard as she clung to his neck. Before he could take her to her mother, the woman was in front of him in an instant, pulling on her daughter. He released her into her mother's arms.

Stepping back, Raphael took in the scene. Nine men stood in a line, their hands secured behind their backs, each holding an expression of either pure hatred or fury. Several dozen women and children stood near the trucks they'd been transported in, the expressions on their faces running the gamut of emotions. The majority of them looked both exhausted and elated. The hopelessness had disappeared.

Peace swept through Raphael. No doubt about it, he was exactly where he belonged.

CHAPTER THREE

Alexandria, Virginia

"Samara, seriously?" Mary Lyons held up the scarlet-red cocktail dress. "You don't think this looks too…I don't know, bold for me?"

Samara McCall shook her head vehemently. "Absolutely not, Mom. You're going to look fabulous in it. You'll knock Daddy's socks off."

"Hmm. Maybe." Mary walked over to one of the store's full-length mirrors, held the dress up to her body, and turned every which way.

"Why don't you at least try it on?" Samara asked.

"Okay. Can't hurt."

Smiling a little, Samara watched her mom head into the dressing room. This vacation was the first one her parents had been on in years. Samara and her four brothers had given them a sixteen-day European cruise for their fortieth wedding anniversary. It was a trip of a lifetime, and while both her parents had insisted it was way too expensive, they'd been almost beside themselves with excitement.

Sighing with satisfaction, she checked the GPS location of Micah's phone. Her son had texted her a few minutes ago to let her know that he and his sister had arrived home from school. She considered once more if she should call her dad to remind him he had promised to stay with them until she got home. Though Micah was ten years old and sometimes acted twice his age, she didn't like leaving him and his sister by themselves. Her work schedule allowed her to be at home most days when they arrived from school, but when she couldn't, either her mom or dad pitched in.

Given the choice of going shopping with his wife to help her pick out cruise clothes or spending time with Micah and Evie, her dad hadn't hesitated to offer his help. Not only was shopping akin to torture for Sam Lyons, alone time with his grandkids was a treat for him. She knew her dad well. Within five minutes of arriving, he would be loading the kids into his SUV for a trip to their favorite ice cream parlor.

She slid the phone back into her jacket pocket. He wouldn't forget.

Turning, she picked up a dress in one of her mother's favorite colors. As she checked for the right size, she sensed someone watching her. Having been trained to listen to her gut, Samara took a surreptitious glance around. Saw no one. Another person might have dismissed the feeling and moved on. She wasn't that kind of person. She trusted her instincts. Plus, she'd seen too much to not take notice. Something felt off.

She looked up again, this time quickly. And saw him. About five foot ten, weight about one seventy-five, beefy, wide shoulders. Gleaming bald head, shaggy black brows, broad nose that was slightly askew, neatly trimmed black beard. Thirty-five to forty years old. The observations took less than five seconds. Noah

McCall trained all his operatives to observe and assess in this manner. His wife was no different. Something else she noticed was the slight bulk beneath his brown leather jacket. He was armed.

When it came to protecting herself and those she loved, there was no such thing as overreaction. There was protocol for such things. She and Noah had practiced numerous times, as had her children.

Sliding her hand into her jacket pocket for her cellphone, Samara pressed the tiny button on the side that was designed specifically for LCR operatives. It would alert Noah, who would take action. Now she just needed to get her mother out of the store without anyone getting hurt.

***

In a nondescript hotel room fifteen miles away, Noah McCall sat across from a couple requesting LCR's help. Though his office was only a couple of blocks from the hotel, he rarely met new clients at that location. Last Chance Rescue had two main head-quarters—one in Alexandria and another in Paris, France—plus multiple satellite locations throughout the world. All locations were carefully guarded secrets, and only those who could be totally trusted were allowed inside. Noah could already tell these people had a long way to go before he would even remotely trust them.

The man, Ronald Tompkins, was a distinguished-looking gentleman in his late fifties. His dark gray suit was of good quality, his manners refined. He had a demeanor that was polite, if some-what aloof. The young woman with him, Mindy Simmons, was his daughter. In her late twenties, Mindy was conservatively dressed, but the way she continually tugged at her skirt and rearranged her blouse made him think the clothing wasn't typical for her.

The two were requesting LCR's assistance in locating Mindy's husband, David Simmons, who had disappeared in South Korea while on a business trip. They both believed he had been kidnapped and taken across the border to North Korea. As of yet, they hadn't provided any evidence other than vague theories.

"And the last time you talked with him, he said he was fine?" Noah asked.

"Yes, but I know my husband's voice, Mr. McCall. He sounded as though he was under extreme duress."

Though she said all the right words, Mindy didn't appear to be all that upset. There wasn't an ounce of sincerity in her tone. On the other hand, Tompkins appeared just a little too anxious.

Noah freely admitted he wasn't the most trusting of people. He'd seen too much to take a stranger's words for truth. Only those closest to him—his wife, his in-laws, and his LCR employees—received that kind honor.

Tompkins and Simmons had looked good on paper, but those kinds of things were all too easy to fake these days. A good computer hacker could create a whole new person in a matter of minutes.

According to public records, Mindy and David Simmons had been married for three years and had no children. Mindy worked at a large law firm in DC, and her husband worked for a defense contractor. Ronald Tompkins worked as an investment counselor at one of the larger investment firms in the DC area.

On first look, Noah had seen no red flags. While Tompkins had no social media presence, his daughter and son-in-law were on a few sites, with Mindy being more active than David. The Simmons' income was commensurate with their job titles, and they spent slightly above their means, which wasn't unusual in today's materialistic world. Their bank accounts had the normal in-and-out flow of an upper-middle-class couple. They had no significant political leanings, at least publicly, that would indicate radical behavior.

All in all, they were a typical, upwardly moving, young, married couple. The case had intrigued him enough to want this meeting, but doubts arose from the moment he met them.

When he'd talked to Mindy on the phone, she had seemed more mature and worried. But her answers to just the few questions he'd asked so far had him concerned. They were both vague and decidedly canned sounding. Was that her typical way of responding to personal questions? Not everyone was comfortable sharing details of their life with a total stranger. Or was there another reason?

"Have you contacted the company David works for? Do they believe he's in any trouble?"

"That's the problem," Ronald said. "They thought he was on vacation."

That was new information that Mrs. Simmons hadn't told him in their initial phone interview.

He turned his attention to Mindy. "Mrs. Simmons, do you know why—" He jerked at the sound of a chime on his phone. Mara's alert.

He surged to his feet. "I'm sorry. We'll have to reschedule." Noah said the words calmly, but a thousand alarms were going off in his mind. Samara would not alert him unless something monumental had happened.

Not waiting to see their reaction to the abrupt termination of the meeting, Noah turned to the door. A blinding, stunning pain slammed into the back of his head. He whirled around, swung his fist toward the person behind him. Didn't matter who it was, his only thought was to get to Mara and his children. He made an impact, but a second later, an electrical charge zoomed through his body. He dropped to the floor, his muscles twitching uncontrollably. Pain reverberated through him, and in a distant part of his mind, he recognized the stinging blows of a man's big, booted foot.

His last conscious thought was his mind screaming for Mara.

***

Noah wasn't responding to her alert. Refusing to even think what that meant, she concentrated on what she needed to do. She had to get her mother out of here and then find Noah and her children. Without showing the alarm she was feeling, Samara eased toward the dressing room.

Out of the corner of her eye, she noted the man watching her hadn't moved from his post. She knew she was likely going to have to confront him, but she wanted her mother out of the way first.

"I wouldn't do that if I were you," a gruff male voice said behind her.

The man who was watching her was still at his post. So there were two of them, possibly more. This had all the earmarks of a joint attack on her and Noah. He would have answered her alert if he were able.

What the hell was going on, and how was she going to keep her mother safe?

As if he knew her thoughts, the man behind her said, "We have no interest in your mother, Samara."

"What is it you want?"

"First let me show you a photo."

An iPhone appeared within her vision, and her heart jolted as if lightning had slammed through her. The photo was of her children, her babies, lying in the trunk of a car. Their eyes were closed.

"Don't worry. They're still alive. For now."

"What do you want?"

"You need to come with us."

Before she could react, he added, "And if you're considering signaling anyone, you might want to know there are four of us here. There's no telling how many people we might have to kill to get you out of here, including your mother. Are you willing to risk that?"

Of course she wasn't.

"Why are you doing this?"

"You'll find out in due time. So, are we going quietly, or should we shed a little blood along the way?"

"What about my mother?"

"Oh, I'm sure she'll worry, but at least she'll still be breathing. I don't guarantee that unless you come along with us right now."

"Fine. All right," she snapped.

"Let's walk out the exit together. Slow and easy."

Samara drew in a shaky breath as she made her way toward the nearest door of the large department store. Two more men, one on either side of the door, were looking pointedly at her, and she knew the man had spoken the truth. There were at least four men here who would apparently do whatever it took to get her to leave with them.

Her world was falling apart around her, and while she could remind herself she had been through hell before, she couldn't get the image of her babies out of her mind. Were they really all right? The man said they were, but how could she trust anything he said?

And Noah. Sweet, sweet Lord, what had happened to her husband?

Chapter Four

St. Mary's Hospital
Alexandria, Virginia

Noah woke with a stunning headache and agony in every part of his body. That pain was nothing compared to what his heart was feeling. Even without anyone telling him, he knew Mara was in grave danger.

He told his body to get up and get moving. Mara was his world. Without her, he and his children wouldn't survive.

"Noah," a familiar female voice said, "can you hear me?"

With difficulty, he turned his head slightly to see Eden St. Claire on the left side of the bed. Standing beside her was Jordan Montgomery, her husband. Eden and Jordan headed up the LCR offices in Paris. When had they gotten here? How long had he been unconscious?

"Tell me," Noah said.

"Here's what we know," Jordan answered. "Samara was at a shopping mall with her mother. When Mrs. Lyons returned from the dressing room, Samara had disappeared and didn't answer her phone when her mother called. The mall security cameras inside the store were down for over an hour. There's no footage of Samara leaving the mall. We've tried tracing her phone, but it's either been disabled or turned off.

"Your father-in-law arrived at your house and except for your pets, found it empty. Micah and Evie weren't there. Your home security cameras were dismantled."

His kids. His wife. Damn them, they had taken his entire family.

Only by sheer force of will was he able to shut down the panic. It would do no one any good. He had to think clearly, rationally. This was no random kidnapping. This had been planned and executed with the precision of a professional, well-paid team. Whoever was behind this had money and resources.

"How long ago?"

"Nine hours."

"Any word from the kidnappers?"

"Not yet."

"How'd I get here?"

"Housekeeping at the hotel found you when they came in to clean. Mr. Alvarez called us."

Horatio Alvarez, the owner of the hotel, had been a friend to LCR for several years. Thankfully, Alvarez had followed his instincts and contacted LCR instead of the police. Noah might have to involve the authorities at some point. For right now, it was better if LCR took the lead.

"What are my injuries?"

"Concussion, bruised ribs, a couple of broken fingers, and multiple contusions. Whoever did this, kicked the hell out of you."

He remembered each blow until he lost consciousness. "Why was I unconscious so long?"

"You had some brain swelling. Doctors kept you unconscious for a few hours to try to reduce it."

Another good reason for the vicious pounding in his skull. "Prognosis?"

"They want to keep you a few days for observation. We can work from here as much as possible."

"Taking my family…in a coordinated attack. Someone's out for revenge."

"That's our take, too," Eden said. "We hopped on the jet as soon as Horatio called. The Elite team is headed back home. The op in Colombia finished up early and went well. We'll get the entire Elite team on it and call in as many other operatives as needed. We'll get them back."

Gritting his teeth, Noah moved to pull the IV from his left hand. "Dammit. I can't just lie here and—"

"Yes, you can, McCall," Jordan said. "You're in no shape to do anything. We're meeting at headquarters in an hour. Every available operative will be there. We will find your family, Noah. I promise."

"Give me my phone."

The minute he held the phone in his hand, he felt a little more control return. He might not be able to move, but he could damn well make calls. He would call every person he had ever met, if it would help him find his family. But first he had an important list that he needed to access.

He entered a code, then his thumbprint, and pulled up a file. "I'm sending everyone a list of suspects."

"Do you have anyone specific in mind?" Eden asked.

"Could be any of these people." He winced, noticing the list was larger than he remembered. "Most of them are in prison, but that means nothing. The first eight are the most likely, but don't rule anyone out without checking."

"We'll get on these," Jordan said. He glanced over at the door. "Your in-laws are wanting to see you."

"Yeah. I figured. Send them in."

Eden opened the door and then said, "We'll keep you updated hourly, more if there's news."

"Thank you."

Noah barely had a chance for a shallow, painful breath before Sam and Mary Lyons burst into the room.

"What the hell is going on, Noah?" Sam shouted.

"Sam, calm down." Though it was obvious Mary had been crying, her typical stoicism was keeping her emotions in check.

She reminded him so much of his brave Mara. Wherever she was, he knew she would be strong in the face of evil. She had stared it down more than once. And he hoped to God she was with the children. They would be terrified. Being together would give all of them strength.

"Fine," Sam snapped. "Where are my grandchildren and my daughter?"

"I don't know, Sam. That's what I'm working on finding out."

"Do you know who attacked you?" Mary asked.

"The same people who took Mara and the kids. I'll find them, Mary. I promise."

"Is this related to your organization?" Sam asked. "Somebody out for revenge?"

Not for the first time, he acknowledged that his father-in-law was both smart and savvy.

Noah and Samara had told her parents about Last Chance Rescue when they'd first moved to the US from Paris. They knew he was often involved in dangerous situations. What they likely hadn't anticipated was their daughter and grandchildren being targeted.

"I met with some prospective clients yesterday. I could tell something was off and was about to call an end to the meeting when I got an alarm signal from Mara. Before I could answer, I was knocked out. That's all I know. Mary, you were with Samara. What can you tell me?"

"I was in the dressing room. I came out, and Samara wasn't anywhere around. I didn't really worry. I thought maybe she went to the restroom or to another part of the store. I called her cell, and she didn't answer. That's when I began to worry."

"And that's when Mary called me," Sam said. "I had gone to pick up Evie and Micah. Except for Roscoe and Sassy, who were barking like crazy, the house was empty." He swallowed hard, and tears flooded his eyes. "I'm sorry, Noah. I should have gotten there sooner. Been waiting for them when they got home."

"It's not your fault, Sam." It would do no good to tell his father-in-law that they might have beaten him up, or worse. These people were on a mission and didn't mind hurting others to get the job done.

Noah had to force his own emotions away. If he gave in to them, then he'd be no good. Imagining the terror of what his children and wife were going through would not help save them.

His biggest hope was that this was about ransom, but he already knew that was a useless wish. He had the money to pay a substantial ransom, and while money might be a secondary goal for these bastards, it wasn't going to be the primary one. He'd angered and helped put away too many sleazebags for this to be about anything but revenge.

The need to get out of the bed and start looking for them was almost unbearable. Mara and his children were his entire world. He could not, would not, lose them. The only thing that remotely made him feel better was the knowledge that he had a cadre of experts who would do whatever it took to find them.

This was an attack on him personally. He would pay every cent he'd ever earned to get them back, but the person behind this would want blood. *His.* And while he'd give his life for his family, Noah already knew it wasn't going to be that easy.

***

Darkness surrounded them. Except for the sound of water gently lapping against the sides of the boat and the slight creak of the vessel, everything was silent. Samara breathed in the air, trying to get a sense of her surroundings. She knew they were on a boat, knew they were on the water. Was it the ocean, river, lake?

The men who had taken her had refused to answer any questions. A van had been waiting for them when they'd exited the mall. She had been shoved inside. Her purse had been taken from her, and she had been bound and blindfolded. All questions she had asked, demanded, had been ignored. They hadn't hurt her, had barely acknowledged her existence. The thought of struggling and resisting was there, but she had held back. Even though she was trained to fight, four against one weren't good odds. Besides, she would have done anything they told her to do as long as she could get to her children.

About an hour into the drive, she had felt a tiny pinprick on her neck. She had fought against the drug, screamed curses, but it had done no good. When she woke, the van was stopped. She had been vaguely aware of someone carrying her onto a boat. A few minutes later, she'd woken to the feeling of both her children beside her. Despite her worry, she had felt immediate comfort.

"Mama?"

"Yes, Micah?"

"What do we need to do to get out of here?"

Their circumstances were too grim to smile, but Samara felt a lift to her heart at her son's question. Micah sounded so much like his dad. Noah would be so proud. And though he was taking after his father in his height as well, already towering over her five-foot-two frame, he was only ten years old, still just a child.

"We're going to do what we've trained to do."

"How, Mama?" Evie asked.

"I don't know yet, baby, but I promise, we'll find a way."

"Okay."

The trembling in her daughter's voice made her want to scream. How dare these bastards terrorize her children? A seven-year-old child should not be worrying about escaping from bad men with guns. No child should have to endure such things. Once they were out of danger, she would make sure every one of these bastards paid for what they had done to her children.

Neither she nor Noah had ever taken their safety for granted. With their jobs, they had encountered some of the most evil people in the world. Their work hadn't made them necessarily paranoid, but they were always hyperaware of the risks. When their children were old enough, they'd included them in being ultra-aware. They'd always made the training enjoyable, like a game. They had sworn their children would never be victims.

They had failed this time, though. No doubt about it, this was a well-organized attack. Someone wanted something from Noah and was using his family to make that happen.

They were likely making the demands to him right now. She refused to think otherwise. No way in hell was she even going to contemplate that he wasn't alive. She loved her husband, body and soul. If he was no longer in this world, she would know. Their connection was that strong. Besides, killing Noah made no sense. If they wanted him dead, there was no reason to kidnap his family.

Micah had described his and Evie's abduction. They had arrived home from school. Both were on the porch, seconds away from entering the house, when they'd been grabbed. If they had been able to get inside, they would have been safe. Sassy, their Maltese, couldn't have done much damage. But Roscoe, their black Lab, would have taken down anyone who tried to touch her children.

The implications were infuriating. How had these people found where her family lived? If there was one thing they had made sure of, it was hiding their location and identities from anyone they didn't know. Records showed Noah and Samara Stoddard owned the house. No one should be able to trace that name back to Noah McCall or Last Chance Rescue. How had they found them? And who were "they"?

Samara took a breath and used her knowledge to assess their situation. No one was hurt, only scared. That was a good sign. That didn't mean they weren't in danger. Things went awry in kidnappings all the time. She and her children would not be statistics.

Noah and LCR would be doing everything on their end to rescue them, and she needed to do everything possible to escape.

For an abduction, there had been a surprising number of people involved. Four men had been involved in taking her. At least two others had kidnapped her children. Plus however many had delayed Noah from answering her alert.

It would do no good for her to speculate who was responsible. That was for Noah and LCR to determine. What she could and would do was try to figure a way out. She wouldn't put her children more at risk, though. If ransom would satisfy their kidnappers, then Noah would pay what was necessary.

Her gut told her something else, though. The people they had crossed and helped bring to justice would be more inclined to want revenge, not money. She had to figure a way out of here.

Gathering her children, one under each arm, Samara whispered words of love and assurances and then began to pray in earnest.

Chapter Five

St. Mary's Hospital
Alexandria, Virginia

Raphael exploded out of the elevator. Ignoring the admonishments from a couple of nurses, he ran down the hallway and pushed open the door to Noah's room. Seeing the man who had been like a father to him bruised and pale twisted his gut into knots. One of Noah's eyes was swollen completely closed. Several nasty bruises mottled his face.

All in all, he was lucky to be alive, but Raphael knew Noah wasn't feeling lucky.

Knowing the man well, Raphael didn't waste time on platitudes. "You look like hell."

As if carved from granite, Noah's expression remained unchanged. "Feel like it, too."

Raphael nodded an acknowledgment to Eden and Jordan and asked, "What do we know?"

"Not much," Jordan said. "Still no ransom demand. And a ton of suspects."

Raphael frowned at the news. "It's been almost twenty-four hours. Why are they taking so long?"

"To make me sweat," Noah said. "No way they're not going to contact me soon."

Raphael didn't know if Noah believed this or was telling himself that because the alternative was too horrific to contemplate.

"I agree," Eden said. "Whoever is behind this is out to hurt you. The longer he waits, the more likely you are to suffer. He's getting off on it."

"So what are we doing in the meantime?" Raphael asked.

"We had an initial meeting at headquarters last night," Jordan said. "We've got all our tech analysts running down every suspect on McCall's list. We should have some more solid suspects this afternoon.

"There's another meeting scheduled for three this afternoon. The hospital has loaned us the use of a conference room. We've got plenty of space to coordinate a rescue operation. We'll—"

Jordan broke off when a chime sounded. The cellphone on the swing table attached to Noah's bed indicated an incoming call. Raphael leaned forward and caught a glimpse of the display screen. *Unknown caller.*

Noah grabbed the phone, but waited a second to answer. Jordan was on his phone to one of their LCR analysts, who would try to trace the location of the caller. The instant Jordan nodded that this was in place, Noah answered, putting the call on speaker.

"McCall."

"Mr. McCall? I just heard the news about your family's untimely tragedy."

His heart sinking, Raphael met Noah's eyes and saw acknowledgment in them. That deep, resonant voice was undeniably familiar.

Noah said coolly, "And you are?"

"I guess it makes sense that you don't recognize my voice, although I've been told it's memorable. I'm sure mine is just one of many lives you've ruined. Tell me, how many other families have you destroyed, McCall?"

"How do you know my family was taken?"

"One hears things...you know. Prisons are rife with gossip and rumors. I just had to call and see if this one was true."

"Do you have my family?"

A burst of laughter, sounding dry and slightly off-balance, blasted over the phone. "But of course I don't. What a delightfully amusing accusation. Alas, thanks to you, I'm incarcerated. How could I, a simple prisoner, a man told when to eat, sleep, and eliminate body waste, be responsible for committing such a heinous crime? I have no power. There must be thousands of other people who have cause to despise you. One of them has finally found a way to punish you."

"So you're just calling out of interest or curiosity?"

"Oh, no, Mr. McCall. I'm calling to express my deepest sympathies. You see, I know how it feels to lose your loved ones due to someone else's machinations. I can completely empathize with the pain you must be going through."

Though his face was a mask of fury, Noah kept his voice calm. "And there's nothing I can do for you?"

"Well...now that you mention it, there is one thing."

Jordan raised a hand to signal that the call had been traced. He said softly, "Fieldstone prison."

Apparently seeing no need to keep up the pretense, Noah said, "What is it you want, Reddington?"

"Aw, good. I'm so glad you had the call traced. Now we can talk more freely. And you'll know that I had no way of abducting your family. I have nothing left, you made sure of that. No, my concern for you and the welfare of your family is the only reason I called."

"Of course it is. But there is something I can do for you?"

"Well, of course. We all want something, don't we?"

"What is—"

"Oh dear. My time is up. I must go. We'll talk soon."

"No!" Noah barked. "Tell me what—"

The line went dead.

Cursing viciously, Noah squeezed the phone in his hand until Raphael was certain it would break. Showing why he was the best at what he did, Noah carefully placed the phone on the table in front of him. "At least we know who and why. He'll want his family in exchange for mine."

Jordan was texting the others that the man responsible had been identified.

"Eden," Noah said, "send Maddox and Bishop to Fieldstone prison in Nebraska. Tell them to do whatever they have to do to get the man to talk."

"Will do."

Raphael approved of the strategic move. Sending Ethan Bishop and Gabe Maddox to confront Reddington was brilliant. The two men had been LCR operatives for several years and would intimidate an army, much less a sniveling weasel like Stanford Reddington.

Reddington. His gut twisted with all the implications.

Forcing his mind away from the painful memories of the past, Raphael concentrated on the here and now. "Do you know where Sarah and her children live?"

"No. Only the US Marshals assigned to their case know."

"And Giselle? She still married to Daniel Fletcher III?"

"You don't know?"

Despite himself, his heart stuttered. "Know what?"

"Her husband died a year or so ago."

"Of what?"

"Car accident. Family released a statement, but there was very little media coverage."

No surprise there. The wealth of the Fletcher family was matched only by their intense privacy.

"Where's Giselle? Is she still living with them?"

"Last I heard, she was. Getting credible intel on that family is almost impossible."

That was likely true. Not that he had tried. What was done was done.

Despite his determination to not dwell on the past, Raphael had often wondered how Giselle was faring with such an intensely secretive family. She had been controlled and manipulated by her father, held a virtual prisoner on that island of his. And then she had chosen to marry a man whose wealth would not only rival a midsize country, but he was ultraprivate to boot. Had she exchanged one prison for another?

Eden ended her call. "Gabe and Ethan are on the way to the airport. They'll call you as soon as they see Reddington. Also, I'll contact the US Marshals' office and have them notify the people in charge of Sarah and her children's protection." Eden's gaze skittered to Raphael and then returned to Noah. "Someone needs to let Giselle know what's going on."

"Raphael will go."

Though his voice was somewhat stiff, Raphael managed an even reply. "I'll head out as soon as possible."

Noah gave Jordan and Eden a look. "Would you guys mind giving us some privacy?"

"Of course," Eden said. She gave Raphael a quick smile of encouragement and opened the door. Jordan followed her, stopping on the way to offer his own support with a slap on the back.

The instant the door closed, Noah said, "You okay with this?"

Was he okay with seeing the woman who'd ripped out his heart and stomped all over it? Not really. He'd had much tougher assignments, but none he had dreaded more. Didn't matter. It needed to be done. He was the man for the job.

"It's not a problem. That was a long time ago. We've both moved on."

Thankfully, Noah took him at his word and didn't remind him of how he'd acted when he'd learned Giselle had left him. It hadn't been his finest hour.

"She may offer to help. If she does, see if she will come back with you. Assure her that we'll protect her."

That hadn't been on his radar, but it made sense. If Reddington's plan was to initiate an exchange, his family for Noah's, having Giselle's assistance would be beneficial.

So not only would he be seeing Giselle again, he would likely be traveling with her, spending time with her. His heart rate picked up. He told himself it had nothing to do with seeing her again.

Yeah, and he was a piss-poor liar.

***

Fieldstone Correctional Facility
Omaha, Nebraska

It had begun.

From his fourth-floor cell, Stanford stared out the small window into the courtyard below. He tried to feel satisfaction.

Knowing that the man he'd hated for so long was finally experiencing the pain he deserved should have at least lifted his spirits. Unfortunately, happiness was an elusive dream these days. For so long, vengeance had been his only motivation to stay alive.

Even though he had been waiting for this day for years, he knew his life would still never be the same. He could never regain what they took from him. All the things he valued were gone. But there were still things he wanted, things he could get. He still had power and influence. They hadn't completely destroyed those, even though they had tried. They thought they'd succeeded.

Years ago, it would have galled him to accept assistance. He didn't do favors for other people and didn't like being in anyone's debt. But in this...in this, it felt right. Didn't really matter what they wanted in return. As far as he was concerned, everything and everyone else could go to hell. His objectives were his only focus.

In a different time, he would have found out the reason for it all and used that knowledge to his advantage. Years ago, it had been a game, and no one had been better at playing to win. Now he just didn't give a damn.

A small smile curved his thin lips. This was a coup like no other, though. They believed he was just a sickly, old man locked up in prison, waiting to die. They were wrong. He had a plan and he had goals. With the help of his new associates, he would win once again.

Noah McCall and the bastards at Last Chance Rescue would rue the day they ever crossed paths with Stanford Reddington.

CHAPTER SIX

The drone of the plane barely penetrated Raphael's consciousness. Frowning, he stared at the minute amount of information LCR's best tech analyst had sent him. Even though she'd had only an hour or so to dig into Giselle's life, he had expected more than this. Yes, the Fletcher family was private, but this went several degrees beyond that.

Following a hunch, Raphael typed Giselle's name into a search engine. Five screens later, he found a small blip about her marriage to Daniel Fletcher III. What had happened to all the articles written right after the marriage? The news that one of the most revered families in the country was now connected in marriage to a former human trafficker and murderer had been plastered everywhere.

Three screens after that small notation was a brief blurb indicating that Daniel had died in a car accident, leaving his young wife a widow.

That was all. Giselle's life had been summarized in less than six lines.

The Internet had been scrubbed clean, almost as if Giselle never existed. He went back to the intel he'd been given. There was nothing substantial there either. Even the university she and

Raphael attended together, before her family went into WITSEC, showed no record of her.

He did some quick searches on her mother and found various articles about her testimony against Reddington, along with an article about her captivity on the island. The author had referenced that she had been forced to bear Reddington's children, but no names were mentioned.

Nothing recent had been written. Sarah Reddington no longer used that name. She, along with her children, had assumed new names when they had disappeared with the government's help.

And then they'd had to do it all over again.

It boggled the mind to think about what a mess that must have been. When news of Giselle and Fletcher's marriage exploded in the tabloids, Sarah, Amelia, and Eric had been exposed. He and Noah had spoken about it just that once. Noah hadn't known any details other than Sarah and her children had once again been uprooted, forced to flee and start all over again. New names, new everything.

Had Giselle even considered that when she'd married Fletcher? The sheer selfishness of that one act was final proof that he hadn't known her at all. The girl he had thought she was would never have done something so utterly wrong.

Raphael glanced out the window, but instead of the dark night skies, he saw Giselle the first day he met her. She had been seventeen and the most beautiful thing he'd ever seen in his entire life. He'd been dry-mouthed and speechless, stunned by not only her beauty but also her so obvious innocence.

Stanford Reddington was one of the most vile, inhumane bastards Raphael had ever come across. The man had been involved in several shady businesses, but his human trafficking organization was his biggest source of income. Reddington's own father had been a sleazy human trafficker and had passed that business on to his son. And Stanford had been in the process of teaching his son, Lance, to do the very same thing. Raphael had incorrectly assumed the entire family was corrupt. Nothing could have been further from the truth.

Sarah, Giselle's mother, had been Stanford Reddington's first victim. He had kept her and her children a prisoner on an island in the Canary Islands. Everything was closely monitored, and they were fed only information and news that Reddington deemed appropriate. Giselle had been living in a mansion and a virtual paradise, but she had been a prisoner. No matter how pretty her surroundings, she'd had no choices, no freedom.

Despite all of that, she had been the most natural and unaffected person he'd ever known. Her smile could light up a room and soften the hardest of hearts. He lost his heart, along with his sanity, early on.

Their relationship was doomed from the start, though. He'd just been too stupid in love to see the signs.

As Dear John letters went, the one she'd left him was short and coldhearted. He'd put most of it out of his mind, but he remembered the gist of it. Blah, blah, blah. Empty platitudes. Shit like that meant nothing when it took every effort just to breathe through the pain.

If she'd said those things to his face, maybe he would've handled things better. He would've at least respected that. But she'd left him a lousy letter, and that had been that. What he had believed was the beginning of their forever had turned into a thanks-for-the-memories kind of parting.

Had he understood the need for her and her family to enter the WITSEC program? Hell yeah. What he did not, could not, understand was her decision to just leave him behind. As if he meant nothing. As if *they* meant nothing. He would have gone with her. They could have continued to have the life they'd been living. She had made that choice for him.

Bitterness had arrived early, washing over the hurt, which had been a helluva lot more palatable. Apathy followed, and he'd taken comfort in simply not giving a damn.

Seeing her again might be a little awkward, but their brief romance ended years ago. He'd had a couple of semiserious relationships since then, and she'd been married. Couldn't get more water under the bridge than that.

So he'd go there, see her. Tell her that her asshole of a father was causing havoc once more and to beware. He'd also ask for her help. If she said yes, fine. He'd bring her back, and other operatives could deal with her. If she refused to help—which, considering her track record of self-centeredness, he was sure she would—he'd go back home and do what was needed. Saving Noah's family was his only priority right now.

The chime of his cellphone had him quickly checking the display. Seeing the name of an old friend, he felt a smile soften his grim mouth.

"Hey you," he answered.

"How are you?"

"Worried."

"We all are, but we'll get them back. There's no one better to do the job."

That was true. Jamie Kendrick Savage knew that from experience. She'd once been one of Reddington's captives. LCR operative Dylan Savage, the man who was now her husband, had rescued her.

"I'm sure he's just using them as leverage. I know they're terrified, but he's not going to let them be hurt. He'll lose his advantage if something happens to them. Besides, Samara is one of the strongest people I know, and those kids are amazing. They'll be fine until we can get to them."

Raphael didn't know if she said the words to reassure him or herself. While it was true that Reddington's people might not plan any harm now, no one knew for sure. Jamie knew better than most what the bastard was capable of doing.

"You're going to go see Giselle?"

"Yes. She needs to know."

"I tried calling her several times and could never get through. I'm astonished you're being allowed to see her."

He was a little surprised, too. When he'd asked to speak with Giselle, he'd been told she wasn't available. That had been no shocker. He'd been prepared for her refusal. Before he could explain that speaking to her was imperative, he'd been told to show up at the Fletcher Compound in East Hampton, New York, at ten o'clock tomorrow morning.

That's what he planned to do.

"Even though I've been invited to the estate, she still may refuse to see me."

"I doubt that. You two might not have ended things in the best way, but you have a history. I remember how you guys used to look at each other. As if no one else existed."

"That was a long time ago."

"Maybe." She paused, then added, "I understand her husband is gone."

"Yes." Raphael left it at that. There was speculation in Jamie's tone that he wouldn't address. This wasn't some kind of reunion between old lovers or friends. It was a business matter and nothing more.

Jamie being Jamie didn't take the hint. "I know things didn't end well between you two. Things are different now. You might—"

"We're about to land. I'll give her your regards."

"I'm sorry. I didn't mean—"

"It's okay. We're good. Just gotta go."

This time, thankfully, she dropped it. "Stay in touch."

"Will do."

Raphael ended the call, settled back in his seat, and closed his eyes. Reliving past mistakes and old feelings accomplished nothing. His mission was to warn Giselle that her father was on the rampage again and ask for her help. Once she gave her answer, he'd know how to proceed. Either way, he'd return home and help figure out a way to rescue Samara, Micah, and Evie. They were his family. Giselle was no one other than someone he used to know.

***

Fletcher Compound
East Hampton, New York

Raphael stood before the oversize door of the massive mansion. At six-four, he was used to towering over most things, but had to admit he felt like a mouse knocking on a giant's house.

The mile-long drive, with its towering trees and decorative shrubbery, gave him an idea of the wealth he was about to face. Large amounts of money neither intimidated nor impressed him, but he had known too many wealthy people who put their money above their integrity. Making snap judgments wasn't necessarily his way, but he couldn't deny the feeling of bias that was already developing. He told himself it had nothing to do with Giselle, but he wasn't buying it. These negative feelings had everything to do with her.

Within seconds, the door opened, and a middle-aged, dour-faced butler stared up at him. "May I help you?"

"I'm here to see Giselle."

Though the man's expression never changed, Raphael swore there was the slightest hint of alarm in his eyes. He recovered quickly and intoned, "And you are?"

"A friend of the family."

"What family?"

"Her mother's family."

Another brief flicker of…something. What the hell was it?

In case the man needed more information, Raphael said, "I called yesterday. I am expected."

"Of course, sir. And your name?"

"Raphael Sanchez."

The butler backed away, saying, "Please come in and have a seat in the parlor. I'll go…" Mumbling something Raphael couldn't quite make out, the man pointed toward a room to the right and then hurried away.

Even though the family was known for their extreme privacy and eccentricities, the butler's behavior was still damn odd.

Shrugging away the moment, he crossed the giant marble foyer and headed to the room the butler had indicated. He stopped at the door, getting a brief glimpse of the kind of affluence few could imagine. Giselle had grown up surrounded by wealth, but Reddington's measly millions were nothing compared to what this family was worth.

Raphael walked to the middle of the room and stood, waiting. There were plenty of places to sit…three sofas, four chairs, and an uncomfortable-looking chaise to be exact, but he preferred to stand.

"Mr. Sanchez, please come with me."

Following the butler, Raphael felt eyes on him. Though he saw no one else, he knew he was being watched. Security? Or curious family members?

The butler stopped at a large cherrywood door and knocked softly. On hearing a voice say, "Enter," the butler pushed the door open and stepped back. Raphael entered the large office, noting there was only one occupant. He hadn't expected to see Daniel Fletcher, Jr. himself. The secretary hadn't mentioned he would be meeting with anyone else, especially not her father-in-law. He had stupidly assumed it would be Giselle. Hell, maybe this was for the best.

Fletcher stood and walked around his desk. The man was impressive in photographs and even more so in real life. He was just a little over six feet, movie-star handsome, with a bit of silver crowding out the honey-gold hair. Fletcher was reportedly a little over sixty but moved toward Raphael with the energy of a much younger man.

"How wonderful to meet an old friend of Giselle's. She never talked about her past a lot. Understandably, considering what her father put them through."

Raphael shook the man's hand, noting the smoothness. His own were callused and likely felt like tree bark.

"We were friends a long time ago. I haven't seen her in years."

"Please, have a seat."

Raphael sat in the chair Fletcher nodded toward, unsurprised that the man settled into one across from him. The older man's demeanor was friendly, inviting, and almost grandfatherly.

Raphael couldn't put his finger on why, but he didn't trust him. Maybe because he seemed to be trying too hard to be nice.

"Now, tell me how I can help you."

Though Raphael wanted to be the one to tell Giselle about her father's newest evil deeds, he saw no reason not to give a brief explanation. "My employer's family has been abducted. We believe Stanford Reddington is responsible and that he plans to use them as a bargaining chip to get to his own family."

"How horrifying." A puzzled frown appeared on the older man's face. "I wonder why I haven't seen any news reports. Surely an abduction of this magnitude would bring reporters from everywhere."

Considering the man likely squelched ninety percent of media stories on himself, Raphael was surprised at the question.

"We're keeping it out of the press. LCR specializes in rescuing kidnap victims. We're handling this in-house."

"Of course. Of course. That makes sense. But are you sure the culprit is Reddington? Isn't he still in prison? Don't tell me some fool has let him escape."

"No. He's still there. We're not quite sure yet what the man's agenda is, but we felt it important to alert Giselle of what her father has done. If he's got people working for him on the outside, he could very well find another way to get to her."

"And you're absolutely sure her father is responsible? There's no doubt?"

"None whatsoever."

Fletcher released a powerful sigh, shook his head. "What a tragic upbringing that poor girl endured. She was such a blessing as a daughter-in-law. She and my son loved each other deeply. When Giselle lost the love of her life, she was, understandably, inconsolable."

Like a wild animal sensing danger, Raphael felt the hair on the back of his neck stand up. Every instinct he had was blaring a warning. There was something wrong. Why did the man keep referring to Giselle in the past tense?

"Where is Giselle? Is she here?"

"No." Fletcher gave a deep sigh. "I wish there was an easier way to say this, and I'm sorry to be the one to tell you, because I can see you really cared for her." He drew in a breath and said, "Giselle is dead. She passed away several months ago."

CHAPTER SEVEN

Raphael couldn't breathe, couldn't think. He could hear a voice in his head repeatedly saying, *No, no, no*. He was surprised his frozen lips managed to mumble, "What happened?"

Tears glistened in Fletcher's eyes. "We were so focused on our own grief, we missed how devastated Giselle was. She held back her despair, didn't share how she was really feeling. By the time we realized, it was too late to save her."

"I—" Raphael's voice croaked. He cleared his throat, tried again. "How did it happen?"

"My wife went to her bedroom to wake her. She thought a girls' day out, shopping and a spa session, would help them both. She found our darling Giselle in the bathtub. She had cut her wrists and was long gone."

No, he refused to believe it. She might have hurt him when she left, sliced his heart into a million pieces, but he knew Giselle, knew her heart. Despondency was not part of her personality, no matter what life threw at her.

"That doesn't sound like Giselle."

"We didn't think so either." Fletcher's expression was grave with grief as he explained, "But she loved our son so very much. They were inseparable up until the end. She was lost without him."

"Does Sarah, her mother, know?"

"No. I'm sure she doesn't. We kept it very private. We're not ones to share our personal grief with others. And since we had no way to get in touch with her, I don't see how her mother could know."

Standing, still numb from shock, Raphael said woodenly, "I would like to go to her gravesite, pay my respects."

"That's not possible, I'm afraid. Her body was cremated. We spread her ashes in the same place we distributed our son's. In the ocean behind our house. We thought the location the most appropriate, as it was one of their favorite places to go together."

He had to get out of here. A thick wave of grief threatened to engulf him, swallow him whole. He could not spend one more moment in this man's suffocating presence.

He managed, somehow, to thank Fletcher for the information and get out of the house before he lost it. He got into his rental car, managed to drive almost a quarter mile down the road before he had to pull over. He pushed open the car door seconds before losing the contents of his stomach.

Giselle was dead? Had killed herself? How was that possible?

***

The instant Sanchez's vehicle moved away from the house, Daniel Fletcher breathed an easier breath. The matter was far from resolved, but he thought this part had gone rather well.

The door behind him opened, and his longtime friend and confidant Hugh Rawlings strolled into his office. "Well, that was a bit of a shocker."

"So you saw him?"

"Yes. Uncanny. Did you expect that?"

"No, I had no idea. Changes things a bit."

"Not really." Seeing Daniel's surprise, Hugh shook his head. "Don't make it more complicated than it needs to be. We've known from the beginning what needs to be done."

Daniel sighed. "I know. It's just all so messy...so tawdry."

He slapped his old friend on the back. "It'll work itself out."

"I suppose. Cavendar's not pleased."

"So?" Hugh gave a careless shrug. "He works for us, not the other way around."

"I wish I had listened to you from the beginning."

"You had your reasons."

A wave of gratitude engulfed Daniel. Out of all the people he'd known in his life, his longtime friend and associate was the only person who had never disappointed him.

"What's next? Is there anything more I need to do?"

"No." Walking over to Daniel's desk, Hugh grabbed the item he needed. "You just relax and let me take care of the rest. We have more than enough people to handle the situation. By this time next week, all of this will be like a bad dream, and you can go on as you planned."

One hundred percent confident, Daniel nodded his approval. "Excellent."

***

The flight back to Virginia was a blur of images of Giselle—when he first met her, when they were together. Raphael's gut felt as though hot embers were burning him from the inside out. The hideous words kept reverberating through his mind.

Giselle is dead.

How could a healthy twenty-six-year-old woman be dead, just like that? Yeah, it happened, but not to the woman he had once known and loved. Just, no.

As Raphael stared sightlessly out the window of the plane, he tried to reconcile the young, vivacious girl he had known with a woman so despondent over her husband's death that she would choose to end her own life.

Had she changed that much? With her mother and family far away and unable to communicate with them, who had she been able to turn to? Had she had no friends? A priest, a minister? *Someone* to talk to?

He could not get his head wrapped around the concept that Giselle was actually gone. How had his gut—the one thing he'd relied on for so many years—not let him know in some way that she was no longer on this earth?

From personal experience, he knew that grief could ravage even the strongest of souls. His own mother had lost her will to live early in life.

Raphael remembered nothing about his father, but he had no problem remembering the men who came after him—so many of them. The last one had broken his mother, not just her heart but also her spirit. He had watched the woman who used to love and care for him become someone else. The alcohol and drugs dimmed the pain, and she all but forgot she had a son. By the time he was ten, he was on the streets, rummaging in garbage bins for food, stealing when he could get away with it.

When he was about twelve or so, he went back to their rat-infested hole-in-the-wall apartment to find her dead from an overdose. For two days, he had sat in the corner beside the mattress she'd died on and wept his heart out. Then he'd covered her body with a blanket and walked out the door. He'd stopped long enough to make an anonymous tip to the police about a dead body, and then he'd used the small amount of money he had left to buy a bus ticket to the next town over.

Those were the years he preferred to forget, from the constant hunger to the near miss of becoming Donald Rosemount's drugged-out zombie slave. Then LCR had happened, and his life had never been the same.

He had survived. His mother hadn't. And somehow, something similar had happened to Giselle.

Guilt slithered through him. At one time, he was her friend. Her only friend. Even though she abandoned him, he should have found a way to make sure she was okay. Yes, she had changed her name, and it would have been hard to find her, but perhaps Noah might've been able to find something out. He had blamed her for abandoning him, but maybe he'd been the one to do the abandoning. To know she had suffered so badly that she felt taking her own life was her only option sickened him. How alone she must have felt.

Would things have been different if he had returned her call that day? On the same day that news of her marriage was exploding across the tabloids, she had called him, leaving a mysterious voice mail that she needed to talk with him. He'd been thrown for a loop. When he'd heard her voice, he'd still been reeling from learning about her marriage. Bitter and angry, he had deleted the message. What was the point in calling a newly married woman?

But now, looking back, he couldn't help but think about that moment and wish he'd made a different decision.

Images long buried resurfaced in his mind. He remembered her smile, her beautiful laugh, the way she saw wonder in every living thing. To know that that light had been snuffed out ripped at his insides.

He shook his head. No, just no. Damn if he would just accept her death without getting all the facts. He owed it to Giselle to find out the truth.

For right now, the priority was getting Samara, Micah, and Evie back home, safe and sound. But when that had been accomplished, he would be launching another investigation.

Something was off here—way off. And he was going to find out what.

CHAPTER EIGHT

Gardner-Vicks Cemetery
Queens, New York

The young man drove down the narrow, graveled road. Spotting the now familiar clearing in the distance, he headed there. The late afternoon sun struggled to brighten up the dreariness of the day. He always chose the late afternoons to come. Not too many people wanted to hang around a graveyard after the sun went down. It didn't bother him. He actually enjoyed the quiet.

He pulled off into a clearing, parked the vehicle, and got out. Fighting the almost overwhelming anxiousness inside him, he went around to the back of the vehicle and pulled the gardening equipment from the trunk. A hoe, shearing scissors, a small broom, and an empty garbage bag—tools of the trade for a maintenance man in charge of clearing debris from graves and tombstones.

If anyone happened to see him, they might think he was too young for the job or that the slenderness of his physique would prevent him from doing anything too strenuous. They would be wrong. Beneath the worn clothes, he was much fitter than anyone could imagine. It had taken him longer than he'd ever anticipated, but he was healthy once again. And he was ready to face the challenges ahead. No matter what.

Carrying his equipment, he went about clearing the gravesites of overgrown weeds. He threw away dead flowers left by grieving loved ones and gently swept away dirt and moss that obscured names and epitaphs from the headstones. This was his ninth visit in as many days. The thought that he would once again leave empty-handed hounded his every step.

It was coming on dusk now, and the storm clouds rolling in from the east made it even darker. Gloom was settling, turning the headstones into dark, indistinct forms. The larger ones loomed over him like giants. The thunder rumbling in the distance warned of the impending storm.

The surroundings were eerie and creepy, reminiscent of a horror movie. He felt no fear. The dead couldn't hurt him. Ghosts and goblins and things that go bump in the night were figments of an overactive imagination. Real monsters roamed among the living. Evil people with ulterior motives and no consciences preyed on the vulnerable and the innocent.

He usually started his work about three rows from his ultimate destination, and while he wanted to get to that one particular grave with almost manic intensity, he forced himself to do the job. No one looking would ever suspect him of being anything other than a meticulous and competent employee hired to maintain the cemetery. A part of him actually found peace in his efforts. He hoped that when family members visited, they were comforted that the final resting place for their loved ones was being cared for so diligently. No one need know that he was never paid for the work he performed or that he'd never been hired to do this job.

An hour later, he finally reached his destination. His breath coming in short spurts had nothing to do with his labors and everything to do with the anticipation of what he might find. What if there was nothing there once again? What if she'd told someone? What if she didn't keep her word? Those questions hounded him every time he came.

He pushed aside the panic. Before he searched the hiding place, his gaze made a casual sweep around the cemetery. He saw no one. Saying a prayer that there would be something for him this time, he pulled the loose brick from the crumbling tombstone and searched. His fingers touched something solid, and relief made him dizzy. Hanging on to the headstone with one hand, he pulled the treasure out with the other. A larger envelope than he had expected. Its heaviness gave an additional concern.

There was no point in worrying and speculating. He couldn't open the package here. He would need to be in his room, behind closed doors.

Wrapping his arms around himself, he turned away from the headstone. The sound of gravel crunching beneath his feet barely penetrated his consciousness. The urgency to get to his vehicle and his hideaway was almost more than he could bear.

As he loaded his tools in the trunk, he stayed alert, hyperaware of his surroundings. He might feel as though thousands of bees were inside him, urging him to flee, but he couldn't break his routine. If anyone recognized him, they would kill him.

Ten miles from the cemetery, he pulled into the small motel parking lot and drove to the back of the building. He had paid cash for the room and given a fake name. Even though he wanted to go inside and examine every morsel of information in the packet, he would allow himself only a brief review. When he got back to his apartment, he'd pore over everything. But for now, he needed to know what the packet held.

Assured he was alone, he grabbed the envelope, stepped out of the car, and took a second for another sweeping gaze around. An icy, cold wind whipped out of the north, causing the rickety motel sign to swing back and forth, creating an eerie squeaking noise. No sane person was about. He laughed at the irony of the thought, the sound hollow and humorless.

Hurrying to the motel door, he slid in the keycard. The light indicator clicked green, and he pushed the door open and closed it quickly behind him. Locks secured, he dashed to the small desk in the corner.

Dumping the contents of the envelope onto the desk, he pulled the note from the small stack and read:

Sorry for the delay. He had a visitor. Thought you would want to see.

Taking his eyes from the words on the page, he glanced down at the desk. A few photographs lay on the surface. His heart lurched in his chest, and it took all his willpower not to sit down and exam each one, savoring them. His eyes shifted to something else that had fallen from the envelope. A USB drive. What could be on it? Had something happened? Who was the visitor?

Grabbing his laptop from beneath the mattress of the bed, he opened it and inserted the drive. His heart pounding for whatever he was about to see, he clicked the icon. It was a recording. The room was a large, masculine office. The colors muted and austere, the room was easily identifiable as the home office of Daniel Fletcher. The older man sat at his desk, seemingly working.

A knock sounded, and Daniel called out, "Enter."

A tall, well-built man walked inside and closed the door behind him. Inside the motel room, a small cry escaped the young man's lips. He stopped breathing as myriad emotions swirled within him. Tears he didn't know he could still shed flowed down his face.

It took several moments to regain his composure enough to realize he'd missed half the conversation between the two men. Drawing in a breath, he restarted the recording and watched it from the beginning.

Alarm mounted with every word he heard, and fury followed. The recording lasted about ten minutes, and with every moment that passed, the anger increased. The son of a bitch. How dare he!

Slamming the laptop shut, he slid it into the small duffle bag holding his clothes. Grabbing the envelope and the bag, he marched to the door.

He knew what he had to do. It had been inevitable, but these new circumstances made it more imperative than ever. The consequences he would face were unavoidable as well. That wouldn't stop him.

As he closed the door behind him, a hideous thought whirled around in his head, making his worry increase a thousandfold. After coming to see Daniel Fletcher, Raphael had no idea that he, too, was now marked for death.

CHAPTER NINE

St. Mary's Hospital

Raphael leaned against the back wall and waited for the meeting to start. Fully in charge, Noah stood at the front of the borrowed conference room. Except for the bruises on his forehead and both jaws, his face was colorless. Raphael knew that sheer will alone kept him on his feet. Just because the hospital had refused to release their patient didn't mean they could keep him from doing what needed to be done.

The conference table had been removed, and though the room was a good size, it was still standing room only. Every available operative wanted in on this mission. The mood was a hundred degrees past grim. Bishop and Maddox had called from the prison in Nebraska, where they had gone to interview Reddington. They had arrived to learn that Reddington had been released from prison. The day after Noah's family was taken.

How the hell a man serving life in prison without possibility of parole could be released was not yet clear. Everyone involved pointed a finger at someone else. Bottom line was Stanford Reddington was loose somewhere, and he had Noah's family.

It had been three days since Reddington had called. Three days and no demands. The theory that Reddington wanted to exchange his family for Noah's was becoming less likely. No one had yet spoken of another reason for the abductions, but fear hung in the air like a bad stench. Could it be that Reddington would disappear completely and never return Noah's family to him?

The very idea of such a horrific event was almost too terrible to contemplate, but it was their job. Every person at LCR was determined that this would not be the outcome.

Giselle's death still hovered like a thick, dark cloud over Raphael's consciousness, and he had been only partially successful in shoving back his grief. As fiercely as he wanted to know what had happened, nothing could be done about it right now. His total focus had to be on this mission. After that, he swore, he would dig all the way to hell to find the answers.

Noah had been almost as disturbed as Raphael on learning about Giselle. LCR prided itself on keeping tabs on the people they rescued. Once Giselle and her family had gone into WITSEC, their information line had been cut off. Still, Raphael knew Noah felt a heavy responsibility. He would want to know all the details and facts, too.

But first they would find Samara and the kids.

"Here's what we know," Noah said. "Until a few days ago, Reddington was still in prison. He had no visitors the entire time of his incarceration. Not even Lancelot Reddington, the man's oldest son, went to see him."

"Then how did he pull this off?" Raphael asked.

Justin Kelly shrugged. "Getting a cellphone in prison isn't difficult."

"True," Raphael said, "but putting something of this magnitude together took some major planning. The number of people alone would make coordination a must."

"We've always figured he has money stashed that no one knew about," Noah said.

"Even if Lance didn't visit his father in prison, I don't see Reddington doing this without his son's involvement," Dylan said. "Lance is too much like his old man not to want to be in on it."

"I agree," Raphael said. "But he's also lazy. Lance was always more about the money than doing any actual work. There's no way he could coordinate this on his own. Nor is he intelligent enough. "

"It's not Lance," Angela said. "Unless he has a doppelganger."

"What do you mean?"

She looked up from the iPad she was holding. "According to one of my most reliable sources, Lancelot Reddington has been in jail in Frankfurt, Germany, for almost six months."

"For what?" Dylan asked.

"Bar fight. Almost killed a man. I can dig some more, but it's doubtful he could have helped his father pull this off while he's incarcerated himself."

"I agree," Raphael said.

"So we know who isn't involved," Justin said. "And we know Reddington's getting help from someone. Question is, what's Reddington's endgame? What does he want from you, McCall?"

The room went quiet. That was everyone's biggest question. How far was the bastard willing to go to get his revenge?

"We're going to work toward the idea that he's going to want to negotiate a trade. His family for mine. If it's otherwise…" Noah broke off, swallowed audibly. The room went silent. No one could bear to comprehend any other outcome.

No. Raphael refused to believe taking McCall's family and disappearing was the man's endgame. He knew Stanford Reddington better than anyone. "It's got to be about seeing his family again. The man's too devious to want things to end quickly. If he had wanted that, he could have easily taken out your entire family without all the extra work. He's going to want something for his trouble."

The cellphone lying on the table in front of Noah chimed. Grabbing it, he turned his back to the room, walked to a corner, listened intently to the caller.

The longer Noah stayed on the call, the grimmer everyone's expressions became. Anxiety and anger were living entities inside the room. LCR operatives were hard-core, tough as nails—the most disciplined and focused people Raphael had ever known. They didn't flinch or overreact, and their success rate was off-the-charts crazy-good because of how they did their jobs. But this was different... way different. This was personal. There wasn't a person in the room who didn't look upon McCall's family as their own.

Noah ended his call and turned around. Raphael hadn't believed his face could get any paler or any grimmer.

"Noah? What's happened?" Riley asked.

"Reddington is dying. Has only a few months to live."

"So that means that either he's wanting to see his family one last time and is planning an exchange. Or—" Eden broke off, obviously not wanting to say the words everyone was thinking.

McCall finished for her, "Or he has nothing to lose and is planning to kill them as his last evil act."

***

His blond head covered with a Washington Nationals baseball cap, slender body hidden beneath a bulky army-green jacket, the young man shuffled into the hospital. A bouquet of flowers in his hand, he walked along with five other people as if he were part of the crowd. He had waited outside the hospital a few minutes until he saw a larger group getting ready to enter and had joined them.

Once inside, the group of people disbursed in several directions. He had thought about coming in last night when there were fewer people around, but changed his mind. Security would be tight. Noah McCall wasn't a celebrity, but he would no doubt have plenty of operatives on watch. Better to try to blend in with others who were visiting relatives and friends.

Instead, he'd used his time last night to study the hospital. The noncritical patients were located on floors six and seven. He recalled from the recording of the meeting with Daniel Fletcher that Raphael had mentioned McCall's injuries as serious but not life-threatening. A regular patient would likely stay on either of those floors. But Noah McCall wasn't a regular patient. He had enemies. With so many politicians in this area, the odds were good that there was another floor for patients who needed extra privacy and protection. After looking at the blueprints and websites last night, he had determined that was the eighth floor. If he were wrong, he would search every nook and cranny of the hospital, but he would start on the eighth floor.

He was unarmed and felt naked without at least one weapon. If he was caught, it would be a lot easier to explain he was lost if he wasn't carrying. He had learned, though, that in a pinch the most innocuous items could be used to defend oneself. He vowed never to be caught off guard again.

The elevator was already half full when he and a few others stepped inside. Noting that the button for the sixth floor was already highlighted, he placed himself in the center of the group, toward the back. He would get out on the sixth floor and take the stairs to the eighth.

No one paid attention to him. He had gotten used to being ignored. Most people were so caught up in their own worries and problems, it was easy to disappear, blend into the background. A helpful talent, considering he was likely being hunted all over the world.

The elevator dinged and then opened. Several people disembarked, and he slid out right along with them. Spotting the stairway door a few yards away, he headed toward it. Two flights later, he was at the eighth floor. It might take him a few minutes to determine the location of Noah McCall's room, but he'd find it. There was no other option.

His hand touched the door handle, and he clenched his fist when he noticed the trembling. He'd been doing so well, but now it was all hitting him. There would be no going back after this.

Reminding himself how far he'd come, what he had overcome, and what he was working to achieve, he took one last shaky breath and opened the door to the eighth floor.

***

Raphael paced up and down the small area of the hospital room. While others were running down leads and digging deep for information, he and Dylan had stayed back to talk with Noah. The three of them knew more about Reddington than anyone outside of law enforcement.

"Okay, until we know different, we're going with the scenario that he'll want a trade. You think he's going to want more than that?" Dylan asked.

"Yeah, he'll want my blood. And that of anyone else who gets in the way. We'll play it his way for right now, but if he's hurt Mara or one of my kids?" Noah shook his head. "All bets are off. The bastard is going down."

"Hurting them just doesn't fit him," Raphael said. "Women and children are nothing but a means to an end to Reddington. He's going to ask for an exchange. He'll never see what we've got planned coming."

"Eden and Jordan have already put together a list of operatives who could pass as his family. Amelia is about sixteen, and Eric is around eleven. There's no way to know if he knows about Giselle, so we'll have to be ready to make an adjustment."

Dylan turned to Raphael. "I was sorry to hear about Giselle."

A deep stab went through his heart. Giving Dylan a nod of thanks, he returned his focus to Noah. "You don't think Sarah would help if we found a way to contact her?"

A flash of fire flared in McCall's eyes. "Using a victim goes against everything LCR stands for. I'll get my family back, but it won't be by victimizing the victims. Neither Sarah nor her children need to be involved."

"What if one of them wants to be involved?"

All three heads turned at the sound of a new voice in the room. A young man stood at the doorway, dressed in a light blue denim shirt, wrinkled khakis, and a battered-looking army jacket. A Washington Nationals baseball cap covered his longish bleach-blond hair. The black-rimmed round glasses made his brown eyes look large and gave him a serious, studious air. Slender to the point of being skinny, he was medium height and slouched with poor posture.

There was something familiar about him, but Raphael couldn't decide exactly what that something was.

"Who are you?" Dylan asked.

A slender hand pulled the ball cap from his head, revealing the messy blond cap of hair. His fingers tugged, and the blond hair slid off his head. Long, lustrous black hair fell in dark waves to his shoulders.

Dark eyes swept over the room and then zeroed in on Raphael. "Giselle Reddington."

CHAPTER TEN

Three stunned faces stared back at her. If she had any sense of humor left at all, she might have smiled at their reactions. They hadn't had any idea. Even Raphael hadn't recognized her.

Raphael took a step toward her. "Giselle… How did…" He took a raspy breath, continued, "I thought you were dead."

"That's what they wanted you to think. What they wish was true."

"Who are *they*?" Dylan asked.

"Daniel and Clarissa Fletcher, my in-laws. Former in-laws."

"Why would they want you dead?"

She leaned against the doorframe to brace herself and get her bearings. Seeing Raphael in person was even more of a shock than she had anticipated. The brief recording of him in Daniel's office hadn't prepared her for the impact. He looked so much like the young man she'd once known, but he looked totally different, too. He was now all man—tough, strong, confident. It was both heaven and hell to be this close to him again. Despite distrusting almost every living person, she found herself wanting to throw herself into his arms. She couldn't do that. Not only did she not know him now, he likely hated her.

And if he didn't now, he would soon.

Apparently interpreting her struggle as exhaustion, Raphael pushed a chair toward her. Since her legs were decidedly weak, she collapsed into the chair with a grateful sigh.

Before walking away from her, he squeezed her hand gently. A weight lifted from her heart. Maybe he didn't hate her after all. When he turned to face her again, all traces of emotion were gone as if that small, affectionate gesture had never occurred.

"Tell us what the hell's going on," Noah said. "Why did Daniel Fletcher tell Raphael you were dead?"

"It's a long story. One I'll be happy to share with you, as I need your help, too."

"Are you in contact with your father?"

She inwardly flinched at the word *father*. Stanford Reddington had no idea what it took to be a father, nor did he care.

"I haven't seen or heard from Reddington in years."

"Then how did you know about my family's abduction?"

The question came from Noah, but both Raphael and Dylan shared the same suspicious expression. She understood their confusion as well as their anger. Someone precious had been taken from them. She knew that feeling all too well.

"I didn't until yesterday." Her gaze strayed to Raphael. "When I saw a recording of your meeting with Daniel Fletcher."

"How did you see a recording?"

"I have a contact inside Fletcher's household. I had asked for…information on what was going on inside the house. She left me the recording, claiming she thought I might be interested."

"You don't believe her?" Dylan asked.

"No. I think it was a setup." She sent a grimace of apology toward Noah. "And I think the abduction of your family is all part of a larger picture. Mainly to get to me."

"What the hell are you talking about?" Noah barked.

"My in-laws had me committed to a mental institution. I managed to escape, but I know they're looking for me."

"And you think they're trying to lure you out of hiding by abducting my family? That's a helluva stretch, Giselle."

Yes, it was, and she knew she had some major hills to climb before they believed anything she said.

"Why the hell would your in-laws have you committed?" Raphael asked.

"They claimed I tried to kill myself. That I was a danger to myself and my...and others."

"Kill yourself how?" Dylan asked.

"An overdose." She shook her head. "I have never willingly taken anything other than antibiotics or over-the-counter pain meds for a headache."

"What happened?"

"I had a meeting with my in-laws. I told them I was leaving. Clarissa gave me a glass of lemonade. It must've been drugged. The next thing I knew, I was in a mental hospital."

They made no effort to hide the doubt in their eyes. She couldn't blame them. If she hadn't lived it, she wouldn't believe it herself. Who would believe that one of the most prominent and respected families in the United States could be guilty of drugging their daughter-in-law and committing her to a mental institution? No one. And that was the reason she had given up on anyone helping her.

The Fletchers were known all over the world. Not a hint of scandal or impropriety had ever been written about them. Even her ill-advised marriage to their son had ended up making them look like paragons of virtue and acceptance.

How they did this, she didn't know. What she did know—knew to her soul—was that they were as evil as any hardened criminal. Money, influence, and power had a way of hiding a multitude of sins.

"Do you have any proof of this?" Noah asked.

Of course she didn't. "No."

"Why would they do this?"

There were many answers to that question, and for now, there was only one she was willing to answer.

"From the moment I married their son, they wanted to get rid of me. After he died, it became easier."

"If what you say is true, why not just have you killed? Why put you in the hospital?"

"I've asked myself that question a thousand times. I don't know the answer."

"How did you get away from the hospital?" Raphael asked.

"I hit one of the guards over the head and ran away."

"When?"

She closed her eyes as she whispered, "Almost five months ago."

"Where have you been all this time?"

"For several weeks, I could do nothing. I was given drugs at the hospital, and it took a long time to overcome the effects."

"If you left the hospital with nothing, how have you been living? Where have you been staying? Someone must have helped you."

She wasn't sure which one of them was looking at her with more distrust. She knew how this looked. She could easily be working with Reddington. He could have sent her here to learn their plan so he could be ready for them.

It was likely a more believable explanation than the truth.

Talking about what happened after she escaped was difficult. Some of it she didn't really remember other than vague images and soft voices of encouragement. Her recovery had been long, arduous, and the most physically painful experience she'd ever endured. Though it wasn't something she planned to describe in detail, she gave them what she could. "I stayed in a homeless shelter for a while. Made up a story about hiding from my abusive ex-husband. They had medical staff who helped me with the effects of the drugs."

"If Fletcher's people were looking for you and have as much influence as you say, I'm surprised they didn't find you."

"Their priority at the shelter was protecting me from my abusive husband. Only a few people even knew I was there. When I was strong enough, I left the shelter. I knew if I stayed, I could be putting everyone in danger."

She made her recovery sound a lot more simplistic than it had been. Weeks had gone by before she finally remembered everything—who she was and what had been taken from her. After that, she worked her ass off to get healthy.

"And then what?" Dylan asked.

"My mother had to move again after my marriage." She couldn't look anyone in the eye as she spoke those words. What she had done to her mother...done to her family was one of the biggest sorrows and regrets of her life.

She cleared her throat and continued, "Before she left, she gave me the location of a lockbox. She told me to use it only if I had no other choice. She left me money. Fake IDs. Anything I might need if I needed to hide."

Having lived as Stanford Reddington's prisoner had made Sarah determined that neither she nor her children would ever have to endure imprisonment again.

If not for that safety net, Giselle wasn't sure what she would have done. It enabled her to stay hidden until she was able to face what she needed to do.

All three men continued to look at her with varying levels of distrust. She couldn't blame them. Considering who her father was and the family she was accusing of trying to destroy her, she could certainly understand their feelings. The truth was often harder to believe.

As they fired questions at her, she kept her eyes focused on Dylan as she answered. Though his expression was just as wary, she found his distrust easier to handle. Looking at the bruises on Noah's face, the agony in his eyes, made her feel ill. Reddington was responsible for his pain—the man she once called Papa. She might not be responsible for what had happened, but the stench of his existence was inside her. As was his blood.

Looking at Raphael was even more painful, but in a different way. Seeing him again after all these years called to mind what he had once meant to her. What they had meant to each other. Seven years was a long time to hang on to a dream you knew could never come true. She was surprised and not altogether pleased that those feelings lingered. She could not and would not let that impair her thinking.

She answered each question as succinctly as she could without giving everything away. No, she didn't go to the police. Who would believe her? If she had gone to the authorities, she would be dead right now. Of that, she had no doubt.

When the questions became repetitive, she tried to stay patient. She knew the drill. They were trying to trip her up. It didn't matter. She had nothing to hide. Well, almost nothing.

"This person who gave you the recording of my meeting with Fletcher. Who is she?"

She forced herself to look directly at Raphael when she answered. "An employee of the Fletchers. We became friends while I lived with them. After I recovered, I approached her and asked for her help."

"What kind of help did you think she could provide?"

"I needed to know what was going on in the household."

Though her answer was an obvious deflection, thankfully no one delved deeper for a more complete answer.

"Why do you think she's betrayed you?"

"It's the only thing that makes sense. Why would she leave me a recording of you meeting with Fletcher? She knows nothing about my history with you."

"And you think Fletcher teamed up with Reddington to get you out in the open?"

"Yes. Daniel will stop at nothing to get to me."

When none of them looked convinced, she leaned forward, zeroed her gaze in on Noah. "What are the chances of your family being taken at the same time I am being hunted? I believe with all my heart that Daniel set up this entire scenario to draw me out."

"How would they know that you would even show up to offer your help?"

"It's a chance they were willing to take. My seeing that recording almost ensured that I would come to you."

"And you played right into their hands. You came running to help?"

She detected no sarcasm in Dylan's question, but she felt defensive all the same. She hated that McCall's family was going through hell, and she would do whatever she could to help them, but she did have an ulterior motive as well. One that Daniel was all too aware of and would use to his advantage any way that he could. However, until she was sure they would help her, she would wait on revealing her true reason.

"Yes, I thought I could help."

"Help how?"

"The abduction of your family might be a ruse to get to me, but Reddington likely believes he is in control. Hurting you, causing you grief, is part of this, but his ultimate goal is to get to his family, specifically my mother. He'll want to see her, possibly exchange your family for his."

"So everyone gets what they want. Reddington gets to see your mother. Noah is hurt in the process."

"And Daniel Fletcher finds me."

"You think all of this was done in an effort to get you to a certain place for an assassination attempt," Dylan said.

"Yes." Surprisingly, considering the subject matter, the tension in her body lessened a little. At least they were considering her theory.

"Then, if that's the case, you don't need to be involved in this at all," Raphael said. "We'll do this without you."

"No. I want to be involved. This is because of me. I need to help."

"You would do this for me?" Noah asked. "Why?"

For the first time in she didn't know how long, she was able to smile sincerely. "You saved my mother's life—all of our lives. I owe you. We all owe you a debt of gratitude. I'd like to repay you by helping you get your family back."

"Or you could be part of Reddington's plan, and you're here to find out what we know."

Fury erupted within Giselle, and she sprang to her feet. "I am in no way associated with that bastard. He raped and abused my mother for years, and I want nothing to do with him."

After all she had told them, they still didn't believe her. Why had she expected anything different? Anger burning pure and bright, she strode with furious indignation to the door. "I hope you get your family back, Mr. McCall."

When her hand touched the door, Noah barked out, "Stop."

She turned, glaring at them all. Daring them to throw another accusation her way.

"I'm sorry, Giselle," Noah said. "I needed to know for sure."

It had been a test, one she had apparently passed. That realization didn't lessen the hurt, but it did diminish her anger. This was Noah's family. It was stupid of her to expect him to give her his blind faith. And her explanation, though perfectly valid in her mind, was definitely out there.

She noted that they were all looking at her with less suspicion and something that looked like acceptance. Without warning, her legs went out from under her, and everything dimmed around her. She felt strong arms holding her up and looked up into dark, beautiful eyes. Eyes she used to dream about.

"I'm fine." She tried to pull away, but the hands holding her didn't let go. Instead, he pushed her gently into the chair she'd jumped up from moments ago.

Relieved that she hadn't made a total fool of herself by passing out, she managed a small smile of thanks to Raphael. He squeezed her shoulder gently and stepped back. She still felt the warmth of those large hands and she looked away, afraid of the feelings she was suddenly having. She had no time for any tender emotions. She had an agenda. Nothing else mattered.

"It's time to put your cards on the table, Giselle." McCall's voice, raspy from the strain of the last few days, broke her out of her trance. "We'll gladly accept your help, but there's something you're keeping from us."

Raphael had once told her that Noah McCall had a sixth sense about people. That he could read them, seemed to know what they were thinking. She now saw what he meant. But these people didn't know her, and she didn't know them...not even Raphael. Not anymore.

"If you expect us to help you, Giselle, we need to know everything."

She focused on each of their faces, saw the determination, the strength. They saved people, rescued innocents. If she didn't trust them, who then was she going to trust?

Taking a breath, she took another huge gamble and answered softly, "They have my son."

CHAPTER ELEVEN

"What?" Raphael found himself grappling on several different levels. Giselle was alive. Dammit, she was alive, sitting here in front of him. In the deepest part of his soul, he had been grieving. He hadn't realized quite how much until she'd walked through the door and taken that ridiculous wig off. Seeing her again, especially after thinking she was dead, had almost brought him to his knees.

Daniel and Clarissa Fletcher, her in-laws, the bastion of American society—a height that others only dreamed about attaining—were in cahoots with Stanford Reddington, convicted human trafficker, in an effort to find and kill their daughter-in-law? As farfetched conspiracy theories went, this was at the top. As unbelievable as it seemed, he saw some truth to it. And it was clear that Giselle believed it to her soul.

And her in-laws had her son? Nowhere in LCR's research had a child been mentioned. Admittedly, that was no major surprise. Hiding a grandson should be no real problem for the Fletchers. Question was, why would they even want to hide the fact that they had a grandson? Typical grandparents carried photos of their grandkids on their phones and in their wallets. They talked about them to anyone and everyone. They didn't hide them away as if they were ashamed of them. Unless they had cause to keep him a secret.

"Start from the beginning," Noah said calmly. "Why do the Fletchers have your son? And why do they hate you enough to want to see you dead?"

Giselle was twice as pale than when she first arrived. Recalling trauma was damn difficult. Doing so in front of three doubting Thomases would be worse. Even though every protective instinct told him to demand that they lay off for a while, give her a break, he wouldn't. Keeping her on edge, pushing for information, was the best way to get to the truth. LCR would do everything possible to help her if she was telling them the truth. If not, this kind of questioning would reveal the holes in her story.

As if accepting the inevitability of spilling her guts, she stared sightlessly at the wall and began to recount what had happened. She started where she met Danny Fletcher. Their whirlwind romance had resulted in an elopement to Las Vegas right before they were both scheduled to graduate from college.

What she said tracked with what Raphael had read in the tabloids. He told himself to listen dispassionately. Anger was a useless emotion. This wasn't about him or what they'd once had. A child could be at risk.

"The Fletchers were never unfriendly to me. In fact, they were downright cordial. After Danny died, the pretense stopped."

"In what way?" Noah asked.

"Small things at first. I didn't pick up on them. After Danny's death…" She cleared her throat. "I think I was numb, just trying to get through the day. I had a lot of decisions I needed to make. I—"

As if realizing she'd gotten off track, she shook her head quickly, then continued, "At first it was just Clarissa. Petty little insults I let slide. From my appearance to the way I ate. I was focused on my son. He adored Danny and didn't understand why he never came home.

"I'm not sure if I finally woke up from my numbness, or if Clarissa decided she wasn't being direct enough. Her remarks became meaner, more pointed. I knew I needed to move out. That kind of environment wasn't healthy for my son. Then she told me I should go away for a while, get a fresh perspective. She said she would see to 'the boy.' That's what she called him most of the time—the boy."

"It doesn't sound like she has much affection for your child. Why would—"

"No." She cut Dylan's question off. "She has a great deal of affection for him. Or what passes for affection in her world. From the moment she saw him… I saw it, but I was grateful that she was so fond of him that I ignored the warning signals. She's obsessed with him."

Raphael frowned at her words. "Any grandmother would be fond of her first grandchild."

She shook her head. "It was more than that. It was like she wanted to claim him as hers."

"And she wanted you out of the picture," Dylan said.

"Yes. I made a stupid mistake. I told them I was leaving and taking my son with me."

"I'm assuming that didn't go over well."

"On the contrary. We were at dinner when I told them. They were calm. Said they supported whatever I decided to do. That we would be missed." She gave a humorless laugh. "Clarissa even went so far as to say she hoped I would find a place close-by so she could see 'the boy.'

"The next morning, Joan, one of the maids, brought me coffee, as she had for as long as I'd lived there. I drank maybe three swallows and began to feel dizzy. I think, maybe, that was the first time they drugged me."

All of this sounded unbelievable, but it was obvious Giselle was convinced, and Raphael saw no reason to doubt her. Barely thirty-six hours ago, he sat across from Daniel Fletcher and was told Giselle was dead. Did he tell Raphael the lie with the hope that very soon it would be true?

"How long did this go on?" Noah asked.

"I don't know exactly. It could have been weeks or only days. I've never fully regained my memory of that time. I have flashbacks…nightmares. I don't know if they're real or not. What I do know is that one morning I woke, semi-clearheaded, and discovered I was incarcerated.

"I don't know how long I was there. Maybe only a few weeks, but I have a feeling it was longer. I was drugged daily…remembered nothing. I only knew I didn't belong there and needed to escape. Once I did…as soon as I was able, I went back to New York. I knew I couldn't just show up at their house. They would have either had me carted away, or worse, but I needed to find out about my son.

"Mavis Tenpenny is his nanny. I remembered that on her days off she often visited the cemetery where her parents are buried. I went to the cemetery every day until she showed up. I explained what happened. What the Fletchers did."

"She believed you," Raphael asked.

"I don't know. I thought she did, but now I'm not sure. She was my only hope on getting news. I had to take the chance."

"What did you ask the nanny to do?" Dylan asked.

"I wanted to know about my son. How he was. I wanted photographs. Any kind of information she could give me."

"You didn't ask her to bring him to you?"

"Of course I did, but she refused. I wasn't surprised. She would be putting her career on the line, possibly her life. At that point, I had to settle for what I could get. Photographs and information."

"But you got more than that," Noah said. "You got a recording of Fletcher telling Raphael that you were dead."

"Yes. The minute I watched it, I knew it was a ruse to get to me."

Raphael hadn't thought she could get paler. The telling had taken a toll. He gave Noah a look that his boss correctly interpreted as, *That's enough for now.*

He came to stand in front of her. Noah and Dylan were behind him, each on his phone, barking out orders for intel on the Fletchers. He couldn't take his eyes off Giselle. Her skin was so translucent, she looked as though she could keel over any moment.

"I'll be right back." He strode out of the room and was back within a minute with a bottle of water. Opening the bottle, he handed it to her and watched her take small sips.

"Better?"

"Yes. Thanks."

"No problem."

The silence that followed was both uncomfortable and painful. He wanted to say more. He wanted to ask her why she hadn't contacted him. Even though they'd ended badly, she had to know she could have come to him.

"Are you happy?"

Her softly worded question came out of left field and temporarily froze his brain.

"Happy? Not sure what you mean."

"I mean…in your life. With LCR? Is it what you thought it would be?"

"Yeah, it is."

"I'm glad."

She looked different but the same. Her dark brown eyes were still beautiful, but they used to glimmer with laughter. Now they were dull and lifeless. Her heart-shaped face had thinned out, making her cheekbones more prominent. Her lips were still full, but there were little lines around them, showing the tension and stress she was under. Her hair was much shorter, just brushing her shoulders. Years ago, it had reached the small of her back.

She had suffered. There was no question about that.

"Raphael…don't."

"Don't what?"

"None of this is your fault."

She had always been able to read him. It bothered him that she still could. He'd been through hours of training on how to remove all emotion from his face. A part of him did feel guilty for not checking to make sure she was okay. Another part told him he had nothing to feel guilty about. She was the one who'd left him, not the other way around.

He went on to a safer subject. "How old is your son?"

"Almost four."

"What's his name?"

"Giovanni." A slight smile curved her lips. "Gio for short."

"I like it."

A brief flash of grief swept across her face. She quickly replaced it with the stoicism she'd displayed since she arrived. Giselle was no longer the innocent, naïve young woman he had once known.

She was a mature woman…a mother, grieving for the loss of her son. And her husband.

"I was sorry to hear about your husband's death."

"Thank you."

He wanted to say more. He wanted to ask if he had been good to her. If she had loved him. Inappropriate questions and none of his damn business.

"All right." Noah's voice called him back from things best not dwelled on.

Straightening to his full height, he faced Noah, noting that at some point Dylan had left the room.

"What'd you find out?"

"Nothing and a lot, depending on how you look at it. As we figured, there is no death certificate on Giselle. I don't know what Fletcher thought to gain by telling you she was dead, other than the hope that you'd leave it alone."

"Or buying them time to actually make it real," Raphael said grimly.

"Possibly." Noah's gaze went to Giselle. "Do you think your son is in any immediate danger?"

"No. They won't hurt him physically. But I'm worried…very worried about his emotional well-being." She swallowed hard and continued, "I don't know what they've told him about me. Not really. Mavis said he believes I'm on a long trip…a holiday. I cannot imagine what he's thinking. He's just a little boy. He doesn't understand what's going on."

"We'll do everything we can to get him back for you," Noah said.

She pressed her fingers to her eyes and breathed out a long, sobbing sigh. "Thank you, Noah." Collecting herself, she straight ened her shoulders, lifted her chin. "Now, tell me what you need me to do to help you get your family back."

CHAPTER TWELVE

Giselle walked with Dylan to the parking lot. She was being taken to an LCR safe house. Noah had told her that his first order of business was to get her safely settled, away from anyone who might recognize her. She was feeling exposed and couldn't deny the relief. The Fletchers could have spies everywhere.

Raphael stayed behind. She told herself she was glad of that. Every ounce of her reserve had been used up. Facing him alone would be more than she could handle right now. She needed some time to prepare herself again. She thought she'd done a good job of handling her emotions, but that could end at any moment. A few hours away from him would help prepare her for the next meeting.

They weren't friends any longer. Still, she had felt bereft, empty, the moment she'd walked out of the room without him. She snarled at those feelings now. This wasn't a reunion to catch up with an old friend. She had ended their relationship the day she left him. Something he had acknowledged, and quite painfully, when he hadn't returned her call. It was over—had been over for a long time.

Her reason for calling him that day would have to be addressed soon. Would he regret not returning her call? She hoped he didn't. Even though many things would be different now if he had, she was learning that regret was just another form of torture.

She needed to focus on the positive. She finally had people who could help her. Highly trained operatives who rescued people on a daily basis. They had the skills to get her son back.

She wasn't ready to feel optimistic, wasn't really sure there was any optimism left inside her. But there was a glimmer of hope. For right now, she would settle for that. It was much more than she'd had in a long time.

She glanced toward her car. "I parked in the visitor lot across the street."

"We'll have someone get your car for you later. For right now, let's get you hidden."

Nodding, she followed him to a charcoal-gray Jeep Grand Cherokee not far from the entrance. Before she'd walked out of Noah's hospital room, she had covered her hair again. Someone could be watching, waiting for her to come to Noah. She could take no chances. She had walked into the hospital as a man. Anyone watching would recognize her immediately. She couldn't take the risk.

With a sigh, Giselle settled into the front seat, but couldn't make her body relax. Dylan's demeanor wasn't threatening, but his harsh expression hadn't changed. When she had met him, he had been undercover as John Wheeler, an LCR operative working to bring her father to justice. He looked only slightly less dangerous now.

As the Jeep moved out of the parking lot and onto the main road, she searched for something to say. Polite conversation often flummoxed her. Growing up with only her family to converse with had left her at a disadvantage when it came to everyday discussion. With the exception of today, her lengthiest exchange in months had been with a motel night clerk, and that had been about changing rooms because the heating didn't work.

"You could have called Jamie."

Startled at the break in silence, she jumped slightly. "What?"

"Jamie would have helped you."

Yes, she would have. Without going into the gory and humiliating details, how could she explain what she had gone through? The weakness, the sickness. The extreme paranoia. After escaping from the hospital, she had lived with the fear that she really was crazy. She hadn't trusted herself and was too afraid to trust anyone else.

Having no choice, she had given what little trust she'd had left to the people who had cared for her. Without them, she wouldn't have survived. They had gone a long way in reestablishing her belief that there were still good people in the world. But she had lost all confidence in being able to discern who those people were.

When she'd finally regained her mind, and her strength somewhat, she had been physically better but without an ounce of confidence. Her only focus after that had been to get to her son.

Knowing whatever she said wouldn't settle anything, she said, "How is Jamie? Is she still teaching?"

For the first time, she saw his expression change, soften. She knew Jamie and Dylan had married—that had happened not too long after her father's arrest.

"Doing great. Teaches part-time now. We've got two girls, four years old and seven months."

"That's lovely." And she meant that with all her heart. It was nice to know that some people did fall in love and live happily ever after. She had once believed in that for her and Raphael.

"Raphael." She swallowed. "Is he…um…married?"

She hated to be so obvious, but she wanted to know. Needed the answer like she needed her next breath. She told herself it didn't matter, not really. But she couldn't allow herself a breath until she heard Dylan's answer.

"No. He's not married."

She kept her face averted, her gaze focused out the window. She knew Dylan was looking at her, that he had questions. She was glad he didn't ask. She didn't have any answers.

She had no right to be glad that Raphael wasn't married. She had given up that right when she'd walked away from him. She should want him to be happy...settled. And she did.

Still...

***

Raphael paced the confines of Noah's hospital room. He wouldn't be able to settle again until he joined Giselle at the safe house. Just watching her walk out of the hospital room without him had been painful. He needed to make sure she was safe. But first, he and Noah needed to talk.

"You believe her?" Raphael asked.

"Yes and no. We knew Reddington has some major backing. Having Fletcher's money and influence behind him would get him through doors he'd have no way of opening on his own."

"Which might explain how he got out of prison without anyone having a clear answer about why."

"Exactly."

"What's the part of Giselle's story you don't believe?"

"I'm not sure I disbelieve her as much as I think she's holding back."

Raphael nodded. "I agree. She's not telling us everything."

"I need you to find out what that is. She's going to trust you more than anyone. If she's going to help us get my family back, we need to know everything. And if we're going to get her son back, we need everything she's got on her in-laws. Why the hell do they hate her so much? Enough to want her dead?" Noah's eyes narrowed into slits. "Think you can be objective?"

The automatic answer that came to his mind was yes, of course, he could be objective. He was an LCR operative, trained to interrogate people, to ferret out secrets they didn't want to give up. It was his job. But this was Giselle, the girl he'd once loved.

Instead of answering right away, he took a moment for a gut check. Satisfied, he nodded. "Yeah, I can."

"Spend some time with her. The more we know, the better our chances of getting my family back without anyone getting hurt. Then we'll concentrate on rescuing her son."

Before he could respond, the cellphone in front of Noah chimed. They both glanced at the display, noting the unidentified caller. Had to be Reddington. He hoped like hell the bastard was calling to move this thing forward.

"McCall," Noah answered.

"Delightful to talk with you again, Mr. McCall."

"You ready to deal, Reddington?"

"Do you have something to deal with?"

"I do."

"Excellent. Perhaps you and I could satisfy a mutual need."

"LCR isn't in the habit of bartering one life for another, Reddington. You know I can't give your family back to you, right?"

"That's not my intent. I'm sure you know I'm ill, likely only have a few months left. But it would give me such joy to see them one last time."

Raphael barely refrained from an eye roll at Reddington's overdramatic speech. The bastard was enjoying himself. The idiot thought he was in control. Playing it his way until Noah's family was back safely was the only way to go. Once they were within LCR's grasp, the tables would be turned. Reddington wouldn't know what hit him.

"Where and when?" Noah said.

Reddington's voice, formerly soft and mellow, went hard. "I'll make the arrangements. I would hate to be disappointed, McCall."

"You won't be."

"I'll be in touch."

Snarling a vicious curse, Noah dropped the phone on the table in front of him before he could throw it across the room. Fury zoomed through his veins. Closing his eyes, he searched for the famous control he was known for. He and Mara had been through rough times, absolute hell. They had survived then, they would survive now. No son of a bitch bastard freak was going to destroy his family. They were counting on him to rescue them, and he damn well would not let them down.

"Noah?"

Resolved, calmer, he opened his eyes. "Let's get everyone ready. When he calls with the location, I want everything in order. Get it started. Then get what else you can from Giselle."

Raphael gave a solemn nod and walked out the door. Noah blew out a ragged sigh. He didn't like using anyone other than LCR operatives. Putting an innocent in danger went against everything LCR stood for, and if Giselle was right, this entire elaborate scenario had been done to draw her out of hiding. If that was the case, after this was over, he would not rest until he dug up every speck of dirt on Daniel Fletcher.

Did Reddington realize he had set up his own daughter to be murdered? Noah had long ago stopped being surprised at the shit people did to one another. The very reason he'd started LCR was to help people who got caught up in other people's evil deeds. But if Reddington had agreed to this with the full knowledge that his daughter would die, Noah had to admit even he was shocked.

Either way, Giselle would be protected. This he swore.

Focusing on what needed to be done had kept his mind from going to what Mara and his children were going through. He tried to tell himself that now that he knew Reddington wanted to make a trade, his family for Noah's, they were being treated well. But he didn't know that. Lying to himself wasn't his thing, but he had no choice. If he started thinking anything else, he wouldn't be able to focus on getting them back.

He stared at the door and thought about the young man who'd just left. This was rough on him, too. Raphael was part of the McCall family. He was hurting, worried. And now the girl who'd broken his heart was back in his life. How that would play out, he didn't know. Raphael had exceeded every expectation Noah had had for him. He was an exceptional man in every way, but it was Raphael Sanchez's heart that Noah admired the most. Yes, he could be ruthless and had a stubborn streak a mile long, but Raphael had a heart for rescue unlike anyone he'd ever hired. In fact, he reminded Noah of himself.

Raphael had chosen LCR. He'd wanted to be an operative almost from the moment Noah had met him. Although Noah had opened some doors for him early on, everything he had accomplished was Raphael's alone. His tenacity and determination had made him the man he was. He'd had numerous opportunities and talents for other careers, but he'd never changed his focus from his original dream—to work for Last Chance Rescue.

When Giselle had left Raphael, though, Noah had worried. Optimism had always been one of Raphael's core qualities, but he had changed after that. In a way, he'd become even more focused, more determined, but he had also lost a lot of that bright shine of optimism.

Noah couldn't help but wonder what kind of impact Giselle's reappearance would have on Raphael. Or what it would do to him if she left again.

Giving in to exhaustion and pain, his head pounding, body aching, Noah closed his eyes. What was Mara doing right now? Were she and the kids together? Were they being mistreated?

He wasn't one to believe in psychic connections, but as he lay there, he put every ounce of his energy into thinking about her, communicating his love and commitment to her and their children. From their first meeting, he and Samara had shared an amazing connection. His love for her had only grown stronger through the years, and their bond was deeper than ever.

In the darkest of dark despairs, he prayed that their bond was strong enough to break through all barriers so she could know he was coming for her, that he would do whatever it took to get her and the kids safely home. In his mind, he told her to stay strong, to believe.

He would be with her soon.

***

Samara woke with a start. She had been dreaming of Noah. His soft growl had been whispering in her ear. She couldn't remember all the things he'd said, but for some odd reason she was warm all over. And despite the fact that tears seeped from her eyes, she felt surprisingly optimistic. She knew it was only a dream, but it had been so real, as if Noah had been right beside her. She could almost feel his arms around her, his warm breath in her ear, whispering everything would be okay. That they would be together again soon.

"Mama?"

Hurriedly wiping tears from her face, she turned to Evie. "Yes, darling?"

"I gotta go to the bathroom again."

Her poor baby. On top of everything else, Evie had an upset tummy. She had a sensitive stomach already, and the stress had exacerbated her issues. Between the greasy food they'd been given to eat and the stress, her little girl was hurting. Just one more reason she wanted to make these people pay.

"I'll call them." Standing, she pushed Evie behind her. "Micah, come stand beside your sister."

So far, the men had been mostly accommodating, allowing bathroom breaks three times a day. This would be the fifth time today she'd had to request a trip to the bathroom. She and the children always went together. No way was she leaving either of them here by themselves. The men hadn't physically hurt them, but she would take no chances.

Rapping on the door, she called out, "We need to go to the bathroom."

There was no answer.

She knocked on the door again, called out louder, "We need to go to the bathroom."

Still no answer.

"Mama." The distress in her daughter's voice punched her anger to the top.

Pounding on the door, Samara used every expletive and curse she could come up with. When this was over, she was going to owe the bad-word jar they kept in the kitchen a good twenty-five bucks.

The door swung open, and the man who usually took them to the bathroom stood there. He was usually accommodating, if not terribly friendly. The glint in his light hazel eyes said he wasn't in the best of spirits.

"We need to go to the bathroom."

"You've used up all your bathroom allowances. Now shut up before I shut you up."

"My daughter has an upset stomach."

"Tough shit." He didn't laugh, but she saw a trace of amusement at his own joke.

At barely five two and a hundred and seven pounds on a good day, Samara knew she could do no real physical harm to this six-foot, two-hundred-fifty-pound man. And while she had no problem using shame and reproach with lavish flair, this big jerk would likely not be moved, no matter how much she piled on the shame factor.

Giving him details of the consequences of not doing as she asked was her best bet.

"In about five minutes, maybe less, there is going to be an ungodly stench in here. If you don't allow us to go to the bathroom, the smell will get worse, permeating the entire boat. Even a shithead like you won't be able to handle it."

He glowered as the facts sank into his thick skull. "Fine. But only the kid."

"No. Absolutely not. We all go together."

He looked like he was about to argue, but when Evie started crying, he snarled, "Okay. Come on."

They followed him, single file, with Samara in the front, Evie behind her, and Micah in the rear. This was the third day of their imprisonment, and they had gotten used to the routine. That didn't stop Samara from looking for something, anything that would give her an advantage over her captors. They had been rude, crude, and careless, but as yet had not physically hurt them. She hoped it would stay that way, but a weapon would give her a better chance if things changed.

As they walked down the narrow passageway, she was aware of eyes watching her. She knew there were at least four men on the boat, but she suspected there were more. The stark reality of their situation had come to light the first time they had been allowed to go to the bathroom. She had looked out a porthole and had seen nothing but water. She had been prepared to fight, but trying to take on a half-dozen men or more in the middle of a large body of water would be stupid. If anything happened to her, her children would be left alone. No way could she take the risk.

"Mommy, hurry!"

Before she could turn to reassure Evie that they were almost there, the man leading them snarled out a curse and reached back for her daughter. He never got the chance to touch her. Grabbing his arm, Samara twisted hard and quick, stomped on his foot with her left foot, and brought her left knee to his groin. It was a move her brothers had taught her and Noah had helped her perfect with skillful precision.

Howling a curse, the man backhanded her, knocking her against the wall.

The man hadn't counted on the McCall children.

Micah flew at the man, managing to clock him in the jaw and then the gut in a one-two punch his father had taught him.

Though unable to deliver the punch her brother could, Evie let loose an ear-piercing shriek as she went for the man's knee, kicking with all her might.

Horrified, Samara sprang toward her children. Ringing ears and a throbbing jaw were nothing compared to her need to protect them. Pulling them away from the furious, cursing man, she pushed them behind her and stood before him, her entire body trembling with the force of her anger.

"You touch my children, you will die. You understand that?"

The man reared back as if to slug her again, but another man's voice, harsh with command, snapped, "Enough," stopping him cold.

She kept her children behind her as she faced this new man, one she hadn't seen before. He was shorter by several inches than most of the muscled men that surrounded him, but he had such a commanding presence it was easy to assume he was the one in charge. Light blond hair with a few strands of gray, a thin, narrow nose, and full thick lips gave the impression that he was both cold and merciless.

"My apologies, Mrs. McCall. Clark here had no right to put his hands on you or your children."

"Who are you? What do you want?"

"That will be answered in time. Rest assured, our business is not with you, but with your husband. As soon as he obliges us, you and your children will be set free."

She tried not to show it—giving this man any advantage was not a good idea—but as relief flooded through her, she couldn't stop the words, "So Noah is okay?"

"But of course he is. Perhaps a few bruises and, I'm sure, quite a bit of worry, but otherwise he's fine. We're not barbarians."

"No, you're just child abductors."

He made no move toward her, but the icy humor in his eyes gave her chills. The other men were conscienceless mercenaries, paid to do a job but without any kind of real malice. This man with his slick suit and expensive haircut was evil personified.

"Evan," the man said in a mild tone, "please take Mrs. McCall and her children to the bathroom and see that they have everything they need to make their stay as pleasant as possible."

Before she could respond, another man came to stand in front of her, blocking her view. He gestured toward the direction they had been headed. "This way."

Taking each of her children's hands, she continued her walk down the corridor toward the bathroom. As they turned a corner, she dared a look back. The man in the suit was gone and so was Clark, the man who had hit her.

She was in the process of assisting Evie when she heard the unmistakable blast of a gun and then a large splash.

Samara had a feeling they wouldn't be seeing Clark again.

CHAPTER THIRTEEN

Dusk was settling in when Raphael arrived at the safe house. Located in a more rural area of Northern Virginia between Warrenton and Culpeper, the cabin was one of three safe houses LCR owned in the area. The closest neighbor was a small farm three miles away.

Things were in place, ready for the meet. Reddington just needed to give them a location. LCR would pretend to play the bastard's game and then turn the tables once Noah's family was safe.

With the exception of Giselle, all people playing Reddington's family were LCR operatives. It'd taken more than a little creative magic to find an operative who could pass as an eleven-year-old boy. Fortunately, one of their female operatives, Mia Ryker, was game. With the help of an award-winning makeup artist known only as Cleo, Mia had been transformed into a believable Eric Reddington. Since Reddington hadn't seen his youngest son since the kid was three years old, creating a convincing facsimile had been easier than it might have been.

Cleo had come to LCR a couple of years ago. Retired from the movie business, she now offered her services to aid in helping others. LCR had used her several times, and her immense skill had saved lives.

When Reddington saw his family, he would have no doubts that they were Sarah, Amelia, and Eric. By the time he realized they were well-trained, highly dangerous operatives, it would be too late.

Their biggest concern now was protecting Giselle. If her theory was right and this was a ruse to get her out in the open, they needed to be prepared for anything.

Raphael pulled into the graveled drive and parked. The guard at the front of the house acknowledged his arrival with a nod. Raphael returned the nod but stayed inside his vehicle. He'd been so focused on what needed to be done, he hadn't allowed himself to deal with the reality of what had happened. Giselle was here—actually here—behind those walls.

Now that he was about to see her again, spend time with her alone, he needed to get his head on straight. Truth was, he felt numb. Yesterday he'd thought she was dead. He had barely begun to deal with that blow when she had appeared, alive and well. Surreal didn't even come close to describing the situation.

Having her back in his life made him remember things he'd forced himself to forget. The way her hair fell across her brow, the little half gasp she would give when she was surprised, the tender curve of her jaw and how it felt when he cupped her face in the palm of his hand. Her silky skin, joyful laugh, the way she—

Aw, shit.

Rubbing his hand down his face, he released a disgusted snort. So much for being objective.

With more determination than energy, he got out of the car and headed toward the house. On the porch, he asked the guard, "Any trouble?"

"Quiet as a mouse."

"You guys need anything?"

"We're good."

Nodding his thanks, he opened the door. "Giselle?"

"I'm in the den."

The house wasn't large. Just two bedrooms, two baths, a kitchen, and a den. Raphael figured it had once been used as a hunting lodge or weekend getaway for a small family. The decor was rustic and basic but comfortable enough for a short stay.

He found Giselle sitting in a rocking chair beside a cold fireplace. He noted that her pallor was still a little off, and the shadows beneath her eyes were more pronounced. As he stood there, staring at her, he also noticed she was shivering.

"I'll build a fire if you're cold."

"That's not necessary. I just caught a bit of a chill from the rain earlier."

Grabbing a throw from the sofa, he draped it over her body and then stepped away quickly before temptation got the best of him. No use going down a road to nowhere. He'd traveled it once already.

"You get anything to eat?"

She grimaced. "Tried to, but just couldn't eat anything."

A good meal would help both of them get through the next hour, but he felt the same way. Eating right now didn't appeal to him either.

He sat on the sofa, which was the closest to her chair. He wanted her to be as comfortable as possible when he started with the questions. She had been too vague earlier. The information had been enough to get them started, but if they were going to help her, they needed details. And admittedly, there were a helluva lot more things he wanted to know.

"You need anything while you're here, let me or one of your guards know. We'll do our best to get it for you."

"Thank you. Is there any news?"

"Yes. Reddington called. Mostly to taunt Noah, I think, but he said he'd call back with a time and place for a meet."

"He did say he wants my family for Noah's?"

"Not outright, but it was clear nonetheless. That's what this is all about...at least for him. "

"I can meet him alone. Explain that Mama—"

"We've got this handled. Reddington will see what he wants to see."

"How is that possible?"

He wanted to trust her, but at this point he just didn't. Not totally. Yes, he believed most of what she'd said, but there was more. Both he and Noah had felt it. Until she told him everything, he'd keep the details of the op to a minimum.

"Don't worry about it."

"You don't trust me." There was resignation in her tone.

He didn't like seeing Giselle look so defeated or sad, but neither would he lie. Those days were over.

"The things you told us earlier only grazed the surface. If we're going to succeed, pull this off, you need to tell me everything. Starting now."

"I know," Giselle said softly. There were things she hadn't revealed. There was just so much, and what she'd told them earlier had given them only a brief glimpse of Daniel Fletcher's treachery.

They needed to be prepared, ready for whatever Fletcher and Reddington had planned. Telling Raphael everything would be painful, but she could no longer keep her secrets. Not when they could cost lives.

Raphael remained silent, allowing her to go at her own pace.

She breathed a shaky sigh. "I'll start from the beginning, since there's a lot that happened before I met Danny. Maybe you'll see some things that might be relevant." She swallowed and added, "After we left and went into the WITSEC program."

His expression never changed, showing none of the anger and hurt she knew he must have felt back then. Maybe he had recovered quickly. She hoped so.

"We moved around a lot. They warned us we might have to for at least the first few months. Turned out to be more like a year. It wasn't until our fifth move that they found the mole within their organization."

"Reddington had a mole in the WITSEC program?"

"No, not exactly. A contractor they used—it was a long, involved process to suss him out. Once they did, it got much better. We settled close to Wilmington, North Carolina.

"Mama worked in a bookstore. A day care center was right next door, so she could work and be close to Eric, too. Amelia started public school, and I was accepted at UNC."

"So you had some kind of normal life?"

"Our actions weren't totally limited, but we couldn't just go anywhere we wanted."

Not that they had wanted to. Having been hunted had made all of them paranoid.

That's all she would say about that first year. The other information wasn't relevant—at least not yet. She looked down, noticed that she was literally wringing her hands, and forced herself to stop. Raphael would be trained to pick up nonverbal clues.

"Things were good for a while. It got to the point that Mama would only hear from Mackie, the US marshal protecting us, every other day. And then, after that, less and less."

Those first few years of safety had been both heaven and hell. She had ached for Raphael like he was a missing appendage, but there had been other reasons to be happy. She had learned that there were a number of ways to be fulfilled in life.

"We were safe."

And if not for her, they would have stayed safe. Everything was her fault…all of it. She swallowed past a dry throat, remembered she had a glass of water on the table beside her. She took several sips.

"When did you meet Fletcher?"

"My senior year. We had a psych class together. I didn't know who he was." She grimaced. "I didn't have a lot of friends. He was nice to me. Made me laugh. I didn't realize he was off-limits until it was too late."

"Why would he be off-limits?"

"His family." Her shoulders lifted in a halfhearted shrug. "They were in a different class of society."

"Bullshit."

Despite the circumstances, Raphael's curse gave her heart a lift. Social status had never meant anything to him. She was glad to see that that hadn't changed.

"I was so serious about doing everything right. Making sure I didn't attract attention. Danny couldn't have cared less about being proper."

And if she were being honest with herself, she could admit that his lack of propriety was the thing that had attracted her the most. She had been so serious, so afraid of doing anything wrong.

"We started dating. He never talked about his family, and I didn't want to talk about mine. We lived in a bubble, and that worked for both of us.

"We dated for only a few months. I was young, so very naïve. I couldn't be honest—tell him who I really was, who my father was—but I did try to tell him that we shouldn't get serious. That there were things he didn't know."

She shook her head. There was naïve and then there was just plain stupid. She had definitely been in the latter category.

"None of that seemed to bother him. A few weeks later, he asked me to go with him and a group of his friends to Las Vegas for spring break. It seemed innocent enough. There would be a lot of other people going. Just a group of young people having a good time."

She paused. The next part of the story was one of her deepest, most profound regrets, but hiding from her mistakes would do her no good. It had happened, and she was still dealing with the consequences.

"On our first night there, I…guess I had too much to drink. I woke up the next morning and discovered that we had gotten married.

"I had never done anything so reckless or foolish in my life. I knew my mother would be devastated that I'd gotten married without telling her." She closed her eyes. "She found out before I could call her. The news was out."

"How did the news get out?"

"He's a Fletcher. He was newsworthy no matter what he was doing. Daniel Fletcher the Third marrying the daughter of a convicted human trafficker and murderer? It was salacious, lurid. Perfect for the tabloids."

"Did you know who his family was?"

"Yes and no. Mackie had told me his family was wealthy and influential. At the time, it didn't really mean anything to me. Danny made it seem like it was no big deal. When I saw my real name and photograph splashed across the front pages of tabloid magazines, I realized it was a very big deal.

"Legitimate news services wouldn't have reported it without verifying the info. The Fletchers have some sort of hold over what kind of publicity is printed or said about them. The tabloids didn't care. They weren't beholden to the family and, for once, had the truth on their side.

"After it was out, the major news outlets picked it up as a 'we haven't confirmed this report' kind of story. The damage was already done. My mother and his parents found out in the worst way possible."

"Did Fletcher realize how dangerous this was for you and your family?"

"I had to tell him then—about WITSEC and the difficulties we'd caused. He said his parents were so powerful and so wealthy that no one, including Reddington, would dare touch me now that I was a Fletcher."

"And to hell with the rest of your family."

She didn't flinch but felt the shame all the same.

"Yes. Once the story of our marriage got out, our cover was blown. I went home and said goodbye to my mother, Amelia, and Eric. They were relocated."

"You didn't want to go with them?"

Of course she had. It had taken every bit of strength she had left to let them go. "I was married. I stayed with Danny."

She couldn't deny that shame had played a big role in her decision to stay. To know that she was responsible for not only putting her family in danger, but also for destroying the life they'd built in North Carolina.

"My new in-laws, as you might imagine, were not exactly thrilled."

"I thought you said they were cordial to you."

"They were. That's the Fletcher style. Play the role until it's no longer necessary. I had no idea that they felt any antipathy toward me until after Danny died. They were as welcoming as if they had arranged the marriage themselves."

She had been so clueless, so happy that they weren't angry, so eager to please, she hadn't read between the lines. She was married, determined to try to make her marriage work. They had been the only family she had left.

In the end, she realized it had been just another monumental mistake. And she had no one to blame but herself.

Chapter Fourteen

Having been trained to never show an emotion he didn't want to reveal, Raphael hid his hands at his sides so Giselle couldn't see them fisted with rage. The more he heard, the more difficult it was for him to hold himself back. She clearly believed herself responsible for everything. And that was wrong. Damn wrong.

He put the blame where it belonged—squarely on the shoulders of Daniel Fletcher III. Yeah, he knew he had more than a few unresolved issues, but those had nothing to do with seeing the facts. Giselle had been a babe in the woods when it came to detecting deceit and evil. She had met a player and never had a chance.

No way Fletcher hadn't known who she was. They might never know how he'd found out. But Giselle had been played whether she knew it or not. The quickie marriage sounded all too contrived for it to be anything other than a setup. Just how far had Fletcher gone? Considering who his parents were and what they were capable of, the bastard had likely gone as far as he needed to get Giselle's compliance.

Raphael remembered the first time he met Giselle, how artless and innocent she had been, believing the best in everyone. Even though Reddington had shattered many of those illusions, she'd still been naïve about the world. And that same naïve, young girl had been thrown into an ocean of sharks, expected to fend for herself.

From the moment of her birth until she'd left that island, she had been sheltered, protected…virtually smothered. Every ounce of information she had received had been carefully filtered. She hadn't been allowed access to newspapers or the Internet. The only things she knew were the things Stanford Reddington had deemed appropriate.

Life lessons were learned out in the world through firsthand experience, but Giselle had received no preparation for that. With the right amount of money and influence, the scum of the earth could make themselves look like paragons of virtue and goodness. And she had fallen into their trap.

It only made sense that Fletcher had seen her, wanted her. A beautiful innocent who'd had no clue who he was and what his family was capable of doing. He had betrayed her, put her entire family in danger. That sure as hell hadn't been love.

In truth, Raphael placed some of the blame on his own shoulders. It didn't matter that she had left him. He should have put his bruised heart aside and made sure she was okay.

She had said she didn't make friends easily, but she'd had one friend—him—and he'd betrayed that friendship.

"You called me after you married."

"Yes," she said softly.

"I'm sorry, Giselle. I should have called you back. Been there for you."

She frowned, shook her head vehemently. "You have nothing to apologize for, Raphael. None of what happened is your fault. It's taken me a long time to come to terms with my bad decisions.

Don't take that away from me by trying to place the blame on yourself or anyone else."

Since she looked so miserable, he saw no point in arguing.

"What happened after your family moved away? You stayed in college? Got your degree?"

"Yes. We were only a few weeks from graduation, so we both went back and finished. After graduation, we moved to New York and lived with his parents."

"That couldn't have been pleasant."

"It was actually quite nice for the first few months. In both public and private, they were very kind to me. There was never a hint at how much they resented or hated me."

"It didn't stay that way."

"No. Danny grew bored with staying at home. We traveled a lot, which was fun at first. I had traveled so little, and it was exciting to see the places I'd only ever read about. But eventually, that became a bone of contention between us."

"How so?"

"I wanted to settle down for good and raise a family. Have roots. Buy a house, make friends our own age. Live a normal life. Danny was always looking for the next grand adventure. It wasn't until later that I realized how very much he hated his life. Traveling was just a way for him to escape."

"Having a child didn't settle him down?"

"Danny loved Gio, but being a father didn't hold his attention for long."

"There's nothing wrong with wanting a home and a family."

Years ago, that had been his hope for them. Marriage, a family, sharing their life together. He shoved aside those thoughts. They sure as hell didn't help.

"And your in-laws? They were okay with you living with them?"

"Yes. Although we didn't see each other that much. Daniel and Clarissa have an active social life. Gio and I stayed to ourselves much of the time. It was fine."

And she had been lonely. That much was easy to see.

"When did you realize how your in-laws felt about you?"

"It wasn't until after Danny died that I knew for sure, but things changed a few days before that."

"How so?"

Giselle took another sip of water before answering. In her mind's eye, she saw herself back then and wanted to shake that naïve young fool until her teeth rattled. She had still been so very foolish, so very stupid.

"I overheard something I wasn't supposed to hear. As you know, the Fletchers' house is a monstrously huge place. For a little boy of Gio's boundless energy and curiosity, it was a wonderland waiting to be explored. One of his favorite games is hide-and-seek. One day it was raining, and we were playing. Daniel, my father-in-law, was rarely at home during the day. I was behind a sofa in one of the living rooms not far from his office, hiding from Gio. Daniel and another man came into the room."

She shrugged. "I would have made my presence known, but the other man was Hugh Rawlings, Daniel's closest friend. Rawlings has always made me nervous. There's just something about him that makes me uncomfortable. I decided to stay silent, hoping they would leave quickly and would never know I was there.

"They didn't, of course. They thought they were alone and began to discuss the murder of a family the year before. A woman and three children had been found dead, murdered in a seemingly random home invasion. They talked about how it disrupted the life of the husband and father. He was out of town when it happened and was a suspect for a while, but was finally cleared. No one was charged with the murders, but the husband was destroyed by them. A merger his company was working on with another company fell through.

"At first, I thought Daniel was expressing sympathy. How you would when it's someone you don't personally know, but you identify with them on a human level of how awful life can be. It wasn't until they continued on that I realized they were calmly talking about how successful the ploy had been and how much money Daniel and Hugh made off the man's tragedy.

"I don't exactly know how that worked. What I do know is that Daniel was responsible. He, along with Rawlings, arranged the murders to destroy the man. Killing this man's family prevented the merger, and Daniel and Hugh somehow profited."

The sheer horror of that moment often replayed in her mind. After hearing the damning conversation, she'd planned to stay hidden until they left. Her greatest fear had been realized when she'd seen a small, dark head appear at the doorway. Gio was still playing the game and had come to the room seeking his mama.

Neither Daniel nor Rawlings had realized what was going on. Daniel had swept Gio into his arms, and both men had left with her son. Gio had seen her, though. Her heart had been in her throat, knowing if the men saw her while they had her son, she would have done anything they asked. But her beautiful boy had continued to play their game. She had put her finger to her mouth in a shushing motion. His dark brown eyes, so like his father's, had twinkled with mischievous merriment, and he had said nothing. The men had walked out of the room, and she had dashed out another door.

She had thought she was safe.

"How did they find out?" Raphael asked.

"There's a camera in almost every room. I didn't know that. One of Daniel's security people saw the footage and went to him."

She had replayed over and over in her mind how that moment could have gone differently. In her fantasy, she jumped up before they could start talking, apologized for being there, and left quickly. Having the knowledge of what Daniel Fletcher was capable of, what he had done, had destroyed her life.

"What happened when he found out?"

"He came to me, told me to keep my mouth shut, or he'd make sure I regretted it. I acted like I didn't know what he was talking about. He just nodded and smiled, told me to keep it that way."

"Did you tell anyone?"

"I told Danny." It had taken her forever to be able to find a private spot to do so. She had no clue whether their bedroom was bugged, but she couldn't take the chance.

"I managed to get him to agree to a walk on the beach. I told him what happened. What I heard and the threats his father made."

"What did he say?"

The shock of that brief meeting still haunted her. "He told me almost exactly what his father told me. That I should forget about it. That it wasn't any of my business."

"He wasn't surprised."

"No. Apparently, doing away with people who get in their way was an accepted practice in the Fletcher household. Something he was very aware of."

"What happened after that?"

"I told him I wanted to leave, to take Gio away from them. He surprised me by agreeing. He said he had a quick trip to make, and when he returned, we would leave. I didn't believe him. I knew I was going to have to get out on my own. Before I could do anything, Danny was dead."

"Car accident?"

"That's what they said. I don't know. His parents had him cremated before I even got the chance to say goodbye."

"Do you think Daniel arranged for his son's death?"

"I wondered, but I don't know for sure. I certainly never asked. But why would he? Danny accepted the Fletcher way of doing business. He was no real threat."

"Did you try to leave on your own?"

"I didn't have a car. The only option was to have one of their drivers take us somewhere. If I'd called a taxi, it wouldn't have been allowed inside the compound. If we'd left on foot, I knew we wouldn't get far."

"There was no one you trusted to tell?"

"Not really. The Fletchers hold an enormous amount of influence everywhere, including over law enforcement. Every dinner party they gave was filled with judges, police chiefs, even a couple of state Supreme Court justices. Going to the authorities would have meant certain death. I couldn't take the risk."

"And then things changed between you and your in-laws?"

"Yes. All I wanted to do was take my son and leave. They, of course, wouldn't let me."

"Is Fletcher's wife, Clarissa, involved? Does she know about the murders?"

"I don't know. Possibly. And even if she doesn't, I don't think it would really matter to her. She has her own priorities and agenda. What I told you before is the truth. Clarissa has an obsession with Gio. Maybe it's because she failed so miserably with her own son and sees Gio as her second chance. I don't know."

"Either way, having you out of the picture would be beneficial to both of them."

"Yes."

"We'll protect you, Giselle. You don't have to worry about that. And we'll get your son back, too."

"I believe you, Raphael. You've never let me down. And I know you never will."

"What happened after Danny's death?"

"Nothing at first. They included me in everything related to his memorial. They waited until things settled, and then it started. I was so focused on Gio, on comforting him, I didn't notice it at first.

"Clarissa's remarks became more pointed, snide. I passed them off as a consequence of grief. When it became worse, I confronted her."

"How did that go?"

"She denied it. Said it was my imagination. Or my own feelings of guilt."

"What would you have to feel guilty about?"

"She needed someone to blame. I was a convenient target. If I had been a better wife, Danny would have been home instead of looking for his next adventure."

"Bullshit."

She sent him a grim smile. "I told her I thought it best that Gio and I leave. And that's when I began to lose control over my life, my child. I became sick. The doctor said I could be contagious, so they kept Gio from me. The last thing I wanted was to make my son ill. I couldn't think straight.

"Late one afternoon, I woke and had no real idea where I was or what was going on. I only knew I needed to find my child. I went looking for him and couldn't find him. I ended up outside. They were having a party. I probably looked like a ghostly wraith or something. I think I had my nightgown on, and I'd lost so much weight by then I probably looked like death. I was too distraught to care about my appearance."

It took every bit of Raphael's willpower not to reach out to comfort her. He could tell the experience was devastating to her.

"I'll spare you the dramatic details. Suffice to say that several people saw me, heard my tearful ranting. I don't really remember much. I think someone must have carried me back to my room. It wasn't too long after that when I woke up in the mental hospital."

Raphael closed his eyes and cursed himself once more. She had been going through hell, and all the while he'd thought she was living this full, happy life.

"I am so sorry, Giselle. If I could—"

"No, stop it, Raphael. I'm at fault. The choices I made got me into the trouble I'm in."

"Like hell. You trusted people who should have been your biggest supporters and instead became your jailers and torturers. This is not your fault."

"When I became a mother, my priority should have been my child. I might have depended upon my in-laws to be kind and loving, but it was up to me to take care of my son. I failed.

"I know LCR is the best chance I have for getting Gio back to me safely. I had planned to come to you soon, ask for your help. Reddington's perfidy just made that happen quicker."

To know that she had intended to contact him helped ease the anger somewhat. He wished she hadn't delayed. He wished it hadn't been necessary. Hell, he wished for a lot of things.

"We're good at what we do, Giselle. We'll get your son back to you."

She took a breath and leaned forward, locking her gaze with Raphael's. Her face was now ghostly pale, but a fierce light glowed in her eyes. It was as if sheer will alone kept her going.

"If something happens and we can't get Gio back, I would like Noah to consider something else."

"What?"

"I'd like him to negotiate a trade."

"What kind of trade?"

"My son for me."

"Never in a million years," Raphael growled.

"It's certainly not my first choice either, but my son is the most important thing in my life, and he's in danger. Being cared for by murderers. Just because I don't think they'll physically harm him doesn't mean he's not being hurt. He needs to be with his family."

"Yeah, only you'd be dead. And you have no idea where his other family is. He'd be alone."

"No, he wouldn't. He would still have his father."

"What?"

"You, Raphael," she said softly. "You're Giovanni's father."

CHAPTER FIFTEEN

"Raphael. Say something."

Unable to sit calmly, as if his world had not just been turned upside down, Raphael stood and began moving.

"Where are you going? We need to talk."

He was almost to the kitchen but stopped abruptly. Not turning, his voice almost hoarse, he said, "I don't know about you, but I've had about as much as I'm going to take today on an empty stomach. We'll eat, and then we'll talk. Maybe by then you'll have come up with an explanation that won't make me hate you."

"I don't blame you for hating me."

He whirled around. "And that's supposed to make me feel better?"

"No. I just—"

He turned his back on her. Yeah, eating right now would likely make him puke, but if he didn't get away from her for a few minutes, he would say things he would regret later. Fury boiled within him, and he would spew that venom all over her. Yes, he would make sure she knew how he felt, but he'd do so when he was able to think straight. Right now, concentrating on making a meal would help.

Of course she followed him anyway.

"Please let me explain. I didn't have a choice. Didn't know what else to do. When we left—"

"Did you know you were pregnant? Is that the reason you left me behind?"

"No. Of course not. I would never do that to you."

"Excuse me for not believing a damn thing you say right now."

She grabbed his hand, and he pulled away quickly. "Don't touch me right now, Giselle. It's not safe."

As her dark eyes dulled with sorrow, she backed away. "All right. I'll wait. I'm going to take a shower."

"Wait." He opened the fridge and pulled out the milk carton and poured a small glass. "Drink this. I'd rather not have you passing out in the shower."

She took the milk and walked out of the room. The instant she disappeared, Raphael turned and slammed his fist into a cabinet door. The impact vibrated through him. Numb from shock, he was glad for the pain. It grounded him, helping him to focus.

When she had left him before, he'd lost himself for a while. His focus, his goals…everything. He'd been angry, yes, but the hurt had overwhelmed everything else. That gut-wrenching, soul-destroying hurt that could only come from being betrayed by the one person you loved more than any other.

That feeling of betrayal had returned now, but in a different way. The feelings he'd once felt for her had blurred, changed. The betrayal should be different, too, but he could say with all forthright honesty that it felt similar to what he'd gone through before. Dammit, how could she have kept this a secret? Kept him from his child?

By rote, he made them something to eat. Scrambled eggs were a safe bet. Protein for energy, filling and easy on the stomach.

When he heard the shower turn off, he waited for a few minutes. Was she just going to stay in her room, or was she going to face him?

The bedroom door swung open, and she appeared in the doorway of the kitchen.

"Sit down and eat."

She didn't argue, but sat down and ate from the plate he put before her. Raphael consumed his meal standing up.

They finished the simple meal quickly and quietly. When he reached for her empty plate, she touched his hand. "Can we talk now?"

"Go on into the living room. I'll be there in a minute."

Giselle walked into the living room and sat on the sofa. She was out of tears, so she just stared at the empty fireplace and thought about regret. What a strange emotion it was. It hovered like a dark cloud, and no matter how much you tried to get rid of it, it stayed, lingered, taunted.

Hurting Raphael was the very last thing she had ever wanted to do. And she had probably hurt him worse than anyone else ever had. Twice. This last one was one he'd never forgive.

Her reason for not telling him was valid, but she doubted he'd ever see it that way.

Minutes later, Raphael dropped into the chair across from her and asked in a cool tone, "When did you find out you were pregnant?"

"Two months or so after my family was relocated. I thought my nausea was from stress. We had to move several times those first few weeks, and we were all exhausted. Mama suspected and asked me. Maybe deep down I suspected but couldn't face the knowing. I don't know. Anyway, she sent for a pregnancy test and we confirmed it."

"So you lied about his age?"

"Yes. Giovanni is six years old," she whispered.

He didn't say anything for several moments. Giselle knew he was still trying to absorb everything. She wanted, needed to make him understand her choices, but she could already see in his eyes that she had a long way to go before that happened.

"We used protection. Every damn time. I—"

"That last time," she said softly. "We didn't."

She saw the heat in his eyes before he allowed it to ice over. Yes, he remembered. That night, their last night together, had been magical, beautiful. Just before dawn, when they were warm, exhausted from not sleeping, and so very much in love, he had slid inside her and made love to her with exquisite tenderness. Even after all these years, she felt a hot flush of desire at the memory.

"One screw-up and you got pregnant?"

She flinched at the way he said the words, but couldn't blame him. She deserved every bit of his wrath.

"Yes. It only takes one time."

"Did you consider for one moment letting me know?"

"I could have no contact with anyone I had known before. That was their number one rule. I couldn't put my family at risk."

It had been a lot more complicated than that. The instant she had revealed her pregnancy to the US marshal in charge of their protection, things had gone sour. He had always been professional before, but when she had pleaded with him to let her contact Raphael, he'd gone from polite to downright icy. Even though she had understood his job, and a part of her had agreed with him, her heart had never gotten on board. Not telling Raphael he was going to be a father was one of the hardest things she'd ever endured.

"Does Giovanni believe that Fletcher was his father?"

"No, he was three years old when I met Danny."

"Tell me about him."

The tension in her muscles eased a minute amount. Nothing was settled. Raphael's anger was a living thing, like a caged, hungry lion, but talking about Gio always lightened her being. "He weighed seven pounds, six ounces and was twenty-three inches long. He came into the world squalling. Mama said that was a good sign.

"He was a good baby. Hardly cried at all. Slept through the night. Mama said that wasn't quite fair, since she swore that I cried every night my first two years."

"Your mother was a big help to you."

"I couldn't have managed without her."

"Who does he look like?"

"He's a miniature version of you."

Pain flashed in his eyes, and Giselle almost regretted telling him. She had photographs, but she would wait. They had a long way to go before they could sit comfortably and talk about the absolute joy of having a son like Gio.

"When I showed up at Fletcher's house, I thought I saw shock in his eyes. Now I know why. He knew who I was."

"Yes, I'm sure he did."

"This makes no sense, Giselle. Why the hell would your in-laws want to keep a child that's not even related to them? Looks nothing like them."

"Because of Clarissa. Daniel's acceptance of Gio was careless and vague, occasionally affectionate. Clarissa, on the other hand, was entranced the moment she met him. As I said, I think she saw him as her second chance."

He eyed her then, reading between the lines. Seeing things she wasn't ready for him to see. "At some point, I want to know about your marriage to Danny."

"Not tonight, though."

"All right."

She didn't bother to tell him it wasn't any of his business. For almost two years, Danny played father to Gio. Raphael had every right to know what went on in their marriage. Besides, she had accepted that when it came to Raphael, she couldn't keep secrets. When she did, everything got messed up.

"So the basic gist is Fletcher wants to get rid of you for what you overheard, and Clarissa wants you gone so she can keep Gio for herself."

"Yes."

With startling abruptness, Raphael went to his feet. His expression was one she'd never seen before. He had been trained to expect and deal with the unexpected, but today had been filled with too many twists and turns. Finding out he had a six-year-old son was likely his limit.

She wasn't surprised to hear him say, "I've got to get out of here. You've got guards in front and back. You're safe here. I'll see you tomorrow."

Without giving her a chance to respond, Raphael walked out the back door and into the night.

She sat in the chair for the longest time after he left. Sadness lay heavy on her shoulders, and all she wanted to do was curl up into a ball and sob her heart out. How could choices made for the right reasons turn out so badly? In one way or another, she had hurt every single person she loved.

She might not stop making mistakes, but she could damn well make sure no one else paid for them. She had to get her son away from the Fletchers. No matter what happened to her, she had to save him.

Feeling much older than her twenty-six years, Giselle went into the bedroom. She didn't pull off her clothes to change into nightwear. Though her bags had been delivered to her from her car, and she had other clothes, she wanted to stay prepared. She was dressed in light sweats and a long-sleeved cotton T-shirt. They were comfortable enough. If something happened and she needed to move fast, already having clothes on would give her extra time.

She lay on the bed and drew the comforter over her. It had been months since she had slept through an entire night. Nightmares often woke her. On other nights, torturous thoughts kept her awake. Her child was being held captive. Even though she could tell herself that they wouldn't physically harm him, the psychological damage could be irreparable. Daniel and Clarissa Fletcher were evil. She had brought that evil into her son's life. It was up to her to get him out. With LCR's help…with Raphael's help, she would.

She closed her eyes, and Raphael's image appeared in her mind. His body was muscular, much more defined, and he'd gotten even taller than before. There were lines around his mouth and eyes that hadn't been there seven years ago. He had been beautiful to her back then, and though maturity and life had changed him from a beautiful young boy into a ruggedly handsome man, he was still the same person she had fallen in love with.

Despite the heaviness of her heart, she smiled to herself, thinking about those early days. There were many good memories of her time with Raphael. They had shared laughter, secrets, and Raphael had shared his dreams with her. Those beautiful, magical moments had coalesced into a strong, unbreakable bond. One that would have lasted a lifetime if evil hadn't arrived to tear it apart.

She pushed all of that from her mind and concentrated on one of her most precious memories—their first kiss. It had been the night of her eighteenth birthday and had been the sweetest, most precious gift she could imagine receiving. His kiss was everything she'd dreamed about and so much more.

The memories of that lovely night wrapped themselves around her, comforting her. Her nervousness, his tenderness. And then that bright, shining moment when his lips had finally met hers and everything had been right with her world at last.

She should have known the nightmares wouldn't allow her even that momentary happiness. They attacked with a vengeance.

Darkness rolled around her, through her. Her head, her entire being felt heavy and useless, as if tons of water pressed down upon her. Something wasn't right...this wasn't right.

The voice, thin and high, penetrated the darkness. "You're sick, Giselle. You need to go away, get healthy again."

"No." She shook her head and then almost cried at the pounding in her skull. "I'm not sick. You did this to me, and you know it."

"Don't be ridiculous. You did this to yourself. You should have kept your nose out of my business. You're responsible for everything."

She refused to listen to their lies any longer. She had to get out of here. She would take Giovanni and run.

"We think you should go away for a while."

"Yes." For once, she agreed. "Giovanni and I will leave immediately."

"No, you misunderstand. We believe you could harm the child or yourself."

"That's ridiculous!" She surged to her feet, and the room swirled around her. She glanced down at the empty glass of lemonade her mother-in-law had poured her.

"It's for your own good, my dear."

No! Giselle tore out of the room. Every step she took grew harder and harder. Darkness edged her vision, and she fought its depths with every ounce of her strength.

"Gio!" she screamed.

"Mama!"

There he was, in his playroom. His smile beaming, his beautiful dark eyes gleaming with tears. He lifted his arms toward her. She reached out for him, and something, someone, pulled her away. Screaming, she fought against the hands that kept her from her son. She could hear him calling for her.

She screamed his name over and over. She had to get to him, had to save him.

"Giselle." Firm, hard hands shook her gently and then harder. "It's a nightmare. You're fine. You're here with me now. You're fine."

Blinking her eyes open, she looked up into Raphael's worried face. Shuddering out a breath, she shook her head. She should have warned him.

"Sorry. That happens sometimes." She sat up in the bed, putting distance between them so he had to drop his hands away from her. The temptation to throw herself into his arms was too great. If she did that, she'd never want to let go. And as angry as he was with her, having him reject her right now would be more than she could handle.

Pushing the nightmares as far from her mind as possible, she rubbed at her eyes and then looked blearily at the man sitting on her bed. "I thought you'd left."

Raphael shrugged. He hadn't gone far. Just a good hard walk around the property. Even as infuriated and hurt as he was, he wouldn't leave her alone.

"I didn't leave. Took a walk."

"I hope I didn't wake you."

"No." Sleeping tonight was out of the question anyway. "You want to talk about your nightmare?"

"No, not really. But thank you for asking."

He told himself he had no reason to be offended by her refusal to share. It wasn't like they had anything between them other than a past that no longer mattered. Except they had a son. Dammit, he had a son.

"It's...they're hard to describe anyway."

Yeah, he knew all about nightmares. He'd had plenty of them through the years. Horrific memories jumbled with fears could create vivid ones. You ended up not knowing the difference between what had really happened and what you feared might happen.

"Raphael, about before. When I left you, I should have told you in person. I know reading it in a letter was painful. I thought I was going about it the right way."

"Water under the bridge. That was a long time ago."

"And I'm so sorry for not telling you about Gio. I wanted to, I really did."

"Let's not go there again tonight. We're going to get McCall's family back, and then we'll get Gio back. Then we'll find a way to make sure the Fletchers pay for what they've done. That's all we need to focus on."

"But you need—"

"Let it go, Giselle."

She breathed out a ragged sigh. "Okay. All right."

He glanced at the bedside clock. "It's still early. Think you can go back to sleep?"

"I'll be fine. Thank you for your kindness."

The stiffness in her tone, her body told him he had hurt her. Maybe he should've let her get it all out. Let her have her say. But then, where would that lead them? What would it solve?

No, if he stayed longer and they talked, it would end one of two ways. Either they would argue, and he'd say things he'd regret. Or even worse, he would kiss her. Hell if he needed that complication.

CHAPTER SIXTEEN

East Hampton, New York

Daniel Fletcher took a sip of his brandy nightcap and eyed Clarissa, who was gazing into the fire with a small smile on her face. She seemed content, happy. That was a good thing. Unless it went against a specific goal for business, he strived to make her happy.

He and Clarissa had been married for thirty-nine years, but they'd been together much longer than that. Almost from the moment of his birth, he had known they would marry. Clarissa's parents, Marvin and Millicent Potter, had been his parents' best friends. It made sense that their only son, Daniel, and the Potters' oldest daughter should marry. Social class notwithstanding, they had so much in common that not marrying would have gone against all logic.

It had been a good match. What they lacked in warmth, they more than made up for in shared interests and goals. Carrying on the family name, the family heritage, was a full-time job. Few people realized how time-consuming and burdensome their responsibilities were. Not that he minded—they were, after all, his destiny.

That destiny had been passed on to his son, but Danny had squandered the right. The boy had been spoiled, that much was obvious, but other children were spoiled and ended up making something of themselves. Danny never got to that point. And now he was dead, leaving them with a worthless and classless daughter-in-law to handle.

He had never asked his son why Giselle had caught his eye. He really didn't care. He imagined it had been a combination of things. The girl was a beauty—there was no denying that—and surprisingly sweet. She had a pleasing manner and, other than a few social blunders, had carried her role off rather well. It was unfortunate that she was the exact opposite of any girl they would have chosen for their son. Her family! It sickened him to think of it. She was the daughter of a pervert—a sleazy, low-life human trafficker.

Danny's marriage to the girl had been the first Fletcher scandal in decades that he had not been able to bury.

The two had married in secret, without his knowledge or consent, which, of course, was the only way Danny could have gotten away with it. The boy had possessed a wild streak that could not be tamed. They had bailed him out of numerous scrapes and scandals, always hoping that would be the last one. But no, their son never learned his lesson. He had gone against everything he had been taught. Members of privileged society had codes and standards to uphold. Danny had known this, and the sheer defiance of those codes had resulted in a mockery and sham of a marriage. By the time they had learned the truth, nothing could be done to stop the damage.

He and Clarissa had done the only thing they could by embracing the girl and her marriage to their only son. They had acknowledged her tragic past, heralded her courage and strength.

Talked about how she and her family had been so abused and mistreated. Clarissa had made a substantial donation in Giselle's name to an organization known to fight against human trafficking. It had played well in the press. Though the blight on their name was still there, eventually the scandal had faded away, leaving both he and Clarissa looking like paragons of charity and tolerance.

Unfortunately, marriage hadn't changed Danny. In only a few months, he had been up to his old antics. His death had been inevitable, he supposed.

He had considered an overdose for the girl early on. A young wife, grieving over the death of her one true love, devastated and distraught, takes her own life, unable to live without the man she adores. A scandal to be sure—there had never been a suicide in the Fletcher family. However, it could have played well in the media. Another donation to another charity, a couple of public appearances showing their grief, and that would have been that.

Why he had changed his mind he couldn't really say. The girl certainly deserved what she got. Lurking in the shadows, overhearing a private business conversation, had been an unforgivable offense.

He thought maybe the boy was the one who'd stopped him from taking that route. Every time he looked into the child's eyes, he saw innocence and something…he couldn't explain it. Whatever it was, it had saved his mother's life. Putting her in an asylum had been a concession, but had she appreciated him sparing her life? Of course not. She had escaped. Death was the only option now. The child would forget her soon enough, and they could go on as before. Clarissa was exceedingly fond of the young fellow, and Daniel couldn't deny a little affection himself for the little imp.

Yes, he would rectify his son's ridiculous error very soon, and then everything would be right again.

Chapter Seventeen

LCR Headquarters
Alexandria, Virginia

It was barely seven in the morning when Raphael arrived at Noah's office. It didn't surprise him in the least to find Noah, along with Jordan and Eden, already there. All of them looked as though they'd gotten as much sleep as he had the night before. Which had been none at all.

Noah had apparently just dropped the bomb about Daniel Fletcher's involvement in this mess.

"Okay," Eden said, "I can get on board that Reddington has help. But Daniel Fletcher? That's insane."

"Not if you'd heard Giselle's description of them," Raphael said.

"In-laws from hell, I get. But this? The kidnappings? The Simmons couple faking the abduction in North Korea to gain access to Noah?" She turned to him. "Getting your home address would have taken months."

"Not if you know the right people."

"Raphael's right," Noah said. "I've kept my family's location as private as possible, but somehow someone found out."

"Someone with avenues to information no ordinary citizen could get," Jordan said.

"Okay. But how could Fletcher even be sure Giselle would hear about the abduction? There's been nothing on the news."

"Fletcher asked about that when I met with him. About why he hadn't seen reports of the abductions." Raphael shrugged. "I assumed it was mere curiosity, but now I don't think so. That's probably the one thing that didn't go in his favor. He was counting on the abductions being reported everywhere. If we hadn't kept a lid on it, Samara's, Micah's, and Evie's faces would be splashed across every news outlet in the world."

Understanding dawned in Eden's gray eyes. "And when that didn't happen, they had to improvise. That's why the recording of your meeting with Fletcher got to Giselle."

"Yeah," Raphael agreed. "I think the nanny told Fletcher that Giselle contacted her. Once Giselle saw the recording, they counted on her contacting Noah."

Jordan still wasn't on board. "Why go to all that trouble? Why not just grab her at the cemetery?"

"Beats the hell out of me. Maybe the way she was dressed kept them from identifying her. I didn't recognize her either."

"So is Reddington Daniel Fletcher's pawn?" Eden asked.

Raphael shook his head. The bastard had his own agenda. "If he is, he doesn't know it. He's too arrogant not to think he's the one in control."

"Do you think he has any idea the danger he's put his daughter in?"

"I don't know, but I doubt he'd care. Getting to Sarah and hurting Noah are more important to him than protecting his daughter."

"Okay." Jordan nodded. "I can see it now. They're using each other to get what they want. Reddington gets to see his family, hurting Noah in the process. And Fletcher gets Giselle out in the open."

"I've known many powerful and wealthy people, plenty of whom were corrupt. However, most of them have a reason for wanting someone dead. I'm sure Giselle's son is a beautiful little boy, but putting his mother in a mental institution and then going to all this trouble of arranging Noah's family's abduction? Just to get custody of the child?" Eden shook her head. "That's extreme even for a narcissistic sociopath. There's got to be more to this."

"You're right. There is." Raphael told them what he had learned from Giselle last night. He didn't tell them everything. He was still having trouble getting his head wrapped around what she had revealed. He had a son. A six-year-old little boy he had never seen who was in the clutches of an egomaniacal family that seemed both impenetrable and untouchable. As bombshells went, this was a major one.

"He couldn't pay her off or blackmail her," Noah said. "To him, his only recourse is to kill her. I'm surprised he had her committed. Seems like a staged suicide would have been easy enough."

"Giselle agrees. Says she doesn't know why they didn't. Fletcher knows it was a mistake, too. One he intends to rectify."

Eden shot a concerned glance at Noah and then Raphael. "This could get sticky."

"Protecting Giselle will be a top priority," Raphael said.

"We have a few hours," Jordan said. "We can work on finding another operative to pose as Giselle."

"I made that offer last night. She refused." Before anyone could argue, he added, "I'll protect her. Reddington won't be surprised to see me with her. I'll make sure she's safe."

Noah's cellphone chimed, and everyone held their breath.

Putting the call on speaker, Noah answered, "Yes?"

"Mr. McCall?" Reddington's voice had gotten stronger the last few days. The arrogance he'd lost during his imprisonment was quickly returning.

"Yes."

"I wonder if we could arrange a visit."

"At the prison?"

"No. Due to special circumstances, I've been released."

Even though they already knew that, questioning how that happened was useless. The bastard wouldn't tell the truth. The people helping Reddington had enough influence to get a man serving a life sentence in prison released. Which made Giselle's story all the more believable.

"Where and when?"

"I have a few details to iron out, but for right now, let's plan on a week from Tuesday. I'll—"

"Like hell, Reddington. You play your games all you want, but if I don't have my family back by tomorrow, I'm going to—"

"You're going to what, Mr. McCall?" There was amusement in the voice and more than a little smugness. "Regarding your family, I'm afraid I don't know what you're talking about. Whoever is listening to this conversation might think I had something to do with their disappearance, and we both know that's just not possible. I'm just one weak, broken man wanting to console another one. Having you bring my family with you is simply something you're doing to boost my spirits. Correct?"

"Yes," Noah bit out. "Correct."

"Excellent. And since you've been so cooperative, let's move up the date of your visit to me. Would tomorrow be soon enough?"

"Yes."

"Excellent. I'll be in touch."

Noah stood in the middle of his office and rubbed his temple where Raphael figured a headache was pounding. The man hadn't recovered from his assault and was planning the rescue of his family, plus the takedown of the bastard responsible. Not to mention the new worry that this was all a setup to get to Giselle.

"Okay. We're moving forward." Taking an audible breath, Noah turned to Jordan. "Are we ready for the first showing?"

"Yeah. They worked through the night to get this right. I think you'll be surprised. I know I was." He walked over to the conference room door, knocked, and stuck his head inside. "Each of you come out one at a time. Let's see what we've got. Sarah, you first."

The door opened wider, and a tall, middle-aged woman emerged. If Raphael hadn't known for sure, he never would have guessed she wasn't Sarah Reddington. The woman coming toward them walked with the slightly stiff gait of an older woman. Her ink-black hair carried a few gray strands. Lines at the corners of her rich brown eyes could be attributed to either stress or age. Her face was slightly fuller than it had been eight years ago. She was still slender, but carried a bit more weight than she had when she was younger. The makeup artist had worked wonders. No one, not even Jake Mallory, would recognize his much younger wife, Angela Delvecchio, behind the façade.

Raphael felt a slight loosening of the muscles in his neck and shoulders. This was going to work. "Amazing. I think even Giselle might be fooled into thinking this is her mother."

"I agree," Noah answered. "We haven't seen Sarah in years, but we ran an age-progression program on her photo." He gave Jordan a nod. "Let's see Amelia."

A young woman walked out. Riley Ingram was several years older than sixteen-year-old Amelia Reddington, but once again the makeup artist had accomplished wonders. A young girl would change dramatically during her teen years, but the artist had used some of Sarah Reddington's most pronounced features and given them to Riley Ingram. Not only did Riley look years younger, she was a miniature version of Sarah. Raphael thought she looked a lot like Giselle had when he'd first met her.

"Excellent. Now Eric."

This was the one who concerned everyone the most. Reddington placed a higher value on males than females. He would pay attention to Sarah simply because he considered her his property and would assess her as such. He might or might not even glance at Giselle or Amelia. He would, however, want to see Eric, his youngest son.

Having Mia Ryker pose as an eleven-year-old boy was a chance they'd had no choice but to take. Mia was a trained LCR operative. If things went bad, she, like the other fake members of Reddington's family, would know how to react.

Mia walked through the door, and Raphael felt his tension ease considerably more. Mia had even adopted a slight, boyish swagger. A short, dark brown wig covered her hair. Her chin was narrower, her mouth less full. Her shoulders were broader, her chest flat. She wore tan slacks and a button-down white shirt. She looked like a preteen boy. More important, she looked like she could be Reddington's son.

"That's incredible," Eden said and then laughed. "Jared will not believe his eyes."

Mia grinned, and Raphael saw a glimpse of the pretty Mia behind the boyish disguise. "It'll freak him out, which is exactly why I'm getting some photos made."

"Stay in costume," Noah advised. "When Reddington calls with the location, I want to make sure we're ready to go on a moment's notice." He shot a glance at Raphael. "Will Giselle be ready?"

"Yes. She'll be ready."

He thought about how she'd looked this morning. Before he left the cabin, he'd checked in on her. She'd been sitting in a chair by the window, already dressed. The terror he'd seen in her eyes after her nightmare the night before had been replaced with resolve. Though she had still looked pale and exhausted, he had seen she was determined to see this through.

"She okay with what's on her agenda today?"

"Loretta and her team arrived just before I left. She's getting the full treatment."

***

LCR Safe House

Of all the things Giselle thought she would be doing this morning, getting a spa treatment hadn't been one of them. She understood the reasoning behind it, but considering everything that was going on in her life, it seemed almost ridiculous.

After Raphael had left her last night, she'd been unable to go back to sleep. After tossing and turning for hours, she'd gotten up, showered, and dressed, ignoring the fact that it was only a little after four in the morning.

She knew she looked like a worn-out shell of the girl she used to be. Raphael had stopped in before he'd left this morning, and though he hadn't said anything, she had seen the concern behind the anger. Having Reddington see her looking like a zombie would not help.

For the most part, she had put the memories of her life with the man who fathered her out of her mind. Despite his evilness, there weren't that many bad ones—at least not for her. It wasn't until later that she'd realized the reason. She simply hadn't mattered to him. As long as she had behaved herself and stayed out of his way, her existence had been superfluous. His only requirement of her, other than to cause him no problems, had been to always look pretty. Anything else, like her intellect, hopes, wishes, or dreams, had been unimportant.

So, despite her distaste for doing anything that would please Reddington, looking healthy and pretty was an important component of a successful mission. She would do everything LCR asked of her. Ensuring Noah McCall's family was returned safe and sound was of utmost importance to her.

The people LCR had sent over to make her look the total opposite of how she felt had agreed with her assessment of her looks. The woman in charge, Loretta Foster, had shrieked in dramatic horror and then assured Giselle that she was a beauty miracle worker. Her face wreathed with a kind smile, she'd told Giselle to sit back, relax, and let the magic begin.

After an hour-long massage, plus a facial, manicure, pedicure, and a full-body skin refinement treatment, Giselle had to admit she did feel more relaxed than she had in months. Loretta's deft hands had cut and styled her hair, and the results were amazing.

She stood before the mirror, stunned at the transformation. She looked like she used to look, before her hell began.

"Now none of that, darling. That mouth gets any droopier, you're going to be mistaken for a basset hound."

"Sorry."

She gave Giselle's shoulder a motherly pat. "There, there. Nobody's better at rescuing and saving people than Last Chance Rescue. They saved my nephew and his girlfriend a couple years back from something awful. Whoever they're working to save for you, they'll pull it off. Don't you worry."

She wanted to believe that with all her heart. Even though neither Raphael nor Noah McCall had told her how they would help her get Giovanni back, she had to believe they would. She had no one else to turn to.

"I'll come by in the morning to do your makeup and bring a couple of outfits for you to try."

"In the morning?" Her heart pounded faster. This was going to happen tomorrow?

"Oh dear, I hope I didn't spoil the surprise. I received a text from Mr. McCall's office asking if I could be available for you in the morning."

"That's fine. Really." She gave Loretta an encouraging smile. "I knew they were working hard to get this done as soon as possible."

Loretta placed her hands on Giselle's shoulders and turned her to face the mirror. "Look at that woman in the mirror. See her strength, her endurance. She is a survivor, she is a warrior. No matter what she has to face, she will win."

"Thank you, Loretta. I needed to hear those words."

She squeezed Giselle's shoulders one more time. "Get some rest. I'll see you in the morning."

Loretta walked out of the room. Giselle heard her tell her assistants that it was time to go. She heard her say goodbye to one of the guards, heard a car engine start up and the crunch of gravel under the tires as the stylists drove away.

She didn't move from the mirror. It had been a long time since she'd bothered to do more than glance at her reflection to ensure that her disguise was in place. She hadn't *seen* this Giselle in a long time. Even when she'd been married, she hadn't been *Giselle*. Not really. She'd been the wife of Daniel Fletcher III. The proper daughter-in-law the Fletchers had expected her to be. Somewhere during that time, the real Giselle disappeared.

She wanted that girl back. That Giselle was optimistic, full of laughter and joy. That girl fell in love with a boy who was everything she'd ever dreamed of in a man. It hadn't worked out for them, but she wanted to believe in love again. It did exist. It must.

The woman before her stood straighter. Loretta's words penetrated a frozen part of her that had been hiding, afraid to live. She *was* brave, strong, and courageous. She had survived against unbearable odds. She was a mother. One of the many things she'd learned from her own mother was the knowledge that she was her children's number one protector. There was no better example to follow than that of her own mother, who had sacrificed so much to keep her children safe.

She would save Giovanni and in the process become even stronger. Her sweet baby boy was waiting on her to be his hero. She had let him down once. She would not let him down again. She would get her son back, no matter what.

What happened after that was up in the air. Raphael would want to be a part of his son's life. She wanted that, too. Whether he would want anything else was a question she refused to even consider. Hoping for anything more was a sure path to heartbreak. She'd already been down that path once—she refused to travel it again.

CHAPTER EIGHTEEN

Noah walked the perimeter one more time. Reddington and his cohorts had likely chosen this rural area of Virginia because of its remoteness. Situated between Roanoke and Lynchburg, the abandoned park likely had few visitors anymore. A few old buildings surrounded the campgrounds, but for the most part it was a desolate and uninviting place for any living thing other than local wildlife.

It was, however, the perfect spot for clandestine meetings and other unsavory events.

Though his ribs ached with an unceasing throb and his head pounded in an answering rhythm, he ignored them both. This op had an off-the-chart stink factor. Hell, he didn't even know if Mara and his kids would be brought here. This could be a setup to eliminate him and as many operatives as possible. He had no choice but to take the chance. Getting his family back meant everything. Without them, he could not exist.

And if Giselle was right and Fletcher was behind everything, her life was on the line as well. He had made arrangements to ensure everyone's safety. Things could still go awry, but they'd gone through several scenarios. This was what they did. The mission might mean more to him than any others, but that didn't mean he and his people didn't know how to do their jobs.

Ten operatives had arrived yesterday afternoon and scoped out the location. He had gotten here a couple hours later, bringing five more operatives with him. If Reddington and his people wanted to play rough, he would give him what he wanted. He had more than a few tricks up his sleeve.

As long as he got his family back and none of his people were hurt, then he'd be well satisfied. Nothing else would be acceptable.

"We'll get them back, Noah," Angela said.

Angela Delvecchio had been with LCR almost from the beginning. Having gone from receptionist to tech analyst to Elite operative, she knew the ins and outs of the organization almost as well as he did. After her first shaky start as an operative, she'd become one of LCR's most versatile team members. She and her husband, Jake Mallory, were two of his most valuable assets.

He was used to seeing her in various disguises—she'd become amazingly adept in role-playing and working undercover. Becoming Sarah Reddington, a woman almost twenty years her senior, might have been a major challenge for some, but Angela had eased into the older woman's persona as if she were channeling Sarah.

"I know we will."

"This isn't your fault, you know. Reddington and whoever else he's in cahoots with are responsible."

She had read him well, as always. "That doesn't mean I'm without blame. They found my family…that part is all on me. I got too comfortable. Thought we were safe."

"Do you have any clue how they found you?"

"I have some ideas. Once I have them back, I'll make damn sure it never happens again."

He glanced down at his watch and spoke into a mic attached to his collar. "We're a few hours away from the meeting time, but I want everyone in place now. Reddington isn't going to come without some major firepower. Let's make sure he doesn't see us until it's time."

He turned back to Angela. "Everyone ready on your end?"

"We're ready. Putting us in the building away from the main area is a good idea. If he even tries to take one of us, he won't know what hit him."

"You think Giselle will hold up?"

Angela glanced over at the young woman she'd heard about but met only a few hours ago.

She was standing in front of the building they were going to wait in until Reddington showed. Mia and Riley were close-by, but Giselle stood several feet away from them, as if she didn't feel she belonged. They needed to work on that.

Both Mia and Riley were dressed for their roles, unrecognizable as their true selves. Mia, especially, was a shock. The petite operative who could take down a man three times her size was a marvel of modern makeup and ingenuity. Mia's own husband, Jared Livingston, had nodded at her as if she were a stranger and then had done a double take. That moment had lightened the entire atmosphere.

"I'm going to talk with her a little more…get her more comfortable with her fake family. But she'll stand. She's a lot stronger than anyone has given her credit for."

"You talked with her already?"

"A little. I think she needed a woman to talk to." She smiled, but her eyes remained solemn. "Not only do I look like her mother, I talk and act like her. I spent hours yesterday viewing the recording of Sarah's testimony against Reddington. I wanted to make sure my voice and mannerisms were as close as possible."

Sighing, she shook her head. "She's been through a lot, Noah. More than she revealed to you or Raphael. I don't think she's even hit the surface of what happened to her. I'm surprised she's as stable as she is. They drugged her for a long time. Took her months to get that shit out of her system."

"Once this is over, we're going to make them pay."

"They're powerful people. It's not going to be easy."

His smile was grim. "Easy has never been our way. If we wanted easy, none of us would be here."

"You ever think about getting out? You've been in the game a long time. Ever think about taking Samara and the kids, moving to a deserted island?"

"And let evil win? Hell no. As long as I have breath in my body, this is what I'll be doing."

A little surprised at the turn of the conversation, he sent her a quizzical look. "You and Jake thinking about doing something like that?"

"Moving to a deserted island? No, never. I'm too social for that, but…" She smiled, her delight obvious. "I was going to wait till this is over to tell you. Jake and I are expecting."

Delighted, he threw an arm around her and drew her in for a strong hug. "I'm happy for you two. You've come a long way, Angela Delvecchio."

Drawing back, her dark eyes misty, she gazed up at him. "Thanks to you, Noah McCall. Now let's kick some bad guys' asses and get our family back."

He kissed her forehead. "Sounds like a plan."

Noah watched her walk over to the others, glad to see her engage Giselle in a conversation with the other two operatives.

He couldn't deny a certain amount of guilt regarding Giselle. He should have followed her more closely. One of the things he prided himself on was making sure the victims that LCR rescued were safe. Once this was over, he would right that wrong.

***

Ten miles away from the meeting site, Stanford stood before a full-length mirror. He had exchanged his prison garb for a tailored suit from his favorite designer. It galled him that he was down two sizes from what he had been before prison. For the moment, he was temporarily free. After this event finished, he would have total freedom. It paid to know the right people and to be able to deliver the goods.

McCall and his team of self-righteous do-gooders wouldn't know what hit them. It pleased him immensely that they had no idea what this was all about. They thought this was nothing more than an effort to have his family returned to him. Nothing could be further from the truth. Sarah was likely a dried-up old hag. She'd be in her forties now. When they'd been married, he'd been a devoted husband, willing to put up with the flaws that came with aging. He didn't have to do that now. She'd ended his commitment to her when she'd betrayed him. He had the money and the smarts to find someone younger, better. So, no, this had nothing to do with Sarah.

The children, Amelia and Eric, he was slightly curious about… especially Eric. A man liked to see what his seed produced. Was he as strong as Stanford, or would he be a disappointment like his firstborn son, Lance? Didn't matter that the boy was only eleven or so. His own father had started him out early…given him his first girl at thirteen. Eric might well turn out to be the son he'd always wanted. He'd keep an eye on him, see what he could see.

His oldest daughter, Giselle, was the key to everything. The plans he'd had for her had never panned out, but damn if she hadn't landed on her feet by marrying into one of the most influential families of this century. Too bad she took after her mother and pissed all that away.

Shrugging his bony shoulders, he turned away from the mirror. His bitch of a wife would get what she deserved, and so would her daughter.

And Stanford would get the two things he'd been working on for years— vengeance and freedom.

***

Uncharacteristically self-conscious, Giselle smoothed her hands down her dress once more. For someone who used to wear dresses and makeup every day, she felt surprisingly uncomfortable. The last few months, her survival had meant dressing in a way that didn't draw attention to herself. Being inconspicuous had become her comfort zone. Dressed this way, she felt as vulnerable as if she had put a target on her forehead.

The people around her acted as if they did this kind of thing every day, which she supposed they did.

Her gaze immediately went to Raphael, who stood talking with two other male operatives who had been introduced to her as Jared Livingston and Jake Mallory. Raphael's stance was relaxed but alert, his eyes both hard and wary, his mouth flat. He looked dangerous; he *was* dangerous.

A shiver zipped up her spine. How was it that she had adored the younger Raphael because of his sweetness and gentleness, but found this new Raphael both exciting and sexy? Looking at him now, it was hard to believe he was the same man. There was nothing sweet or gentle looking about him. He was all man, and despite all her fears for the future, she felt a zing of warmth zipping through her that had nothing to do with nerves and everything to do with sexual attraction.

She told herself that having these feelings was a crazy, useless fantasy. There was no way he would ever forgive her for keeping him from his son. No matter what reasons she gave, all valid, he could not see past the anger.

Last night when he had returned to the safe house, she had been waiting for him. If she pushed aside all the pain and anger over the last few years, she could almost imagine she had been waiting for him to come home from work after a hard day. Could imagine she'd already put Gio and their other children to bed, and she and Raphael would sit down to a nice romantic dinner where they would talk and share their days. After dinner, they'd sit by the fire and make out. Then he would take her by the hand and lead her to bed, where they would make love for hours on end.

That fantasy had lived in her head for only a few moments. It had ended when he'd barely nodded at her, told her to be ready to see Reddington the next day, and then headed outside to talk with the men guarding the house. She had gone to bed, and though she'd been woken by the usual nightmares, she had been able to catch herself before she had screamed for Raphael. He had made it clear that they no longer had a relationship beyond this. She told herself to accept that and just be happy he wasn't outright hateful to her. Once all of this was over, she anticipated the hatred would come.

"You okay? Have any questions?"

The question came from LCR operative Riley Ingram, but the face belonged to Giselle's sister, Amelia. The shock had finally passed, but the first time she'd seen the operatives posing as her mother, sister, and brother, she'd almost lost all composure. She'd had the surreal moment that her family was standing directly in front of her, and it had taken every bit of her strength not to throw herself into their arms. She hadn't seen them in years, but these operatives were almost identical to how she remembered them.

"I'm good, thank you."

"You have your vest on, right?"

"Yes." Thankfully, her dress was loose enough that the vest molded to her body and didn't feel the least bit confining.

"Does this happen very often? Having someone want to make some kind of family exchange?"

"On occasion."

"Does it usually turn out okay?"

"Yes. We've never had one that didn't work out our way. Just keep close to Raphael and do whatever he says. He'll keep you safe."

Having Raphael beside her during the meeting with Reddington would be a comfort. No matter how little he thought of her now, she knew he wouldn't let anything happen to her. But what about him? By bringing him into this, had she made him a target as well?

Apparently hearing his name, Raphael headed toward her. The look on his face was so intense she wondered if something had happened.

"Is everything all right?"

"Everything's fine. You stick to me like glue. Understand?"

"Yes."

"Just keep your head down, and don't draw attention to yourself."

"Has Reddington made any further contact?"

"No. The meeting is still on for three. We have lookouts all around the perimeter. As soon as he's spotted, they'll let us know."

"But we won't go out until he asks to see us?"

"No. We'll try to keep it contained to the building. If that doesn't work, Angela will go out first. His main goal will likely be to see your mother. If he wants to see the rest of his family, he'll have to ask for you by name."

"What happens after that?"

"We'll have to see how it plays out. Just do what I say, and you'll be fine."

"Listen up." Noah's voice came through her earbud. "Everyone in place."

Every muscle in her body went taut. Was Reddington close? Was this about to happen?

Raphael could practically feel the nerves bouncing off Giselle, but her expression was calm and composed. He had barely acknowledged her since she had arrived, and anything he'd said to her had been brusque and businesslike. Despite his best intentions, he felt bad about that. Didn't matter that he was still furious with her. She was under his protection, and part of that meant making her comfortable.

"If Reddington asks to see you, I'll be right beside you."

"I know you don't want to talk about…things right now, but what I told you last night…that Gio looks just like you. If Fletcher is behind this to bring me out in the open, don't you think he might try to target you, too? Having both of Gio's parents gone would make things easier for him and Clarissa."

"He, or whoever he's sending, won't get a chance to target either of us. We'll be fully protected at all times."

"Good. That's good."

"You nervous about seeing Reddington again?"

"Yes and no. Seeing him again, knowing what he did to my mother, will be hard, but I feel nothing for him but contempt."

"Hold those feelings inside as much as possible. Unless I tell you different. We want him to think he's in charge until he realizes he isn't."

"Don't worry. I've become accustomed to hiding my feelings."

He knew she had to be experiencing all sorts of emotions. She hadn't seen Reddington since the day they carted him off his private island in chains and handcuffs. Coming face-to-face with a man who was the epitome of evil was one thing, but Stanford Reddington was her biological father. Did she still feel any degree of affection for the bastard? She'd said she hated him, but what would she feel when she faced him?

She looked lovely, and Raphael would imagine Reddington would take pride in that, if nothing else. Her hair gleamed blue-black under the bright sunshine, and her face glowed. Loretta had done wonders making her appear much healthier than she likely was. The dark crimson dress she wore was both sleek and sophisticated, and though designed for fashion, he noted with approval that the bulletproof vest she wore underneath made her slender frame look fuller but not bulky.

He glanced over at the other women masquerading as Reddington's family. Their expressions were operation-ready, fierce resolve stamped on their faces. When the time came, each of them would become her character. Raphael had complete faith that each woman would play her part perfectly.

Reddington wouldn't know until the last minute that it was all an elaborate lie. By then, Samara, Micah, and Evie would be safely with Noah. With twenty operatives and a battalion of reinforcements on standby, there was no way this meet would go in Reddington's favor. This time tomorrow, the bastard would be back in a prison cell, rotting like the diseased vermin he was.

And if this really was all a ruse to get Giselle out in the open, they had a contingency plan for that, too. The plan was for no one to die today. But if anyone did, it would damn well not be anyone he cared about, including Giselle.

"I appreciate the concession Noah made to allow me to have a weapon."

It wasn't the norm. If disaster struck, an armed civilian could make things worse. Even a trained civilian could get in the way of a successful op. But having Giselle be the only person here unarmed hadn't sat right with him. This morning, he'd planned to give her a cursory review of how to handle a small handgun. He didn't plan for her to have to use it, but he refused to allow her to go into this without added protection.

Instead of looking shocked or uneasy, she had surprised the hell out of him when she'd shown she was way ahead of him. Her Glock 43 was easy to conceal and a good size for Giselle's small hand. He was both pleased and surprised to learn she not only had no fear of handguns, but could handle one quite competently. They'd performed a brief shooting exercise, and she had hit the target every single time.

"I'm glad you're trained."

"Mama insisted that I learn." Her eyes searched his, and though he knew she was looking for a softening, an understanding, he couldn't give it to her. He wasn't sure he ever could.

"Mic check." Noah's voice came through loud and clear in Raphael's ear. As each operative sounded off with an affirmative, his adrenaline increased.

"I'm good."

The last person to speak was Cole Mathison. It was good to hear his friend's voice. He hadn't seen the man in over a year.

Cole had moved his family to Knoxville, Tennessee, not long after he married Keeley. They had four kids now, and Raphael had yet to meet the youngest member of the Mathison family.

Cole worked out of the East Tennessee branch of LCR, along with Ethan Bishop; Ethan's wife and partner, Shea Monroe; and Gabe Maddox.

Skylar James, Gabe's wife, and Kacie Dane, Brennan Sinclair's wife, were heavily involved in the prevention of child trafficking and worked closely with LCR.

The operatives were often on the other side of the world from him. When word came that Noah's family had been taken, nothing would have stopped them from being involved.

"Heads up, everyone. We've got activity heading your way."

Cole was two miles up the road. He, along with five other operatives, was on standby. Not knowing how many men Reddington would bring, Noah wanted to be prepared for as few or as many as needed. If he brought an army, then that's what he'd be met with.

"Five…make that six vehicles. I see…" Excitement filled Cole's voice. "Noah, I see Samara in the back of one of the vehicles. It's a white Ford Taurus."

"Thank God," Noah whispered. "What about my kids?"

"Just a sec. Yeah. They're in another car…a light blue Toyota Camry. It's right behind the Taurus… but yeah, it's definitely them."

More than a dozen sighs came through Raphael's earbud as every operative expressed that moment of relief. No one had been sure this would actually happen.

A cellphone rang, and Noah's voice said, "Yes?"

"My family is here, McCall?"

"They are."

"This is how we'll play this. Once we park, I want my family to walk toward the black SUV. When I am assured it's them, your family will be released."

"There's a small brick building on the right side of the roadway. They'll be waiting for you there."

"No. I want to meet them outside. All of them together."

"That's not the way this works, Reddington," Noah growled. "We—"

"You want your family back, we play by my rules, McCall."

There was a long pause. Giving in too easily would alert Reddington that things would not go as the bastard expected.

Finally, Noah said, "Very well, Reddington."

A tense moment later, Noah growled, "Okay, it's a go. Bring the trucks in. Once they're in position, everyone step out as we practiced. Take it slow and easy. As soon as we have my family safe, I'll give the signal."

Reddington's insistence of meeting out in the open was telling. While the man could just be paranoid about being inside an enclosure, Raphael's gut told him there was more to his demands. If he had indeed set up his daughter for execution, having her exposed was a good way that someone could take a shot at her.

Damned if that would happen.

Hearing the powerful engines of the semi trucks coming toward them, Raphael peeked out the window. Once their shield was in place, they'd continue their plan.

"McCall," Reddington shouted. "What's the meaning of this? I never approved this kind of setup."

Showing his confidence that things were going exactly as planned and the rescue of his wife and children was already in progress, Noah responded calmly, "Just a little extra insurance, Reddington. Your family will come out as soon as we're assured this isn't a trap."

There was silence as Reddington was apparently trying to reconfigure his own plans. Seconds later, he replied, bitterness in his tone, "Very well. We shall play it your way for now, McCall."

"All right," Noah said. "Everything's in place. Let's do this."

Adrenaline surging, Raphael opened the door and walked out. Two semi trucks were parked on either side of the small roadway. There was plenty of room for Reddington's vehicles to come through, but the protection of the giant trucks gave them the cover they needed.

Four cars and three SUVs were stopped along the roadway. No one exited the vehicles, and Raphael figured they were waiting to see if this was an ambush.

Spotting the black SUV in the middle, the one holding Reddington, Raphael and Angela walked out together with Giselle right behind them. Both Riley and Mia came behind them, ensuring that Giselle was safely covered on all sides.

This was it.

Chapter Nineteen

Trying to keep a calm demeanor as she followed Raphael and Angela, Giselle told herself that a panic attack right now would be a really bad idea. Now if she could only get her breathing and heart rate to get that message. She had been so focused on what needed to be done that she hadn't given herself a chance to prepare herself for the actual event. How many eyes were on them? How did they see this going down? How could LCR anticipate what might happen? The questions whirled dizzily through her mind.

They were about twenty yards from the black SUV, moving at a slow pace, when the front passenger door opened, and a smallish, older-looking man stepped out. Her feet stuttered as she got her first glimpse of Stanford Reddington. He looked nothing like the man Giselle remembered. He had never been tall—average height at best—but his sheer presence and personality had always made him seem much larger. That man was no more. Now he was shrunken, hollow-eyed, and the skin stretched over his thin face had a sallow cast. But his eyes were familiar, as was his thick silver hair.

"Hello, my loves."

Reddington's voice boomed out as if he had a microphone. That was another thing that hadn't changed. She remembered that big voice, which sounded as if he'd been trained for the theater.

About ten yards from Reddington's SUV, Raphael came to a halt. She and the rest of her "family" stopped behind him. No one spoke for several seconds. Finally, Angela said, "Hello, Stanford."

Reddington smiled and opened his arms in welcome. "You're still lovely as ever, Sarah. Come closer."

"That's not the deal, Reddington," Raphael said.

Reddington tore his eyes from his faux wife and focused on Raphael. "I must admit, I'm surprised to see you again. Does this mean you and Giselle have continued your relationship?"

Negating Raphael's need to answer the question, Angela moved aside, allowing him to see his children. "Have you nothing to say to your children, Stanford?"

Distracted, his gaze moved from Giselle to Amelia and then targeted Eric. "Come here, boy. Let me see you."

Doing what most eleven-year-old boys would do when confronted with such a commanding voice, Mia took a tentative step forward, but Giselle reached out a hand to stop her.

"Have you nothing to say to me, Papa?"

Yes, she was calling attention to herself, but since she was the only real member of Reddington's screwed-up family in attendance, she wanted to keep him so distracted he wouldn't be able to detect the deception. Having him see through the ruse too soon would ruin everything.

"Giselle…yes." Disappointment dripped from his voice. "You've made quite the mess of things, haven't you?"

Her heart almost stopped at Reddington's words. Had the man unknowingly revealed he had a secret partner in this setup?

Raphael kept his gaze on the man in front of him, but in his peripheral vision, he watched the rescue of Noah's family take place. As the arrogant Reddington focused on his pseudo-family, ten operatives stealthily surrounded the other vehicles in the caravan. In less than a minute, Reddington's men quietly stepped out, hands above their heads. Not a whisper of sound was issued.

Samara emerged from the white Taurus and was immediately engulfed in Noah's arms. With admirable silence, they raced to their children, who were being plucked from their vehicle by Fox and Thorne. One arm around his wife and the other around his children, Noah hurried them out of sight.

Now the real fun could begin.

LCR came from all over, swarming the campground like an army of ants. At least fifty men and women covered the area, inside and outside the enclosure.

Several seconds passed before Reddington, still distracted, realized what was happening.

"What the hell!" His voice boomed, bouncing off the trucks that surrounded them.

Angela pulled her weapon from a hidden pocket of her dress, pointed it at the man. "Time for you to go back to the sewer, asshole."

"Sarah!" he snapped. "You will not speak to me in that manner." His face stamped with a cruel glower, he pointed at the gun Angela held on him. "And what are you doing with that gun? Put it down before you hurt someone."

"Not a chance in hell," Angela snarled.

Shock and fury glimmering in his eyes, he roared, "Sarah! Kneel!"

Not only had the bastard not figured out that the woman before him was not Sarah, he was expecting her to submit to him as he obviously used to make her.

Raphael felt Giselle's body jerk in response to her father's demand. Even though she knew much of what Reddington had done to her mother, the words had been a reminder of the hell Sarah had gone through.

He gave her hand a quick glance, glad to see she had pulled out her own weapon. In the grand scheme of things, this meant nothing, as there were more than enough weapons trained on Reddington to fill him with numerous holes. But there was enormous satisfaction in having Reddington's entire family hold a gun on the man who had tortured and abused their mother.

Aiming his own weapon at the bastard's cold heart, Raphael snarled, "Hands up, Reddington."

Apparently slower on the mark than he used to be, Reddington turned, likely to issue an order to his men. A rasping gasp left his lungs. All his men were on the ground, handcuffed. Several LCR operatives stood guard over them. His eyes zeroed in on the vehicles that had held McCall's family, which were now empty.

Whirling around, his eyes wild, he shouted, "McCall! This was not our agreement!"

Noah emerged from the tree line and strode toward Reddington. Raphael had seen the LCR leader angry on various occasions. The dark look in his eyes was unlike anything he'd ever seen. His big body was tense, vibrating with violence.

Standing before the man responsible for taking his family, Noah felt the fury beat at him as though an electrical charge zipped through his body. He had hated before, and he had killed. Not once had he ever been pleased that he had ended a life. This time, though. Yeah, this time he knew if he took down Stanford Reddington, he would not regret the killing.

"You're not a man of your word, McCall. You—"

His fist, fast and fierce, slammed into Reddington's jaw. Blood exploded, and Noah felt a brutal satisfaction as the bastard went airborne and landed several feet away.

Striding toward the prone, semiconscious man, he thought about how easy it would be. One shot to the head, and the son of a bitch would stop breathing. For all the agony he'd put Mara, Micah, and Evie through, he deserved nothing less than death.

That could not happen, at least not by his hand. In an agreement with the Virginia State Police and the FBI, he had agreed that Reddington would be surrendered to them. They would see to it that the few months or years he had left were spent behind bars.

With that thought, Noah turned his back on the man and walked away. He listened as Reddington was handcuffed and hauled to his feet. The man was likely addled and didn't even know what was going on anymore. He hoped he woke up soon, though. Hoped he realized just how dire his situation was.

Surprising him, Reddington let loose an ugly, slightly mad laugh. "You think you know what this was about, McCall, but you don't know anything."

Without looking at Reddington, Noah jerked his head toward Thorne. "Get him out of here before I change my mind and decide killing him would be worth the trouble."

Cursing and shouting, Reddington was shuttled away, and for the first time in days, Noah felt the weight lift from him. His family, though slightly bruised and very exhausted, was alive and back with him. As rescue missions went, this one had gone off without the slightest hitch. Almost too easy.

He turned to see Raphael leading Giselle away just as the sound of a high-powered rifle shot blasted through the air.

"Everybody down!"

CHAPTER TWENTY

Giselle opened her eyes, blinking up at the clear blue sky. Shouting and gunfire blasted around her. Vehicles zoomed and then screeched to a halt. Her mind scrambled to come up with an explanation for all the chaos. One moment, she'd been walking with Raphael back to the building, and the next, her world had upended.

Something big and heavy covered her. Shifting her head, she recognized Raphael's ink-black hair. It hit her then. Raphael had tackled her, shielding her. Had he been shot?

She pushed on his shoulders, panicking when she realized he was motionless. "Raphael?"

Hands pulled on Raphael's shoulders, lifting him away from her. She stared up at Noah's worried face.

"Stay down, Giselle. The bastard's still out there."

"But Raphael. Is he—"

Noah slapped Raphael's face, shook him hard. "Raphael?"

Releasing a gasping breath, Raphael opened his eyes and then twisted his head to see her. "You're okay?"

"I'm fine. Are you okay? Did you get shot?"

"Not sure." He grimaced. "Something slammed into my back. Hurts like the devil."

"Oh no." Tears sprang to her eyes. "Let me—"

"Stay down," Noah snapped. Twisting his head around, he looked up at an area in the distance. "Son of a bitch. We've got snipers."

"As in more than one? The fuckers weren't shooting randomly. They were aiming for Giselle." Surprising her, Raphael's eyes skittered over to hers. "Sorry," he muttered.

"Sorry? For what?"

"Bad language."

The fact that he could apologize about cursing in front of her when he was injured and chaos surrounded them was suddenly the funniest thing she'd heard in a long time. Pressing her forehead against his cheek, she laughed softly. "I think I'll survive."

Raphael winced again. "Damn, that hurts. Take a look at my back, McCall. Tell me what you see."

Still on his knees, Noah gently rolled Raphael over. "Half a rearview mirror is sticking out of your jacket. Don't move." He turned and shouted, "Thorne! Get over here!"

When Raphael had introduced her to Aidan Thorne, he told her that Aidan was not only an Elite operative but also a doctor. Barely able to breathe, she watched as Aidan examined Raphael's back.

"Good thing you were wearing a vest and jacket. The mirror only penetrated the Kevlar. If your back hadn't been protected, it would've sliced right through you."

"Still hurts like hell."

"Yeah," Aidan said cheerfully. "You're gonna have a good-sized bruise. Gonna need a new jacket, too."

Raphael turned his attention to Dylan, who crab-crawled toward them. "Tell me you found him."

"Not yet. As soon as the shots were fired, we sent a hail of bullets toward the areas they came from. Sinclair, Gates, and Fox took off after them."

"They're long gone," Noah predicted. "Just in case, let's get the hell out of here."

Dylan opened the back door of a vehicle and held out a hand to Giselle. She took it and was practically airborne as he shoved her inside. She glanced over her shoulder. Raphael was getting into the other vehicle, and despite having a huge hole in the back of his leather jacket, he moved quickly as if he felt no pain.

Noah got into the vehicle and sat beside her. "Let's get out of here. We'll sort things out once we're away."

"Where are Samara and your children?"

His smile grim, he said, "Where nobody in their right minds would even consider going."

As they sped down the drive and onto the highway, Giselle's heart rate finally settled into a less-panicked mode as she allowed her mind to go over the last half hour. Noah's family had been recovered and were safe. A blessing she had feared wouldn't happen.

And there had been snipers. Raphael believed they had been aiming at her. How he knew that, she wasn't sure. If he was right, though, it reinforced her belief that Daniel Fletcher was behind all of this.

"Reddington said something to me…before things got crazy. He told me I made quite a mess of things."

Noah nodded slowly. "Proves he definitely knows something about Fletcher."

"He's behind it all, isn't he? Daniel, I mean."

"Yeah. He is."

She already knew this, but on hearing Noah's agreement, an odd combination of joy and sadness filled her. It had been so long since anyone believed anything she said, having his affirmation that she had been right went a long way in restoring her confidence.

She couldn't help but be sad, too. Because of her, Noah's family had been taken. They had been used like chess pieces in a deadly game with her father-in-law. The man was merciless when it came to something he wanted. And he wanted her dead.

"I'm sorry, Noah. This was all my fault."

"The hell it was, Giselle. Don't play into Fletcher's hands by believing any of this is your fault. The bastard is evil, and he needs to be stopped."

"But how can he be stopped? He's got so many people on his side."

He offered her a grim smile. "Everyone has a weakness. We'll find his. Don't worry."

It hit her then how phenomenal this man really was. As much as he likely wanted to be with his family, he was here with her, reassuring her. The dedication of purpose in that one act showed her the nature of Noah McCall.

Raphael wasn't related by blood to Noah, but she had witnessed the same dedication in him. What made men like Daniel Fletcher and Stanford Reddington evil, and what made other men like Raphael and Noah good and honorable? That was a question with many answers. She was just glad there were men like Raphael and Noah in the world.

"I'm going to send you back to the safe house. Raphael will join you soon. Then we need to talk. We're going to need every ounce of information you can give us on both Fletcher and this Rawlings character. You up for it?"

To save Giovanni? She would give up everything, including her life, to make that happen.

***

It was long past midnight when she finally arrived back at the safe house. They had stopped in Alexandria and dropped off Noah. She knew he was aching to see Samara and his children. Before exiting the vehicle, he squeezed her hand gently. "Raphael told me that he's Giovanni's father. He's hurt and angry right now, but don't give up on him."

Before she could find an answer that wouldn't have her sobbing her heart out in his arms, he continued, "I'll see you tomorrow."

She spent the rest of the trip to the safe house with her mind in exhausted limbo. She ached everywhere, body and soul, and could think of nothing she'd rather do than take a hot shower and then fall into bed. The oblivion of sleep would be so comforting. That couldn't happen. Not only would she suffer from nightmares, but she wanted to know the next step. How were they going to get Giovanni away from the Fletchers, and how in the world would either of them ever be safe?

She wasn't surprised that Raphael was already there, standing on the porch waiting for them. She thanked her driver, a tall, middle-aged man who was introduced to her only as Dexter, and got out of the car. Noting how grim the man on the porch looked, she asked, "Don't you think you need to go to the hospital and get checked out?"

"Thorne was right. It's just a bruise. I'm okay. How are you?"

"I'm fine, but I'm not the one who was shot by a mirror."

His dark eyes glimmered with amusement. "Technically, the mirror wasn't at fault. It was the guy who shot the mirror I'm pissed at."

"You saved my life."

"It never should have happened. Let's get inside, and then we'll talk."

The instant the door closed behind them, she faced him. "What happened proves my theory. That Daniel Fletcher was working with Reddington. Noah agrees."

Instead of answering, he headed to the fireplace. "I'm going to build a fire. Why don't you make us something warm to drink? There's cocoa and sugar in the pantry."

"I don't want hot chocolate."

"Yeah, well, I do."

When she didn't move, he threw a look over his shoulder that she recognized all too well. If stubborn had a face, it would look like Raphael Sanchez.

"Fine."

Turning back to the fireplace, Raphael grunted his thanks.

Blowing out an exasperated sigh, Giselle went to the kitchen and forced herself to think about something other than that someone tried to kill her today and that Raphael almost died because of her. Concentrating on making the hot chocolate the way her mother used to make it, she felt her nerves calm, her emotions level out.

By the time she carried two mugs of steaming hot cocoa into the living room, a fire was roaring in the fireplace and Raphael was sitting in a chair waiting for her.

Handing him a mug, she took her own drink and settled on the sofa. She took a sip, sighed at the delightful memories the thick, sweet chocolate evoked, and felt herself relax even more.

She sent him a wry smile. "You did that on purpose."

"What?"

"Made me focus on something else."

"Did it work?"

"Yes."

"Good. Besides, I wanted hot chocolate."

"Thank you for always taking care of me, Raphael."

"It's my job."

She wanted to ask him what he meant by that. Was it his job because he was an LCR operative? Or did she still mean something to him? She didn't ask his meaning, because she greatly feared the answer. Raphael had no reason to be anything but furious with her. What if Noah was wrong and he never forgave her?

Fighting off the chill of that thought, she took another sip of her cocoa and then asked, "Where do we go from here?"

Swallowing the last of his chocolate, Raphael set the mug aside and stood. He still didn't know if he could ever forgive Giselle for keeping him from his son, but seeing her look so damn miserable didn't sit right with him. Yeah, she'd made mistakes, but she sure as hell didn't deserve what had been done to her.

Easing onto the sofa beside her, he ignored the ache in his back as he drew her into his arms. "We're going to get our son back."

Whether it was his words or his actions, he didn't know, but seconds later she turned to him, buried her face against his chest, and burst into tears.

Raphael pulled her closer and let her cry. He had a feeling she hadn't allowed herself to let go like this in a long time. And he couldn't deny the pleasure he felt at having her in his arms. There were obstacles to get over, and he couldn't say things would ever be right between them again, but for now this was enough.

When her sobs finally turned to hiccupping sighs, he stretched out his hand, snagged a couple of tissues from the box beside him, and handed them to her. "Feel better?"

She took the tissues, wiped her face, blew her nose, and nodded. "Yes. Thanks. I needed that."

"Everyone deserves a good cry every now and then. Does a body good."

She peeked up at him, her swollen eyes and red nose doing nothing to dim her beauty. "Do you ever cry?"

"Nah. Cracking a couple of heads together or kicking an ass or two usually does it for me."

She giggled softly.

"What's so funny?"

"You sound so very American."

"I am an American. Got my citizenship a few years back. Getting into the slang was more the army's doing than anything else."

"You went into the army? I thought you were going to be an operative as soon as you graduated college."

No point going down that avenue of discussion. It would only bring back the bitterness he'd felt back then.

"Changed my mind. Instead of college, I did a four-year stint in the army. As soon as I got out, I started with LCR."

"You've done a lot in seven years."

That was because he'd been motivated. Focusing on what he needed to do kept him from thinking about what he had lost. Heartbreak had been a powerful impetus. Those first few weeks after she left had definitely not been his best. Noah had finally done a little McCall-style ass-kicking, which had gone a long way in moving Raphael forward.

"I've had some good experiences. Learned a lot."

"I'm glad." She snuggled closer to him, and in seconds he realized her shallow, even breaths were an indication that she'd fallen asleep.

He needed to get up, and they needed to talk about their plans. He needed to get more information from her on the Fletchers. That would have to wait. When was the last time she'd gotten a decent night's sleep? How often did she wake screaming from the nightmare of having her son taken from her? Of being incarcerated in an insane asylum?

He might not be able to give her his forgiveness, but he could damn well offer her this. Settling more comfortably against the back of the sofa, Raphael closed his eyes and allowed himself to doze.

Morning would come soon enough with a new set of problems. For now, he would savor that the woman he'd been obsessed with for close to ten years was in his arms. He'd deal with the rest tomorrow.

CHAPTER TWENTY-ONE

Rockwell, New Jersey

Cato Cavendar was about as pissed off as his kind could get. He had no conscience and very little temper. In his line of work, he could afford neither. You let your emotions take control, you got dead a whole lot quicker than necessary. He was a problem fixer and was damn good at his job.

What should've been an easy assignment had been screwed up from the get-go. Damn idiots thought they could handle things on their own, and now it was as fubared up the ying-yang as it could get.

He had been handling problems for the Fletchers for years. This was the first time he could remember that he'd just as soon shoot them instead of handling the situation. If Daniel Fletcher and Hugh Rawlings had left it alone, let him do his thing, the girl would already be dead. Noah McCall and his organization wouldn't have even been involved.

All it would have taken was a little nudge, and the girl could have gone over the deep end. They'd started off the right way—giving her drugs to make her sick had been working just fine. Her showing up at that party looking like death warmed over and spouting all sorts of nonsense had been unexpected, but it could've worked in their favor. Widow overcome with grief ends her own life—simple, uncomplicated.

In his vast experience, keeping death simple was always the best way to go. Try to make it something more, something bigger, always muddled things up.

Instead of using the party incident as a springboard, they'd shipped her off to some kind of asylum. Arranging for people to disappear was his job, not theirs. If they'd stayed out of it, all their worries would have been over by now. Instead, he was going around trying to clean up their mess. And, oh hell, what a mess.

Not only had they screwed the pooch with the girl, they'd gotten in bed with Stanford Reddington. When it came to sleaze, Reddington was king. Wasn't much the man hadn't done. Cato respected a man like that, but that didn't mean he wanted to do business with him. Especially since it involved going up against an organization like Last Chance Rescue.

Taking McCall's family? The instant he'd heard about it, he gotten a gut-deep bad feeling. Fletcher had seen it as brilliant, and Hugh Rawlings had gotten on board. Talking the men out of the idea had been impossible. His only choice had been to work with what he was given and try to make the best of it.

Reddington's job was to get his family to the meet. His only job. None of it had worked out. McCall had his family back. The girl was still alive. And now McCall knew that someone other than Reddington was involved.

Damn, what a shitfest.

But it was up to him to clean up said mess, and he got paid a more than decent salary to get it done. He was off to a good start, having already arranged for one death this morning. That should be taken care of within the next forty-eight hours. Next thing to do was get the girl dead as soon as possible. And since they now wanted Sanchez dead, too, he'd make it a twofer.

After that, he'd have to deal with the fallout from McCall and his people. They'd eventually go away, or he'd figure out something.

After that was all settled, he'd have a chat with both Fletcher and Rawlings about staying out of things that didn't concern them. Killing was his job, not theirs. And he was damn good at it.

***

LCR Safe House
Virginia

Giselle woke, feeling more refreshed than she had in months. She owed Raphael for that, too. She had fallen asleep in his arms. She wasn't sure for how long, but she vaguely remembered him carrying her to bed, where she had continued to sleep deeply.

Now she was ready to face the day, ready to do whatever she had to do to get her son back. She took a quick shower, eager to see Raphael and discuss their options. Her optimism stayed high until she walked into the kitchen and found a note from him.

I'll be back in a few hours to get you.

Her optimism slowly faded as she acknowledged what else she had to face. The frustrating thing about admitting your mistakes was the knowledge that admitting them didn't make them go away. They were still there, still hers.

Despite their closeness last night, Raphael would never forgive her. Even as she had made the decision to ask LCR for help, knowing it would bring her face-to-face with her past, she had known that. Accepting that he would never forgive her was a lot easier than the knowledge of how much she had hurt him. The pain on his face when she had told him Giovanni was his son would remain with her forever.

Though he now knew everything, she hadn't told him how very hard she'd tried to be allowed to contact him about her pregnancy. She had pleaded and then railed at the US marshal and their other handlers to no avail. They would not budge. Finally, they had painted such a grim and horrific picture of what Reddington would do if he had the chance to grab her child or her family, she had relented. She had always thought they had been a little over the top in their warnings, but now she knew they had been right. Reddington had set up his own daughter to be killed. There was nothing the man would not do to get what he wanted.

Would it help if she told him everything? Probably not, especially when, given another chance, she would make the same decisions. Protecting her loved ones would always come first. She pushed aside the snide inner voice that reminded her what a piss-poor job she had done in that area.

Her eyes roamed around the kitchen. Even though she had no appetite, she needed to eat something. She was going to have to be strong to face what came next. Getting Gio back was the most important thing right now. He needed his mother healthy so she could fight for him.

The sound of the front door opening had her heartbeat in overdrive. She turned. Raphael came toward her, his long legs eating the distance with the determined stride she recognized all too well. His face looked as if it had been carved from stone. The softness she had glimpsed in him last night was no more.

He stopped at the doorway. "Here's the deal. I'm going to get Giovanni back, not only because he's my son, but because it's what I do."

"Thank you, Raphael. I—"

"Save your thanks. It's not needed. As for your explanations and excuses, save them, too. Bottom line, I can't forgive you for what you did, but that won't stop me from doing my job."

In just a few sentences, he had dashed any hope she'd had for them. His attitude wasn't unexpected, but that didn't keep the hurt away.

"I understand."

His eyes swept around the room. "Have you eaten?"

"No."

"We'll stop on the way to headquarters. Noah wants a meeting."

"I'll do whatever it takes…whatever you need."

"We'll leave as soon as you're ready."

Raphael didn't bother to watch her leave the room. The fact that she looked as miserable as he felt gave him little comfort. He'd woken this morning and had it slam into his face once more. He had a child. A six-year-old little boy he had never met. The thought of that was still staggering. Everything he had believed about his life, about his purpose, had been upended.

Dwelling on Giselle's deceit was not helpful. Neither was the knowledge that his son didn't even know who his father was. What kind of relationship could they form? He had to push all of that aside. His priority was getting his son away from the people who held him. And keep Giselle alive in the process.

Even as furious as he was with her, he knew his priorities. Knew what needed to be done. Once this was over, once his son was safe, he'd worry about the rest.

"I'm ready."

Fragile, scared, sick with worry. All those things were reflected in her eyes. Calling himself seven kinds of a fool didn't stop him from opening his arms. "Come here."

Surprising him, the vulnerable Giselle disappeared, and in her place was a coolly composed woman. A mother determined to get her son back, no matter what. "I don't need to be coddled or consoled, Raphael. I'll do everything LCR asks of me to get Gio back."

"Very well. Let's go."

They didn't talk as he drove them back to the city. What he wanted to say would only hurt her more. Coming in like the asshole from hell had only made things worse. Telling her how he felt had done nothing but shut her down.

Pulling into the parking lot of a diner not far from LCR headquarters, he parked and sat, staring at the restaurant without really seeing it. In his mind's eye, he saw a vulnerable young woman who had been slammed left and right by circumstances beyond her control. And he had been just one more to slam her.

"I'm sorry for what I said."

"Did you mean it?"

He wasn't going to lie. "Yeah, but I could've said it better."

"The truth is better. Even when it hurts, it's better."

Maybe, but it didn't keep him from feeling like shit. "Stay there. I'll come around for you. Stay in front of me at all times."

She didn't question the caution. She did as he asked, and they walked into the diner and were seated in a corner booth, far away from the windows.

In seconds, a server arrived to give them menus. Raphael declined the menus and, circumventing what he knew would be Giselle's order of toast and coffee, said, "Bring us both the number three special. Eggs, over easy. Orange juice and coffee, too."

Though the waitress sent Giselle a little frown of concern, she wrote the order down and walked away.

A half smile twitched at her mouth. "She thinks you're bossy."

"I am."

"You've changed, Raphael."

"I grew up."

"No. You were already grown up. When we first met, I recognized that. But you are tougher."

He couldn't argue with that. He'd seen things that would haunt him forever, but he'd also had experiences he never wanted to forget.

"Before we get to the meeting, before Noah begins his questions, I'd like for you to do one thing."

"What's that?"

"You started this the other night, and I interrupted you. I won't today. Tell me about my son."

The quiet way he said those words brought a lump to Giselle's throat. Refusing to give in to the emotions as she had last night, she said, "He's bright, articulate, funny. Has a delightful sense of humor. Loves silly jokes and Saturday-morning cartoons. He's already reading books well above his age level."

She swallowed hard, damning the lump. Opening her purse, she took out an envelope and slid it across the table. "I have some photographs."

He held the envelope in his hand but didn't open it. His jaw clenched, and for the first time ever, she saw he was nervous. Introducing his son to him this way was a mockery of what it should have been. No man wanted the first glimpse of his child to be in a photograph. An honorable man like Raphael Sanchez, with the integrity and goodness of ten men combined, deserved so much more.

The photos slid from the envelope, and Raphael saw his son for the first time. The look in his eyes when he raised his head sent a spear through her heart. There was both wonder and agony in them.

"He's beautiful."

She laughed through her tears. "Just like I told you. He's a miniature version of his father."

Their breakfast arrived, and Raphael grabbed the photos, holding them out of the way so the waitress could set the plates down. "What a cute kid."

Giselle sent her a grateful smile. "Thank you. He's my…" Her eyes met Raphael's. "He's our son."

***

LCR Headquarters

Noah had seen some miserable people. In his line of work, that was a given. The couple who sat in front of him today had despair written all over their faces. Well, he amended, Raphael actually just looked stone-cold furious.

Hoping to diffuse the volatile emotions somewhat, he said, "Giselle, Samara and I both want to thank you again for your help yesterday. Without you being there, I'm not sure Reddington would have believed we'd brought his family."

"It was my honor to help. How are they doing?"

"Better than I hoped. They weren't physically harmed, which was a blessing."

"That's a relief. Thank you for allowing me to be involved. Odd as it seems, seeing Reddington again gave me closure I didn't know I needed."

"Your mother was a victim of the bastard. Letting him see how you and your family have thrived without him was a good thing."

"And he's definitely back in prison?"

"Yes. A different prison this time. Maximum security. No matter who tries to arrange his release, he will never be free again."

There was no need to tell her about the face-to-face meeting he'd had with Reddington. Bitterness had spewed like lava from the bastard's mouth, and every other sentence had included invectives about his oldest daughter. Though he refused to reveal that he had been working with the Fletchers, he didn't mind admitting that he'd set up his daughter. Said she'd made one too many enemies.

"He has no idea that he didn't really see my mother, Amelia, and Eric?"

"There was no need to tell him. Seeing them happy and healthy will be torture for him. Besides, having others know that we have this ability wouldn't be a good idea."

Noah had to admit that it had been difficult not to throw the truth in Reddington's face. Telling the bastard how badly he had been fooled would have been an enjoyable moment but completely selfish on his part. That the man actually believed his family had all drawn weapons on him was enough.

Raphael broke his stony silence. "Did Reddington admit to working with Fletcher?"

"No. I didn't expect that he would."

"Why can't we just go there and demand Giovanni's return?" Raphael asked. "They're not even related to him."

"With any other family, I'd say that's exactly what we should do. The Fletchers aren't like any other family. They've got influence in every sector of society."

"No one's above the law. They still have no right to—"

"I agree, Raphael, but going in blind is not our way. We'll learn as much as we can, and then we'll make our move." He turned to Giselle. "You said you don't believe he's in any kind of danger. Correct?"

"No. They won't hurt him physically. Clarissa wouldn't allow it. Neither would his nanny, Mavis."

"I'm going to find a way to get one of our people inside the mansion, just to give you both some proof that he's really okay. In the meantime, Giselle, you are going to have to disappear. They proved yesterday that they'll do whatever it takes to get rid of you."

"Raphael is a target, too."

"How's that?"

Taking the envelope Giselle had given him, he slid it across Noah's desk. "Take a look."

The smile of delight that spread over Noah's face would have surprised most of his enemies, but no one who knew him well. "He looks just like you."

"Yeah. I'm sure the instant Fletcher saw me, he knew exactly who I am."

"Then I agree. You're both targets."

"I'm so sorry, Raphael. I never wanted you involved in this," Giselle said.

"Yeah, that's pretty obvious."

Shooting Raphael a hard look, Noah turned the focus back to their earlier discussion. "Let's move forward. Let's find out what we can about them so we can not only get the bullseye off both your heads but get your son back, too."

"Where do you want me to start?" Giselle asked.

He started the interview as he would for any victim, and whether Giselle knew it or the hardheaded Raphael wanted to admit it, that's exactly what she was. She had made some bad choices, but who the hell hadn't?

Giselle straightened in her chair and took a deep breath. Noah was right. She had to think about how to move forward. Apologizing to Raphael when it was obvious he had no plans to forgive her would get them nowhere. She would do anything necessary to get her son out of the Fletchers' clutches.

She told Noah what she had told Raphael. How she'd met Danny in college. She hadn't known who he was and had also assumed he hadn't known about her background.

She sent a cautious look toward Raphael when she talked about introducing Danny to Gio for the first time. Both of them had been charmed with each other. In many ways, Danny had been a child in a man's body. He had made her son laugh, and she had realized too late that Gio had been one of the biggest reasons she had been attracted to Danny.

"When did you meet his parents?"

"It was after we married. He took me to their apartment in New York."

Danny hadn't seen fit to call them. He said they already knew because of the tabloids. News of the wealthy and respected Fletchers being associated with the daughter of a convicted murderer and human trafficker had enthralled tabloid readers for days. If there had been one thing she had been thankful for, it was that Gio was never mentioned. Only the Fletchers knew that the woman their son had married had a child.

"And how did they treat you?" Noah asked.

Though she wasn't sure how this related, she answered truth-fully, "They were incredibly polite and kind." She almost cringed as she said it, but that was the truth. They had treated her like family from the moment she met them. And it had all been a lie.

"When did things begin to change?"

"With Daniel, it started right after he found out I overheard his conversation with Hugh Rawlings. It wasn't until after Danny's death that Clarissa began treating me with disdain. Nothing overt, mind you. At least not at first. Just subtle criticisms. I attributed it to grief. I know his death hit her hard."

"And how did they treat Gio?"

"The same…maybe a little more possessive than before. Especially Clarissa. Again, I thought it was due to losing their son. I had no idea they were looking at Gio as theirs."

"When did you realize it?"

"When they wanted to take him on a trip without me. I told them I appreciated how good they were to him, but I preferred that Gio stay with me. Losing Danny was hard on him, too. I offered to go with them, but they made it clear, not so subtly this time, that I wasn't invited."

"Where did they want to take him?"

"To their villa off the coast of Italy. I knew they were angry with me, but they acquiesced and didn't take him. I hoped they'd go by themselves, but they decided to stay home, too.

"I knew I needed to leave. It wasn't a healthy environment for Gio. I told them I thought it best that Gio and I live somewhere else. It wasn't long after that that I began to feel ill. Nausea, severe headaches. They insisted that Gio shouldn't see me in case I was contagious. I didn't want him to get sick, so I agreed."

"And you believe they were drugging you?"

"I do now. I didn't then. I just assumed I had a virus of some sort. It was a week, maybe more, before I started feeling better. I was finally able to get out of bed and dress. I went in to see Gio and—"

She had to stop and take a deep breath. Remembering that day was still one of the most frightening moments of her life. Little had she known that the horror had just begun.

"What happened?"

The question came from Raphael, and his gentle tone surprised her.

"He wasn't there. Some of his clothes were gone, along with his favorite toys and stuffed animals. I knew immediately that they'd taken him away. Gio's nanny was gone, too. I called Clarissa immediately. When she answered, I demanded to know where Gio was. She accused me of being hysterical. Said I was being ridiculous."

She shrugged. "I can't deny that claim. I was hysterical. I demanded they return him immediately. Threatened to call the police."

"I take it that didn't go over well," Noah said.

"An understatement. They were livid. But they came back." She swallowed back the tears as she remembered. Gio had raced up the stairs and thrown his arms around her. She had held him, kissed his cheeks, delighting in his little-boy scent, his laughter. He'd had no idea of the drama unfolding around him.

"They asked to speak with me alone. Because I didn't want to make a scene in front of Gio, I agreed. Mavis took him to his room.

"I followed them to their private den. I wanted to give them a piece of my mind. They, of course, took me off guard by apologizing. I thought then that they were going to be very civilized about us leaving. I told them how much I appreciated their support, but I thought it was time for Gio and me to go off on our own. Begin a new life."

Wrapping her arms around herself, Giselle cursed herself again for her sheer stupidity. Some might have called it naïveté, but she refused to soften the terminology. Once she became a mother, being naïve was no excuse. She had failed her son in the worst possible way.

"Clarissa handed me a glass of lemonade." Her laugh was painful to her own ears. "I thought we were being so adult, so mature. I drank some and passed out. When I woke, I was in a bedroom. Not my regular one. I didn't realize I was in a hospital until a doctor and nurse came in."

She looked down, surprised to see a glass of water in her hand. Raphael had apparently given her one, and she'd been so lost in the past she hadn't noticed. She sent him a grateful look and took several sips.

"The rest is mostly a blur."

"Have you seen either of them since then?"

"Yes, but only from a distance. When I finally got away from the asylum, and after I recovered somewhat, I went to their compound in the Hamptons. I knew I couldn't just walk in. They'd have me arrested, or worse."

She grimaced as she remembered. "I climbed a tree and watched the house for hours. I saw them both. Clarissa got into a car and drove away. And Daniel stood out front, talking on his cell, and then went back inside. I was afraid someone would see me, so I left."

That had been a hard moment for her. Knowing her son was behind those walls and not being able to get to him. She had brought her gun with her that day, and it had taken every bit of her willpower not to use it to break into the mansion. Finally, reason had won, and she had walked away, her heart breaking.

She took another swallow of water. "What can we do, Noah, to get Gio back home? I'll do anything."

"I'm sending you and Raphael to another safe house, out of state. I know you want to be involved, but for right now, information is our most powerful tool. You lived with them for almost three years. You may not know it, but you have knowledge that will help us. What you know about them and about this Rawlings guy will help us. While Raphael gathers that information from you, the rest of us will be working from here."

The thought of not being directly involved or close-by was worrisome. What if Gio needed her and she was too far away to get to him? She opened her mouth to protest, and Noah, anticipating her argument, said, "Keeping both of you alive is just as important as getting Gio out of there."

Swallowing her protests, she nodded and then glanced over at Raphael. He looked about as excited as she was to be going away together.

CHAPTER TWENTY-TWO

Manhattan, New York

The Fletchers' New York apartment, in a high-rise on one of the most exclusive blocks in Manhattan, occupied the entire twelfth floor. The decor was elegant but unpretentious. At first, Noah was surprised they didn't live in the penthouse, but the more he studied the family, the more he realized that these people did not flaunt their wealth. They lived a low-key, sedate-looking lifestyle, but from what he had discovered so far, their influence and power went realms beyond what should exist for any one person or family.

His people were in place all over the world, on watch. On his order, they would move. Mara and his kids were safe and out of harm's way. Raphael and Giselle were already hidden away.

Now it was his play. Depending on how this went down, he'd know how to proceed next. One way or the other, Daniel Fletcher was about to get a comeuppance like never before.

A full minute after he rang the doorbell, a butler with an impressive snobbish air about him opened the door. His nose lifted in the air and wrinkled slightly as if he smelled something not to his liking. This particular attitude was one that Fletcher had likely encouraged. Any other time, Noah would find the experience amusing. There was nothing the least amusing about this meeting.

"I'm here to see Daniel Fletcher."

"You have an appointment?"

"Nope."

"Then may I suggest that you—"

Getting in the man's face, Noah snarled, "I suggest that you go and get your boss before something very nasty happens."

"Sir, I will call the police."

"Please do. I will be talking with them soon, so you can save me some time."

His demeanor slightly less certain, the butler stared for several more seconds. Apparently realizing Noah would not back down, he intoned in his starchy voice, "I'll check with Mr. Fletcher."

"You do that."

Thirty seconds later, the butler reappeared, looking three shades paler. "Mr. Fletcher is in the middle of something important. He suggests that you either make an appointment for another time, or that you wait here until he has the time to see you."

"Tell him he has two minutes to free his ass up and get out here."

A slight widening of his nostrils was the only indication that the butler understood his threats. He stiffly turned and walked away again.

One minute and fifty seconds later, Daniel Fletcher appeared. Haughtiness dripped from him like poison. The man made no effort to hide his hostility, and Noah was glad for it. Straight-on hatred was easier to face than fake politeness.

Fletcher's eyes snapped with arrogance as he demanded, "Mr. McCall, what is the meaning of this?"

Noah made a tactical decision. He strode forward, stopped an inch from the man's face, crowding him. "Are you in cahoots with Reddington? Did you arrange to have my family kidnapped? My people shot at?"

Startled, Fletcher stumbled back into a table behind him, knocking over what Noah was sure were priceless antiques. "I don't know what you're talking about, and I resent—"

"Resent all you want, asshole. Did you have anything to do with my family being taken?"

Fletcher recovered somewhat, the arrogance leaping back into his eyes. "Do you know who you're talking to? How dare you?"

"I dare plenty."

"Get out of my house. Now."

"When I get proof, and I will, that you were involved in my family's abduction, you and your goons are going down. You got that?"

"I have no idea what you're talking about. I—"

"Have you got Giovanni stashed here or at another place?"

"Who? I don't know who you're talking about."

"The kid isn't yours."

"If some woman is making claims that I am the father of her—"

"Stow it, Fletcher." Even knowing it wouldn't happen, Noah made the offer anyway. "You have one day to return Giovanni to his mother." Grabbing the man's smooth, manicured hand, Noah shoved a piece of paper into the sweaty palm. "Bring him to this location at two o'clock tomorrow. You don't show, you'll regret it. That's a promise."

Raising his own arrogant brow, Noah gave the man one last insulting look and stalked out the door.

Quivering with a rage he'd never known before, Daniel dropped into a chair. *How dare he?* How. Dare. He? The man was a lunatic. He would have him arrested. Have him torn apart in the media. By the time he was through with him, his organization would be disintegrated, destroyed. He—

No. He couldn't do that. Common sense washed away the initial rage. Media attention was the last thing he wanted. This had to be done silently. If he involved too many people, questions would be asked. The boy was a closely guarded secret. Clarissa hadn't yet decided how she wanted to bring him to the forefront. Daniel had promised her this concession. Until she decided, no one could know. For right now, everything had to be done in secret.

Involving Reddington had been a mistake, he would admit that to himself. The man was not only pond scum, he had failed to deliver what he promised. Giselle and the boy's father were still alive. The moment he'd seen Sanchez, he had known who he was. Seeing the grown-up version of the boy had been a shock.

He took a long, deep breath. He was back in control now and knew exactly what needed to be done. He also knew the man who could make it happen.

Standing, he went to his desk and pressed an intercom button. "Get me Cato Cavendar. And tell my attorney I want to see him immediately."

Feeling more settled now that he had plans in place, he strode to the window and looked out at the city, at the people milling around like ants. Though he was only twelve stories higher than they were, he was realms above them where it really counted. They went about their day-to-day lives never knowing that they were being used, manipulated, or simply ignored. Those little cogs in the wheel of life believed they had control over their destinies. He guessed in some sense they did, since he couldn't care less about most of them. They made tiny little decisions for their tiny little lives. They meant nothing to him. Most of them were superfluous, a waste of space and oxygen.

The cellphone in his pocket chimed with a familiar tune, reminding him that a few of those small cogs were necessary to put things in order. Holding the phone to his ear, and with the arrogance of the generations of power and wealth behind him, he said, "Mr. Cavendar, I have several new assignments for you and your people."

CHAPTER
TWENTY-THREE

New Orleans, Louisiana

Giselle gazed up at the house that would be her home until this was over. She had never been to New Orleans, but had always wanted to visit. Considering they had flown from Virginia to Louisiana under the cover of night and, after landing, were hustled into an SUV with darkened windows, she had little hope of actually being able to see anything of the city.

According to Raphael, the safe house belonged to a secret government entity and was as secure as any place on earth. The house was a white, two-story structure that looked as though a fresh coat of paint hadn't been applied in a couple of decades. In its day, the house had likely been lovely and grand. Now it looked sad, lonely, and unloved.

From what she could tell, it had balconies on all sides and both floors. She spotted several rocking chairs on the first-floor balconies, along with an ancient-looking swing. The house was nestled in a small, swampy forest, and Giselle thought that was likely the biggest reason it was considered so safe. No one, unless they were specifically looking for a house, would even know it was here. Nor would anyone believe it was inhabited.

"Let's get inside."

A hand barely touched her elbow to urge her forward. When Raphael had told her they were going to a safe house and would have to remain there until the danger passed, his cool expression had told her all she needed to know about how he felt about the arrangements. He had no desire to be with her.

She told herself that was fine. She wasn't here for a vacation or a cozy hookup with a former lover. She was here to work tirelessly on finding a way to get her son back to her safely. If it involved staying with a man who hated her, then so be it. She'd been through much worse.

She stepped up onto the rickety steps, wincing slightly at the loose-looking boards. "You're sure this is safe?"

"Yes. You'll see why."

He opened the door, and the instant she walked inside, she realized what he meant. The outside was all for show. The inside was a lovely, vibrant, updated house that anyone would love. She felt instantly at home.

She turned to face the man behind her, ready to get started. "Okay. What now?"

Dropping their bags onto the shiny hardwood floor, Raphael gave a quick nod, as if appreciating her all-business demeanor. "The information you've already given us was just preliminary stuff. I need it all. Impressions, theories, conjecture. I want to know where you think their money is tied up, where they put it, who they trust. We're already digging into Hugh Rawlings. But there might be more just like him. I need names. People who dropped by, attended their dinner parties, rubbed elbows with them."

"What good will that do?"

"I won't know till I hear it."

She gritted her teeth. Okay. Fine. It didn't sound helpful to her, but she would trust LCR's judgment. She opened her mouth to respond in the same cool, businesslike demeanor and then stopped. His eyes were glazed with fatigue, and his mouth was a straight, grim line. How much sleep had he had in the last few days?

"We could take a few hours and rest, if you like."

"Not unless you need it. I'm fine."

His tone told her everything she needed to know. He was used to being in the thick of things. Not only had she made him a target, he was having to babysit her instead. The least she could do was what he asked of her.

"No, I'm good. Where do you want me to start?"

They walked into a small comfortable-looking sitting room. Giselle headed to a cozy rocking chair in the corner. Raphael continued to stand, and she wondered if he thought he might keel over if he got too comfortable.

Standing by an empty fireplace, Raphael propped an arm along the mantel and said, "Start at the beginning, when you first met Fletcher. You said you didn't know who he was, or his family."

How many times was she going to have to go over the same thing? "As I said, I had no idea who he was. If I had, I would have stayed as far away from him as possible."

"How old was Giovanni when you met Fletcher?"

"How does this relate to finding out more about the family?"

"Giovanni is my son, something you so conveniently tried to forget. I believe I have a right to know when my son met your husband."

Though something shriveled within her at his words, she answered evenly, "Giovanni was three when I first introduced him to Danny."

"Was he good to him?"

"Yes. He was."

"Care to expand on that statement?"

She rose from her chair, pacing in front of him. "What exactly do you want me to say, Raphael? Did he call him Papa? No. He called him Danny. Did Danny teach him things a father teaches his son? Yes, probably. Maybe. Since I didn't have a very good example, I can't really say."

She stopped in front of him. "What exactly is it you're looking for, other than to punish me?"

The repressed anger in his eyes was an awesome thing, frightening her and thrilling her at the same time. Without warning, he gripped her arms and pulled her against him. Glaring down at her, his black eyes flashed brilliantly with both fury and something else. Something she dared not hope to see. Maybe something lingered between them after all.

"Raphael?" His name came out soft as a whisper, filled with that hope.

Raphael ground his teeth until he thought his jaw would crack. He wanted her. How the hell could he even justify this passion after what she had done? Keeping his son a secret for all these years was unforgivable. He shouldn't want to have anything else to do with her.

"Would you ever have told me about him?"

"What?" she asked in a soft whisper that went straight to his groin as if she had caressed him.

Ignoring the demands of his body, he gritted out, "If the Fletchers hadn't taken him away from you, would you have ever come to me, told me about my son?"

Before she could answer, he released the grip on her arms and walked away. He didn't want to know the answer.

Stalking to the window, he peered out. "Forget I asked that. Let's continue," he said. "You married in Vegas, and the first notice you received of his family's identity was the articles in the tabloids. Correct?"

She sat on the sofa again, silent for several seconds. "Yes and no. I don't read the tabloids. We were staying in a penthouse suite at one of the hotels on the Strip. I knew Danny was well-off. He had a very nice apartment close to the university, drove an expensive car. Mackie, our WITSEC handler, told me he was from a wealthy family. But he was throwing money around lavishly in Vegas. It all just seemed over the top. Almost manic. I mentioned to him that perhaps we should talk about finances."

She paused for several more seconds, and he knew this had to be difficult and humiliating to not only remember but to have to share it with him.

"He slid a couple of newspapers toward me. Said, 'Surprise!'" She huffed out an angry breath. "It was all there, in black and white. The son of the wealthy and powerful Fletchers had married Giselle Reddington, the daughter of a convicted murderer and human trafficker. That was my first clue."

"Son of a bitch."

She laughed at his words. "That's one thing I know firsthand. Clarissa Fletcher is indeed a bitch."

All humor gone, she continued, "When he showed me the papers, I told him he had put my family in terrible jeopardy. He laughed. Said that no one would ever dare touch a Fletcher. Now that I was one of them, I was safer than anyone in the world."

"And to hell with the rest of your family."

The sheer carelessness and arrogance of the bastard made Raphael wish he weren't dead so he could beat the hell out of him.

"What about his parents? That's how they found out, too? From the tabloids?"

"No." Her voice held a minute amount of dry humor. "As you might imagine, the Fletchers don't read what they call gossip rags. Some of the more legitimate news outlets called his parents' PR people to ask them to confirm or deny."

Forcing himself to ignore the pain in her voice was hard. "Did you go see them?"

"Not immediately. I had to fly home and see my family. Mama was devastated, but she had no choice. They had to get new identities, leave North Carolina. She had to think of Amelia and Eric, and herself." A closed look came over her face, and she shook her head. "I said goodbye, picked up Gio, and then we went to New York."

Even though he'd like nothing better than to hear her talk more about their son, Raphael continued, "And Danny? How did he act?"

She shrugged. "Like a child who was bored with his new toy. Once his parents knew, the surprise was over. The fun had been taken out of the game."

From what he could tell, the asshole hadn't been much more than a spoiled brat who thought of no one but himself.

"Were his parents furious?"

"You would think, wouldn't you? Again, I had no concept of their antipathy. They were polite, almost kind. Since Danny and I were both about to graduate college, we talked about where we would live after graduation. They suggested we come there for the summer, and we could decide then what we wanted to do."

Raphael heard her move and turned. She'd gotten up from the sofa and, with her arms wrapped around herself, began to pace around the room.

"And so after graduation, you went to live with them."

"Yes. There was plenty of room. Fifteen bedrooms, eighteen baths, and three living rooms made it easy to avoid each other."

"How was Gio during that time? Did he understand what was going on?"

"Gio is incredibly adaptable. He's amazingly self-assured and wise beyond his years."

Love softened the strain on her face. Whatever her mistakes, Raphael knew that she loved her son with all her heart. He hadn't doubted it, but seeing the physical proof did something to him… something that made him wary. Softening toward her was not a good idea. If he let his guard down, he couldn't do his job.

"He looked upon everything as a new adventure. He already loved Danny. When he met his new grandparents, it was like Christmas for him. They gave him presents, treated him as if he were their own."

"Do you think they really love him?"

"Daniel? No, not at all. He's a tool to be used. I do think Clarissa loves him, but it's a terrible kind of love. The kind that smothers and destroys. I saw what that kind of love did to Danny. I don't want that for my son. She wants to control him, manipulate him. Turn him into them. I won't have it. They—"

She stopped, sent him a mutinous look. "He doesn't belong to them."

"No, he doesn't."

At least that was one thing they could agree upon. Gio was their child. The Fletchers had no claim on him. All they had was the sheer arrogance that whatever they wanted, they could have.

He was reminded of the text he had received from McCall a few moments before they'd landed at the airport. He hadn't yet said anything to Giselle, but he would have to soon.

"And their friends. How did they treat you?"

"Standoffish at first. They were taking the lead from Daniel and Clarissa, but they were careful, as if they weren't quite sure everything was legitimate. They were smarter than me. I believed everything. Even though I was still furious with Danny, I thought things were falling into place. That I had a real family again."

There was no bitterness or self-pity in her voice. She stated it in a matter-of-fact manner. He could certainly understand why she had longed for a family. Having had her family taken from her, her entire world ripped apart not once but twice, had to have made her long for stability and a loving family once again.

His own experience with family was different, but when he'd found LCR, all of that had changed. They weren't a traditional family, but there was love, respect, and caring. All the elements of what a family was meant to be.

"Their friends. The Fletchers have a lot?"

"Friends? Yes and no. More like acquaintances, I think. They know a lot of influential people. There were parties and events at least once a month at one of their homes. And they attended several throughout the month at other people's homes."

"You attended them?"

"Some of them. Yes."

Walking over to a desk, he grabbed a notepad and pen and took them to her. "Write down every person you met that you can remember. Something in the mass of information you have in your head about the Fletchers is what's going to get Gio back for you."

"How?"

"Because we need to find their weaknesses. One of those people might be the key to that weakness."

"But Gio is my son…our son. Why can't we just demand they give him to us? I couldn't do it myself. I knew they would kill me. And neither can you, since they want to kill you, too. There's got to be someone that LCR trusts that can demand…" Her voice trailed off as she caught the expression on his face. "What aren't you telling me?"

He gave her a condensed version of Noah's confrontation with Daniel Fletcher. He had known Noah planned to confront Fletcher and, with all his might, had wanted to be there, too. He had forced himself to follow their plan. Confronting Fletcher would have been for his ego only. He wanted to slam his fist into Daniel Fletcher's face and demand the return of his son. That likely wouldn't have gotten him anything but a stint in jail. The Fletchers were too damn powerful to be treated like the scumbags they were.

"I don't imagine Daniel has ever had anyone talk to him like that."

"McCall said he didn't expect it to happen, but before he left, he demanded that Gio be brought to a location the next day."

She gasped, hope gleaming in her eyes. "What happened? Did anyone show up? Did he bring Gio?"

He told himself to be quick. "Do you remember signing a document before they locked you in that asylum?"

"What kind of document?"

"An adoption agreement. Giving Daniel and Clarissa full custody of Giovanni. They brought a copy of it to McCall, or their lawyers did. You relinquished all parental rights."

Her face drained to stark white. "What? I most certainly did not."

"It's a legal document."

"How dare they?"

She started toward the door. Raphael grabbed her arm, and she swung around toward him.

"You can't stop me, Raphael. I'm going there to demand my son back. They can't get away with this." Tears pooled in her eyes, but they were formed from fury, not despair. "I never would have done this, Raphael. You have to believe me."

"I do, Giselle. Unfortunately, it's a legally binding document until we can prove otherwise."

"How can it be legal when I was drugged? Coerced?"

"Because it's their word against yours."

"But I'm his mother. If I say I didn't knowingly sign such a thing, they have to believe me. They can't…" She shook her head. "I'm so stupid, so very, very stupid. Of course no one is going to believe me. They've got dozens of witnesses who saw me appear at their party looking like a drugged-out wraith. No judge would believe me, would he?"

"I don't know. As Gio's father, I could try on my own. But if we fail, what then? We've got to play the game until we find their weakness. They have one…everyone does. We will find it."

"How is that going to get Giovanni back to me…to us? Clarissa will not give him up without a fight."

"Then that's what we'll give them. The fight of their lives. The Fletchers might be powerful, but they've never come up against Last Chance Rescue. They won't win this time, Giselle. I promise."

She released a shaky breath, stared into the distance for several seconds, and then settled. "Yes. All right, fine. I'll do anything… anything it takes."

"Then let's keep going."

Chapter
Twenty-Four

LCR Headquarters

Noah stood at the front of the conference room and faced his Elite team. He was using the biggest conference room they had, not for the number of people in attendance, but for the massive amount of paper loaded on the table. All of it pertaining to the Fletcher family.

His confrontational meeting with Daniel Fletcher had yielded results, though not the ones he wanted. He hadn't expected the man to admit his collusion with Reddington. Nor had he thought he'd just give Giovanni back to his mother. That would've been too damn easy. The hand he had played, though, was both surprising and infuriating. They were going to have to go about this a different way.

His voice carrying the fury seething just beneath the surface, he said, "Every operative not assigned to an active case will be involved in this one. These people were responsible for taking my family. They tortured Giselle, held her against her will. Drugged her, had her incarcerated. They're holding her son."

"How can they—"

Noah held up his hand to stop Riley's interruption. He understood her frustration—she'd lived with something similar herself.

"I gave Fletcher an ultimatum. Demanded he return the child. Instead of doing that, his attorneys arrived with a document stating that Giselle agreed to allow the Fletchers to legally adopt her son. She gave them full custody."

Before anyone could argue against its legitimacy, he continued, "Even though we know it's either a fake signature or Giselle was drugged when she signed it, if we go to court, we won't win. I've had our attorneys review it, and they agree that though it's not legally binding, Fletcher's got too many damn people in his pocket. We get a wrong judge, we've got more problems.

"Proving any of this is impossible right now. Who these people are and how the hell they've been able to get away with what they've done all these years is something we're going to find out. And when we do, we're going to bury the son of a bitch."

He met each person's eyes as his gaze roamed the room. "I've always said never make it personal. To be able to focus and do the job, you have to keep a distance. That's bullshit. I'm here to tell you, this is as personal as it gets. I can't see it any other way.

"One way or the other, the Fletchers are going down."

He shot a glance toward Angela, who had taken the lead role on research. "Angela's going to take you through the basics."

Angela stood and went to a whiteboard. Flipping it around, she revealed what she and Jake had spent most of the night working on. "Since we don't know what kind of technology the Fletchers have access to, we're going old-school on this op. So far, we've managed to dig out a ton of info, but I've got a feeling we've barely scratched the surface.

"The Fletcher family has been around for centuries. They didn't come over on the Mayflower, but it's close. The money they had when they came was earned in the shipping industry. Through the years, they've diversified into dozens of different kinds of businesses. They have an amazing knack for knowing what to invest in and when to buy, when to get out. They look like risk takers, and it's paid off in a big way.

"Most everyone has heard of the wealthiest people in the country and in the world. There are magazines, newspapers, and websites devoted to revealing those kinds of things. The Fletchers appear on none of those lists, but it's my estimation that they're wealthier than any of those publicized billionaires.

"Their business interests still include the shipping company they're originally known for, but it's spread across a variety of corporations and companies, including tech, pharmaceutical, and oil. They also own a massive amount of real estate throughout the world. So far, everything looks completely legitimate."

"How do they keep all this hidden?" Thorne asked.

"That's what we're still digging for. Right now, I'm following a thread. I think they've got multiple companies and entities under names other than Fletcher. These are likely shell companies, moving, selling, disintegrating, and then reappearing under something else. I'm hoping that'll lead us somewhere."

She shook her head. "Have to say, though, whoever is in charge of their investments portfolio is scary good."

"How can they get away with that... taxwise, I mean?"

"One of the main things we're exploring," Noah answered.

"They've filed every year, and though their yearly income is more money than most people see in a lifetime, it all looks legit."

"What about this Rawlings guy Giselle mentioned?" Sinclair asked. "We got anything on him yet?"

"Just basic background stuff so far. He's been friends with Daniel since college. He doesn't have the pedigree that Fletcher grew up with. Looks like he had to claw and scrape for everything he had, but when he met Daniel, things changed for him. They've been fast friends for years."

"He might be our weak link," Noah put in.

Angela grinned and then winked. "Gotcha. We're on it."

"Okay, I get where we're going with this," Riley said. "But why can't we just go in and rescue the kid?"

"It may come to that, and we'll do it if we have no other choice. Problem is, that means that Giselle and her son might never be safe. I'd like to see both of them living their lives free from fear."

"Not to mention," Eden added dryly, "that with the adoption papers, legit or otherwise, Fletcher could accuse LCR of kidnapping."

"Yes. As bizarre as that seems, I could see him getting away with that. Daniel Fletcher won't accept defeat. He'll do whatever it takes to win. No matter how much time or money is involved." His smile mean, Noah added, "What the bastard doesn't know is LCR doesn't accept defeat either."

***

His operatives long gone, Noah continued to study the intel. LCR analysts were working night and day and coming up with an astounding amount of data. Problem was, there was nothing here to hang his hat on. Nothing he could use to make the Fletchers the least bit uncomfortable.

The custody document Fletcher's attorney had sent over had been scrutinized by the brightest legal minds in the country. Daniel Fletcher might have excellent lawyers, but so did LCR. Problem was, no one could find an iota of evidence that the document wasn't real. Giselle, at some point in her time with the Fletchers, had given them sole custody of her son.

They could go to court and fight it, but Noah was coming to understand something about the Fletchers. Their influence reached further than anyone he'd ever seen. For every inch of progress, obstacles were being thrown in their way to prevent any kind of hearing. If it weren't so damn infuriating, Noah would be impressed with their uncanny ability to manipulate the masses. He liked a challenge, but damn if he could see a light in the darkness.

"Can we talk?"

He looked up to see Olivia Gates standing at the doorway.

"Sure. Come on in."

When she closed the door behind her, he knew this was going to be an off-the-record meeting.

She settled into a chair across from his desk, but looked out the window instead of at him. Her gray-blue eyes far off and unfocused, her shoulders slightly slumped, she definitely had something on her mind.

"Gates? Everything okay?"

"I'm just trying to decide if I should open a can of worms that I'd really rather stay closed."

"All right." Knowing when to push and when to wait was a lesson he'd learned the hard way. "Just let me know when and if you decide."

She was silent for a moment more and then expelled a huge sigh. "You know it'd be a lot easier if you'd just insist on knowing why I'm here."

"I'm not known for easy, but if you like, very well. What's going on, Olivia? Why are you here?"

She gave a short, humorless chuckle. "Thanks." Releasing another sigh, she stood and began to pace.

"Gates?"

"You know that I have some contacts…off the books."

"Yes." Like several of his most-skilled operatives, Olivia had come to LCR fully trained. He didn't have to know everything about an operative's past when he hired them. Their commitment to rescuing innocents was his number one concern. Having them able to kick ass on their first day of employment was an advantage he gladly accepted without too many questions. He had a code of ethics and morals he insisted his people follow, but what they had done in their past lives was on them. Everyone had their demons to conquer.

"My contacts…these people…they're hard to describe. The man in charge of them, even harder. What they do…how they go about accomplishing their goals isn't within the realm of what many people would find acceptable.

"Point is, they can find out things in a manner that ordinary people might consider invasive, illegal, and downright wrong."

"Not unlike some of the things LCR has been accused of."

"True. But you place limits on LCR. These people don't ascribe to such limits."

"Do these people or their organization have a name?"

"Unofficially, they call themselves OZ, or Option Zero. Officially, they don't exist. On paper or anywhere else."

"And you think they can help?"

"I know they can. Whether they will isn't a sure thing, but I won't know unless I ask."

"Do it."

She stopped pacing, took a shaky breath. "I'll leave on the next flight out."

"You can take the plane."

"No. It's best if I travel completely beneath the radar."

"Are you putting yourself at risk by asking for their help?"

"No. None of them would physically hurt me."

She walked out the door, and Noah knew she likely was facing a past she didn't want to have to deal with, but for the sake of this mission, she would. Just one more reason he would make sure Daniel Fletcher paid.

"Everything okay? I just saw Olivia leaving, and she looked upset."

Samara came toward him, his light in the darkness. Just the sight of her created a hopeful calmness inside him. Being without her had been like he'd lost a part of himself, the very best part of himself. He'd done his damnedest to give the appearance of control, but inside he'd been coming apart.

"Everything's fine. She's just going to see some old friends she's not too excited to see."

Even though it had only been a few days, Mara had recovered quickly. The dark bruise on her face was healing, but every time he saw it, fury zoomed through his bloodstream. Someone had touched her, hurt her. He wanted to rip the arms off every person involved in the abduction of his family, but most especially those of the man who had given her that bruise.

His kids, amazingly resilient considering, continued to suffer from nightmares, though with each day that passed, the bad dreams seemed less and less severe. Bringing their pets, Roscoe and Sassy, from his in-laws house had helped enormously with their anxiety. He smiled as he remembered the joyous reunion between the dogs and their best friends.

They would recover…they all would, and for this, he was exceedingly grateful his prayers were answered. But this wasn't over by a long shot.

Having Mara and his children back with him gave him energy and stamina to do what needed to be done. Never again. His family was his everything. Nothing like that would ever happen again. He would make sure of that.

She sat on the arm of his chair, put her arm around his shoulders. "Anything yet?"

"No, but they've been at this too long for it to be simple. People with this kind of power and influence have layers of protection."

She squeezed his shoulder, pressed a kiss to his cheek. "If anyone can find a hole in their network, it's LCR."

"You got that right." Turning slightly, he pulled her down until she settled in his lap. Burying his face against her neck, he breathed in deeply. "They'll pay for what they put you, Evie, and Micah through. I'll make sure of it."

"We're fine. Evie only woke up once last night from a nightmare. Micah slept the night through. They're tough like their father."

"And their mother."

She didn't mention the number of times she woke up to check on them. Nor did she say anything about her own nightmares. But he'd been there, right beside her, holding her. He knew. She had suffered, she still suffered. Not only had she been worried about her children, she hadn't known for sure if Noah was alive. She had been put through hell and might never feel safe again. Yeah, someone would pay.

"Have you talked any more with your mom and dad?"

"No. I'm giving them some space. They've gone through so much. I don't want to push them."

"You think you can convince them to go on their vacation?"

"I'm hoping this will all be over before they have to make that decision."

"They don't like not being able to see you every day, but we'll see them as often as possible."

"They know it's only temporary. And they know this has to be done."

"I just can't take another chance. I grew too comfortable here."

"We both did."

His fingers caressed the tender curve of her jaw and then tilted her chin so he could see her as he quietly said, "I can quit. You know money's not a problem. We don't have to live like this."

"Money isn't the issue, and you know it, Noah. And yes, we do have to do this. I'd no sooner ask you to give up LCR than I would ask you to give up a limb. You need LCR and it needs you."

"Others can do the job I do."

"I would definitely argue that fact, but the point is, LCR is your heart and soul."

"But you, Micah, and Evie are my life. I can do without LCR. I can't do without you three."

He considered keeping his family safe his primary responsibility, and no matter what anyone said, he'd failed. While he wanted his kids to be able to enjoy themselves and be free, he had to weigh that against the evil that would always threaten. They were taking new precautions, setting up additional safety features, creating new protocols to ensure something like this never happened again.

"We'll do what we need to do to stay safe," Samara said.

"Yes, we will. We'll—" His cellphone chimed with a text, and his wife adjusted herself in his lap so he could check the message.

As he read the grim words, Noah felt no surprise. Obstacles were being removed. This particular event had been less of an obstacle and more like a loose end.

Having read the message, too, Samara said softly, "Fletcher's tying up loose ends, isn't he?"

"Yes. I wonder if Reddington had any idea what he unleashed when he agreed to their terms."

"I'd say at some point he did."

"Ah, well, I'll give Raphael the news."

With one last kiss on his cheek, Samara rose and headed toward the door. "I'll leave you to do that. Give them both my love."

"Giselle, too?"

"None of this is her fault."

He already had formed that opinion, but he wanted Samara's take. "What about the fact that she concealed her son from Raphael? If the Fletchers hadn't turned out to be the amoral family they are, would he have ever known about Giovanni?"

"Yes. She would have found a way to tell him at some point. I have no doubt about that."

As she closed the door, Noah looked out the window as he considered Mara's words. She was a good judge of character. On this, he agreed with her, too. Problem was, Raphael didn't believe that.

On occasion, Noah had manipulated events to encourage his operatives to see what was in front of them. This time, though, he had his doubts that things would work out.

Pushing aside that worry, Noah sent a text to Raphael. Breaking this kind of news, no matter the circumstances, was never pleasant. Perhaps it would put a slight crack in the iron veneer Raphael had wrapped himself in.

Time would tell.

CHAPTER TWENTY-FIVE

New Orleans, Louisiana

Sitting on the back porch, looking out into the untamed, ever-changing wilderness of a Louisiana night brought out her reflective side. It was chillier here than she'd thought it would be. To her mind, the deepest parts of the South were always hot and sultry. Tonight was clear, cold, and slightly damp. She was covered in a blanket and wore sweats and still felt chilled. She could get up and go inside, but the cool weather was much more warming than Raphael's cold silence. The only time he spoke to her was to ask a question about the Fletchers. Nothing else seemed to matter to him.

Giselle closed her eyes. That wasn't fair of her. He had every right to his feelings. She didn't blame him for his anger or distrust.

Looking back on that time, when she'd first learned she was pregnant, she had never consciously considered that years would go by before she told Raphael he had a son. There had been the hope, albeit vague, that she would be able to contact him and let him know. And though that moment had actually come, it hadn't worked out the way she had envisioned.

And now the Fletchers had a legitimate-looking legal document saying she had given her son to them. She knew things had happened that she couldn't remember. But there was no way she ever would have signed any such thing if she had been in her right mind. How long had they drugged her before she even realized it? What else might she have done that she had no memory of doing? Just the thought sent nausea roiling in her stomach.

And her baby had been alone with those monsters for months. What was going through Gio's mind? Was he worried, afraid? Did he believe she had abandoned him? What had Clarissa told him about his mama's absence?

In the midst of those torturous thoughts, she saw Raphael step out on the porch. Giselle drew herself up, preparing herself. There were only two reasons they spoke to each other. Either he had more questions about the Fletchers, or he asked her what she wanted to eat. Since they had just finished an early dinner, she braced herself for more questions.

Surprising her, he handed her a mug of steaming tea. "Thought you might need this."

She accepted the drink with a grateful smile, relishing the warmth. "Thank you."

"Your father is dead."

Raphael grabbed for the cup that slipped from her fingers. Cursing the careless way he had announced the news, he ignored the burning liquid on his hands. He was lucky she hadn't thrown the cup in his face.

"How?"

Setting the cup on the table beside her, he took the napkin he'd handed her with the tea and dabbed at her hands. "Did you burn yourself?"

"No. I'm fine. Are you okay? Did you burn your hands?"

"No. I—" He shook his head. "That was a shitty way to tell you. I'm sorry."

"It's okay. It's not like I have any feelings for him anymore. He ceased to be my father when I learned what he did to my mother, to other women. What happened?"

"Someone stabbed him in prison. He bled out before they got him help."

"Do you think Daniel is responsible? That he arranged for it?"

"Yes. So does Noah. Reddington managed to stay alive all these years without a single threat against him. Even though he was in a different prison this time, he was under a lot more security than before. He hooked up with the wrong people this time. Fletcher didn't need him anymore, and the likelihood of him revealing information wasn't a risk he wanted to take."

"And it didn't work out the way it was supposed to. I'm still alive."

"Yeah, there is that."

"It's so odd, but I used to dream about this. I don't think I consciously wished death on him, but I thought how nice it would be if he didn't exist. Mama, Amelia, and Eric would no longer be afraid for their lives. We could all have normal lives and finally be together again."

"You can—"

"Don't lie to me, Raphael. Things haven't changed. Not really. The faces have changed, but the threat is as real as ever. Reddington might be out of the picture, but thanks to me, my family is still in danger. Daniel would use them to get to me."

He couldn't argue with the truth. That's exactly what they would do. Reddington was no longer useful, but her mother, sister, and brother would be fair game.

"Noah contacted the US Marshals' office. They're aware of the new threat. They're on guard in case Fletcher tries to find them and use them."

"That's something, I guess."

"This won't be forever, Giselle. We'll find what we need to destroy Fletcher, and we'll get Gio back. Then you can reunite with your family. "

The hopeless look she gave him went straight to his heart. He had done his best to keep his distance. He still didn't know if he'd ever forgive her, but those feelings he'd had for her had never gone away. He'd been fooling himself, telling himself he wasn't attracted to her like he'd once been. Bullshit. If anything, the feelings were stronger.

He could fight them, had no choice. What they'd had before could never be regained. But that didn't mean he wanted her to suffer. She had suffered enough.

Telling himself he was a fool didn't stop him from pulling her up and into his arms. She fit him just as he remembered, felt perfect in his arms.

She didn't resist him, and he was glad for that. He hadn't exactly been gentle with her the last few days. When he felt her soften against him, he sat down, holding her on his lap. They stayed like that awhile, absorbing each other's warmth. Raphael couldn't help but remember the many times he'd held her like this. How blessed he'd felt at the time.

"Why did you call me, Giselle?"

He felt her stiffen and almost regretted asking, but the question needed to be asked and answered. It had been hammering at him for days. He hadn't asked before because it wasn't pertinent to getting the goods on Fletcher. But in the quiet, with darkness surrounding them, secrets could be shared.

"What?"

"Right after you got married. The day after, I think, you called and left me a message."

"I wasn't sure you got it."

"I did. I—" He closed his eyes, feeling more than a little stupid. He should have returned her call.

"It doesn't really matter anymore."

Yes, it did, and the more he thought about it, this might be the most important conversation they would have.

"Tell me."

"I called to tell you about Gio."

As the truth slammed into his stubborn brain, Raphael closed his eyes. And he hadn't called her back out of ridiculous pride and anger. He'd seen the reports of her marriage, and the bitterness had prevented him from doing the right thing.

Though he already knew what she was going to say, he asked anyway. "Why then?"

"I was no longer in the witness protection program."

So she could finally do what she had wanted to do all along. She had told him she wanted to call and had been prevented from doing so. He had ignored her words, even though he had recognized the truth in them. He knew the number one rule of WITSEC. To protect her family and their son, Giselle had had no choice but to abide by that rule. The moment she was no longer bound by that rule, she had reached out to Raphael. And what had he done? Acted like the number one asswipe of the century and ignored her call.

"If I had called you back, none of this would have happened. Gio would be with you...with us. I am sorry, Giselle."

"I don't blame you, Raphael."

Yeah, that much was obvious. She was too busy blaming herself to put the blame on anyone else. And he had done everything to make things worse.

"How about we put the blame where it belongs? First your father and now the Fletchers."

The sound she made, part shaky sigh, part giggle, cheered his heart. "It does feel good to do that."

"Then let's do that. We both made mistakes, but none of this would have happened if the bastards weren't corrupt and evil."

A soft hand touched his face as she tilted his head downward. "Thank you, Raphael." Her mouth touched his, and Raphael felt a million things in the soft kiss. Forgiveness and apology, and for the first time in a very long time, he felt hope.

CHAPTER TWENTY-SIX

Montana

Olivia stood several yards away from the entrance to the underground bunker that housed the headquarters of one of the most secretive covert op organizations in existence. That she had once worked for them was a nonissue. The moment she'd walked out the door, they had erased all evidence of her past with them. Only a few would remember her. One of those few was the man she was coming to see...to ask a favor. It was a sixty-forty split whether he'd let her inside, much less agree to her request.

She hadn't left under good circumstances, but that was the nature of the beast. People left OZ for only two reasons. Either you got dead, or you messed up big-time. She counted herself lucky that she had left for the second reason, but she was quite sure not everyone agreed. Especially the man she was about to see.

He knew she was here. Most likely knew the moment she'd gotten on a flight to Montana. Cameras were situated unobtrusively outside the compound. She imagined he was sitting at his desk watching, waiting to see if she'd actually have the guts to walk up to the gate and request entrance. He was right to doubt her. Her knees were shaking, and what felt like giant mothlike creatures were having a field day in her stomach. She had sworn she would never return. Since she'd been practically shoved out the door and told not to return, coming back here could be a hopeless endeavor. But she had to try.

Working for Last Chance Rescue these last few years had returned some of the humanity she had lost. Before LCR, she had been in limbo, going through the motions of living. No, not living—she'd barely been existing. LCR had saved her life, her sanity. If she could help them, despite the pain it might cause herself, that's what she needed to do. Doing the right thing often involved sacrifice. She owed it to LCR, and she owed it to herself to try, no matter the consequences.

"Are you coming in?"

The voice was his, and despite her resolve, it took every bit of her willpower not to turn tail and run. Heaven help her.

Steeling her spine, she answered calmly, "If you'll let me."

The sound of a door opening brought her head around. He had come from another entrance behind her. Olivia braced herself.

"Hello, Liv."

"Hello, Ash."

"Been a long time."

Since she had never planned to see him again, a long time wasn't long enough. However, she had come to ask a favor. "Yes, it has."

"You come to kill another one of my people?"

She didn't outwardly flinch—she was too well trained for that—but he'd know full well that his words had landed and bruised. Asher Drake never said anything without being assured of the outcome he wanted.

"I've come to ask for your help."

"Is that right?"

She heard the meaning behind the words. Yes, there would be consequences. This man did not give without taking. She would deal with that at another time. A child was at risk, and if there was one thing Ash would not abide, it was an innocent being harmed. Yes, he was ruthless, but never without cause.

"Okay if I come in and tell you about it?"

Something like amusement glinted in his deep-blue eyes. "But of course." He moved aside and waved his hand. "You know the way."

Feeling like a lamb heading into a lion's den, Olivia walked through a door she'd sworn she'd never go through again.

***

LCR Headquarters

Disgusted, Jordan threw a mass of papers down on the table. "We still have a whole lot of nothing."

"No," Eden said evenly, her frustration evident but less volatile. "We have a whole lot of something, just nothing that's going to help us, at least not yet."

"Okay," Noah said, "let's go over it one more time." Moving his eyes around the room, he noted the same level of frustration in everyone's faces. They'd been at this for several days.

"Angela?"

Taking her cue, Angela stood. Before becoming an operative, Angela had been LCR's best tech analyst. With this part of the op, until they could find their needle in the haystack that they could use against the Fletchers, she was leading the charge on getting the goods on them.

"Let's review." She walked over to the whiteboard and the mass of information they'd uncovered. "The family is old money. Railroads, shipping, oil, banking. You name it, they've had their fingers in it, or still do. Most recently, it's been the tech industry. Even though they had a good foundation when they came to the US over three centuries ago, their wealth accumulation has been phenomenal. Daniel Fletcher is as savvy and discerning as his father before him. Whoever taught these people how to make money taught them well."

She gestured toward a long list of well-known companies in which the Fletchers held stock, and sometimes even a controlling share. "These are only a small percentage of their investments."

"It's a veneer," Sabrina said.

"Yes and no." Angela shot her Elite team member a smug smile. "If someone was printing up a PR brochure for the family, this is what they would use. It's all legit, and there's not a missing dot over an i, or even a crooked cross over a t. It's perfection to the nth degree."

"In other words, it's too clean," Justin said.

"Yep. But still all true."

"So how does that help us?" Riley asked. "If there's nothing there?"

"Because no one is that clean," Olivia Gates answered, a world of knowledge in her statement. "Everyone has garbage stored somewhere."

"That's an awfully cynical attitude you've got there, Gates." Brennan Sinclair gave Olivia a toothy smile. "Damn proud to have you as my partner."

"So how do we find the dirt?" Justin asked. He glanced over at his partner, who last year became his wife. "Riley's question is a valid one. Just because we know that no one is that squeaky clean doesn't mean the dirt will be easy to find."

Angela gave Noah the look, and he took his cue. Standing, he met each operative's eyes unflinchingly. Most of the operatives who'd assisted with his family's rescue had returned to their regular locations. Several were already involved in new ops. For now, he would rely on the Elite team. They, along with Eden and Jordan, would do the bulk of the work. If necessary, he could have many more operatives available within a matter of hours. It might come to that, but not yet.

"We've faced some of the shittiest and evilest people on the planet. Monsters who have done unspeakable things. We've had a few stumbles here and there, but for the most part, we've managed to stop them.

"These people are different. They've got layers upon layers. Every time we think we've got a thread, it disappears down a rabbit hole."

"So what you're saying, McCall," Aidan Thorne said, "is that they can't be taken down in our usual damn-the-torpedoes manner."

"Exactly. We're not known for our subtlety, but in this matter we have no choice. We're going in covert and undercover in every area. These people have a rare level of power and influence. Politicians of every party, numerous members of several royal families, along with some of the wealthiest and most-influential people in the world, have given their endorsement and support. Yet there's no indication of money being exchanged.

"I want to know how. More than that, I want to know why. Why do they have this fearsome protection and loyalty? How the hell do they get away with what they get away with?

"And I want to know how we can penetrate their seemingly impenetrable veneer. Everyone has a weakness. They have theirs. We need to find it."

He would mention nothing about the avenue that Olivia Gates had traveled. Looking both haunted and pale, she had returned with the cryptic news that things were in place. Whatever that meant, only time would tell if her idea would pan out. For now, they would proceed as if they were on their own.

"In the meantime, we need to make sure Giovanni is not in danger. Giselle doesn't believe he is, but we all know that people who feel threatened don't always react in a predictable manner."

"How are we going to get inside and find that out?" Riley asked.

Shooting Olivia a smile, he said, "Gates will explain how that part of the op has already begun."

CHAPTER TWENTY-SEVEN

Two days later
London, England

His eyes gleaming with appreciation, Lucas Kane looked down at his wife. "If I haven't told you already, you look absolutely stunning tonight."

Standing in the long hallway, waiting for their arrival to be announced, McKenna Sloane Kane peeked up at her husband. "Thank you. You look pretty good yourself." That was an understatement. Eight years of marriage, and she could still get lost in those mesmerizing eyes. The day she came to rescue him, Lucas Kane had stolen her heart.

"It feels strange to be wearing something so elegant on an op."

He grinned down at her. "That's because the Ghost's usual superhero costume always ran to ragged jeans and running shoes." He glanced down at her feet. "Shoes aren't too uncomfortable?"

She winced slightly and then laughed softly. This was the first public event they had attended since their daughter, Madeline, had been born. Getting dressed up had been fun, but she had groaned when she'd slipped her spoiled feet into the three-inch heels. Though she was sure they were ridiculously expensive, they still weren't the trainers she was accustomed to wearing.

"They're fine." She glanced around the crowded room. "I just hope this works."

"I've put bugs in a couple of ears to make sure we're seated close to them. By the time they leave tonight, they'll be suitably impressed with the Kanes of London, England."

Her nose wrinkled with distaste. Putting on a different persona for an undercover mission was second nature to her, and she usually had no trouble getting into the role. This felt odd for a different reason. She was married to a ridiculously wealthy man, and their assignment tonight was to use that wealth to hobnob with other ridiculously wealthy people and pretend a snobbery she would never feel. The Fletchers were part of the upper echelons of American society. It was up to her and Lucas to not only impress them, but to have them so enamored of their elite sophistication that they would follow their lead in one very specific area.

"I'm going to let you take the lead with them," she said. "Not only will your accent and Prince Charming good looks impress them, you're better at being pretentious than I am."

"I don't know if I feel complimented or insulted."

"Ha. No insult intended. You just sound fancier than me. Plus, you're more diplomatic than I am. My first instinct will be to grab a hank of her hair and his earlobe, clank their heads together, and demand they return Giselle and Raphael's son to them immediately."

"As much as I would like to see that, I think finesse is our best option for now."

"Spoilsport."

"Lord Lucas Kane and Lady McKenna Kane!"

She allowed one more wrinkle of her nose and then giggled when she felt Lucas's suppressed laughter vibrate through him. "You're the one who insisted I accept the title, Lady McKenna," he growled softly.

"I know," she whispered as she took her husband's arm and walked through the double doors. "I just didn't realize how it would sound when someone yells it out. Be sure to kick me if I start giggling like a hyena."

And on that note, with her husband's soft chuckle comforting her, they entered the grand ballroom and looked out into a sea of unfamiliar faces. When she spotted the couple they'd come to impress, she settled. This was a job, and no matter how differently she'd like to handle the situation, she would make sure she accomplished her goal. The Fletchers wouldn't know what hit them.

There were a million and one reasons why he loved and admired his wife, but tonight he was reminded of one more. She was an amazingly talented actress. Not once did she indicate even the slightest antagonism toward some of the more priggish people they met. Many of them were kind, if somewhat eccentric, but on occasion one would offer an acerbic comment or observation. McKenna was the sweetest and kindest person in the world, but she also had definite opinions and was known to share them whenever she liked. It was one of the things that had drawn him to her. There wasn't a pretentious bone in her lovely body. Tonight sugar wouldn't melt in her mouth.

Fortunately, there were a few people they knew, and the crowd wasn't a total gathering of strangers. They made their way through the masses, stopping on occasion to offer a greeting or join a discussion briefly. Since they were here for one purpose, he didn't feel obligated to linger. When he spotted the Fletchers, he bent close to his wife's ear. "Targets spotted at two o'clock."

In the middle of issuing a greeting to an elderly gentleman with a slight hearing problem, she seamlessly transitioned from courteous and kind to full-on LCR operative without changing her expression. No one but Lucas would see the change, but he felt her take on the persona as if cloaking herself in a protective veneer.

"Got 'em in my sights," she murmured. "Why don't we schmooze a little closer? See if we can pick up what others might say about them."

His hand at her lower back, he nodded at an acquaintance as he guided her toward their destination. From their intel, the Fletchers were in London only for this particular event and would be heading back to their home in the US soon. This was their one shot to make the impression. Although, if necessary, they could invite them to a smaller gathering at their home and pile on more bullshit. Neither he nor McKenna wanted that. The sooner they got their part over with, the sooner Olivia Gates could do hers.

As they drew closer to their targets, Lucas took in their appearances. Daniel Fletcher had the looks of an old-time movie star. Tall, broad-shouldered, slender, with an upright posture that would rival a military man. He was aging well, with a slight graying at the temples and several creases around his eyes and mouth to give him an air of both maturity and character.

Mrs. Fletcher was equally impressive. She looked to be a few years younger and had a slender, youthful appearance many women half her age would envy. Her golden hair, which gently curled at her shoulders, flattered both her unlined face and her swanlike neck. Only a few inches shorter than her husband, she wore a designer gown of silk with silver sequins that was neither staid nor provocative but perfect for the occasion.

Having been a covert agent for the British government and currently a successful businessman as well as an LCR operative, Lucas was good at snap-judgment analyses. He saw arrogance and entitlement. They were a power couple and enjoyed that status immensely.

As he watched them, he noted something else. If he wasn't mistaken, he spotted a small amount of insecurity as they were introduced to several of the more notable aristocracy in attendance. Being amongst the upper crust of British society might have made them feel a little less superior. As much as he would have liked to go in with a full-blown arrogance, that wasn't his or McKenna's mission.

Making nice with evil was one of his least favorite jobs, but he was damn good at it. And so was his lovely wife.

"Lord Lucas, how good to see you. And Lady McKenna, my dear, don't you look divine. How is your darling daughter, Maddie? Why, she must be two years old by now."

As he shook Sir Gerald Wexley's hand, Lucas could barely hold back his grin of admiration. Wexley had a way of getting to the heart of a matter with the smoothness of glass. Anyone else would have taken half an hour to build up to the information he'd dispensed in just a few sentences.

"Wexley, it's good to see you."

As McKenna played her part, smiling prettily when Wexley kissed her hand, Lucas watched the Fletchers. They were intrigued. Hard not to be when one of the most well-known men in England stops in the middle of a conversation to greet newcomers so warmly.

Gerald Wexley had been recently knighted, but it wasn't his knighthood that made him famous. A renowned physician, Wexley had been part of a team of civilians who had held off a group of terrorists who had attacked an orphanage just outside London. Though he was well into his seventies, he had single-handedly saved four children and captured one of the rebels.

Lucas had known Wexley all his life, as Gerald had been one of Lucas's father's best friends. He was one of the few who knew Lucas's background and the work he did for LCR. When Lucas had asked to be introduced to the Fletchers, Gerald had been delighted to oblige.

"Fletcher, do you know the Kanes? Rather, Lord Lucas and Lady McKenna?"

"I don't believe we've had the pleasure."

As introductions were made, Lucas noted their expressions were exactly as he had hoped. Even though his companies were well known and he made no secret of his wealth, he wasn't one to pursue publicity—something the Fletchers would definitely identify with.

He had heard of the Fletchers before LCR became involved, but had given them little consideration other than the fact that he knew they were wealthy and influential. After digging deeper, he was surprised at how little could be found. LCR analysts were experts at finding out things people didn't want known. He had no doubt they would do the same with the Fletchers. It was just going to take a little longer, and that's where he and McKenna came in.

"I knew your father," Daniel Fletcher said. "Brilliant businessman."

"Indeed, he was." But his father had been something Daniel Fletcher was not. Phillip Kane had been a kind and decent human being.

Not wanting to make it appear that they considered the Fletchers any different than any of the other guests, Lucas murmured in his wife's ear, "Darling, there's Felicia Dutton. Didn't you mention you wanted to chat with her about one of her upcoming charity events?"

Taking his cue, she said, "Indeed, I do." Giving one of her most winning smiles to both Fletchers, she said, "So lovely to meet you both," as she followed Lucas to another small group gathered close-by.

They made their rounds, once again engaging in brief conversations, but all the while keeping an eye on the Fletchers. The couple seemed to be enjoying themselves. He had heard Daniel's booming laughter and Clarissa's twittering laughs several times.

Her smile adoring, McKenna looked up at her husband. "Think we made a good impression?"

"I do. And when they find themselves seated at our table, we'll make sure they're even more impressed."

Holding up her champagne flute, she tipped it toward him. "Operation Snobbery is in full swing."

Unable to stop himself, Lucas swooped down and lightly kissed his wife's luscious lips. "I adore you, Lady McKenna."

"As I do you, Lord Lucas."

***

The hotel door had barely closed behind them before Clarissa turned to her husband. "We have to contact this Susanna Wainwright immediately."

"It's quite late, dear. I doubt that she would be pleased to be woken in the middle of the night for a job offer."

"Then you'll have to make sure we offer her enough to overcome being woken. The Kanes made it clear they were going to contact her tomorrow. If we don't do it tonight, she'll take their offer. The British are known for their loyalty. No matter how much more we offer, she'll feel obligated to work for the Kanes. We must move tonight."

"But we know nothing about this girl other than what the Kanes told you. She might—"

"We don't need more information. Don't you think she's been vetted already? It's obvious the Kanes have thoroughly researched her. After the way they went on and on about their little girl, you'd think no child had ever drawn a picture of a horse before. Giovanni is much more gifted, and he's older than their daughter. He needs to have the best teacher to bring that intelligence to the forefront.

"The Kanes believe Susanna Wainwright is the best governess for their daughter. We absolutely have to have the best for him."

"Fine, fine." Retrieving his cellphone, Daniel dropped onto the sofa and began to make calls.

Assured that her husband would handle that business, Clarissa went to her laptop and did a little research of her own. She had known of the Kanes before meeting them, but wanted to learn a bit more. It was always good to know your rivals.

If she needed to, she could have one or more of her assistants to do a more in-depth analysis. She doubted that would be necessary. She knew quality people when she met them.

There wasn't as much information on the Kanes as she had thought there would be, but from what she could tell, they had a sterling reputation. Lady McKenna was involved in an enormous amount of charities, and Lucas was considered one of the most brilliant business minds in Europe. There was no way they wouldn't have thoroughly and carefully researched the governess.

Susanna Wainwright was even more interesting. Master's degrees in both child development and psychology, she had attended Oxford and Cambridge. She was thirty-four years old, moderately attractive, and single. She even had, though several generations in the past, a hint of royal blood. She was a British citizen, but her family was from Germany. Father a history professor, mother a psychologist. No siblings.

She was perfect. Nothing would stop Clarissa once her mind was made up. She had to have Susanna Wainwright for the boy.

Before she could turn around and insist Daniel hurry with her request, she heard him coming up behind her.

"All right, my dear. Here's Wainwright's number. Do you want me to handle it?"

Triumphant and smug, she snatched the slip of paper from her husband's fingers. "I'll take care of it."

***

When the phone rang at one fifteen in the morning, it was rarely good news. For Elite operative Olivia Gates, who had been waiting for hours for this particular call, it was a delight.

Since grogginess would be expected, Olivia Gates answered the phone sounding both startled and sleepy. "Hello...yes?"

"Is this Susanna Wainwright?"

"Yes, this is Susanna. What is...Who is this?"

"This is Clarissa Fletcher. I would like to talk with you about a job."

"A job? How did you..." Thoroughly enjoying herself, Olivia put confusion in her tone. "Who did you say this is?"

"Clarissa Fletcher of the New York Fletchers. Surely you've heard of me."

Knowing how to play the game, Olivia said, "Well…yes, of course. Um…how can I help you, Mrs. Fletcher? You're calling about a job, you say?"

"Yes. I have a position for which I'd like to employ you."

"I see. Well, that's awfully kind of you, and while it's true that I've recently left my position and am considering several offers, I had planned to take a holiday prior to committing to another family. When I return, I can meet—"

"No. We need you now."

"Now? But—"

"We will pay you twice what you were earning with your last employer."

"That's frightfully generous, but—"

"Three times, then."

"Three?" Olivia allowed a little squeak to come into her tone. "Well, I don't know. I'd have to know exactly what you expect. What the child needs and who—"

"Fine," Clarissa cut in. "Can you be at the Connaught Hotel at noon tomorrow?"

"Yes. I believe so."

"Ask for the Fletchers' suite. I'll explain everything then."

"Yes. All right. Goodbye."

The instant the call ended, Olivia took another phone from her small bag of burners and sent a text: *Game on!*

Crossing her long legs, she took a sip of the excellent brandy she had been enjoying as she had waited for the call. Things were definitely looking up, and she could not wait to start her job as governess for a beautiful little boy named Giovanni.

CHAPTER TWENTY-EIGHT

New Orleans, Louisiana

"How's everyone doing?" Noah asked.

Holding the phone to his ear, Raphael shoved his fingers through his hair for about the tenth time that day. "Going stir-crazy. Any developments?"

"Yes. Gates interviewed with them this morning. They're headed back to the States. She'll be going to their estate later this week for a more comprehensive interview."

"Just like that?"

"They see something they want, not much stops them."

"Olivia must've made a helluva impression."

"Everything went as planned. We've got good people."

"Yeah, I know. Tell everyone thanks."

"Will do. Now tell me how you're really feeling."

"Like a dick."

"Uh-oh, what did you do?"

"Basically told her all of this is her fault and I'll never forgive her."

"Is that how you really feel?"

"No, not really. Not anymore. Did I ever tell you that she called me after she got married?"

"No, you didn't."

"She left a message, asking me to call her. I never did."

"She tell you why she called?"

"Yes. To tell me I have a son. She was no longer bound by the WITSEC rules. Her first thought was to call me, let me know."

"Aw, hell."

"Yeah. My thought exactly. If I had called her back...hadn't been so busy being a prick, none of this would have happened."

"Not a thing you can do about that now. But you have a chance to make it right."

Yes, he did, but could he? Had too much time passed? Or had too much happened for them to regain what they'd had? Even as much as he knew he'd messed up, an old resentment lingered. She had left him cold turkey. Would she do it again?

"Raphael, you need to remember that this won't be forever. You will get your son back. You'll be a father. You'll need to have the right kind of relationship with his mother."

"I don't know what that will look like."

"You've been given time to figure that out. Take it."

"What if we can't get past it?"

"Then you learn to deal. Just remember, our mistakes don't define us. It's what we do with what we learned from them."

"Thanks for the advice, Pop."

Noah snorted. "Ha. Talk to you soon."

After ending the call with Noah, Raphael walked onto the screened-in back porch. The forest beyond the small yard was teeming with a variety of wildness and life. The sounds, some soothing, some dangerous, filled the night.

Here, they were isolated, far away from danger. Noah was right. He needed to take this time and figure out how to go forward. This would be over at some point. When it was, he would be a father to a little boy he'd never met. A little boy who knew nothing about him. And he would share parenthood with a woman he had once loved with an all-consuming passion. Could they get past the hurt and the anger and be the kind of parents their son needed?

His early childhood had given him only a glimpse of what a good father should be. It wasn't until he had been rescued by LCR that he had been exposed to what kind of man, what kind of father, he wanted to be.

The rain came in, silent as a whisper, shimmering in the dim glow from the porch light. He didn't hear her approach, but he felt her presence, a delicate stir of air.

"And the night weeps," she spoke softly, dreamily.

"How's that?"

Her smile was sad, but her eyes looked far away, almost unfocused. "My mama's words. When I was a little girl, she used to make up stories. One of my favorites was about a cricket named Horatio. He was a talented violinist, and whenever he played, it would move all the hearts of nature, including the night. Together, they would weep at the lovely music he made.

"So whenever it rained, my mother would tell me that Horatio was playing music for his family and friends." She shrugged. "It made me feel less lonely."

And that loneliness had only increased for her. Had Fletcher seen that loneliness? Had he spotted a lonely and vulnerable young woman, preyed upon her? And when he'd discovered, somehow, that she was the daughter of a convicted felon, he had used that, used her.

Her soft voice cut into his thoughts. "I guess you had a lot of loneliness, too. Growing up, I mean."

Had he? He didn't remember being alone as much as being determined to get away from all that he had known.

"It was different for me. I had choices. Places I could go, things I wanted to do."

"We've led different lives. Before and after."

"And now we're parents together."

"I don't know how many times I can say I'm sorry."

"No, we're past that. That's not what I'm looking for."

"Then what?" She took his hand, squeezed it. "What can I do? What do I need to do?"

Unable to resist the temptation, he pulled her into his arms. Burying his face in her hair, he stifled a groan at her familiar scent. How he had missed it.

"When this is over…when Giovanni is safe, we'll figure things out."

"Will we?" Pulling slightly away so she could see his face, she said softly, "Raphael?" There was a wealth of meaning in her voice. It was an invitation, a plea.

He looked down at her for the longest time, his need for her fighting against the sense of betrayal he still felt. It would be so easy to lose himself in her soft, giving body, to forget, even for a little while. Every instinct told him to take what she offered. He saw no guile in her eyes. They were open, honest. She wanted him. The expression on her face told him that whatever he decided, she understood.

His jaw clenched with need. Yes, he wanted her. Had never stopped. But if he did this, it would be for purely selfish reasons, and though he was no saint, he wasn't a user either. The gulf they had between them was too wide, too fraught with hurt and misunderstandings. Giving in to his needs would solve nothing more than easing a physical ache. The problems would still be there.

Taking a steadying breath, he stepped back, away from temptation. "Get some sleep. We'll start again tomorrow."

"No."

"What?"

Her voice, her entire demeanor, held resolve. "You heard me. It's taken me a long time to realize something. Something I'm profoundly ashamed to admit. I don't speak up for myself. Don't tell others what I want. If I did, maybe I could have done something to help my mother all those years we were stuck on Reddington's island. If I had spoken up for us, fought for us, we never would have been apart. And I most certainly could have prevented what my son is going through now.

"Every time I accepted what others said without fighting for what I wanted, I lost. Those I care about lost. I'm tired of losing, Raphael. I want you. I want this. If you don't, then say so. But I—"

She never got to finish her sentence. His mouth was on hers, ravishing it tenderly, thoroughly. Hard, steely arms wrapped around her, and he said her name, part growl, part groan, causing a flood of need to swamp her senses, almost swallow her whole.

She pulled away, breathing heavily, wanting to make sure he knew. "I'm not asking for promises. I know that we have a lot to get through."

"Hush. This is what I want. You are what I want. Hang on."

Surprising her with both his speed and strength, he swung her into his arms and carried her into the house. Giselle's heart was pounding so hard, she could barely hear the hard rain that was now pouring from the heavens. They entered the bedroom and closed the world out. Soft darkness surrounded them as he laid her on the bed. She reached for him, and he said thickly, "Let me love you."

He started at her feet, taking off her shoes and socks, tenderly kissing each naked foot. His hands slid up the outside of her legs, amping up the anticipation. Quickly unzipping her jeans, he slid them off but left her underwear. Going back to her feet, he started all over, his mouth moving up one leg, stopping close to her core. When he went back to her feet again, Giselle groaned and twisted on the bed.

Raphael chuckled, the sexy sound vibrating through her. "Raphael...please."

"Patience, sweetheart."

"I've been waiting too long already. I need you."

"Shh." Proving that his self-control was much stronger than hers, he started at her other foot, moving slowly up her leg. When he stopped once again, she reached for him. He took advantage of her arms being raised and slipped her shirt over her head. Now wearing only panties and a bra, Giselle was sure the delicious torture was almost over. She was wrong.

His fingers hooked in her panties, dragging them from her legs, and then slowly, leisurely his caressing hands moved up to unclasp her bra. She was so lost in need, she hardly realized she was completely nude until his mouth covered her left breast and at the same time one of his long, hard fingers gently penetrated her. The twin sensations sent her soaring.

She wasn't sure how long it was before he finally slid into her. She had lost count of the number of times she had climaxed. Lost count of the times she begged him to come inside her. When he finally did, Giselle wrapped her legs around him and held on tight. But the torture she had thought was over had only begun.

Showing once again that his self-control had grown through the years, Raphael set up a series of hard, fast thrusts and then tempered them with the occasional long, slow glides. Just when she didn't think she could take it anymore, he would withdraw and then start again.

Giselle groaned with both frustration and need. "Why are you torturing me like this?"

"I don't want it to end. Do you know how I've dreamed of this night? How many nights I'd go to bed, aching and hurting, needing you?"

"I'm here now, Raphael. I'm not going anywhere." She pulled him down and whispered against his ear, "Let go."

His breath rattled through his lungs as he fought for control. "I don't have any protection."

"It's not a problem. It's taken care of."

She barely got the words out before Raphael plunged deep again, pounding and thrusting. This time they exploded together.

Other than their heavy breathing, the room was silent. If at all possible, she would be holding her breath because she really didn't know what she should say. Had this been just a momentary moment of madness for him? For her, she had no doubts. She had never stopped loving him. No matter how much time passed, that would never change.

From Raphael's perspective, things were understandably different. Not only had she left him, she had kept their son from him. He had so much to forgive, and she didn't know if he would ever get there. She didn't blame him for his anger, but that didn't negate her wishing he could get past it. They'd once had something remarkable between them. She had messed that up, but did that have to be the end?

Unable to bear the suspense any longer, she said, "Raphael, I—"

The buzz of Raphael's cellphone came at an opportune moment. They both scrambled in the dark, trying to find its location. Giggling at how silly they must look, Giselle groped for the light but couldn't find it. Raphael gave a grunt, and she turned to see he'd found the thing and was answering it.

She heard what sounded like someone yelling. Was that Noah's voice? She reached again for the bedside light and froze at Raphael's bark, "Don't turn on the light."

"What's wrong?"

"Our location has been compromised. Get your clothes on. I'll get our go bags. We've got to get out of here."

The urgency in his voice kept her from questioning him. Grabbing her clothes from the floor, she slid into them.

Just as she finished tying the laces on her track shoes, Raphael came to the door. Holding a bag in one hand and his gun in the other, he snapped, "Let's go."

Sweeping her hair up in a messy ponytail, she followed him out the door and through the house.

"We'll drive to—" He jerked to a stop.

"What's wrong?" she whispered.

Instead of answering, he grabbed hold of her hand and pushed open the back door. They were halfway across the porch when she heard a buzzing noise above them.

"What's that sound?"

Cursing, Raphael grabbed her by the waist and hauled her down the steps.

They were only a few yards away when the house behind them exploded.

CHAPTER
TWENTY-NINE

LCR Headquarters

"I'm so damn sorry, McCall. I believed they'd be safe there."

The fury burning in Declan Steele's eyes was the only thing holding Noah back from shouting with rage. Steele was just as pissed as Noah.

"What the hell happened?" Noah asked.

"One of my techs intercepted a text. Thought it looked fishy. Sent it up to me. I agreed, so we checked the guy out. Found texts going back several weeks, relating to a target not yet identified. This man doesn't have the clearance or the intelligence for that kind of intel or op. We dug more, found where he'd communicated with someone yesterday, revealing the location of the target."

"The safe house in New Orleans."

"Yes."

"Raphael's not answering his cell."

"He's likely on the move, evading. He'll get in touch when he's able."

The sick feeling in Noah's gut said something else. Something was wrong, he knew it.

Declan's cellphone rang, and as he answered, Noah tried once more to reach Raphael. When there was still no answer, he texted him, asking him to call. Stupid, really. He knew Raphael would call as soon as he could, but it made him feel better, so what the hell.

"Trouble," Steele said.

Noah whirled around. "What?"

"Somehow, someway, there was a drone strike on the house. It's demolished."

No, he refused to believe it had hit while they were still inside. "Raphael would have gotten out before then. I'm sure of it." As he texted a message to operatives closest to New Orleans, he said, "I'm sending a team there. We should know soon."

"They'll have someone there, making sure they hit their target."

"Yeah. Maybe we can pull some of them in, have a chat."

He stared out the window, barely able to form the next words. "He's still not answering his cell."

A hand landed on his shoulder. "You trained him, McCall. Sabrina says he's one of your best. He's fine…they're both fine."

Steele was right. Raphael was trained, had excellent instincts and great survival skills. He and Giselle had escaped in time. Any other option was not acceptable.

"Who the hell are these people, McCall?"

Noah rarely invited other organizations, especially governmental ones, into LCR operations. Declan Steele was the exception. Not only was he married to Sabrina Fox, one of his most-talented Elite team members, Declan was the team leader of a clandestine government agency. The man had intel even those in high government positions never knew.

By necessity, Noah had shared intel on the Fletchers, but he would share more. He was long past treating these bastards like ordinary evil. They had both power and influence, evidenced by what had happened at the safe house. Who had that much influence that they could commandeer a drone strike on American soil?

Noah gave Steele everything he knew on Daniel Fletcher. All the while, in the back of his mind, was the worry. Had Raphael and Giselle made it out? Were they still alive?

***

Louisiana

The sound of someone urgently saying his name woke Raphael. Blinking rapidly, he struggled to get his bearings. Pain throbbed in several areas of his body, but they were distant and bearable.

"Raphael? Can you hear me?"

"Giselle?" He blinked again. "Are you all right?"

"I'm fine. Just a few cuts and bruises."

He tried to rise, groaned as the pain went from a dull thud to a herd of a thousand cattle stampeding in his head.

"Take it easy. You're bleeding from a wound on your temple. You've been unconscious."

"How long?"

"It's hard to say. Maybe two or three minutes. I don't—"

Gritting his teeth, he sat up.

"What are you doing?"

When he tried to get to his feet, she pulled on his arm to stop him. "Raphael, no. You can't move. You may have internal injuries. We need—"

"We need to get the hell out of here. Whoever blew up the house will be here soon, checking to make sure the job was done. We have to be long gone before that happens."

He got to his feet, felt a little shaky, but he'd hold. Reaching his hand out, he pulled her up. She swayed and caught herself.

"You're hurt."

"No. Just kind of wobbly. I'm fine. I just…" She turned to look at the burning embers, all that was left of the house. "Someone blew up the house?"

The house continued to burn, but the steady rain was slowing its progress, which meant things would be easily identifiable, revealing no people had died there.

Turning back to her, he roamed his gaze over her. Her hair hung in wet tangles around her pale face. Something dark, besides the mud, gleamed dully on her face. He reached out, touched her, and she flinched.

"You're cut."

"It's nothing. Just a scrape. I'm fine."

Treating the cut, whether it was nothing or serious, would have to wait. They needed to be gone from this place. Taking her hand, he led her into the woods. Going down the road would have been preferable but more dangerous. If Fletcher's people were brazen enough to bomb a house, they would damn well check to make sure there were no survivors.

They'd been walking for several moments when he heard the distinct sound of trucks. "Get down," he whispered.

Seconds later, lights from powerful flashlights shone in the distance. Yeah, they were searching, and when they didn't find bodies, they'd come looking.

"Let's get the hell out of here." Still holding her hand, he took off at a run. For right now, speed was their priority. It would take a while, maybe half an hour or so, before the assholes discovered no one had been inside the house when the bomb hit. And then the search would be on. They needed to be as far away as possible when that happened.

He had his Glock and his cellphone. The go bag was filled with food, water, medical supplies, a change of clothing for each of them, and a thermal blanket. It could've been a helluva lot worse.

Without warning, the rain that had been quiet and steady earlier came down on them in torrents, hard and mean. Stopping wasn't an option, but the last thing either of them needed was to break a leg trying to get away.

"Hold on." He stopped and turned. Could see no lights behind them. Risking light was less of a concern than a broken limb. Pulling out his phone, he noted he had a full charge, but also saw what he expected. No signal. No way was he going to be able to contact Noah until they got closer to civilization. He could, however, use the flashlight.

Turning the light on, he first looked at Giselle, wanting to assure himself she was really all right. Her clothes and hair were soaked, and she was shivering. Putting on dry clothes would be pointless, but he could help out a little. Stooping down, he unzipped the duffel and pulled out a rain hat. For no good reason, he'd picked it up a year or so ago when he'd been in Colombia. It was too small for his head, obviously made for a smaller person. "Here." He settled the hat on her head. If he'd been in a better frame of mind, he might've laughed. She looked both ridiculous and adorable.

His fingers touched the bloody scrape on her cheek. "Does it hurt?"

"No. Not really."

"I'll clean and bandage it as soon as it's safe to stop." He looked around at their location. Mostly just dense woods now, but the deeper they went, the swampier it would get.

"Let's keep going." Taking her hand, he pulled her with him.

"Can't we call someone?"

"No signal yet."

"How can anyone get hold of a drone that would drop a bomb?"

"I think we can both agree that the Fletchers' tentacles reach pretty damn far. They're not getting away with it, though. We'll make sure of that."

"I'm so sorry, Raphael. I brought all this trouble to your door."

"Stop blaming yourself, Giselle. You don't deserve what they're putting you through, and you sure as hell don't deserve to have your son taken away from you."

"*Our* son."

Despite himself, a flood of warmth went through him. What they had shared tonight had gone a long way in healing their rift. There were still plenty of issues to get through, plenty of blame on both sides, but tonight felt like a new beginning.

And now they were running for their lives.

Fletcher's ruthlessness was matched only by his ability to know things he shouldn't. Daniel might be providing the money and pulling the strings, but there was someone else in charge of orchestrating all the events. If they could get to him, maybe they could tear away their foundation.

Question was, who the hell was it?

***

Rockwell, New Jersey

"House was empty," a deep voice drawled.

Cato ground his teeth till his jaws ached. "You're sure?"

"We'll double-check as soon as day breaks, but we did a thorough search already. Fire got put out early because of the rain, so it was easier than it would've been. They weren't here when the bomb hit."

"Keep looking." Cato ended the call before he pissed off the only people he had in New Orleans right now. They were independent contractors, and while he didn't mind pissing them off, they had no loyalty to him. They could walk away without a backward glance. Until he had his own people there, he'd play nice with the local talent.

Tucked between a Chinese restaurant and a used-clothing store, the offices of Cato Cavendar Investigations were innocuous and low-key. The outside was a multicolored dull brick façade with a yellowish tinge that made the place look years older than it actually was. The sign on the building, equally innocuous, proclaimed the investigative services of one Elton J. Marks. Cato had used that alias once and, liking the sound of it on the tongue, had chosen that name as his current cover. Elton was always busy and never had room for a new client. They'd turned away dozens since they'd opened the office, but that number had dwindled to only one or two a month. Word had apparently spread that Elton J. Marks was just too busy to take on new clients. No one knew that Elton had only one client, and it was all he and his staff could do to keep up with that client's needs.

Freddy Carlisle shook his head, the mournful look in his beady dark eyes almost comical. "It should've worked, but they must've found out about it."

Cato barely resisted rolling his eyes, but Freddy was a sensitive SOB and didn't like to be made fun of. Still, Cato couldn't resist giving him the blank stare that made most people piss their pants. "You think?"

Standing, he addressed his team. "Okay, here's the deal. Everything goes on the backburner until these assholes are put down. Whatever you're working on can wait."

His staff of seven included two tech whizzes, a political liaison who conveniently had a Harvard Law degree, a public relations expert, two highly skilled mercenaries who were expert sharpshooters, plus an office manager who not only maintained all their schedules but kept her ear to the gossip pipeline like a rabid teenager. Chloe Willis could dig up dirt faster than an undertaker.

Each of them was at the top of their field. He had recruited them himself, and while he appreciated them for their talents in their given jobs, his number one requirement was the thing that had landed each of them a job: Not one of them had an iota of conscience. His two motivations had proven to be his most effective method of retaining all his employees. He paid them well, and if they screwed him over, they were dead.

It helped that he didn't have an iota of conscience either.

He sent a hard look to his mercenaries. "Clive and Franco, get down to New Orleans and find Sanchez and the girl. Don't come back until you do."

"We have a team of five down there already."

"And they haven't done dick. You shouldn't have hired locals. Should've done them yourselves."

Clive looked like he wanted to argue, but Franco must've kicked him under the table, because his big body jerked and he said, "Sure, Cato. We'll take care of it."

He gave both of them a hard, telling look and was happy to see their eyes skitter away. They might be mercenaries, trained to kill on order, but when it came to killing, he wrote the book.

"CeeCee, where are we on finding the girl's family?"

"Good and bad news on that. Breaching WITSEC isn't as easy as it used to be. I'm still working it from my end and have put out some feelers with a few of my best snitches." CeeCee shrugged. "No nibbles yet."

"Was that the good or bad news?"

"Bad news. Good news is we've located her older brother, Lance. He's in prison in Germany. He was a runner for one of the mob bosses there, but got put away for almost killing a guy in a bar fight. We can get to him fairly quickly if need be."

"We'll hold out on that. From what we know, there's no love lost between sister and brother. She probably wouldn't cross the street to save him.

"Keep working on the rest of the family. There's got to be school records, doctors' reports. The boy's only eleven or so. Kids get sick, broken bones, shit like that."

"Do you know how many eleven-year-old boys there are in this country? And we don't know if they are even in this country. Lots of other countries will take them if the money's right."

"I don't want excuses. I want results. *Capisce*?"

CeeCee jerked at his harsh tone. He was usually easier on her than the others, because they sometimes did the nasty when work slowed, or he needed a stress reliever. Work wasn't slow now, though, and she needed to pull her weight.

Since he knew he'd made his point, he softened his tone a bit. "Look, people. Boss is going to give each of us big bonuses when this is wrapped up. This is the most important thing for them right now, so it's gotta be our most important thing, too."

For extra incentive, he added, "Get what we need, or you're off the team."

Off the team for most people would mean losing their job. For his team, it meant something a bit more permanent, and they knew it.

Pep talk behind him, he swept the room with his gaze. "Now, anybody got anything useful?"

CHAPTER THIRTY

Louisiana

They weren't going to make it to civilization today. The forest was giving them the cover they needed, but Raphael wanted to wait another day before heading into a town. Giselle trusted his judgment on this…she trusted him in everything.

As she trudged through the damp forest, she kept her eyes on his back. It could have been worse, he'd told her. In the summertime, mosquitoes as large as birds, snakes longer than his arm, and giant alligators roamed the swamp and forest. At least in the wintertime, they were less prevalent. She didn't know if that was supposed to make her feel better or not. Less prevalent indicated they still existed somewhere. She imagined little beady eyes staring out from behind giant leaves, their stares malevolent and ravenous, as they bided their time, waiting for a chance to pounce.

She stepped over a rotten tree branch, looking around warily. "Were you kidding with me…about the gators and snakes?" She could deal with mosquitoes. She didn't like them, but they could be swatted and batted away. Harder, much harder, to do that to a snake or alligator.

"No." He glanced back at her, and her worried frown must've made him feel guilty. "Okay, maybe a little. I've never seen either one, but I've seen a lot of movies that show some mean-assed creatures hiding in the swamplands."

"So you told me that to what?"

"It gave you something else to think about."

"Oh jeez, thanks. Not only am I looking for bad guys with guns and bombs, I'm on the lookout for gargantuan-sized mosquitoes, alli—"

She didn't shriek or even panic. She just stopped breathing. "Raphael." Odd, but she thought she sounded freakishly calm.

"Yeah...what?"

He turned, and though she wasn't looking at him, she sensed his stillness. "Don't move. Okay?"

She didn't bother to nod and decided she could no longer speak either. The snake at her foot probably wasn't as long as Raphael's arm, but it looked like it could easily take a nasty bite out of her.

She thought he would shoot it, or at the very least try to distract it. Instead, he walked away from her. She finally made a sound, and it was a cross between a squeal of terror and a gasp of indignation. He was leaving her?

He walked maybe three yards away, picked something up, and headed back. Since she hadn't been able to take her eyes off the snake, which thankfully still hadn't bitten her, she didn't know what he had picked up. Whatever it was, she hoped it would take care of the problem.

A thick stick swooped into her line of vision and scooped up the snake. With a smooth jerk, Raphael flung the snake into the woods.

She'd barely taken a breath before Raphael was there, gripping her arms. "Are you okay?"

"Yes." She laughed a little, the relief making her giddy. "Guess since you were right about those snakes, I'd better keep my eye out for those alligators after all."

Raphael shook his head. She was laughing, and he was still shaking. The snake had been a water moccasin. Even though it had likely been sluggish from hibernating all winter, it still could have bitten her. That would have been painful and might even have killed her. They were too far out from any kind of town for him to get her medical care quickly.

"I'm all right, Raphael. Really."

He took a breath. "Okay. Yeah." He looked up at the sky. They weren't going to make it out before nightfall. "We've got a little over an hour before sunset. We'll walk for another half hour or so, and then we'll hunker down for the night."

"We're going to sleep in the woods tonight?" The voice that had held amusement only seconds ago now held uncertainty.

He sent her a grin. "I promise it'll be less scary than getting caught by bad guys with guns." He held up the bag. "I've got everything we need to camp. We'll be fine."

She took a deep breath, let it out slowly. "Okay. All right."

He wanted to hug her for her bravery. She had never been exposed to anything wilder than what she had encountered on the island where she'd been raised. She was not only facing the wilderness surrounding them with determination and grit, she had been amazingly strong through this whole ordeal. Not many people could handle almost being blown up by a bomb or chased into the woods by guys with guns.

"You're doing good, you know."

"I'll take your word for it."

"Just stick close and watch where you step."

She gave him a slight smile. "Understood."

Considering what she'd been through, she looked amazingly upbeat and healthy. When dawn arrived and he'd deemed it safe enough, they'd stopped and tended their wounds. He'd been relieved that what she had described as a scratch on her face was indeed just that. Still, he'd cleaned and put a small bandage on it. There was no telling what kind of bacteria was swimming around in the mud and the muck they were stomping through.

His own injury was nothing more than a small knot on the side of his head and hadn't required anything other than a couple of ibuprofen for a slight headache. All in all they were surprisingly unscathed. He'd like to think their luck would continue but he would take no chances. There was no telling how many were looking for them.

He gave her an encouraging nod. "You're doing great. Let's get moving and find a decent spot to camp."

As they trudged through the woods, he was aware of eyes following them. Most of them were harmless creatures worried for their own safety and keeping a wary eye on the interlopers invading their home. A couple were likely predators. No problem there, as long as they respected each other's territory.

His eyes alert for any danger, he said conversationally, "So what was your major in college?"

"Umm. Journalism."

"So you decided to stick with that?"

"Yes. Although I never did anything with it."

He glanced back at her, curious at her choices. "Once this is over, you'd have a helluva story to write."

"You really think we're going to be able to expose the Fletchers? You don't think they're too powerful?"

"Power doesn't last forever. It's time the Fletchers lost theirs. When the truth comes out about the assassination of that family you overheard Daniel and Rawlings talking about, there's no way they're going to get out of it. And if they've killed once, they likely are responsible for more."

"You're right. Though, for now, I just want us to get Giovanni back."

"We will." He reached out, gave her shoulder a reassuring squeeze. "I promise you, Giselle, we'll get him."

Almost an hour later, Raphael found a relatively dry area to stop for the night. He cleared as much debris as possible, giving Giselle the assignment of digging into their supplies and finding something to eat that sounded remotely appetizing. Since all they'd had for the past almost twenty hours was water and nutrition bars, anything would work for him. His stomach felt as though someone had dug a crater.

As he cleared the area, he glanced over at her from time to time. She'd been unusually quiet since the snake incident. Which, he had to admit, had scared the shit out of him. The very thought of it curled his gut.

She held up a package. "How do you feel about ravioli?"

"Sounds good to me."

"Me, too, but I'm so hungry I think I could eat anything."

"You should have said something. You could've eaten another bar."

She wrinkled her nose. "I take that back, I could eat anything other than one of those energy bars. They're terrible."

"Can't argue with that."

They settled down to eat their dinner. It wasn't the best meal he'd ever had, but having gone without meals many times in his life, he wasn't complaining. It filled a hole and gave both of them much-needed energy.

After their meal and a quick cleanup, they settled onto the large sleeping bag Raphael had spread out for them. Giselle sat with her knees bent and her arms hugging her legs.

"You cold?"

"No, not really." She looked up at the sky. "I'm glad it's not raining."

"Yeah, we lucked out there."

"You don't think we're being followed, do you?"

"No. Our biggest risk will be when we step out of the woods."

"How will we avoid them then?"

"McCall will come through."

He had been texting Noah on and off all day. He'd known the instant his phone had acquired a signal by the number of alerts for voice mails and texts that buzzed. The instant he had texted him back to let him know they were alive, a flurry of texts had come through.

"We'll have a vehicle waiting for us. They can't cover every inch of the road." He wrapped an arm around her shoulders and pulled her close for a comforting hug. "We'll be fine. I promise."

Surprising him, she scooted closer and put her head on his shoulder. "Tell me about your first rescue."

"There's not much to it. Wasn't very dramatic, and I played a small role."

"Stop being modest and tell me about it."

"It was a domestic abduction. The dad had custody of the kids. Mom took them, wouldn't give them back. He contacted LCR and asked for our help."

"Why didn't he call the police? Was this not considered an abduction?"

"Yes, but he didn't want the police involved. That might have required jail time for the wife, plus publicity. She was a prominent figure in the city where they lived. He didn't want to ruin her. The dad was a friend of McCall's, so he asked Noah for his help."

"Sounds like he still loved his wife."

"Yeah. I think they ended up going to counseling after it was over. Not sure it stuck, but at least it worked out that time."

"What happened?"

"We did a simple grab. Mom had the kids in the kitchen, feeding them lunch. One was about three, the other five. Angela and Sabrina knocked on the front door, engaged the mom in a conversation about something. While she was busy, Olivia and I went into the kitchen, grabbed the kids, and were gone. Took less than five minutes."

"Were the children frightened?"

"A little, but we had the dad in a car out back. The instant they saw him, they were fine."

"That's a nice story. I hope they found their way back to each other." She sent him a quizzical smile. "I guess I thought there would be lots more action. Guns, explosions. Things like that."

"There have been plenty of those since then. That one was the first time I was involved in a rescue, though. The first time I felt like a real LCR team member."

"I remember how you used to talk about being an LCR operative. I'm so glad you achieved that dream." She snuggled deeper into his embrace. "Now tell me about your favorite rescue."

"My favorite one will be when we rescue Giovanni."

"You sound so sure that it will happen. That it will work out."

"I am sure. We've got the best people in the world working to make that happen. They'll do whatever it takes to rescue him."

"What happens after that, Raphael? Will the Fletchers ever give up?"

"Yes. Once you have him back with you, they'll stop. They have no claim on him, other than that measly piece of paper they forced you to sign. They have no blood relationship...nothing. That's why they're doing everything they can now. They know you have all the rights and they have none."

"I want to do something... I know I can't walk in there and take him. But I need to do something."

"I have an idea."

"What?"

"Promise to hear me out before you say no."

She lifted her head to look up at him. "Okay."

"We could get married."

She tried to jerk away from his arms, but he wouldn't let her go. "You promised to hear me out."

"Okay." Her body was still tense, but at least she wasn't trying to pull away from him.

"When and if we get this before a judge, if it has to go that far, being married would show a more stable environment for Gio."

"But you don't love me."

"People get married for other reasons besides love."

He couldn't see it—she wouldn't let him see it—but something inside her shriveled at his emotionless tone. What had she expected? She already knew he wouldn't forgive her for what she'd kept from him, had she really thought marriage would be anything other than a convenience?

She squared her shoulders. Didn't matter. She would do whatever it took, including marrying a man who didn't love her to get her son back. Raphael was the most honorable man she'd ever known.

On top of that, showing that Gio had two adoring parents who would love and take care of him, even if one of them had alleged sketchy mental issues, would present a much stronger case if those parents were married.

"All right."

She felt the tenseness go out of him. They'd get Gio back, and then at some point, the marriage would be dissolved, but Gio would still have two parents who loved him. Lots of families didn't live together.

"You have a valid driver's license?"

"Yes, but not with me."

"We can work around that."

"But aren't we supposed to stay off the grid? Wouldn't getting married call attention to us?"

"Not right away. But when it does, we'll be ready. I'll make the arrangements tomorrow."

"Tomorrow?"

"Yeah. The sooner the better. When we get back to Virginia, we'll go see an attorney McCall knows. One he trusts. We'll go from there."

"Okay."

She told herself it could work. Maybe he wasn't ready to admit it yet, but what they had shared last night, the intimacy they'd experienced, wasn't some anomaly. They still had a connection—one that neither time nor betrayal could destroy.

And tomorrow they were to be married.

CHAPTER
THIRTY-ONE

East Hampton, New York

The home office of Clarissa Fletcher matched the woman perfectly. It was coolly sophisticated without an ounce of warmth to soften the pretentious atmosphere. Olivia sat across from the immaculately dressed older woman. The first time she'd met Clarissa, she had seemed softer, less sure of herself. Apparently, now that she was back in her home environment, all the arrogance had returned. The forceful personality was as off-putting as it was impressive. If Daniel Fletcher was her equal in intimidation and snobbery, it was no wonder Giselle had felt overwhelmed.

"Our initial interview was a mere introduction to one another."

Was that a warning? Had Olivia given off vibes that Clarissa had picked up on, or was this just the woman's way of getting down to business?

"I'm told you are the best," Clarissa continued.

"That is true." Arrogance respected arrogance. Her intent was to impress Clarissa, as well as feed her ego. The woman needed to feel as though she had made the perfect decision. When she left here today, Olivia planned for Clarissa Fletcher to give herself a huge pat on the back for being so bloody brilliant.

"The boy needs a strict, structured environment. He may only be six years old, but he has a bright future ahead of him. He needs to be prepared early on for the heavy responsibilities that will be placed on his shoulders."

"You are the young gentleman's grandparents, is that correct?"

Olivia considered herself not only a good judge of character, but also an expert at reading deception, yet she detected absolutely no lie in Clarissa Fletcher's demeanor when she answered, "Yes. We are his grandparents and have full custody."

"Excellent. I, of course, would need to meet him, talk with him. Though I have a standard regimen I use with my charges, I will redesign and refine it based upon my assessment of his needs and abilities."

"He's an exceptional child. Gifted, I believe."

"I'm sure you understand that grandparents have a tendency to be somewhat biased when it comes to their grandchild. If he is gifted, I will design his curriculum with that in mind. I will, however, need to evaluate the child myself."

When Clarissa looked as though she would argue, Olivia, though showing no outward sign of her unease, went tense with concern. What was the woman's hesitation about? Was Giovanni all right?

Taking a risk, Olivia stood. "Perhaps you would prefer another governess? One who is not so rigid regarding excellence and hard work."

"Sit down, Ms. Wainwright."

Not surprised by the arrogance of the command, Olivia sat back down. She would not overplay her hand. She waited in silence as Clarissa grappled with whatever was holding her back from committing to hiring her.

Finally, Clarissa said, "You have an example of your assessment material?"

"Of course." She handed over a folder that Jamie, Dylan Savage's wife, had put together for her. Jamie had told her the curriculum far exceeded what should be expected for a six-year-old, but it should pass muster and impress Clarissa Fletcher with its thoroughness and inflexibility. That was a good thing, since rigidity seemed to be of paramount importance to the woman.

Olivia again waited in silence while Clarissa perused the material.

After several moments of examination, Clarissa closed the folder. "All right. I'm hiring you on a contingent basis. I'm still in the process of having you thoroughly vetted, but I want the best for the boy, and it is my understanding that you are the best. If I find out different, you'll be dismissed and will have great difficulty finding another position. Do I make myself clear?"

Forget warm or cozy, Clarissa Fletcher could make ice feel comfy. "My references are impeccable, as is my record. However, if something displeases you, then I would expect no less."

"The Fletcher name must be protected at all cost. You will be expected to sign a nondisclosure agreement. You will not talk to the press or anyone regarding what goes on in this household. Will that be a problem?"

Olivia took a moment to thoroughly assess Clarissa Fletcher. She had come into this op with an open mind, but she had to admit she had seen Daniel Fletcher as the villain and perhaps viewed Clarissa as less dangerous—maybe even an unwilling participant in all this. She adjusted her evaluation. This woman was no innocent party or second-in-command. Clarissa Fletcher was fully in tune with her husband. They were together, in a partnership.

Olivia would never underestimate the woman again.

"I understand. That won't be a problem."

"Good." She stood. "Come with me, and I'll introduce you to the boy."

"Why is it you refer to him as 'the boy'?" Yeah, she was probably on thin ice here, but dammit, the child had a name. Why didn't they use it?

For the first time since meeting her, Olivia saw actual emotion in Clarissa Fletcher. Not embarrassment and not even anger at the impertinent question. It was confusion, surprise.

Instead of giving her a reason, she said quietly, "His name is John."

Feeling like she'd won a small victory, she followed Clarissa through the house and then up a long, winding stairway. She could only imagine what Giovanni must be feeling. The only father he'd ever known was dead. His mother had mysteriously disappeared. And he had been left with these people—cold, imperialistic, egomaniacal creeps who lived in a museumlike mansion without a hint of warmth or kindness in sight. So yes, just getting the bitch to say the child's name, even the wrong one, felt good.

On the third floor and down a long hallway, they entered a suite that was obviously designed and decorated for a child. A wealthy, overindulged child's dream. Shelves filled with toys and books lined three of the walls. A large-screen television hung on another wall. There was a drafting table, train sets, replicas of ships, model cars. It was like they had purchased a toy store and installed it in the room. The word *overcompensation* came to mind.

"He seems to have a lot of toys."

"He's a bright, imaginative boy and needs a lot of mental stimulation."

Or he was missing his mother, and they were doing everything they could to take his mind off of the loss.

"His psychologist recommended many of these things."

"Psychologist?"

"Of course. He lost his father and then his mother. No matter how unprepared she was to be his mother, he still misses her."

Detecting some defensiveness in Clarissa's tone, Olivia throttled back. "You have provided a stable, loving environment for the child."

"Yes, exactly." Clarissa's eyes roamed the room. "He'll not want for anything."

Olivia imagined that if they had an ounce of conscience, this was what they told themselves if they felt the least guilty for what they'd done to Giselle.

"I look forward to meeting him."

"I believe he's in the game room." She started toward a closed door, and as Olivia followed her, she asked, "Does John have a daily schedule yet?"

"A loose one for now. We wanted to give him time to adjust. That will be your responsibility. From the time he wakes until he goes to bed, his day should be structured. He turned six a few months ago, so we're starting later than I would like. There should be no idle time where he might get into trouble."

Those words clicked inside Olivia's mind. Giselle had indicated that Clarissa looked upon Giovanni as her second chance. By controlling every aspect of his waking hours, did she think that would keep him from being a willful, wild child, as her son had apparently been?

Despite herself, Olivia felt a moment of pity for the woman. She really had no clue, did she? Some people were not designed to have children. In her estimation, Clarissa Fletcher belonged in that category.

They entered a large room, and once again it appeared that the Fletchers had spared no expense. There was so much, it was all she could do not to turn to the woman and ask her just what the hell was wrong with her. She could only imagine what a little boy who'd lost his mother thought of all of this. It had to be overwhelming and scary as hell.

She heard a sound, soft and low, like a little sigh. She turned and was faced with a tiny replica of Raphael. He was sitting at a child's table, crayons neatly organized by shade in front of him.

Going to her knees so she would be on his level, she said, "Hello. You must be John."

Eyes, dark and sweetly innocent, glanced up at Clarissa, and then with a mutinous look on his little face, he looked at Olivia and said, "My name is Giovanni. You can call me Gio."

Clarissa sighed loudly. "That is not your name now. Remember what I told you?"

Ignoring Clarissa for the moment, she said, "Hello, Gio. It's nice to meet you."

"Who are you?"

"My name is Susanna."

"Why are you here?"

"I'm talking to your grandmother about being your teacher."

"I don't want you to be my teacher."

"John, that's an inappropriate thing to stay to an adult. You—"

She smiled up at Clarissa. "I admire honesty above all else. Children are so completely without artifice, don't you think?" Before the woman could respond, she turned back to the courageous little boy. "But honesty must be tempered with good manners."

"You talk funny."

"I have a British accent."

"It's nice. Mommy has an accent like that, too."

"That's enough, John. Go find Ms. Mavis and ask her to take you for a walk."

Looking like he wanted to say something else, he pursed his little mouth for a second. Then, apparently changing his mind, he nodded at Olivia. "Nice to meet you."

The instant Gio ran out of the room, Clarissa said, "As you can see, he has a stubborn streak you'll need to tame."

"Tell me about his mother."

For just an instant, Olivia saw the disdain she figured Giselle had lived with on a daily basis. Clarissa was good, though, and covered it almost immediately with fake sorrow.

"She was just so lost after our son died. We did everything we could for her, but she fell into a deep depression, and no matter what we did, she could never recover. She took her life a few months ago. We haven't found the right time to tell John."

"Where does he think his mother is, then?"

"He believes she's on a long vacation. The doctors advised us to wait a little while longer. When he's used to her being gone, we'll tell him she's gone on to heaven. It'll be easier for him to accept."

Likely, that's what they believed would actually happen. Giselle would be dead, and they could get on with whatever plans they had for the child. This little boy was their pawn. If he didn't please them, would they at some point do away with him, too?

Every protective instinct in Olivia told her to grab Giovanni and get him the hell out of there. But she knew she wouldn't get more than five feet away before she was stopped. There were eyes everywhere. Discreet but easily spotted if one knew what to look for and where to look. She imagined they had been here long before Giselle had come here as a new bride. There were likely no secrets inside this house.

She had done what she'd set out to do today. Her assignment had been to assess Gio and his condition, plus determine if he was in immediate danger. The spirit she'd seen in the little boy told her he was far from being beaten down, but at some point, that bright spirit would diminish. However, he was in no physical danger that she could see.

"Losing his mother will have an impact on his life, but we're doing everything we can to minimize his pain."

Hence the overabundance of toys and entertainment options. "Does he have friends? Perhaps he—"

"For the time being, we are limiting his exposure to other children. At the right time, we'll introduce him to appropriate children of his age group."

Appropriate children. How could there even be such a term? Children were children. Period.

Her training was the only thing that allowed her to nod and say, "I understand." And she did understand, much better than Clarissa Fletcher would ever know.

"Testing could begin immediately, even today, if you like." Olivia held up the folder. "I have what I need to make my initial assessment."

"No, not yet. In one month. No sooner."

She read between the lines. They didn't want her here until Giselle and Raphael were dead and Gio was completely theirs to control and manipulate.

Walking a thin line, Olivia pushed it a little. "My schedule will accommodate now. I'm not sure I'll be available at—"

"We'll pay whatever you require to retain you. Consider yourself hired but with a month's vacation. You said you wanted a holiday before you took another position. Now you have a fully paid one."

Before Olivia could come up with a reasonable reason why she would turn down a paid vacation, Clarissa continued, "Once you're here, you won't have a lot of time to yourself." Clarissa's smile was both condescending and kind, a hard thing to carry off, but this woman did it with style.

"How kind of you."

"In the meantime, I'll send along the child psychologist's reports. As I've already said, John is a gifted child. The more you know about him, the better you'll be able to help him achieve his maximum potential."

Clarissa led the way out of the room, talking as she headed down the hallway. Olivia kept an attentive look on her face, but used the time to once again get a feel for where cameras were set. She spotted three in the ceiling corners of the hallway and one larger one in the chandelier that hung just over the stairway. As she had installed more than her share of secret cameras, these were easy to identify.

There would be others, though. Giselle had told them that cameras were everywhere. That was how Fletcher had learned that Giselle had overheard him and Rawlings discussing murder.

Who was watching them now, and what exactly were they looking for?

Owen Holcomb watched Mrs. Fletcher and the kid's new teacher head down the stairs and toward the door. With those thick round glasses and pale skin, the woman wasn't much of a looker. Not that it was any of his business, but when you sat on your ass and stared at a hundred or so monitors for eight hours a day, you had to stay entertained some way.

He'd been working here for a little over a year now. As long as he stayed out of their way, everything was fine. If he happened to pass them on the way into work, they pretended he wasn't there. Guess it took all kinds. They paid well, and all he was required to do was look at the screens and report any unusual activity.

Didn't take a lot of skills or imagination. He'd kinda taken the job for granted until that one day. Ratting out Giselle, the daughter-in-law, had felt kind of strange. She'd done nothing really wrong. She and her kid were playing hide-and-go-seek. Fun game until it took you places you weren't supposed to be. Since he didn't listen to audio, he had no idea what the girl heard. Whatever it was, her eyes had gone wide and her face had lost all color. When he'd reported the incident to Fletcher, it'd been all he could do not to back away from the man. There was something dangerous in the depths of that man's eyes, and he for one didn't want to have intimate knowledge of what that was.

Later on that day, he'd seen Fletcher and the girl talking. She'd looked even more terrified than before. Whatever Fletcher had told her must've really struck a chord. She'd practically run away from him that day.

Almost made him sorry that he'd had to rat her out for a second time. She had tried to take the kid out. That'd been a near miss that had almost cost him his job. Felt sorry for the girl. Sure, he did. He wasn't a bad person, but a guy had to eat, didn't he? He had a job, just like other folks. When he was told to do something, he did it.

Girl cried like a baby, though. Hated seeing that. He wasn't sure where she was now. Probably dead, like they were telling everyone but the kid. Sad, really. She'd been a pretty thing, but crossing the Fletchers just wasn't a good idea. That's why he never would.

CHAPTER THIRTY-TWO

Louisiana

They emerged from the woods just after dawn. Giselle felt as worn out as an old mop. Her head throbbed, her body ached, and she desperately wanted a hot shower.

And while she felt and likely looked terrible, Raphael had the appearance of a rough, sexy pirate. A dark beard stubbled his face, his thick tangled hair looked like fingers had sexily run through it, and his clothes—black T-shirt and black jeans—just made him look tougher. The young, skinny boy of his youth was now a gorgeously hot and sexy man. And soon he would be her husband.

What had she agreed to? And what choice did she have? Raphael was right. They had to fight with everything they had. If they weren't able to get anyone to believe them about the murder, then they would have to go against the Fletchers in court to regain custody of her son. Having Gio's real parents demanding their son back would be so much more convincing.

The other part of it—the part where she knew he didn't love her—she would deal with later. It wouldn't be the first time she was in a loveless marriage. Only this time, it wouldn't be totally loveless. She had never stopped loving Raphael.

Sweeping a strand of hair from her face, she looked around. "So, where do we go from here?"

"We should be—" He grabbed her shoulder, pushing her back a little, and then she heard what he must have heard. A car engine. Had they been found?

"Hold on," Raphael said.

Standing behind him, she did as he asked, trusting him as she hadn't trusted anyone in a very long time.

Car lights raced toward them, and a vehicle stopped. Her heart thudding in her chest, she stopped breathing.

"Heard you might need a ride."

The gruff voice held mild amusement and sounded vaguely familiar. Giselle stuck her head out from behind Raphael. Brennan Sinclair, one of Raphael's LCR Elite partners, sat behind the wheel.

"Good timing."

Raphael opened the back door of the SUV, gently pushed Giselle forward, and followed her. The instant he was inside, the vehicle took off.

A huge, relieved sigh escaped her. They were safe.

"You guys okay?"

Startled, she leaned forward in her seat. "Noah?"

Turning, he smiled at her. "Been a rough few hours, but you're safe now."

"Anything happen?" Raphael asked.

"We can talk about that later, after we get things settled."

"I didn't expect to see you."

"You didn't think I'd miss your wedding, did you?"

"How did…" She turned to Raphael. "How did he know about that?"

"I texted him last night, after you agreed. Guess he flew down here in the LCR plane."

Feeling overwhelmed, Giselle settled back into the seat. This was moving faster than she had anticipated. She had agreed to the marriage, but having Noah and Brennan here made it seem more real—more authentic.

She wouldn't go back on her word, though. Showing a united front like this should only work in their favor.

Fifteen minutes later, they pulled in front of a large hotel. "We already have rooms here. I figure both of you will want to clean up before we head to the chapel."

She sent a questioning look to Raphael, who appeared to be just as surprised as she was. It was happening today? He shrugged, grinned.

They got out of the vehicle, and with all three men surrounding her, they walked into the giant foyer of the hotel. Noah handed Raphael a keycard. "Top floor. Honeymoon Suite. We're set for two o'clock. I'll come by at one thirty." Giving her a wink and nod, he and Brennan disappeared down a corridor.

Taking her hand, Raphael led her to a bank of elevators. "Guess we'd better get ready."

He knew he was pushing her. The confusion and worry in her eyes had only deepened since they'd gotten in the car. He had to admit he was surprised at all the things that McCall had already done, but he shouldn't be. When he'd texted Noah last night that he and Giselle wanted to get married today, he should have expected this. Coordinating a small wedding within hours should be no problem for LCR. They coordinated major rescue operations in much less time.

Giselle wouldn't back out of this. She knew the importance of showing a united front.

The minute they walked into the suite, she turned to him. "Raphael, they know this isn't a real marriage, right?"

The question infuriated him, hitting him in a spot he hadn't known could still be hurt. "Yes, it is a real marriage, Giselle. That's the whole point."

"Yes, I know it's real in that sense, but Noah is acting as if—" She stumbled over her words, most likely seeing the anger in his eyes.

"How about we take one step at a time? We get married, we get Giovanni back. Then we'll figure out the rest of our lives. Okay?"

"It's not that I'm not grateful. I am. I just wanted to make sure that—"

"Yeah. I get it. You're marrying me for convenience. No need to say any more." He jerked his head toward the bedroom. "Why don't you shower first?"

He turned away from her, well aware that she stood there for several seconds. His coldness had likely hurt her, but right now it was the best he could offer. The only reason she had agreed to marry him was because of their son. He got that. Didn't mean he had to like it, but he got it.

Finally hearing her move and the shower start, Raphael grabbed his cellphone and pressed a key for Noah.

"You guys getting settled in?"

"More or less. Any news?"

"Some. We can go over it now or wait until later."

"If there's no good news, let's wait. I think she's about reached her saturation limit."

"I think you both have."

"You got that right. We need something good to happen."

"You're about to get married to the girl you've loved for almost ten years. That's something good."

There was no point in arguing with Noah. The man knew everything about him, including the gut-wrenching pain he'd felt when Giselle had left him.

"Thanks for putting everything together so fast."

"It was a team effort." There was amusement in his voice.

He could only imagine. The instant Noah gave the word, he figured LCR people had started coordinating.

"You're standing up with me, right?"

"It would be my honor."

Emotion clogged Raphael's throat, so he cleared it and then said gruffly, "Thanks."

Clearly understanding the emotion, Noah said, "Get cleaned up and dressed. You've got wedding clothes in the bedroom closet and there are some sandwiches and snacks in the fridge. The limo will pick you up at one thirty sharp."

After ending the call, Raphael went to the bedroom closet. Sure enough, he found a white dress for Giselle and a black suit for him hanging inside. He also spotted a suitcase that he imagined held other things that might be important for a woman when she's getting dressed for her wedding. He didn't know what those things were, but he trusted the women of LCR to provide everything a bride would need.

Taking the dress and suitcase, he placed them on the bed so she would see them when she came out of the bathroom. He hoped she liked what she saw. Her first wedding had been a cold, emotionless affair, one she barely remembered. He wanted the second one to wipe even the vaguest of those memories from her mind.

Cautiously optimistic, he headed to a second, smaller bathroom to shower. Noah was right. He was finally marrying the girl he'd been obsessed with for years. The circumstances weren't exactly fairy-tale perfect, but that was okay. Fairy tales rarely started out good. The way they ended was all that mattered.

***

Giselle stood at the entrance to the chapel, feeling as though she were in a surreal, alternate universe. Last night she had been running from evil men, while battling mosquitoes and looking out for snakes. Today she was about to marry the man of her dreams. Life could not get any weirder.

This had once been a recurring dream of hers. She used to fantasize that Raphael would somehow find her, sweep her off her feet, and whisk her away somewhere exotic where they would spend the rest of their days in bliss. He would also, of course, forgive her for not telling him about Giovanni and totally understand why she had left him all those years ago.

She had eventually stopped having that dream, as it was just too unrealistic even for a fantasy. But today she could almost imagine it had come true.

The ivory lace wedding dress she wore had been lying on the bed when she'd finished showering. She had lost her breath at its loveliness. It was a Montague, one of the most famous and popular designers in the world. She remembered Raphael mentioning that Brennan Sinclair's wife, Kacie Dane, was a model who worked with Montague. For her to arrange such an amazing gown was a delightful surprise. The princess design, beautiful in its simplicity, was exactly what she would have chosen for herself.

Everything had been provided for her. From makeup to lingerie, she'd had everything a bride needed. Now if only she had the love of her groom.

She forced that thought away. No, she couldn't expect more from Raphael than he was already giving. This marriage was part of the plan to regain custody of her son. Pretending it was for anything else would only bring heartache later on.

As she began her walk down the aisle, she smiled nervously at the man beside her. Having Dylan Savage escort her seemed entirely appropriate. In large part, she owed her life to him, as he'd been instrumental in bringing Stanford Reddington to justice.

She was shocked to see so many people in the audience. For a rushed marriage of convenience, it was surprisingly well attended. As she recognized a few of them, she knew they were likely all LCR operatives or employees. But she knew, to Raphael, they were his family.

Her gaze went to the man waiting for her at the altar. Determination was stamped on his handsome face, and something glittered in his dark eyes she'd never seen before. Whatever it was sent anticipation zipping up her spine. Raphael wore an elegant, dark suit that emphasized his broad shoulders and muscular physique. He looked both powerful and confident. It suddenly hit her, and she stumbled a little. This was really going to happen. She was going to marry Raphael Sanchez!

Dylan must have felt her sudden panic, as he squeezed her arm gently while he moved with her to the altar. The instant they stopped, he whispered in her ear, "Be happy, Giselle. You both deserve it."

She gave Dylan a nervous smile and then stepped forward, taking the hand that Raphael held out for her. She looked down at their joined hands, his large one engulfing hers but holding it so very gently, and felt an amazing sense of rightness. Whatever they had to face to get their son back, they would face together.

CHAPTER
THIRTY-THREE

In a day that had already been filled with surprises, the wedding reception was one more. Raphael couldn't believe all the people who'd made the trip for the wedding and then stayed for the reception. They were all LCR, of course, and he knew they had jobs going on and responsibilities. For them to take the time to come for his wedding was more than he could have ever expected. When he'd said as much to Noah, the LCR leader had just shrugged and said, "We're family."

And for McCall, that's all that needed to be said. Not for the first time, he wondered at the turn of events that had led him to LCR. He'd never wish his experience on anyone, but if that was the only way to get him to these people, then he couldn't regret the experience.

And in their own way, LCR had led him to Giselle. When she'd walked down the aisle toward him tonight, he had literally lost his breath. He didn't think he'd started breathing again until she'd reached him and taken his hand. At her touch, he had felt as if every step in his life had led him to that one moment. From then on, all uncertainty and anger had washed away. This was right. And when they got their son back, it would be even better. The fact that she wasn't looking at this as a real marriage—that she didn't love him? Well, he'd deal with that later. For now, he would concentrate on what was going right.

Hearing a light, musical laugh, he turned to see Giselle talking with Seth Cavanaugh and Honor Stone. Their year-long deep-cover mission had ended last month with the successful rescue of a child who'd been abducted by a cult. One of Honor and Seth's specialties was infiltrating cults and organizations that preyed on children and shutting them down.

Heading over to join his bride, he stopped along the way for hugs and back slaps. LCR employees didn't gather in one place very often. Not only were they usually spread out all over the world, but it also wasn't a good idea. LCR had way too many enemies to make themselves easy targets.

"You look happy."

Accepting a hug from Jamie Savage, he said, "Thank you. I am."

"Dylan showed me photographs of Giovanni. He's adorable."

"I hope we'll have more than photos of him soon."

She rubbed his arm in comfort. "You will."

A soft hand grabbed his arm. "Hey, no sad faces today."

He turned to see a very pregnant Anna Thorne. The glow of happiness on Aidan's wife's face would have made a grizzly smile. Pulling her in for a hug, Raphael forced himself to push the sadness aside. He'd just married the girl of his dreams in the presence of his family and friends. For now…for this moment, life was good.

The fact that he had a wedding night to look forward to was also dancing around in his head. Giselle wasn't looking at this as a real marriage, but Raphael was going to do everything he could to convince her she was wrong.

* * *

Hours later, when they were back in their suite, Giselle nibbled on a grape and watched Raphael out of the corner of her eye. He had offered her a sandwich before the wedding but she had been too nervous to eat. The food at the reception had looked delicious but she'd barely eaten a bite. And now, though she was famished, she still wasn't sure she could eat. What would happen next? She and Raphael had rushed into this marriage for only one reason. Yet, here they were, alone and married, in the Honeymoon Suite.

The intimacy they'd shared the other night seemed like years ago. So much had happened since then. They had made love as lovers that night. If they did anything tonight, it would be as husband and wife. An even deeper commitment. How would he feel about that? How would she?

"Are you hungry?"

"A little. Are you?"

As he walked toward her, she couldn't help but imagine him as a dangerous black panther, stalking toward her. He had taken off his coat and tie, along with his shoes. The white of his shirt contrasting with his olive skin tone made him look both sexy and exotic.

"Starved." He took a grape from the tray, popped it into his mouth, and then followed it with a piece of cheese. "Want to order something besides this?"

A meal would be a good idea. Maybe it would help ease her nervousness and help her to think of something other than how very much she wished he would kiss her. The light, soft kiss they'd shared after their vows hadn't been nearly enough.

"Yes. That sounds good."

He grabbed a menu lying on the table. "You want anything in particular?"

"Nothing too heavy since it's late. Maybe grilled salmon or something light?"

"You got it." He nodded toward her bedroom door. "Why don't you change into something comfortable? I'll order."

Relieved to have something to do other than just stand there and stare, Giselle headed to the bedroom. The instant she closed the door, a new dilemma hit her. What exactly did she have to change into? The wedding dress had been a delightful surprise, but that didn't mean she had other clothes. She pulled opened a drawer and let out a sigh of gratitude. Bras, panties, and socks filled one drawer. In another drawer, she found jeans and tops. And in another drawer, she found three nightgowns—one extremely sheer and sexy, one a little less risqué but equally lovely, and then another that would cover her from her neck to her feet.

Closing the drawer quickly, she settled for a pair of jeans and a light blue long-sleeved T-shirt. Stripping off her wedding dress, she carefully hung it in the closet, noting there were also dresses, blouses, skirts, slacks, and shoes. When she was able to access her accounts again, she would need to reimburse whoever had provided the clothes.

Feeling more comfortable and considerably less nervous, Giselle walked into the living area, noting that room service had been delivered.

"Smells delicious."

"Yeah, it does." He slid a chair out for her. "Come eat."

The nerves she'd been so successful at tamping down rose again. Raphael gave her an encouraging smile, and for the first time she saw that he was nervous, too. Oddly, that made her feel better. At least she wasn't the only one.

Thanking him, she settled into the seat and politely waited until he was seated across from her before she attacked her meal.

Apparently as hungry as she was, Raphael went after his own meal like a starving man.

The food was delicious, and she was almost finished before she looked up and noted he'd already cleaned his plate. "This was wonderful. I didn't realize how hungry I was."

"We haven't had much to eat the last couple of days."

"The wedding was lovely. I'm amazed at how everything was pulled together so quickly."

"Coordinating is one of LCR's strengths, but I have to say I was impressed, too."

"I can't believe so many of them came, especially since it's not—" She broke off. She didn't want to say the words, but they hung in the air.

Instead of commenting, Raphael stood and held out his hand. "I want to show you something."

"What?"

Still holding her hand, he led her to the sofa in the middle of the room. "I didn't get a chance to buy you a wedding present, but McCall gave me this a few hours ago." He handed her a small, silver flash drive.

"What's this?"

"Just plug it in and let's watch together."

Raphael didn't know why he was so nervous, but as she inserted the flash drive into the television set, he was holding his breath.

When Giovanni's little face appeared on the screen, Giselle gave a soft sob and whirled around to look at him. "How?"

"Olivia Gates, one of our operatives, got inside. She's interviewing to be his teacher. The glasses she wore had a hidden camera. It's a long story about how she got in. I'll tell you about it later. For now…" He patted the seat beside him. "Let's watch our son."

She settled on the seat beside him, tears streaking down her face. "He looks good. Healthy. Don't you think he's the most beautiful child in the world?"

Raphael's heart was so full of love and pride, he thought it might burst. "Yes. Without a doubt."

"I think he's lost a tooth." A shaking hand pointed to the screen. "Don't you think?"

"Yes. Looks like."

Her eyes wet with tears, she turned to him. "I miss him so much."

Wrapping his arm around her shoulders, he drew her to him and kissed the top of her head. "I know you do. We'll get him back soon. I promise."

The exchange between Giovanni and Olivia lasted only a couple of minutes. One of LCR's techs had edited out as much of Clarissa Fletcher as possible. The whole point of this video was to highlight Giovanni and show that he was well and healthy. McCall had given him another flash drive that included the interview and Olivia's observations. He would view it later. For right now, he wanted to sit here with his new wife and watch their son. None of it was ideal, but for right now, he would take what he could get.

A while later, Giselle felt herself being lifted and carried. Though groggy, she was awake and aware immediately and knew exactly whose arms held her. She turned her face into Raphael's chest, breathed in his scent. She supposed falling asleep on the sofa after watching a brief recording of their son a half-dozen times wasn't anyone's idea of a proper wedding night. But for who they were and what they'd been through, it felt right. Comforting and soothing after the storm. Another one was coming, a bigger, final one. Knowing they would face it together meant more than she could express in words.

When he settled her on the bed, she whispered softly, "Stay with me, please."

"You're sure?"

Gazing up at his serious, handsome face looking down at her with such tenderness, she wanted to cry. This was what she'd given up all those years ago. Even though she'd had no choice, the pain of that loss continued to hurt. But he was here with her now, and whether it lasted only a few more days or a lifetime, she had to take the chance.

"Never been more sure of anything in my life. I want you, Raphael. All of you."

Lowering himself onto the bed beside her, he wrapped his arms around her and just held her tight.

Growling, his need and frustration obvious, he said, "I can't resist you, Giselle. No matter how hard I've tried, I never forgot you. Never stopped wanting you."

Covering her mouth with his, he thrust his tongue deep, sweeping her into a vortex of swirling, whirling, mad desire. Groaning her approval, she wrapped her arms around him and gave him all that she had. She was his...had been his from the moment they met.

Raphael couldn't stop...didn't want to stop. His mind told him that things needed to be resolved before this happened again. That they still had so much between them. He told his mind to shut the hell up. This was what he wanted, needed.

Clothes ripped as hands found their way beneath, searching for warmth, for heat. Giselle broke away from Raphael's searing kiss and gasped out, "I never stopped wanting you either. I couldn't."

His mouth covered hers again as his hands roamed soft, silken skin. Hating to break the kiss, but unable to stop himself, he followed his mouth with his hands. Every inch of skin he uncovered, he praised with his fingers and then his mouth. Giselle's body arched as his mouth teased her nipple, and then she shrieked when he gently bit, then suckled hard.

The night closed in, cloaking them in shadows. They moved against each other, wanting, seeking, needing. Reconnecting in the most elemental way possible. Gasps of delight filled the room as they once again rediscovered one another. Tasting, taking, giving.

It was like it had been before, only more. The other night had been about reconnecting and satisfying an aching emptiness. Tonight was about commitment…about love. About renewal.

Tonight was a new beginning.

CHAPTER THIRTY-FOUR

LCR Headquarters

"Since we flew in only a few hours ago, most of us had a late night." He shot a wry grin at Raphael and Giselle. "And two of you should be on your honeymoon. However, things are happening quickly, and I felt it important to brief everyone here at headquarters."

He nodded at the half-dozen whiteboards lined up against the wall. "As you can see, we have a lot of information to get through. Took some major digging, as well as assistance from additional resources. If you're curious about specifics, you can read the boards once we're done."

Noah sent Angela a smile. "Special thanks to Angela, who worked tirelessly to put this together."

Raphael sat with the rest of the team. These meetings were usually attended only by the Elite team. On occasion, Samara would attend to give her expert advice on criminal behavior. Today the meeting included one additional person—Giselle. McCall had said, and Raphael agreed, that she needed to be in on the planning stage. Not only could she offer expert insight into the Fletchers, she deserved to know how hard everyone was working on rescuing Giovanni.

Noah had told him they had an enormous amount of information, and the low-tech whiteboards covered in writing were a testament to that fact. Someone had painstakingly written down the information, and there was a lot of it. A rush of gratitude went through him. As a matter of course, LCR went to great lengths for all of their clients. However, he knew that considerable time and expense had gone into this particular case. Against LCR, the Fletchers didn't have a chance in hell.

"From what we can determine," Noah said, "the Fletchers have been conducting business this way for at least two generations. Could be more, but honestly that's for others to dig into if they're interested. We're only interested in the here and now."

"What exactly are they into, McCall?" Brennan waved his hand, indicating the boards. "That's a helluva lot of information, but what does it mean?"

"It means that they have a wealth of information on people. Misdeeds, screw-ups, cover-ups. Information that could and would destroy careers and families. Ruin lives. Maybe even change the trajectory of the country or the world. When and if they need to tap into that information, they use it to their advantage."

"Use it, how?" Riley asked.

"To get what they want."

"So they blackmail or bribe?" Sabrina said.

"That, along with threaten, coerce, maybe even exchange information—tit for tat. Whatever they need to do to accomplish what they want, to acquire what they want. The murder of the family that Giselle overheard them talking about is likely not an anomaly. We haven't run across any other mysterious deaths yet, but I'm betting we will at some point."

Palms on the table, Noah leaned forward. "Land deals mysteriously go their way. Stocks get sold before they go down. Stocks get purchased right before they go up. Real estate gets rezoned. Politicians from both sides of the aisles are friends and acquaintances, along with judges, law enforcement officials, local and federal. The power behind these connections is staggering. If the Fletchers have something on each one of them, it's no wonder that when they ask for something, they get it."

"Which is probably how they found where you live," Sabrina said.

Anger glinted in Noah's eyes. "Yes. There are also celebrities—actors, directors, producers." He pointed to one of the boards filled with writing. "This one lists those names."

"Hell," Aidan growled, "it's like they run their very own tabloid business, but instead of reporting what they find out to the public, they use the information to coerce others to get what they want."

"Exactly."

"And if someone tries to betray them?"

"They wouldn't know who to trust. Whispering into the wrong ear could get someone dead. Sometimes it's safer and easier to do the deed than to fight."

"I guess that also goes along with nothing negative ever being written or reported about them," Raphael said.

"Exactly," Noah said. "When something negative pops up, somehow, someway, it mysteriously disappears. I'm not saying everyone is in bed with them. They probably don't even use a tenth of the information they gather, but if they need it, they've got it at their disposal."

Noah turned to Giselle. "You said that Danny told you about some of the troubles he had before he met you?"

"Yes. He said he was thrown out of three different colleges. That he had been stopped five times for drunken driving and once was even caught with cocaine in his car."

"And he was never arrested?"

"I think he was taken into custody, but all the charges were dropped." She shrugged. "He seemed to take it as a matter of course. Whatever he wanted to do, he could get away with it. All it took was one phone call to his parents, and the problem disappeared."

"So what we have," Noah concluded "is a family who not only believes they're above the law, they have proved that fact on numerous occasions."

"That's a helluva lot of information to have and keep up with," Aidan said. "How do they do that?"

"Thanks to an outside source, we've learned he has a team, headed by one man, who gathers and maintains the intel."

"We know who this person is?" Raphael asked.

"We do."

"Please tell me we're going after him," Justin said.

"Not necessary."

"How so?"

"Someone else is already on him. It's only a matter of time before he's neutralized."

"The good guys?"

"Let's just say they're on our side in this. Now that we know how Fletcher is getting away with everything, we're going to get the man in charge of this intel to tell us everything. He's going to give us what we need to bring these bastards down."

"Noah…everyone." Giselle looked around the room and then back to Noah. "Please know that I am profoundly grateful for all the help you and everyone at LCR have given me. And if you can prove these allegations, it certainly looks like the Fletchers could be imprisoned for years, but…" She swallowed hard, and her eyes sheened with tears. "How can we be sure that this will bring Giovanni back to me…to us?"

"That's where you and Raphael come in. Before we do anything with this information, before this man is even apprehended, we're going to get your son."

"How?"

Noah smiled. "Here's how."

As he laid out the plan, Raphael felt the gigantic boulder of worry fall from his shoulders. This would work…this would definitely work.

Manhattan, New York
Fletcher apartment

Daniel paced back and forth in his office. Hugh sat on the sofa, sipping coffee. His friend had always been the calmer one. Daniel had a quick temper, and Hugh often eased his worry with his low-key temperament.

Their friendship had survived for over forty years, and there was no one he trusted more to unload his worries on than Hugh.

"I can't believe this has gone on so long. Who knew she would be so hard to kill? The girl has been nothing but trouble from the day my son met her."

"It's not as bad as it looks. So what if the girl got married? That should make it easier to catch both of them together."

There was that. When word had come in that the little bitch had gotten married again, it had been all he could do not to go after her himself. After all the aggravation she'd caused, how dare she find happiness? Even temporary happiness was more than she deserved.

"I would, however, recommend you dispose of the problem prior to your spring party. You and Clarissa will enjoy it so much more if that pesky issue isn't hanging over your heads."

"You're right. Neither of us will have a moment of peace until this is settled. And the spring party is our favorite of the year. It'll just give us more to celebrate when the girl is out of the picture."

"Speaking of pictures, have you given thought to how you want to introduce the boy?"

"Clarissa wants to take him to Europe in the late spring. Allow people to speculate a bit and then announce the adoption. Because of the trouble the girl has caused, we can't make a big splash with him. Noah McCall and his people will likely give us flak no matter how we bring him out. However, if we take a more subtle approach, their impact should be minimal."

Hugh was about to comment, but closed his mouth when Daniel's special phone chimed. As only one man had the private number, they both knew the identity of the caller.

Daniel put the call on speaker. He had no secrets from his best friend.

"Mr. Cavendar, things are not working as I instructed. Why is that?"

"We're headed in the right direction, Mr. Fletcher."

"Right direction?" Daniel practically shouted the question. "Not only is the girl still alive, she got married. How is that remotely the right direction?"

Rockwell, New Jersey

Cato counted to five before he replied. He was paid too well to say what was really on his mind, which was, *If you'd let me take care of the matter early on, we wouldn't be having this discussion.* Since he couldn't respond truthfully, he gave his employer the next best thing. "She and Sanchez will be dead within forty-eight hours."

"You can guarantee this?"

"Yes."

It hadn't been easy. He'd had to spend way more money than he liked, made more promises than normal, and threatened a boatload of people, but he now had a location for the honeymooning couple. Being in the middle of wedded bliss, they would never know what hit them.

"Our spring party is next weekend. I want everything taken care of before then. If not, heads will roll. Do you understand me?"

"Yes, sir. I understand."

"You've never disappointed me before this, Cavendar. I know the girl is wily and she's got some powerful friends, but no one is more powerful than we are. You've made certain of that."

Yes, he had. And as long as Fletcher and his sidekick, Rawlings, stayed out of his way, he would continue to do what he did best. He got the goods, and Fletcher used it to manipulate to get his way and annihilate when necessary. The arrangement had worked well for decades.

"I know you and your team are working overtime on this," Fletcher was saying. "I'll make sure you're compensated."

"Thank you, sir."

"Now, let's review some other business issues."

As Cato reviewed the various issues that his boss wanted resolved, he felt a moment of amusement. How many people were able to blend financial and legal matters, security concerns, with a side note of lurid details on a prominent businessman's new love interest, along with a discussion of murder?

Even if he wasn't paid a ton of money to take care of these matters, plus hundreds of other things, Cato knew he'd take less money just for the side benefit of enjoyment. The job was never boring and sometimes just downright fun.

***

Rural Virginia

The newly married couple arrived at their honeymoon hideaway in the dead of night. Like any couple in love, they only had eyes for each other. Deep laughter came from the man, as if his new wife had said something hilarious. A giggle followed the laughter, this from the woman, as she stood on her toes and kissed him full on the mouth.

The giggling increased when he threw her over his shoulder and carried her up the steps and into the cabin. Seconds later, the lights came on. The curtains on the window did nothing to hide the fact that the couple was now locked in a passionate embrace.

A perfect way to go out.

Forty yards from the cabin, hidden behind a couple of giant holly trees, Clive and Franco watched their prey.

"You ready?" Franco asked.

Lowering his field glasses, Clive glanced over at his partner. "You don't want to wait awhile?"

"Wait for what? They're in there. What more do we need to do?"

"I don't know. It's just, Cavendar told us to wait until just before daybreak. They've got a few hours left."

"You get a romantic streak all of a sudden? Or are you getting chickenshit in your old age?"

"Hell no. I just figured we'd do what he said. Don't matter to me if they get dead in five minutes or five hours. Dead's dead."

"Then let's get it done. It's too cold to stay out here and argue."

"Fine," Clive snapped.

And with those words, he picked up the RPG launcher, aimed, and squeezed the trigger. A fireball zoomed to the cabin and struck with magnificent force. The ground shook like an earthquake had hit, and the entire area lit up like it was daylight.

"Oh man!" Clive hooted with laughter. "I got to get me one of these!" Almost nothing he loved better than a good explosion.

Franco stood watching, making sure he saw no movements. They wouldn't be caught with their pants down again. When he was assured there was no way anyone could have survived, he started packing up. "Let's get out of here."

No more encouragement was needed. They needed to be long gone before the fire department got word.

They were half a mile away when Franco made the call to his boss. "It's done."

"You're sure this time?" Cavendar asked.

"Oh yeah. They were kissing in front of the big window when the blast went down."

Clive guffawed beside him and said loudly, "It was a beautiful thing, boss. They went out in a blaze of horny glory."

"Excellent. See you two on Monday."

Ending the call, Franco glanced over at his partner. "Pancakes?"

Clive grinned. "You read my mind."

CHAPTER THIRTY-FIVE

LCR Headquarters Underground Bunker

The sound of dice hitting the board and the resulting laughter made Raphael smile. He hadn't heard Giselle laugh like that in forever.

"I can't believe you rolled another double, Micah."

His dark eyes crinkling like his father's, his smile all Samara's, Micah McCall moved the silver boot eight spaces on the board. "I passed Go, I get two hundred dollars."

Almost the spitting image of her mother, Evie McCall sent her brother a triumphant smile. "And you landed on my property and now owe me two hundred buckaroos."

Watching Giselle play Monopoly with Micah, Evie, and Paulo, Eden and Jordan's teenage son, was a surreal moment in time. While someone was in the process of blowing up a cabin, believing they were killing him and Giselle—again—they were inside the underground barracks of LCR, safe and far from harm.

When Noah had explained the setup and how he and Giselle would have to appear to die, he'd had one major concern. If the heartless Fletchers told Giovanni his mother was dead, it could cause irreparable harm. After talking with Olivia, he felt reassured that they wouldn't tell him, at least not for a while. Before then, Giovanni would be back with his mother.

What happened after that would be up to law enforcement. He had an idea or two that he planned to suggest to Giselle, but those would have to wait. His focus right now was to get their son back safely.

"So how's married life treating you?"

He took the ice-cold beer Jordan Montgomery handed him with a nod of thanks. Dropping into a chair beside Raphael, Jordan took a long swallow from his own bottle and eyed him curiously.

Raphael had known Jordan almost as long as he'd known Noah. Though Jordan and Eden ran the Paris LCR office, he saw them frequently. They were family. Raphael could be close-mouthed with other people, but telling Jordan what was on his mind came naturally.

He kept his voice low. "Not sure you can call this a marriage."

"Why? Because it was rushed? Impromptu? Unexpected? Just because you and Giselle haven't seen each other in some years doesn't mean you stopped loving each other. That's all that counts, you know."

If only it were that easy. "We still have issues between us. Things that are hard to overcome or dismiss."

"True." Jordan nodded slowly, took another long swallow of his beer. "But you have something more important than that."

"You mean Giovanni?"

"Yes, he's important, but he's not what I'm thinking of. You love each other."

Did Giselle love him? Had she ever loved him? The sting of that coldly worded letter from long ago reverberated through him.

Aware that Jordan was waiting for an answer, Raphael shrugged. "Love may not be enough."

"Really? I'm here to tell you that it is."

"There's a lot to forgive—on both sides."

Jordan went quiet for a moment, his eyes tracking to his wife, who sat on the sofa talking with Samara. "Did you know that I've known Eden since she was a little girl?"

"No. I guess I thought you two met through LCR."

A rough laugh escaped Jordan. "Well, in a way we did."

Since LCR had been around for fewer than fifteen years, the math didn't work. "What do you mean?"

A grim smile flattened his mouth. "Let me tell you a story about how two extremely stubborn people can screw up about as badly as they possibly can, but still find their way to love."

As he listened to Jordan's telling of his painful beginning with Eden, Raphael began to see his and Giselle's relationship in a different light. Though their story was completely different, what hindered and kept them apart for years was the pain of betrayal.

"I think back on those days and how far we've come." Jordan sighed, turned back to Raphael. "When I found out the truth, I was furious and so full of stupid pride, I never looked at what she might have gone through, her reasons for what she did." He snorted his disgust. "She was the one who owed me an apology, right?"

His gaze went back to his wife, his expression one of incredible tenderness. "She forgave me. Still blows my mind that she did. The lies she told were never done to hurt me, but to protect herself."

Standing, he took Raphael's empty bottle and his own. "Find out why she did what she did before you decide you can't forgive her. I think you might be surprised."

With that last piece of advice, Jordan walked away.

Her mind only half on the game, Giselle kept Raphael in her peripheral vision. When they had arrived for the meeting, she hadn't known that this was where they would be staying until everything was over. Who knew there was an underground bunker beneath the large, modern office building?

Though they shared the same bed, she and Raphael had not really talked since their wedding night. The next morning things had been awkward. She had woken in his arms, warm and cozy, incredibly hopeful. That hope had eroded the moment Raphael had opened his eyes. The shield he'd let down the night before was back up in full force. And so far, it hadn't shifted.

Other than the coolness from Raphael, everyone else treated her as family. And not one of them had given any indication that they thought her and Raphael's marriage was anything but the real thing. Well, no one but her own husband.

She wished she could say or do something that would make him understand the decisions she had made. Yes, she had made mistakes, but her reasons, at least to her, had been sound.

"Hey, how are you doing?"

She glanced up at Samara, who, she was relieved to see, looked both healthy and lovely. It was hard to believe that barely two weeks ago she had been kidnapped and held hostage. To know that the man Giselle had once called her father was responsible was humiliating.

"I'm doing fine." She gazed around at the people in the room. "I'm just so grateful for everyone's help."

"Not only is this what we do, but you and Raphael are part of our family. You get preferential treatment."

Unexpected tears filled her eyes. She had tried so hard to be strong and not let the powerful emotions overwhelm her, but Samara's words and warm compassion were more than she could handle.

"Hey." Her brow wrinkling with concern, she took Giselle by the hand. "Come with me."

Her eyes blurred, she vaguely pointed toward the game board. "I can't leave."

Eden stooped down beside her. "I've got this," she whispered. "Go talk to Samara."

Before anyone could say anything, Eden announced to the small group of players, "I'm taking Giselle's place, and I won't be nearly as nice."

Giselle heard groans from the others, including Paulo, who said, "She's not kidding. Mom is ruthless when it comes to Monopoly."

Leaving behind the laughter, Giselle made it out of the room and managed to wait until the door closed behind her and Samara before she burst into tears.

Samara wrapped her arms around Giselle and just let her cry. She had been there and knew that getting all the pent-up emotions out would help more than anything. Sometimes nothing cleansed the spirit quite like a good cry.

She whispered comforting words, similar to what she would say to one of her children. Hurt had no age limit and could often make the strongest person as vulnerable as a child.

Finally, after several gulps of air, Giselle pulled away from her arms. "I'm so sorry. I never cry like that."

"Then I would say you're definitely overdue." Taking her hand, she led Giselle to a love seat and then snagged a box of tissues from a side table. As Giselle wiped her face and blew her nose, Samara grabbed a couple of bottles of water from the mini-fridge.

Sitting down beside the still hiccupping young woman, she spoke softly, "Now, tell me what's going on."

Giselle laughed hoarsely. "You know everything there is to know. Giovanni—"

"Yes, and I know you miss him terribly. I cannot imagine being separated from either of my children, but we will get him back. I promise you."

"I know...I just..."

"It's Raphael, isn't it?"

"He's never going to forgive me. Not that I can blame him."

"Have you talked with Raphael about why you left?"

"He knows. It just doesn't matter to him."

"Then you keep talking until he really listens. Look, I've been in love with a stubborn man for several years. Sometimes you have to get in his face and make him listen."

"And tell him what? I deliberately kept him from his son. What else is there to say?"

"The truth, Giselle. I know we don't know each other that well, but I recognize love when I see it. You're in love with him, and I'm pretty damn sure it didn't happen in the last few days. You've been in love with him for years. There's the surface truth, and then there's the God's honest truth. Tell him the real truth. And if he still won't listen, you just keep at him until he accepts it."

"But—"

"There is no 'but' about it. You love Raphael. You share a son with him, one you both love. And whether he's ready to admit it or not, Raphael loves you, too. You're already a family. You just have a few more pieces to connect before you make a complete one."

The instant Raphael saw Giselle walk out of the room with Samara's arm around her waist, he had wanted to follow. She was obviously upset, and he hadn't done a damn thing to try to make her feel better.

He went to his feet, took a step toward the door she had disappeared behind, and then came to a halt when a hand grabbed his arm. "Let her be for now. She needs someone to talk with who's not going to give her attitude."

Stunned, he turned to Noah. "You think that's what I've been doing? Giving her attitude?"

"I think you're hurt, and when people get hurt, they lash out."

The indignation withered like dead grass. What was the point in arguing? Noah was right. All his anger and self-righteous fury were getting him nowhere and making both him and Giselle miserable.

"Besides," Noah continued, "we need to talk. First part of the plan went off without a hitch."

His heartbeat quickened. "They took the bait?"

"Took it...swallowed it whole. Bastards used an RPG."

"They didn't check for bodies?"

"No. With that kind of firepower, they needed to get the hell out of there. The media will report two unidentified bodies were found. They'll be satisfied they were you and Giselle."

"Thorne and Fox are okay?"

"Yeah. Went out through the trapdoor just like we planned. They stayed to watch."

Raphael nodded. He knew they not only stayed to make sure the op worked, but also to make sure no innocents were harmed or other property was damaged.

"It's a good beginning."

"Next steps will be the hardest on you and Giselle. Waiting is always the hardest."

Yeah, he wasn't looking forward to it. Hiding was not in his DNA, but in this, he had no choice. For the mission to work, the Fletchers needed to believe that he and Giselle were dead. So they would stay here until it was time to move to the next phase.

Noah glanced around the rec room. "Not the most romantic of honeymoon spots."

"We're not exactly the typical honeymooning couple."

"You can always have a honeymoon when this is over."

He glanced over at the closed door that Giselle and Samara had walked through. "Not sure that's going to be necessary."

"I've given you all the advice I'm going to give you about that. You're a grown man and make your own choices and mistakes."

Yes, he knew what Noah thought. And considering the looks the rest of the team had given him, he knew what they thought, too. He just wasn't there yet. Didn't know if he ever would be.

The door opened, and Giselle walked out. Her eyes were gleaming bright, and she looked as though she'd been crying. Tired of the long looks and glares from everyone and needing some privacy, he went to her.

"You okay?"

"I'm fine."

Since she looked as though she could burst into tears at any moment, he knew the words were automatic. Taking her hand, he said, "Come with me."

CHAPTER
THIRTY-SIX

Resisting was futile. Not only did Giselle not want to make a scene by refusing, but she also felt buoyed by her talk with Samara. The other woman was right. She did need to make Raphael listen to her. Whether anything she said would change his mind was up in the air. However, the only way over it was to go through it. What was on the other side would be up to Raphael.

They walked together into the bedroom they'd stayed in since coming here. It was a small, lovely suite decorated in various shades of blues and browns. The ambience both soothed and uplifted. They had slept in the king-size bed last night, separate but together. Neither of them had slept well—not like they had on their wedding night.

"We need to talk." She said it fast and first. She wanted to get this finished.

"Yes, we do, but first there's news."

"From Sabrina and Aidan? Are they all right?"

"They're fine."

"Did it happen the way Noah described it?"

"Yeah. Almost verbatim. They had some heavy artillery. No one was hurt. The fire didn't spread."

"And the reports will only be that two bodies were in the house. There will be no mention of names?"

His gaze softened. "No. It will be reported as unidentified remains. If your mother happens to hear the news, there's no way she would connect the story to you."

"Good...good. That's good. So what's next? The Fletchers' party?"

"Yes."

"I wanted to talk to you about that. I think I should go, too."

"No way in hell, Giselle. If either of them were to see you, they—"

She held up her hand to stop his protests. "Listen before you say that. Okay?"

Though his jaw went rigid, he remained silent. She took that as a win and drew in a breath. Presenting her case would require reason and logic; emotions would not help.

"Gio's going to be terrified if he doesn't know the person coming for him. He will fight. I know our son, Raphael. He'll scream and yell, no matter what he's told. There's no way he can be taken out quietly unless I'm there, too. Besides that, I know the mansion quite well. We can slip out without anyone being alerted."

"You can't just sneak in. Security will be tight."

"I'll come in like everyone else. I can go as one of the catering staff."

"If you get caught, they'll kill you."

"They won't catch me. They think I'm dead, so they won't be looking for me. Besides, if your makeup artist can make your LCR people look like my family, they can make me unidentifiable."

She saw the flicker of doubt in his eyes and drove home her point. "He'll be terrified with a stranger. I'll do whatever you tell me to do, however you tell me to play it, but when we find Giovanni, he needs to see his mama. You know I'm right."

Blowing out a ragged breath, he relented enough to say, "I'll talk to McCall. Get his take."

Before she could thank him, he held up his hand. "No promises. We'll take a look and then go from there."

Relief flooded through her. Even though he wasn't sold on the idea, she believed if they could make it work, they would. She trusted him to keep his word. She trusted him.

Squaring her shoulders, she took on the granite-jaw stubbornness Raphael seemed to have perfected and said, "There's something else we need to talk about."

"All right."

Samara had told her to get in his face, make him listen, but there was something else she needed to do first. "I want to ask for your forgiveness. I know I hurt you when I left. The way I left...the things I said. I believed I was doing the right thing at the time. I played it the way I was told."

A lump of emotion threatened her voice, but she cleared her throat, determined not to mess this up again. "The US Marshals' office laid it all out for us. Reddington would not let this go. Revenge against Mama was all he had left. They said that Mama would be his primary target, but that he'd use us to get to her. None of us would be safe. Including you.

"They told us we would have to move multiple times, likely in the middle of the night, often without warning. We wouldn't be able to settle anywhere for a while, if ever. We could have no contact with our past lives."

"I know all of this, Giselle. I know it would have been tough, but—"

"But nothing, Raphael. Do you remember all the dreams you had…all the things you wanted to achieve? Almost from the moment you told me about LCR, you couldn't stop talking about your plans to be an operative. You had every aspect of your life mapped out. Do you think I wanted to take that away from you? If you had gone with us, none of that would have been possible. Think about the people you've rescued, the lives you've saved. I left you because I loved you and for no other reason."

"I would have given those things up for you. We could have created new dreams. New adventures. We—"

"That's exactly it, Raphael. Can't you understand that? I didn't want you to give up your dreams. Before I met you, I never really had any dreams of my own. My life was what it was. I didn't think I'd ever have anything different. You gave me hope…you showed me your dreams. Once I realized what wonderful things they were, how could I take yours away from you?"

"That wasn't your choice to make, Giselle."

She huffed out an exasperated breath. "Yes, it was, Raphael. I'm incredibly sorry I hurt you, but if I had to do it again, I would do the same thing. I know leaving you like that was painful, but having you be with me, not fulfilling your dreams, would have been excruciating.

"I knew I had to make it believable. If I didn't, you wouldn't rest until you found us. So I lied. I told you I didn't want to be with you. That what we had wasn't real. I said the things I needed to say to keep you from searching for me."

"You'll be glad to know it worked."

She didn't flinch, but she inwardly cringed. She had laid it all out for him, and it still didn't matter.

Feeling extraordinarily tired, Giselle dropped onto a small sofa. The painting above the bed, a mountain stream surrounded by spring flowers, soothed her as she spoke about those dark days. "When I found out I was pregnant, we were in the middle of moving to another town.

"I became ill after breakfast one morning. Mama followed me to the bathroom and asked me if I was pregnant. I think deep down I knew I was but was too afraid to face the truth. We faced it together." Her mouth trembled, and she worked to keep it firm. "She was…is an amazing woman. She held me, told me everything would be all right.

"We went together and told the people protecting us. It added a new wrinkle. I needed to see a doctor… There would be medical records, etc. They offered to help me take care of the problem. As if Gio could ever be a problem. I refused the offer, of course.

"They accepted my decision and made it work. We were able to stay in one place long enough for me to get a regular doctor and have the baby at a hospital in Thomasville, Georgia."

"Did you even consider letting me know?"

"I told you, Raphael. They wouldn't let me. We were still in hiding. Any contact with our old life might have put us in jeopardy. I couldn't do that to my family. To my child."

"You called me, though. Later."

"Yes."

"And if I had called you back, things would be different. I would have known about my son."

"Yes," she whispered.

"And Giovanni wouldn't be—"

"Go ahead and say it. It's true. I failed him. Failed to protect him. My number one job was taking care of my son, and I didn't do it."

"I'm not blaming you for what the Fletchers have done. They—"

"You should. I certainly do. I never questioned them until it was too late... I always went along, followed. Did what I was told. What is the saying? 'If you don't stand for something, you'll fall for anything'? I did not take a stand. I fell for their lies, for Danny's lies. I was stupid, and my son is paying the price for my stupidity."

"You were naïve, not stupid."

"Naïveté can't be an excuse. Not when it comes to being a mother. A mother protects her children, looks out for them. The Fletchers may not be child predators, but they're predators all the same. My son is in their clutches because of me."

"You made a mistake by trusting the wrong people. These people have been manipulating and taking advantage of people for a long time. They're experts at it."

"And I was the clueless, green idiot who fell into their trap."

Raphael sat beside her. He was taking a hard look at his own actions, and the harsh truth punched him in the gut. Giselle had owned up to her mistakes. It was time for him to step up and acknowledge his own.

"It's just as much my fault as yours... No, it's more my fault."

"How?"

"I blamed you for leaving. If I had looked hard enough, I would've seen through the things you wrote in that letter. Truth is, I used my pride to ignore the truth. You're right. If I had gone with you, I would never have been able to do the things I wanted. I remember talking incessantly about my goals and dreams. Not once did I consider you or your feelings."

"That's not true. It's just..." Her smile was sad. "Sometimes what you want and what you can have can't be the same thing."

She had been placed in an impossible position. Young and vulnerable. And heartbroken. The decisions she had made had been made out of love.

And the pregnancy? That was his fault, too. He had told her he'd take care of the birth control, and he had failed her.

He imagined how she had felt. Ashamed to tell her mother and terrified to tell the government authorities protecting them. He hadn't been there to support her, and he should have been. Instead, he'd been on his grand adventure, using his hurt pride to ignore the facts.

While he had been living out his dreams, she had been living a nightmare.

He wouldn't regret the son they made together, but he could damn well own up to his responsibilities.

He took her hand, marveled at her soft, silky skin. "I'm sorry, Giselle. For not being there for you."

"You're here now." She leaned her head against his shoulder.

"Where do we go from here?"

"We get our son back."

For a long while, he held her snuggled against him. The past couldn't be changed, but they both had a second chance. Nothing could be decided until Giovanni was safe, and then they would see.

CHAPTER THIRTY-SEVEN

East Hampton, New York

Today was the day. Giselle sat with Raphael in the back of a white van with the name of the catering company the Fletchers had hired for their party. It had taken multiple conversations to get both Raphael and Noah to the point of agreeing to let her participate. When it came down to it, though, they had realized that having her there when Gio was found just made sense. Her baby would come to her the instant he saw his mama.

What had happened to Gio while they'd been separated was something she had forced herself not to dwell on. If she had, she wouldn't have been able to concentrate on anything. She knew the Fletchers would not harm him, but that didn't mean they wouldn't cause emotional or mental trauma. They had separated a child from his mother. That had to have affected him.

No, she wouldn't think about that now. She couldn't. She had to concentrate on the here and now. Today was the day they would be reunited. And today was the day he would meet his papa for the first time.

Giovanni knew exactly who his father was. Though her reasons for not contacting Raphael had been valid, she had at least made sure her son knew all about the man who fathered him. Giovanni knew he had been born out of love. He knew that his father was a courageous and strong man who rescued children. Raphael was already Gio's hero. Today their son would meet his hero for the first time.

His eyes dark with concern, he asked, "You okay?"

"I'm good. A little nervous, but mostly good. I just want to get to him as soon as I can."

"I know you do." Raphael squeezed her hand. "But—"

"I know. I know." They had gone over the plan numerous times over the last couple of days. "I won't deviate, I promise. I know the risks."

"You look good."

She had to laugh at that. Since she hadn't recognized herself in the mirror, there was no way the Fletchers would have a clue. Cleo, the makeup artist who had made LCR operatives look just like her family, had done an amazing job turning Giselle into someone else, too. The honey-blond wig she wore, along with blue contact lenses, a slightly longer nose, and a few lines at her eyes, made her look at least ten years older. A little extra padding had been added to her breasts and bottom, filling her out in a way that Giselle thought was quite attractive.

The instant Raphael had seen her, he had given her a look that sent a zing throughout her body. But then he had pulled Cleo aside and talked with her. Giselle had been in the midst of admiring her new, curvier figure when Cleo had approached her with even more padding.

"Why more?"

"Raphael made the observation that you need to be more matronly. You need to blend in, not stand out."

He had been right. She had seen several catering staff walk into the mansion, and many of them looked just as she did. Having lived with the Fletchers, she knew they looked through servants unless they wanted something. As long as they got what they requested, the servants were dismissed with barely a flicker of acknowledgment.

Once Cleo had finished, she hadn't recognized the woman in the mirror. She now looked at least two decades older and extremely matronly. No one would know her, including her own son. When she had mentioned her concern, Cleo had encouraged her to remove her wig. When she had, her hair had fallen to her shoulders, and though she had still looked different, she looked enough like herself that Giovanni would recognize his mama.

Raphael's transformation was almost as dramatic. Bushy eyebrows, a full beard, and a darkening under his eyes made him look older. The makeup, along with extra padding at his middle, gave him the appearance of an older, less-fit man.

"You know what to do if something goes wrong, right?"

"Yes." She used her other hand to squeeze his hand that was still holding hers. "I'll be fine. I lived here for almost two years. I know this place well. If there's trouble, I know where to hide."

The plan was simple, but would have to remain fluid. She would work with the catering staff and follow orders. Once the party was in full swing, she would use the servants' stairway to get to Giovanni's room.

The back door of the van opened, and Noah stood there. "Are we ready?"

"Just about," Raphael said. Turning back to Giselle, he said quietly, "Remember, any trouble at all, you get the hell out of the way. They can make up any damn story they want and get away with it. Even with hundreds in attendance, covering up a murder would be no trouble for them."

"I will, I promise."

They stepped out of the van together, and Noah gave them the onceover. "Cleo did a good job, as usual. Wouldn't recognize either one of you."

Raphael was part of the crew hired to do the heavy lifting for the decorating company. Though most of them had arrived yesterday, Raphael had said he'd be able to blend in well enough. All he needed was to get inside.

Giving her one last encouraging look, Raphael headed toward a group of men unloading chairs from a large truck. Taking a breath, Giselle walked down the sidewalk toward the kitchen.

This was it. Soon, very soon, she would be seeing her son!

***

Giselle crept to the back stairway. It had taken her much longer to get away than she had anticipated. The head chef had barely even looked at her when he'd put her to work, ordering her to fill pastry puffs with some kind of cream cheese concoction. She had performed her duties, all the while looking for a chance to escape. The giant kitchen had been filled with people, and organized chaos reigned as everyone rushed to do their jobs. When the last puff had been filled and one of the tuxedoed servers had whisked it out of her hand, she had faded quickly into the background. If she wasn't around, chances were no one would miss her. There were more than enough people to do the various tasks.

The instant her foot was on the first step, she flew up the stairway as if she had wings. She was only a few seconds away from seeing her son. Her heart pounded with both elation and fear. If she was caught, this would be over, and she would have failed to protect him once again.

She reached the second landing and ran quickly down the hallway to another stairway that led to the third floor. Noah had assured her the cameras would be down for at least an hour. Though Fletcher's security people were likely panicking at the malfunction of the cameras, they at least wouldn't be looking for her or Raphael. Having everyone think they were dead was genius. No one would be looking for intruders to kidnap a child holed away on the third floor, far away from the multitude of guests.

Her heart still pounding, she almost lost all her composure when she saw who was waiting for her when she reached the door to the third floor. Raphael stood there like a sentinel. Her hero.

"Any problems?" he asked softly.

"None. You?"

"No. I was dismissed until tomorrow." He reached for her hand, squeezing gently. "You ready?"

"Yes."

Still holding hands, they walked down the hallway together to rescue their son.

Raphael had faced armed men who had every intention of killing him with less trepidation than he felt right now. He could honestly say that he had never been more nervous in his life. His nerves had nothing to do with getting caught by Fletcher's security people and everything to do with the fact that he would soon be meeting his son for the first time. How on earth was he going to explain who he was and why he'd never met him before?

What had Giselle told Giovanni about his father? She had said that he knew Fletcher hadn't been his dad, but had she told him anything about Raphael? Kids were inquisitive. He had to have asked questions. Did he think his real father had abandoned him?

At the thought, Raphael glanced over at Giselle, and his heart softened. Her face was glowing with anticipation, with hope. There wasn't a hint of nervousness in her demeanor. She was a mother about to be reunited with her son.

They stopped at the door to his room. Getting Olivia inside so she could meet Gio had been a godsend. They wouldn't have known that his bedroom was on a different floor on the opposite side of the mansion from where it was when Giselle lived here. Having to search for him would have slowed them down, putting everyone at even more risk.

Before opening the door, she smiled up at him. "Thank you, Raphael. For everything."

Squeezing her hand gently, he used his other hand to open the door. Except for a small light coming from the corner of the bedroom, the room was dark. There was a small lump in the bed, and Raphael lost his breath. His son.

Pulling the wig from her head, Giselle rushed toward the bed.

"Giselle? What are you doing here?"

They both whirled at the high-pitched whisper that came from the corner.

A stocky, middle-aged woman sprang up from a chair. "You're in danger here. Don't you know that?"

"I've come for my son, Mavis. Don't try to stop me."

"But Mrs. Fletcher—"

"He's my son. Not theirs."

"Mommy?"

"Gio!" Giselle rushed forward and gathered her son into her arms. As much as Raphael wanted to follow her, he stayed on guard. The nanny didn't look as though she would scream or try to alert anyone, but he would keep an eye on her all the same.

"Where have you been, Mommy? I've missed you."

Her voice thick with tears, Giselle laughed softly, "Oh, baby, I've missed you, too. But we need to hurry. We're leaving."

As if he realized the urgency, he didn't argue but jumped out of bed. Giselle grabbed a thick jacket that was lying on a nearby chair. "Here, sweetie. You can keep your pajamas on, but let's put this on you."

While Giselle hurriedly dressed Gio, Raphael stood in the doorway, keeping one eye on the hallway and one eye on the nanny.

"Okay, let's go."

Giselle stood before him. In her arms was the most beautiful child he'd ever seen in his life. His son.

"Hello, Papa."

Raphael lost his breath. "You know who I am?"

"You're my papa."

Tears filled Giselle's eyes. The shock on Raphael's face was almost her undoing. She had her son in her arms, and he was meeting his father for the first time. Her most heartfelt dreams were coming true.

"Gio's known from the beginning who his father is. No one could ever take your place, Raphael."

Even though she knew he wanted to hold his son, get to know him, they still needed to get away from the mansion.

"Let's get out of here."

Giselle quickly reinstalled the honey-blond wig and headed toward the door.

"I want to come, too."

Stopping, she glared at the woman she'd believed was her friend. "You betrayed me, Mavis."

"I had no choice, Giselle. I didn't know I was being followed. The man who followed me saw you approach me that day. When Mr. Fletcher found out, he threatened me."

This she could believe. And if she was here when they discovered Gio gone, she would likely be killed.

"Okay. Let's go."

Raphael walked out first and then motioned for Giselle. Hanging on to her baby with all her might, Giselle ran forward. Mavis followed behind her.

The party was still going strong. The Fletchers' choice of music was from their generation and played throughout the house. It was loud enough that any noise they made was easily covered.

They were almost to the first-floor stairway when things went sour.

"Hey! Stop right there."

They turned to see a large man heading toward them. Giselle didn't recognize him as one of Fletcher's regular guards. Perhaps he had been hired as an extra for the occasion. Whether he was permanent or only a temp, she didn't know. The gun in his hand said either way he took his job seriously.

Making sure Giselle and Gio were behind him, Raphael held his gun on the man as he spoke into the mic on his lapel. "Giselle, Gio, and the nanny are headed your way."

Her heart stuttered. What did he mean? "Raphael?"

"Go on, Giselle," he said calmly. "Head the way we practiced. Someone from LCR will be waiting for you."

Knowing she had no other choice, she said softly, "We'll see you soon."

Holding Gio closer, she ran down the stairway and into the kitchen. The doorway was open, and she ran through it just as they'd discussed. She figured Mavis was behind her, but didn't stop to check. She didn't know if she believed her story or not, but that would have to wait for later.

She was running down the sidewalk, seconds away from freedom, when something grabbed at her shirt. She whirled and faced her worst nightmare. Refusing to back down, she put Gio on his feet, pushing him behind her.

Before she could speak, something hit her temple. Giselle felt herself falling and heard Gio scream, "Mommy!"

And then everything went dark.

CHAPTER
THIRTY-EIGHT

Raphael had no choice but to focus on the moment. If he thought about Giselle and Gio, about the trouble they might encounter, he wouldn't be able to do what needed to be done. The man in front of him wasn't trained, not like the other security people he'd spotted. Sweat beaded on his forehead, and the hand that held his gun was shaking. The weapon, however, was trained on Raphael, with the man's finger hovering way too close to the trigger for his liking.

Noah had told him once that he'd rather face a half-dozen trained mercenaries than one untrained idiot with a gun. Raphael could definitely see his reasons.

"No one needs to get hurt." Taking one step sideways, out of the path of a wayward bullet, Raphael said calmly, "You can put your gun down and just walk away."

"Can't do that. I need this job. Cameras are down...I don't know what's going on, but I can't get them back up. I'm screwed. I've got a feeling that catching you will go a long way in saving my job, though."

"You do realize that I could just shoot you."

"Not if I shoot you first."

He could almost feel sorry for the guy. His voice shook, and if his breathing got any faster, the man would likely pass out from hyperventilating. Problem was, he didn't have time to let that happen.

"What's your name?" Raphael asked.

"Owen Holcomb."

"Have you worked for the Fletchers for very long?"

"Almost three years."

"Ever had to shoot anyone?"

"No. I man the security cameras."

Yeah, that's what he'd thought. The guy was an amateur. Taking a chance this wouldn't backfire, Raphael slowly lowered his own weapon and placed it on a hallway table.

Confusion furled in the guy's forehead. "What are you doing?"

"Giving up. Isn't that what you want me to do?"

"Well…yeah…sure. I just didn't think you would without a fight."

"That gun looks pretty lethal. I'd rather not get shot." Slowly moving his hands up as if to surrender, Raphael said, "So what now? I don't imagine the Fletchers will thank you for scaring their guests by parading me in front of them."

Uncertainty flickered in Holcomb's eyes. Quick as a snake, Raphael closed one hand over the gun, the other under the guy's wrist and twisted hard, locking the man's arm with the gun pointed downward. Twisting once more, he threw the man to the floor and grabbed the gun. Before the man knew what was happening, Raphael was on him, slamming his fist twice into his face. Holcomb's eyes rolled back into his head, and he was out.

Raphael took off down the hallway. That had taken less than two minutes, but it was more than he had wanted to spare. He said into his mic, "I'm coming out. Everyone secure?"

"Gio is safe, but we've got a problem," Thorne answered.

"What?"

"Giselle's been taken."

***

Of all the things Daniel had planned to do at his spring party, it certainly wasn't this. Heads were going to roll.

He glanced over at Hugh, who was driving the car. "I still don't understand how this happened. How did the girl even get onto the estate?"

"You didn't notice what she was wearing?"

"No. Of course not." Notice her clothing? He had been so shocked to see an unconscious Giselle in the trunk of Hugh's Mercedes, he hadn't bothered to look at anything as mundane as her apparel.

"Her blond wig came off on the way to the car, but she's wearing a servant's uniform. My guess is she came in with the caterers."

Daniel could not get his head wrapped around the course of events. The girl was supposed to be dead. For at least a week, he'd been living under the impression that all the nasty business with his daughter-in-law and her lover was over. That's what he had been told. When he finally got hold of Cato Cavendar, the man wouldn't have a hair left on his head. Daniel would rip it out by the roots.

"I don't understand any of this. Where the hell is Cavendar?"

"I don't know. I tried calling him before I came and got you. Got his voice mail."

"What do you think we should do with her?"

Surprising him, Hugh sent him a sly grin. "Don't you worry about it. I can handle the situation."

"What do you mean?"

"Don't worry about it."

"Of course I'm going to worry about it. You've got an unconscious woman in the trunk of your car, and I've got one hundred and twenty-seven of the most influential people in the country at my home wondering where the hell their host is. How can I not worry?"

"You'll be back before they even know you're gone."

"How's that? Where are we taking her?"

"My beach house."

"For what?"

"I thought you might want to have a chat with her."

"You're not making any sense. I don't want to have a conversation with the woman. I just want her dead."

"And I'm going to help you with that."

"Help me, how?"

The look Hugh sent him was easy to read. Daniel didn't know if he'd ever been more shocked in his life. "You want the girl for yourself?"

"Only for a short while. Then I'll dispose of her. You don't need to worry about any of it. I'll take care of everything."

He knew Hugh had eclectic tastes when it came to relationships. Even in college, it had been whispered that his friend was a deviant. Daniel had never delved deeply into what that meant. Other than a few indiscreet moments at some frat parties where everyone was doing everything under the sun, he hadn't witnessed Hugh doing anything abnormal.

"Don't look so shocked. I'm not going to cut her up into little pieces and feed her to my fish."

Though Hugh's amusement was an attempt to lighten the mood, Daniel didn't respond. Truth was, he wasn't quite sure how he felt about this. Yes, the girl needed to die. And yes, he didn't mind her suffering for a bit first. But this? It was unseemly, almost uncouth.

"But she's my daughter-in-law."

"No, she's not. She's an interloper who horned in on your family. If not for her, Danny would still be alive."

That was the unarguable truth. His son's death was the girl's fault.

"If she hadn't been snooping where she didn't belong, she wouldn't have overheard our conversation. When you threatened her, what did she do? She went to Danny and told him. Forcing you to make the toughest decision you've ever had to make. All because of her."

Daniel remembered that day as if it were only yesterday. Never had he seen his son so upset, and never had Daniel been so incensed. His son had actually called him a murderer, hurling insults at him as if he was disgusted. When he'd left the house, saying he would be back to take the girl and her son away, it was all Daniel had been able to do to keep from going to the girl and shooting her outright. Instead, he'd made a call to Cato Cavendar. The next day, they'd gotten the word that Danny had been killed in a car wreck.

Clarissa didn't know the truth. Though he did his best to share all his business decisions with her, this had been too personal. She had spoiled Danny and loved him dearly. He was quite certain she wouldn't approve of his decision.

Which brought him back to Hugh's point. The girl *was* responsible for his son's death. If she had abided by his warning, kept her mouth shut, none of this would even be necessary. She did deserve to suffer.

"Thank you, my friend. As always, you've helped me to see things more clearly."

Shooting Daniel a mischievous grin, Hugh turned onto the two-lane drive that led to his beach house. "Happy to help."

Scrunched up in the tiny trunk of Hugh Rawlings's sports car, Giselle lay still, barely breathing. She had heard everything. She wasn't shocked that Daniel was responsible for his son's death. She had suspected it, but without any kind of evidence, proving it had seemed as hopeless as proving all the other vile things the Fletchers had done.

Danny *had* planned to come back for them. She hadn't believed in him and was sorry for that. They hadn't had a good marriage, and she had lost faith in him, but she had never wanted to see him hurt. That was one more thing that Daniel Fletcher would pay for.

Where were Gio and Raphael? The last thing she remembered was running down the sidewalk at the back of the house, toward the woods where an LCR operative would be waiting for them. She'd been holding Gio, and someone had pulled on her blouse. When she had turned to see a grinning Hugh Rawlings, she had wanted to scream. Before she could do anything, something had struck her. That was all she remembered. Mavis had been right behind her. Had the woman betrayed her after all? Had she been the one to knock her out? What had happened to Gio?

And Raphael? Was he okay? The man with the gun had looked extremely nervous, but that didn't mean he wouldn't shoot.

She told herself things weren't hopeless. First, other than a slight headache, she was healthy and strong. Second, the two men up front were older and not trained to kill. Yes, they were responsible for having people killed, but they didn't get their own hands dirty. She was half their age and fully prepared to do whatever was necessary to survive. And third, she had a weapon. Rawlings hadn't intended to kidnap anyone tonight. He had dumped her into the trunk without even considering that there might be tools there that she could use.

These men didn't have a chance. She had a child she adored and a man she loved waiting for her.

She was a woman determined to win.

CHAPTER THIRTY-NINE

Raphael stood in the hallway, leaning against the door of his hotel room. His son was inside the room talking with Samara. He had seen his mother knocked out and carried off. When Thorne had found him, he'd been hysterical, but the instant Raphael showed up, he had calmed.

For the first time ever, Raphael had held his son in his arms. Hugging him close, he had promised that his mother would be with him soon, that she was all right. Never had he made a promise that he intended to keep more than this one. He would find Giselle, and she would be okay. This he swore.

Rage filled him, and it was all he could do to contain his fury. Giselle was in the hands of evil, and they had no idea where she had been taken. Mavis Tenpenny, the nanny, claimed not to know. Her explanation that they had taken a different path than what Giselle had intended rang true. A security person had been headed their way, and they had veered down another path toward a wooded area at the back of the estate.

Tenpenny's explanation was sketchy after that. She claimed that Hugh Rawlings, Daniel Fletcher's friend, had been on that path smoking a cigarette and had spotted them. He had knocked Giselle out and commanded Mavis return the boy to his room.

The woman had ignored that order. Justin and Riley had caught her trying to put Gio into a car. They said it had been obvious that Gio hadn't wanted to go. Gio had been kicking and screaming, putting up a hell of a fight.

Whether the nanny was being truthful would have to be determined at another time. Their only focus now was finding Giselle. Where the hell had Rawlings taken her?

They had researched Hugh Rawlings thoroughly. Knew he owned two houses under his own name and one other under an alias. All three homes were hours away from the Fletcher estate. Would he chance taking her that far, or did he have another place close-by that they didn't know about?

They did know a few things. When Rawlings's vehicle left the estate, Daniel Fletcher was in the passenger seat. The security camera at the gatehouse ran on a separate system, and they had elected to not disable it. The video feed showed Rawlings and Fletcher driving down the winding drive, away from the house. Chances were good that Giselle had been with them, but the camera hadn't revealed her whereabouts. Had she been in the backseat? The trunk? Was she alive? Unconscious? What did the men plan to do with her? And where the hell did they take her?

"How's Gio?"

Raphael whirled around, striding toward Noah. "Anything?"

"Not yet. We've got three analysts running down everything they can find on Hugh Rawlings. So far, we've come up with nothing more than what we already have." He nodded toward the door Raphael had been leaning against. "How's Gio doing?"

"Amazing, considering he saw his mother get knocked out and carted away. He finally stopped crying when I told him Giselle was fine and will be with him soon. I hope to hell I didn't lie."

"You didn't. We'll get her back safely."

"Cavendar cooperating?"

"Yes and no. He hasn't given us anything useful on Rawlings yet. Says he took all his orders from Fletcher. Says he knows of the man, but has never had dealings with him."

"And that's bullshit. No way in hell a man that thorough doesn't know everything about his boss, which should include intel on his best friend. The man's lying."

"I agree. Whatever he knows, we'll get. Riley and Justin are still questioning Ms. Tenpenny. She knows more than she's giving us, too. I'm not sure if she's involved up to her neck, or if she's holding out for fear of reprisal from her employers. Intimidation seems to be the Fletchers' MO when it comes to employee motivation."

Raphael shoved his fingers through his hair. "This is my fault. I should never have agreed to let Giselle go in with us."

"No. This isn't your fault. From talking with Riley, Giselle was right on the money. Gio would not have gone with anyone else. He would've put up a protest and alerted the entire household."

"He would've come with me."

"Yes…possibly. What's done is done. Our focus now is rescuing Giselle. Keep your mind on what needs to be done."

"I need to be doing something. Anything. I can't just stand here twiddling my thumbs, waiting. God only knows what they've done to her."

Noah grabbed Raphael's arm. "I need you to take a breath. When we get a location, I need you focused. Understand?"

"Don't worry about me. I'll be focused."

"Raphael, listen to me. There's no one who understands your fear better than I do. I was lucky that cooler heads talked me down before I could rush in and do something stupid."

Raphael took a breath. As much as that made sense, because Noah had definitely gone through something similar more than once, it was almost impossible for Raphael not to get in his car and just go. Yeah, he didn't know where he'd be going, but—

"What about Clarissa Fletcher? Can we question her?"

"Not without tipping our hand. As soon as the party ends, the feds are moving on them. We go in now, chances are she'll find a way to alert her husband and they'll both disappear."

He didn't like it, but it made sense. "And they won't leave Giselle alive."

"No. She's collateral damage they can't afford."

"Okay. All right. I—"

Noah's cellphone chimed, and he put it on speaker before he said, "What do you have?"

"Olivia just called. Cavendar caved. Says Rawlings has a beach house in Water Mill under another alias."

"That's not far from East Hampton."

"Yes. I'll text you the address."

His heart raced, his feet ready to fly out the door. "That's got to be where they'd take her, right?"

"Makes sense. Fletcher wouldn't want to be far from home with his party still going on."

"There's something else." Angela's voice held more than a tinge of worry. "Is Raphael there with you?"

His blood going cold, Raphael met Noah's eyes.

"Yes, he's here. What is it?"

"Cavendar told us some other things about Rawlings that we didn't know."

"What kind of things?"

"Last year, an incident got out of control. Rawlings raped and murdered a young woman. Cavendar helped him cover it up. He dumped the body. Made it look like the girl moved away."

"Let's go." Raphael started running.

Noah followed him. "We'll go together. Thorne and Fox will follow."

Raphael didn't need more encouragement. Gio was safe with Samara. Now it was time to save Giselle. He'd be damned if he found his son only to lose the woman he loved.

Evil had won too many times in the past. It did not get to win this time.

CHAPTER FORTY

Lug wrench in hand, Giselle was ready for them. The instant the trunk lid opened, she sprang up and swung hard at the closest man—Hugh Rawlings. Didn't matter who she hit first. The wrench slammed into his gut. He managed to utter an ugly grunt before collapsing to the ground, gasping and cursing fiercely.

Giselle whirled around, ready to take on Fletcher. She stuttered to a halt. He was holding a gun in his hand, and the look on his face told her he would gladly use it.

"Well, I do have to say, young lady, despite my antipathy for you, you are a resilient one, aren't you?"

"You'll never get away with this, Daniel. Do you know the people you're up against? No matter what you do to me, you're finished."

Smug amusement in his eyes, he shook his head slowly. "Tsk-tsk. You always were a dramatic one. Never knew your place no matter how many times Clarissa and I tried to educate you."

"And your place will soon be in prison. You and your—" She turned to look down at Rawlings, but he was no longer there. Hard arms wrapped around her torso. Giselle lifted her legs, kicked back. At the same time, she jerked her head back. The crunch of

Hugh Rawlings nose and the resounding vibrations of her heels against his shinbones were infinitely satisfying.

His arms loosened again, and Giselle took a step forward. A fist swung toward her. She managed to sidestep it, but came to an abrupt halt when Daniel's gun pressed into the center of her forehead.

"Make one move…just one. Please."

Giselle didn't move. Daniel Fletcher might not be a trained killer, but he would kill her. Of this she had no doubt. She would give him this round, but her fight was far from over.

Not taking his eyes from Giselle, Daniel said, "You okay, Hugh?"

"That bitch is going to die."

"But of course she is," Daniel said soothingly.

Roughly grabbing her hands, Rawlings pulled them behind her and wrapped something around her wrists.

His smile even meaner and smugger, Daniel pressed the gun harder against her forehead.

Her chances for escape had just gone down considerably.

"Let's get her inside."

"Lead the way," Daniel said.

Having no choice but to follow behind Rawlings, Giselle walked down the pathway toward the house. They likely made an odd-looking group. Two elegantly dressed men with a young woman in a catering uniform between them. If that didn't seem strange enough, having her hands tied behind her back and a gun digging into her shoulder most certainly would.

Though it was dark, the sky was clear and a half moon glowed above them, lighting the way. The house was much smaller than the Fletcher mansion and was older. Her gaze moved left and right, looking for anything she might use to escape. Once inside, her chances of surviving would go down even more. Her opportunity came from the bushes. With a meowing squeal, an orange streak darted out and ran between her and Rawlings. Startled, Daniel cursed and took a step back. Giselle took off running. She had no clue where she was going. She knew only that she needed to get away as fast and as far as she could.

A bullet whizzed by her head, and Rawlings snarled in a harsh whisper, "Dammit, Daniel, don't shoot. The neighbors will hear."

If they were worried about someone hearing them, then they were close enough that she could run to a neighbor. Running with her hands behind her back wasn't easy, but she was motivated. Long legs stretched out in front of her, and her feet flew as though they had wings. She saw a light in the distance and shouted at the top of her lungs, "Help! Fire!"

A dark figure hurled itself toward her. Giselle screamed and tried to dodge it in midstride. Rawlings tackled her, taking them both to the ground. She lay on her back, the air completely gone from her lungs.

"You okay?" Daniel whispered above them.

"This bitch is going to pay," Rawlings growled.

"Come on. Let's get her inside."

Without the ability to breathe, Giselle managed only a half-hearted attempt at kicking the man who hauled her to her feet. She opened her mouth to scream again, determined to make some sort of sound, and never got the chance. Rawlings's fist slammed into her face, stunning her.

Hauling her over his shoulder, Rawlings carried her into the house.

***

Daniel slapped the girl's face. She was conscious, but seemed to be someplace else. He wanted her right here, alert and aware of everything. He had a few things to say, and then his friend could have her. Whatever Hugh had in mind, and he had an inkling what that would entail, wouldn't be nearly what she deserved. She had tried to ruin him. Every offer he'd made to her had been rejected. If she had stayed quiet about what she'd heard and agreed to let them keep the boy, none of what happened to her would have been necessary. She was the only one responsible for her plight. Hell, he had even sent her to an asylum as a concession. He could've just had her killed. There wasn't an iota of gratitude in the girl.

After he delivered three resounding slaps, her eyes flickered open, but were glazed and unfocused. He gave her another, harder smack. Her eyes opened wide, and reason returned. Hatred gleamed in the dark depths, and it was all he could do not to just choke her himself. How dare she look at him with such contempt?

"Glare at me all you want, girl. You're the one responsible for your predicament. If you hadn't been snooping around, sticking your nose where it didn't belong, none of this would be necessary."

Instead of responding, she let her gaze roam around the room. When she realized she was tied to the bedposts, she let loose a shriek that pierced his ears, and began to twist and turn, trying to get free.

"No use trying to escape. Hugh and I are expert sailors. There's not a knot we can't tie."

"You won't get away with this, Daniel."

"But of course I will, Giselle. So few people realize just how far and great my influence goes. There's not a person in this world who won't do as I ask."

Footsteps sounded behind him. "Are you almost done? It's getting late. You need to get back to Clarissa, and I want to get on with my evening's entertainment."

"You're right. I didn't tell my wife where I was going. She's likely very put out, but she'll be happy to hear this little problem is being handled." Daniel glanced over his shoulder. "Thank you for taking care of it, my friend."

"What are best friends for?"

Daniel turned back to the girl. "I wish I could stay and list every single thing you did to deserve this, but quite frankly you're just not worth the trouble. My son made some errors in his life, but you were the worst."

"That is about the only thing we could ever agree on. Marrying your son—marrying into the sleaziest family I've ever known—was definitely the worst decision I've ever made."

He hauled off and hit her again. Not nearly as hard as he wanted. She needed to be conscious for the main event.

Straightening to his full height, he walked away. "Make sure she pays, Hugh. All right?"

An unusual fire burned bright in his friend's eyes. "I'll do my best."

Assured that the girl would suffer before she died, Daniel walked toward the bedroom door. He stopped at the entrance and said, "Oh, and Giselle, don't worry about the boy. He'll be brought up to follow in my footsteps."

Chuckling, he closed the door on her screams of rage.

CHAPTER
FORTY-ONE

Giselle glared up at the man who stood over her. His intentions were obvious. She had always felt uneasy when she was in Hugh Rawlings's presence, and now she knew why. The evil in his eyes chilled her to the bone.

She took a moment to assess her situation. Though her jaw ached and her head throbbed, those were the extent of her injuries. She was healthy and strong, more than able to fight. Her hands were tied to the bedposts, but her legs were free. A powerful kick in just the right place would incapacitate the pervert. Problem was, if she didn't get her hands free, she might lie here for hours.

How could she play this? Making nice with a man who wanted to rape and kill her was beyond her acting abilities. Getting him to release her in some sort of mutual-attraction scenario was out, too. She would throw up the instant he touched her.

She could, however, play on his pride. If that didn't work? No, she wouldn't even consider that option.

Raphael and LCR had no idea of her location. What had happened after she was abducted dwelled like a dark entity in her mind, hammered at her heart. What if Raphael hadn't made it out of the house? What if Mavis had been the one to betray her and had taken Gio back inside the mansion before LCR could find him? What if this was the way things were supposed to end for all of them?

No, no, no. She had not survived a freaking insane asylum, found Raphael again, and rescued Gio only to lose it all. That was not happening.

A smarmy smile slid up Rawlings's face. His hand reached out and brushed a strand of hair out of her eyes. "I always envied Danny. Being able to touch that soft, golden skin. Lie between those long, firm legs, suckle those pretty—"

"I always knew you were a pervert."

Though his smile dimmed a bit, he didn't react the way she had expected. "This doesn't have to be unpleasant. I can make it pleasurable for you."

She snorted her disgust. "Rape is rape."

He gave an exaggerated sigh. "Very well." He grabbed her shirt and jerked. Cold air swept over her, chilling her blood. If she didn't do something soon, it would be too late. Problem was, she needed him closer. Could she play the game long enough to get him close enough?

The instant his hand touched her breast, she knew she couldn't do it. If he went further, she'd throw up. She opened her mouth to scream and then stopped. She had something else…something that would stun this man. Would it cause him to completely lose his temper, or would it give her more time?

When his hand slid down her torso, she knew she had no choice but to try. It was now or never. "Cato Cavendar."

Rawlings froze. "How do you know that name?"

"We know everything, Rawlings. *Everything.* The people you and Daniel threatened and bribed. The politicians and reporters who do what you tell them to do. All the illegal deals you've made for profit. All the people you've cheated."

"Who is 'we'?"

"The authorities."

He snorted. "They won't do anything. We have too much power."

"Oh yeah? Why don't you call Daniel and find out what's going on over at his house?" It was past midnight. The raid on the Fletcher estate was already in progress. There was nothing Rawlings could do to stop it.

Looking more amused than worried, he backed away and pulled his cellphone from his pocket. She watched him press a key, heard the call ring, and then Daniel's voice mail saying to leave a message.

"Daniel, Hugh here. Call me, my friend."

"I imagine he's a little too busy calling his lawyers to talk with his partner in crime. If I were you, I'd get in my car and leave town. They'll be coming for you next."

Rawlings shook his head. "He didn't have his cellphone on him. That's the only reason he didn't answer. You must've heard Daniel mention Cavendar's name...probably heard it when you were eavesdropping. There's no way in hell he'd betray either me or Daniel."

She managed a smug smile. "If you say so."

He leaned over her, his hot, sour breath coating her face. "I'm tired of playing around."

"So am I." She lifted her knee, slammed it into his temple, stunning him. He staggered back a few inches, giving her the room she needed. Holding the bedposts for leverage, she lifted both legs, angled them outward, and kicked with all her might. She heard the crunch, felt the gush of blood as it splattered all over her. With barely a grunt, Rawlings dropped like a stone beside the bed.

She lay gasping on the bed, triumphant and hopeful. They would come here, looking for Rawlings. She knew they would. She just needed to hang on. And pray that Rawlings did not wake up before that happened.

***

A huge wave of relief swept through Daniel as he made his way back home. He was thankful Hugh had lent him a car, or he would have had to call a cab. If there were any guests left at the house, that would have looked quite strange.

Things could now go back to normal. Well, almost normal. His tiresome ex-daughter-in-law would no longer be a bother. She had been his most pressing concern. The man, Raphael Sanchez, was still an issue—especially with the powerful Noah McCall as his friend. But no one could match Daniel's influence. He would find a way to rid the earth of Raphael Sanchez. The man would never get the opportunity to claim the boy as his son.

And if McCall continued to cause problems? He knew the man's weakness. Next time, he would make sure to do things right. He'd gotten to McCall's family once, he could do it again. This time, he would make sure they didn't survive.

Cavendar had disappointed him once again. Twice he'd said the girl was dead, and twice he'd been wrong. He should have reprimanded him the first time. The man needed to know that just because he had done good work in the past didn't mean he would be allowed to get away with failure. Daniel had made Cavendar a wealthy man, but that didn't mean he wasn't replaceable. He could easily find someone to take Cavendar's place.

He glanced at the dashboard readout, noting there was a call option. Though new technology stymied him, he wondered if he should figure out how to phone Clarissa. He'd left in such a rush and hadn't had the chance to let her know what was going on. Not wanting to be interrupted during his party, he'd left his cellphone in his bedroom. Daniel made a mental note to never do that again. He felt at a distinct disadvantage and quite out of touch with the rest of the world.

He made the final turn on the road that led to his home. The party had been a roaring success. Even though he'd had to leave early, he had been quite pleased. Every person he had invited had attended. Every influential man and woman he had insisted show up and play nice had done exactly that.

He sighed, this time with supreme contentment. Yes, there were still a few loose ends to tie up, but all in all, things were going magnificently his way.

That warm fuzzy feeling lasted him all the way to the top of his driveway. The lights were so bright at his house, the entire structure looked like it was on fire. The party would have been over a couple of hours ago. Everyone, even the servants, should be heading to bed.

His heart in his throat, he zoomed down the driveway and then jerked to a stop. Two men in suits, holding guns, approached his vehicle.

Fury erupted. How dare they?

Daniel got out of the car, screamed, "What is the meaning of this?"

Another man stepped out of the shadows. This was someone he knew—one of those influential people who, only hours ago, had been enjoying his hospitality. He had made this man cry and curse more than once. He damn well would know the reason all of this was happening, or this man's head would roll.

"Wilkins, what is the meaning of this?"

Instead of the deference he was accustomed to, Wilkins gave him a broad smile and said, "This, Mr. Fletcher, is the very definition of karma."

CHAPTER FORTY-TWO

The house looked quiet, maybe even empty. Raphael had turned off his headlights as he approached. And now, other than one single light in a window on the first floor, everything was in darkness. She had to be in there. He refused to believe otherwise.

A small vintage sports car was parked in front of the house. Records showed that Rawlings owned four vehicles. Having this one parked out front had to mean something.

Raphael opened his car door, stepped out, and grabbed what he needed from the trunk. He barely heard Noah getting out on the other side.

Aidan and Sabrina had parked on the street and approached at a rapid run.

"Fox and Thorne, go around back," Noah said. "Sanchez and I will take the front. We go in on my count of three. We'll check the door and go in quietly if we can. If not, we'll bust down the damn door."

They'd gone through this scenario many times. Raphael knew what to do, how it should go. This was different. No previous situation had been more personal or important.

His heart pounding with both hope and fear, Raphael kept low as he ran to the front of the house. Noah ran beside him. Before stepping onto the porch, they stopped. Saw no movement inside.

With a nod, they stepped up onto the porch. At the door, gun at the ready, Noah said, "Hold on."

Shining a flashlight over the door, they noted not one but three deadbolts. Busting it down was their only option.

"On my count. One. Two. Three."

Swinging with all his might, Raphael slammed the battering ram into the door. It cracked. He went at it again, and it splintered, then crashed open. He threw the tool to the floor, and his gaze swept the room. Saw nothing.

Heading to the room where the lights were shining, his gun at the ready, he pushed the door open. He told himself whatever he found couldn't be worse than his imagination.

The instant his eyes spotted Giselle on the bed, he knew he'd been wrong. This was worse. So much worse.

She lay still, covered in blood, her eyes closed. Her wrists were tied to the bedposts. Though her pants were still on, her torso was bare with the exception of the blood.

Refusing to accept what he was seeing, Raphael rushed forward. "Giselle?"

Spotting Rawlings's body lying a few feet away from the bed, Raphael shouted, "Noah! In here!"

Reaching the bed, he touched Giselle's neck, checking for a pulse. Her skin was warm. The instant he found a pulse, her eyes opened.

"It's about time, Raphael Sanchez. I've been waiting a lifetime for you."

He almost fell to his knees in relief. "I thought I'd lost you."

"Is Gio okay?"

"Yes. He's safe. He's with Samara."

Tears filled her eyes. "You think you could untie me? My arms are numb."

Feeling like he was moving in slow motion, he pulled his knife from the sheath at his waist and cut the rope. She lowered her arms, rubbing circulation back into the numb limbs.

Almost afraid to touch her, he asked, "Where are you hurt?"

"I'm not. Not really. Just some bruises."

"But the blood."

"It's not hers," Noah said behind him. "It's Rawlings's." Grinning at Giselle, he added, "Good job."

"Is he dead?" she whispered.

"No. But he's going to be in a lot of pain when he wakes up."

Knowing Noah would take care of Rawlings, Raphael turned back to Giselle. He helped her sit up and then pulled her into his arms. Closing his eyes, he held her. She was alive. Thank you, God, she was alive. And he was never letting her go again.

"Everything okay?" Aidan Thorne stood at the door.

"I've called an ambulance for Rawlings," Noah said. "Check on Giselle."

A hand touched his shoulder, and he looked up at Thorne. "Let me take a look at her, buddy."

Raphael nodded. Yeah, he needed to let her go, let her get checked out. For the life of him, he couldn't seem to do it.

"Raphael, I'm fine. Really."

Thorne touched his shoulder. "Why don't we go into the living room? Get her away from here."

Lifting Giselle into his arms, Raphael spared a single glance toward Rawlings. He lay on his back, and blood covered his face and neck. His nose was askew, and his eye looked as though someone had taken a hammer to the socket. Giselle had done that. She had been strong and brave enough to not only take the bastard down, but to also save herself.

Turning his back on the bastard, Raphael carried Giselle into the living room. The lights had been turned on all over the house. He strode to a couch in the middle of the room and lay her gently on the cushions. He wasn't sure which one of them was holding on the tightest. He couldn't seem to let her go, and she kept her arms around his neck even after he'd put her on the sofa.

"Okay, you two." Thorne's amused voice broke into Raphael's numbed mind. "I know you're still on your honeymoon, but I really need to check Giselle out."

Pulling himself together, Raphael gently took Giselle's arms from around his neck, whispering in her ear, "I'm right here, sweetheart. I'm not going anywhere."

She nodded and released a sigh. "Okay."

Standing back, he got the full effect of just how bad she looked. Her white shirt and bra were hanging at her waist, and her entire torso was covered in blood. Beneath the paleness of her face and the dried blood, bruises were already forming.

"Hey, Sanchez, why don't you make yourself useful and find something for your wife to wear?"

Unbuckling his Kevlar vest, he dropped it on the floor and unbuttoned his shirt. He was wearing an undershirt, too, which was fine. No way in hell was he putting anything on her that belonged to that bastard.

Finally recognizing that he wasn't going to get Raphael out of the room, Aidan turned to Giselle and began his examination. Raphael stood close-by. He wasn't leaving her again. Ever.

CHAPTER FORTY-THREE

LCR Headquarters Underground Bunker

The sound of her son giggling woke her. Had there ever been a more beautiful sound? When she heard his father's laughter in response, she amended that thought.

They were together. Father and son were together at last. The journey had been long and arduous, but to hear those sounds vanquished all the fear and pain. She hadn't been sure that would ever happen.

She lay in bed, luxuriating in the quiet simplicity of an early Saturday morning. There was nothing more on her agenda today than spending time with her guys. So much had happened over the past week, it was hard to believe that only five days ago a sadistic maniac had held her captive. She hadn't known if she would ever see Raphael or Gio again.

Daniel and Clarissa were in jail. The judge, deeming them both flight risks, had refused to set bail. With the number of people that the Fletchers had threatened or bribed over the years, securing an unbiased jury of their peers would likely be impossible. Giselle couldn't bring herself to care. They were where they belonged. She was through with that family forever.

Hugh Rawlings was still in the hospital. This time, he was the one bound to a bed. The beautiful irony of that wasn't lost on her. Rawlings had been charged not only with some of the same things the Fletchers had, but also with her kidnapping and assault. He had also been charged with murder. Knowing he had killed a woman the year before reminded her how very fortunate she was to have survived.

The Fletchers' main henchman, Cato Cavendar, had spilled every ounce of information he had. From what she could surmise, he was still spilling. Giselle wasn't sure who had questioned him, or what they'd done to get him to talk—she didn't want to know. However, the man had decades of information to share. He had given up so much that she had been told that she might not even need to testify.

She had decided to table her decision about that. Having the Fletchers and Rawlings in jail, facing charges they'd never get out of, was a good start. She had given the authorities her account of everything that had happened to her and Gio, as well as what she had overheard regarding the murder of the family in New Jersey. She had also told them what she had overheard about Danny's death.

To know that Daniel Fletcher was responsible for his own son's murder didn't shock her as much as sadden her. Danny hadn't been a good husband, or an especially honorable man, but he hadn't deserved to be murdered, most especially at his father's orders. She wasn't one who normally placed the blame on parents if their adult children turned out badly. In this case, there was no doubt in her mind that they were at least partially at fault. If Danny had been born to different people, he might have been an entirely different man.

She pushed aside those sad thoughts. Those were things of yesterday. Today she had exactly what she'd always dreamed.

She rolled over, and her heart almost stopped. Raphael stood in the doorway. Tall, ruggedly handsome, he wore a light blue T-shirt, faded jeans, and no shoes. That, combined with the beard stubble on his face and upward curve of his sensuous mouth, sent a zing of delight to every erogenous zone she possessed. But that wasn't what melted her heart into a puddle of goo. He held his son on his shoulders, his big hands holding him steady to keep him from falling.

These two had formed an immediate bond. If she lived a thousand years, this image would remain in her heart as her favorite one of all time.

"Hey, did we wake you?"

"Yes, but I'm glad you did. It was the perfect beginning to my day."

"Feeling better?"

Yes, she was. Even though she had been pronounced physically fine, the first couple of days after her ordeal, she had wanted only to sleep. Seeing Gio and Raphael together, knowing they were both safe, she hadn't been able to deny her body's need for rest. After living with so much fear and grief the past few months, she had been both mentally and physically exhausted. She had been under strict doctor's orders to rest and sleep. And that's exactly what she had done.

But today, for the first time since this had all begun, she felt as if a heavy burden had been lifted from her shoulders. It was a new day, a new beginning.

Where she and Raphael stood, she couldn't say. He had been so tender and protective, pampering her and seeing to her every need. Did that constitute a forever commitment? They were married, but that had been out of necessity. Now that Gio was back with them, safe and sound, where did they go from here?

Had he forgiven her? Could he learn to love her again?

She knew what she wanted. Spending her life with Raphael, raising their son together, having more children, that was her dream. She loved him, had never stopped.

But what did Raphael want?

The pink hue of her cheeks, the curve of her lips, and the gleam in her eyes told Raphael all he needed to know. She really was going to be okay. Even though the doctors had assured him she was physically fine and just needed to rest, he hadn't been entirely sure. Other than to share a few hugs with Gio and eating her meals, she had done nothing but sleep. It made sense that her body was depleted, but still, he hadn't been sure he'd ever see the shadows disappear from her eyes. Today they were completely gone.

Except for a few words here and there, they hadn't had the chance for a real conversation. He had been with her when she'd shared her ordeal with the prosecutor's office. Hearing everything she had gone through had ripped at his guts. She had once told him she didn't think she was particularly strong. He honestly didn't think he'd ever known a stronger person. She had endured so much, fought with all her might, and survived evil, and she didn't look at it as anything extraordinary.

"We were thinking of going out to breakfast."

She sat up in bed, delight curving her mouth. "Really?"

"Papa said I could get waffles and pancakes, too, 'cause I'm a growing boy."

"Is that right?" Her eyes twinkling, she added, "And who's going to get you down when you're climbing the walls from all that sugar?"

"My papa," Gio sweetly replied. "'Cause he's the tallest."

Raphael burst out laughing. "Sounds like a plan to me."

Pulling him from his shoulders, he gave him a quick hug and set him down. He did exactly what Raphael expected him to do. He ran to his mother and threw himself into her arms.

"Feel like going to breakfast with us?"

Still hugging Gio, she smiled at Raphael. "I can't think of anything I'd rather do."

***

Franco scratched his beard. He needed a bath and a shave. Since Cavendar had disappeared, he and Clive had been holed up in an old hunting lodge without running water. He was tired of this shit and ready to get out of Dodge. Just one more thing to do before they left.

"They're not worried anymore," Clive said. "Think the danger's all gone. That they're safe."

"We'll show them they're wrong."

"Didn't know they had a kid."

Franco glanced at his partner. "So? What's the difference? We're not going to kill the kid. We were paid to do a job, and it's not done yet. They've escaped twice. Third time's the charm."

Sitting in a truck across the street from the restaurant, the two men watched their targets. "Be an easy kill from here," Clive said.

"Yeah," Franco agreed. "Wait till they walk out the door. Pop 'em before they even know what's what. We'll be long gone before anyone figures out where the bullets came from."

"Something feels off."

"Know what you mean. I'm out of sorts, too."

They had worked for Cato Cavendar for almost ten years. When they weren't stalking their prey or carrying out contracts, they often got into trouble. Cavendar had kept them busy, and they'd been working for him on an exclusive basis for the last five years.

All that was in the past. They were still trying to get their heads wrapped around what happened. Cavendar had been caught and had given up his employers, told every damn thing about them. The high-and-mighty Fletchers and that sidekick of theirs, Hugh Rawlings, were in jail, shit-deep in trouble.

What Cavendar hadn't done was give up his own employees. From what they knew, nobody was looking for them. That said something about a man.

There was protocol for this kind of thing. They'd learned those rules the first day of hire. If any person on the team was caught, the entire group was to disband, scatter around the world. All contracts were canceled, all business finished.

Other than the promise to never rat out another team member, there were no real loyalties. The other members had skedaddled right after Cavendar had sent up the signal. By now, they were probably spread all the way from Timbuktu to Saskatchewan. That's what the two of them should've done, too. Problem was, both of them hated loose ends.

Franco looked back at the happy couple—the loose ends. They had a kid. It was obvious they were his parents—he looked just like both of them.

"Okay, how 'bout we do this?" Franco said. "If the kid gets pancakes, we do the guy. He gets waffles, we do the girl. That way, he's still got one parent. That's more than either one of us had. That's something."

"Yeah...yeah...okay," Clive said eagerly and then frowned. "What if he gets toast?"

"We do 'em both." Franco shrugged. "Kid's fault, not ours."

"Works for me."

They waited, watched the couple order. Watched the laughter, the happy smiles, the tender touches. Nice picture they made. Still, they had a job to do.

It took longer than either of them thought it would, but finally the waitress came back with a tray loaded with food. When she placed two platters in front of the kid, they looked at each other, laughed, and then shrugged.

The kid would never know that he had saved both his parents' lives.

Starting the car up, the two killers drove away.

CHAPTER FORTY-FOUR

LCR Headquarters

Raphael sat with the other members of the team. For the first time ever, he didn't want to be here. He wanted to be with his family. The early morning breakfast had felt like a new beginning. He wanted more of those days.

He and Giselle had yet to talk about the future. He needed to know where she was in her head, and he sure as hell needed to tell her some things. Things he had held on to far too long.

But this was a debriefing—one he didn't want to miss.

Noah stood at the front of the conference room. Even though he was still banged up, the darkness was gone from his face. He had his family back with him. Raphael understood that feeling even more than ever.

"Thanks to everyone's efforts, both Daniel Fletcher and Hugh Rawlings will be going away for a long time."

"Raphael," Noah said as he looked at him, "as we discussed, unless Giselle specifically wants to, it looks like Cavendar gave enough evidence that she likely won't have to testify."

He nodded his thanks. "She seemed relieved when I told her she might not have to, but I'll ask her again to make sure."

Giselle, above anyone, deserved her day in court. But she had been through so much already. She'd already told her story to the prosecutor. Would going through it more publicly help or hurt?

"What about Clarissa Fletcher?" Riley said. "Wasn't she involved up to her ears, too? What are her charges?"

Noah's face tightened as he shook his head. "Unfortunately, Clarissa chose not to face the charges against her. She was found dead last night. She hanged herself in her cell."

Raphael couldn't find it within himself to be sad about that. She had made her choice. He was sorry, though, that she wouldn't serve time in prison. For what she had done to Giselle and Gio, she'd deserved to be locked up for several years.

"And Cavendar?" Thorne asked. "He may have been a big help, but he was up to his eyeballs, too."

Rage flickered on Noah's face. "Nothing…legally. He made a deal with the prosecutor's office. He won't serve any time."

"What the hell?" Indignant, Raphael glared at Noah. "He might not have been the decision-maker, but he sure as hell is guilty of setting everything in place. He instigated the hits on us. How the hell can he get away with that?"

"I'm not happy about it either. Samara identified Cavendar as one of the men who held my family on the boat. Said he was definitely the one in charge. There's nothing I'd like better than to see him go away for life."

"But instead, he just walks away, free as a bird?"

"Not exactly." Noah's eyes darted to Olivia. "Gates, you want to elaborate on that?"

Her eyes went wide, and her face flushed. The normally unflappable Olivia Gates looked both uncomfortable and flustered. How was she involved in this?

"I can't really say a lot, other than Cavendar won't be completely free to do as he pleases. He will be working for an organization that gathers intel for various...entities. He'll be carefully monitored."

"Gathers intel for who? What kind of intel? Is this a government agency?" Sinclair asked.

Squirming again, she sent a pleading look to Noah, who shrugged and said, "Not a sanctioned one."

"Black ops?" Sabrina asked.

"Close, but deeper than that," Olivia said. "They hire out their services to lots of different people."

"What kind of services?" Raphael asked.

"Whatever is needed to resolve an issue." Olivia shook her head. "I can't really say more than that."

"Then let's cut to the chase," Thorne drawled. "Good guys or bad guys?"

"Neither." When everyone just continued to stare at her, she sighed. "Seriously. I can't go into detail. Suffice to say that Cavendar will be using his talents to help save lives."

"And if he refuses or wants to quit?" Raphael asked.

"Let's just say it won't end well for him."

Raphael told himself he needed to be satisfied with that. Fletcher and Rawlings were locked up, most likely for life. Not a perfect ending, but he would take it as a win.

"What about the people who worked with Cavendar?" Sabrina asked. "No way the man didn't have a cadre of employees."

"They're in the wind. Cavendar admitted that the instant he was caught, he sent out a signal to his people. Their protocol was to disband with no more communications. We'll likely never know who they were."

While it was a relief that no one was gunning for them, it riled Raphael that there were still people out there who had gotten away without consequence.

"And Mavis Tenpenny," Riley said. "What about her trying to get Gio into her car? Are we sure she wasn't in on all of this?"

Raphael took the question for Noah. "Both McCall and I talked to her extensively. She said she was forced to leave the flash drive recording of my meeting with Daniel. He threatened to fire her if she didn't comply. She said she feared for Gio's safety if she left him alone. When you guys caught her, she said she planned to take Gio to safety and had no intention of abducting him.

"McCall and I both believe she's telling the truth. She was afraid for both herself and for my son. Without her, I'm not sure Gio would be as well adjusted as he seems to be. Mavis kept reassuring Gio that his mother would return for him someday. She gave him hope, and I owe her a debt of gratitude for that."

Noah waited for several quiet seconds and then said, "Any more questions before we close this case?"

No one spoke. Raphael had several more questions, but he'd wait until he was alone with Noah before he asked, as they weren't pertinent to anyone but him. These were personal issues.

When there were no questions, Noah said, "Then let's consider this officially closed. Sinclair and Gates, since you're on assignment in France, hook up with Jordan and Eden. They have some new intel for you."

"Will do," Brennan said.

"Delvecchio has asked for in-office duty until further notice. Since she's one of our most gifted researchers, that's a no-brainer. Since Thorne is taking some time off until after his and Anna's baby is born, Mallory will team up with Fox. I've sent some preliminary notes on an abduction in Arizona. Read over it and let's meet tomorrow morning at eight."

"Kelly and Ingram, your flight for Los Angeles has been booked. Your undercover personas are in place. Check with Angela on the way out for details. This is a sensitive case, so tread carefully." Noah's eyes targeted Riley, who had a tendency to speak more bluntly than her more diplomatic partner, Kelly.

Raphael held his breath. He hadn't asked for any time off, but that was on his agenda once he and Noah were alone. He had some time to make up for.

"Sanchez, we'll talk about your assignment in just a minute. Stay safe, everyone."

As the rest of the Elite team left the conference room, with the usual good-natured ribbing and various insults, Raphael kept his focus on Noah.

Once the room was empty, Raphael said, "Any news?"

"Yes. It's in the works. Late next week is the earliest we can set it up."

"That'll work. It will give us some time together."

"Speaking of that, Thorne left some information you might be interested in."

"What's that?"

"He has a place in the Caribbean. A private island. Great place to spend time with loved ones, get reacquainted. He thought you might be interested in going there this week."

Raphael tried to speak, but his throat clogged, and he couldn't get the words out. Never in his life had he known people like his LCR family. Every good thing that had happened to him was because of Noah McCall and Last Chance Rescue. Even meeting Giselle had been the result of his involvement with LCR.

Clearing his throat, he said, "Have I ever thanked you for what you've done for me?"

"Many times, but no thanks are necessary. You're one of the finest men I've had the pleasure of knowing. I'm proud of you."

If he didn't leave, he'd probably start crying, which would definitely ruin his reputation as a tough-assed LCR operative. Still, he grabbed Noah in a hard hug, "You're the best role model I could have ever asked for."

Returning the hug, Noah stepped back, smiling. "And now you have a son."

"Yeah. Scares me to death. The responsibility is mind-boggling."

"Can't think of anyone who's more up for the challenge. How are things with Giselle?"

"Not sure yet. Today's the first day she's looked like the old Giselle. We haven't talked about the future."

"Samara mentioned something about a movie night for the kids. She's going to ask Giselle if Gio can come."

The McCall kids had taken to Gio like he was their long-lost little brother. "He would love that."

"Good. That'll give you time to pack for your vacation and to talk."

With one more slap on Raphael's back, Noah nudged him toward the door. "Go have dinner with your wife."

CHAPTER FORTY-FIVE

She was as nervous as she'd ever been in her life. Raphael had called an hour ago and asked her out to dinner. Like an actual date.

A few minutes before Raphael called, Samara had knocked on their door with an invitation for Gio to have a movie night and sleepover with his new friends, Evie and Micah. Gio had been napping at the time, but the minute he woke and she told him, he'd been ecstatic. He already adored Evie and Micah.

An hour later, Evie and Micah had arrived to pick him up. Gio had barely stopped to blow his mama a kiss before he was out the door with them.

Her little boy was the most amazing child. She was sure all mothers thought that about their children, but Giselle was sure she was right. Other than crying and clinging to her after she'd been rescued, Gio had been amazingly adaptive.

Even though she hated the Fletchers with the fury of a thousand suns, she was grateful that they hadn't damaged him emotionally. Mavis Tenpenny likely had a lot to do with his emotional stability. Giselle believed she had done everything she could to protect Gio from the Fletchers, and Giselle was grateful.

Things were falling into place quickly. She and Raphael still hadn't had time alone with each other to talk. With Gio staying overnight with Noah's family, she knew that time had come. She was both excited and fearful. What if she was misreading the signs? What if he didn't want them to be a family the same way she did?

Knowing worrying would not help, Giselle forced herself to settle down and get ready for her date. She had come this far. She would do everything within her power to make sure she and Raphael had a second chance.

After a long hot bath, in which she gave herself a facial and conditioned her hair, Giselle felt like a new person. The bruises on her face were still there, but were fading. After a little makeup magic, they were barely noticeable.

She slid into one of the dresses she had received on her wedding day. This one, a short, black cocktail dress, was both flirty and sexy. She couldn't wait for Raphael to see her in it. How long had it been since she'd wanted to look pretty? Her life, at least in the last year, had been about survival. Looking nice hadn't mattered. Tonight was a different story. Raphael hadn't given her words of love, but his actions spoke of deep caring. Had he forgiven her for leaving him? For not letting him know right away that he had a son? Could he accept the choices she had made? Could they move on? Together?

A knock on the door pulled her from her worries. Whatever happened, he needed to understand one thing. She loved him and had never stopped. She prayed that would be enough.

The instant she opened the door, Raphael felt a huge weight lift from his shoulders. Giselle not only looked beautiful, but her eyes were free of shadows. The hope that gleamed in their depths matched the hope in his heart. They'd had a rough beginning, but more than anything, he wanted the future he'd always dreamed for them.

"You look beautiful."

"So do you." She took in his gray suit, confusion in her eyes. "Where did you get dressed?"

"My apartment. If you like, I'll take you there after dinner."

"I'd love to see it. Is it far from here?"

"Just a few miles."

He held out the vase filled with flowers he'd stopped to pick up on the way.

Taking the flowers, she sniffed them appreciatively. "Thank you, they're lovely." She turned away and placed them on the table behind her. "They look good there, don't you think?"

He took her arm, swung her around to face him. "Can we start again?"

He almost groaned out loud. He hadn't planned to blurt that out at her. He had a whole night of seduction planned.

She apparently didn't mind as she beamed a smile at him. "I would like that very much."

Slowly pulling her close, he closed his arms around her. She pressed her face against his shoulder. He held her gently, securely, absorbing the fact that he could. That she would let him.

"I never stopped loving you, Raphael."

Tilting her chin up with his fingers, he lowered his head and kissed her softly. She had been his heart from the moment he'd met her. That had never changed.

"There's not a day that's gone by that I haven't thought of you. Even when I thought I hated you, I loved you."

"I'm sorry for—"

"No, baby. We're past that now."

"But after I—"

He pressed his fingers to her lips to stop her. "You have nothing to apologize for. Every decision you made was done out of love. I know that now."

Love shone in her eyes. "You do understand."

"Hardheaded is my middle name. I'm so damn sorry that I was so clueless. All I could talk about was my plans for the future and completely disregarded the facts."

"Never apologize that you had dreams. When Gio grows up, he'll be able to say his father is a hero in every respect."

"And his mother is one of the strongest, bravest people I know. I love you, Giselle. From the moment I met you, I loved you."

She wrapped her arms around him, hugged him hard. "I can't believe we're finally together."

"And we have a son."

"Yes." She smiled softly. "We never talked about children."

"We never talked about a lot of things. I want to know what you want, Giselle."

"I want us to be a family."

"That's a good start, but what else?"

"We'll figure it out along the way." She stood on her toes, spoke against his mouth. "We don't have to go out. We can stay here."

"No. I'm going to ply you with delicious food and drink, and then we're going to my apartment. I want you on my bed, in my bed."

"But Gio—"

"I checked with Samara. Told her my plans. She said Gio was in the middle of scarfing down his second slice of pizza and was very happy. She said if there's any problem at all, she would call us right away. We can be back here in a matter of minutes."

Taking his hand, she said, "Then what are we waiting for?"

They headed toward the door, but Raphael stopped on the way and looked down at her.

"What are you looking at?"

Instead of speaking, he cupped her face with his hands, tilted her head, and then kissed her again, softly, sweetly. This was a new beginning for them. He wanted every moment from here on out to be perfect.

Stepping back, he looked down at her beautiful face and answered, "Perfection."

***

To say it was the best night of her life would be an understatement. She had never been romanced before—not really. Raphael had everything planned out. The restaurant was low-key elegance. They were seated at an intimate table for two, and though the room was filled with people, everyone else seemed to be as she and Raphael were—lost in their own little world.

Soft music played around them, candles glowed, and the food was divine. The muted conversations from the other diners added a pleasant hum to the ambience.

"It seems so strange to be sitting here in public like this."

Raphael squeezed her hand. "You've been in hiding for a long time."

"Even those few years when I was married to Danny, I felt like I was hiding. They were so protective of their privacy. Being seen in public was a rare event and was usually staged for whatever publicity they deemed appropriate."

"You haven't talked much about Danny. Was he good to you?"

She wouldn't lie—those days were over. "No. But neither was he cruel. He simply didn't care. My usefulness passed rather quickly. He ignored me most of the time."

"And Gio?"

"When he remembered him, he was kind to him. I think Gio ended up looking at him as a fun uncle that he saw only occasionally."

She looked away for a moment. She didn't want to spoil the evening, but she wanted to get this said and move on. "Marrying him was one of the biggest mistakes of my life, and I take the blame for being so clueless. I was lonely and naïve. Danny saw an opportunity."

She held up her hand to stop Raphael from protesting. She knew he would give her excuses for what she had done, but she refused to back away and not own her mistakes. And she needed to tell him everything.

"A few weeks before Danny died, we had an argument. The worst we'd ever had. I told him I wanted out of the marriage, that it wasn't really a marriage. He laughed and told me good luck with that. Fletchers don't divorce.

"I told him he didn't want to be married to me. I accused him of not only knowing who I was when we married, but staging the whole thing to hurt his parents. He laughed and said so very casually that he had wondered if I would ever figure that out. He said he knew within a day of meeting me who I was. That his father's people did favors for him, too."

She smiled, though she knew it was a bitter one. "I was just a tool to embarrass his parents. Nothing more."

There was no surprise in Raphael's expression.

"You already knew."

"I suspected. Seemed too damn coincidental. He was the one who called the tabloids and told them, wasn't he?"

"Yes. He said he knew they'd print the story without going to his parents for permission."

"And he didn't give a damn about the danger he put you and your family in." Raphael brought the hand he was holding to his mouth. "You said you woke up the next day and was surprised you were married. Do you think he drugged you?"

"I don't know. I never asked him. It actually never even occurred to me until later, after everything that happened with Daniel and Clarissa. I believed we'd both just had too much to drink. But now..." She shrugged and shook her head. "I don't know. I guess I'll never know."

"I wish he was alive so I could kick his ass."

The thought cheered her. "I would have paid money to see that."

"He's gone, though. And so are the Fletchers. They can't hurt you ever again."

She knew that. It was just going to take some time to regain confidence in herself.

Taking a breath, she said, "There's one more thing I need to tell you."

"What's that?"

"The letter I wrote you. I—"

"Sweetheart, we're past that. I understand why you said those things."

She shook her head. "That's not it. I wrote two letters."

"Two? Why?"

"I knew I had to say things, tell you horrible lies to make sure you didn't try to find me, that you would let me go. One of the handlers for the WITSEC program gave me some advice.

She told me to write what I really wanted to say and get it out of my system. Then write another letter, one that would keep you away. So you would hate me enough to let me go.

"And that's what I did. Before I wrote the letter full of lies, I wrote another one. It helped to be able to tell you the truth, even if you never got to see the letter."

"Do you remember what it said?"

Locking her eyes with his, she quoted the words she'd written and lived with for over seven years: "My darling Raphael, I'm dying inside. My soul is crushed, my heart is broken. There aren't enough tears in the world to overcome this pain. There will never be another love for me but you. You are my everything. From the first moment I met you to the last time I saw you, you were my first, my last, my always. Forever."

She watched him swallow, his mouth tremble, and something hot flared in his eyes. Surprising her, he pulled several bills from his wallet, placed them beside his empty plate, and stood. "Let's go."

She went to her feet beside him and followed him out the door. The promise in his eyes matched the one in her heart. She was his, he was hers. That was the way it had always been. That's the way it would always be. Forever.

EPILOGUE

Tree Top, Nebraska

Thea Ramirez placed the last book on the shelf and turned to survey her surroundings. Her store, Book Notes, had come a long way in a short amount of time. When she had learned she was moving here, she had been determined to make at least one of her dreams come true. She had lived in books most of her life. They had been her escape, her refuge. Owning her own bookstore was her dream. Creating the perfect place for others to come and escape from their own worries was her goal. She had achieved both.

When she had first arrived, she and her family had attended several churches to get a feel for the community. She knew she had found the right church and the right place when the minister at the last church talked about how God leads you where he wants you to go. Those words had set in her mind, settled in her heart, and she knew a peace she hadn't felt in decades. She was where she had been led.

She had a good life here. Her children had settled in better than she had hoped. They had friends and relationships. They had a normal life, and that's what she'd always wanted for them.

And she, after so many years, had started dating. So far, it was just a casual thing. He owned the hardware store across the street. They met for coffee several days a week, and last week they'd had an impromptu picnic in the park. He was a widower and wanted to go slow. And with all her baggage, slow was the only speed she would even consider. Building a relationship one day at a time was a new thing for her, and she wanted to savor the freedom of being able to do so.

Neither she nor her children acted as if they had anything to hide. After all the numerous places they had lived, she had learned that hiding in plain sight was the best way to not attract attention. If you didn't act like you had secrets, then no one tried to find them out and exploit them.

Life wasn't perfect, but it was definitely on the upswing. The phone call she'd received last week increased that optimism to its highest level. She was accustomed to waiting, but had to admit the last few days had been excruciating.

The front door opened on a slight squeak, and she turned. The young couple standing in the doorway, with the small boy in front of them, was the most beautiful sight she could imagine. A dream she'd had for years had finally come true.

Holding out her arms, she held her breath as they all ran toward her. Embracing her precious daughter, grandson, and the man she'd always dreamed Giselle would find again, Sarah knew her life could now be complete.

Standing at the doorway, Noah and Samara watched the family reunion. This was the best outcome and what LCR strived to do every day. Bring loved ones home.

Her eyes gleaming with happy tears, Samara beamed up at him. "You do good work, Noah McCall."

Gazing down at the love of his life, he said softly, "*We* do good work, Samara McCall. And I wouldn't have it any other way."

DEAR READER

Thank you so much for reading **Running Strong, An LCR Elite Novel**. I sincerely hope you enjoyed Raphael and Giselle's love story. If you would be so kind as to leave a review at your favorite online book site to help other readers find this book, I would sincerely appreciate it.

If you would like to be notified when I have a new release, be sure to sign up for my newsletter. http://authornewsletters.com/christyreece/

To learn about my other books and what I'm currently writing, please visit my website. http://www.christyreece.com

Follow me on:
Facebook: https://www.facebook.com/AuthorChristyReece/
Twitter: https://twitter.com/ChristyReece

Books by Christy Reece

LCR ELITE Series

Running On Empty, An LCR Elite Novel

Chance Encounter, An LCR Elite Novel

Running Scared, An LCR Elite Novel

Running Wild, An LCR Elite Novel

Running Strong, An LCR Elite Novel

LCR Elite Box Set: Books 1 - 3

GREY JUSTICE Series

Nothing To Lose, A Grey Justice Novel

Whatever It Takes, A Grey Justice Novel

Too Far Gone, A Grey Justice Novel

A Matter Of Justice, A Grey Justice Novel

A Grey Justice Novel Box Set: Books 1 - 3

LAST CHANCE RESCUE Series

Rescue Me, A Last Chance Rescue Novel

Return To Me, A Last Chance Rescue Novel

Run To Me, A Last Chance Rescue Novel

No Chance, A Last Chance Rescue Novel

Second Chance, A Last Chance Rescue Novel
Last Chance, A Last Chance Rescue Novel
Sweet Justice, A Last Chance Rescue Novel
Sweet Revenge, A Last Chance Rescue Novel
Sweet Reward, A Last Chance Rescue Novel
Chances Are, A Last Chance Rescue Novel

WILDEFIRE Series
writing as Ella Grace

Midnight Secrets, A Wildefire Novel
Midnight Lies, A Wildefire Novel
Midnight Shadows, A Wildefire Novel

Acknowledgments

Special thanks to the following people for helping make this book possible:

My husband, for your love, support, numerous moments of comic relief, and almost always respecting my chocolate stash.

The amazing Joyce Lamb, for your awesome copyediting and fabulous advice.

Marie Force's eBook Formatting Fairies for their great formatting skills.

Tricia Schmitt (Pickyme) for your gorgeous cover art.

The Reece's Readers Facebook groups, for all your support and encouragement.

Anne, always my first reader, who goes above and beyond, and then goes the extra mile, too.

My beta readers, Crystal, Hope, Julie, Alison, and Kris for their encouragement and great suggestions.

Kara for reading the finished version and finding those things I missed even after reading it a thousand times.

Linda Clarkson of Black Opal Editing, who, as always, did an amazing job of finding those superfluous words. So appreciate your eagle eye, Linda.

Special thanks to Hope for your help and assistance in a multitude of things. Thank you for your generous heart and for keeping me on track.

To all my readers, thank you for your patience. Your emails, Facebook, and Twitter messages about Raphael and Giselle's love story were very much appreciated. Though their story was years in the making, I hope you feel it was worth the wait.

An extra special shout-out to those readers who have followed Noah McCall and the Last Chance Rescue gang from the beginning. Thank you so much for your support!

ABOUT THE AUTHOR

Christy Reece is the award winning, NYT Bestselling Author of dark romantic suspense. She lives in Alabama with her husband and a menagerie of pets.

Christy loves hearing from readers and can be contacted at Christy@ChristyReece.com.

Have you met Grey Justice?

Don't miss the romantic suspense series readers have called "A phenomenal series with twists, turns, and surprises galore!"

The Grey Justice Group

There's more than one path to justice

Justice isn't always swift or fair and only those who have felt the pain of denied justice can truly understand its bitter taste. But justice delayed doesn't have to be justice denied. Enter the Grey Justice Group, ordinary citizens swept up in extraordinary circumstances. Led by billionaire philanthropist Grey Justice, this small group of operatives gains justice for victims when other paths have failed.

No one escapes justice.

Turn the page to learn more.

NOTHING TO LOSE
A Grey Justice Novel
Book One

Choices Are Easy When You Have Nothing Left To Lose

Kennedy O'Connell had all the happiness she'd ever dreamed—until someone stole it away. Now on the run for her life, she has a choice to make—disappear forever or make those responsible pay. Her choice is easy.

Two men want to help her, each with their own agenda.

Detective Nick Gallagher is accustomed to pursuing killers within the law. Targeted for death, his life turned inside out, Nick vows to bring down those responsible, no matter the cost. But the beautiful and innocent Kennedy O'Connell brings out every protective instinct. Putting aside his own need for vengeance, he'll do whatever is necessary to keep her safe and help her achieve her goals.

Billionaire philanthropist Grey Justice has a mission, too. Dubbed the 'White Knight' of those in need of a champion, few people are aware of his dark side. Having seen and experienced injustice—Grey knows its bitter taste. Gaining justice for those who have been wronged is a small price to pay for a man's humanity.

With the help of a surprising accomplice, the three embark on a dangerous game of cat and mouse. The stage is set, the players are ready...the game is on. But someone is playing with another set of rules and survivors are not an option.

WHATEVER IT TAKES
A Grey Justice Novel
Book Two

To Save His Family, She May Be His Only Hope

Working for the shadowy division of the Grey Justice Group is the perfect job for Kathleen Callahan. Compartmentalizing and staying detached is her specialty. Get in, do the job, get out, her motto. Wealthy businessman Eli Slater is the only man to penetrate her implacable defenses and she fights to resist him at every turn.

Eli Slater has worked hard to overcome his family's past and repair the damage they caused. A new light comes into his life in the form of security specialist Kathleen Callahan. Even though she rejects him and everything he makes her feel, Eli is relentless in his pursuit, determined to make her his own.

Darkness has a way of finding and destroying light and Eli learns his family's troubles are far from over. Dealing with threats and attempts on his own life is one thing, but when those he loves are threatened, it's a whole new game. And he'll stop at nothing to win.

But evil has a familiar face, along with an unimaginable goal of destruction, putting both Eli and Kathleen in the crosshairs and threatening the happiness they never believed they'd find.

TOO FAR GONE
A Grey Justice Novel
Book Three

Some Obsessions Can Be Deadly

Gabriella Mendoza has lived her life in seclusion. Guarded by the most corrupt men in the world, she has no chance for escape until an unexpected meeting with the mysterious Grey Justice Group changes everything. Gabriella is free for the first time in her life, but is that freedom all a lie?

Vengeance is Jonah Slater's only purpose. Finding the man who killed his fiancée and making him pay is his only goal. Babysitting the pampered princess of a crime boss is not part of his agenda. But the more he gets to know Gabriella, the more he realizes that protecting her might be the most worthwhile thing he's ever done.

They thought they knew the threats, believed they were contained. Jonah and Gabriella soon learn that evil has varying degrees and many faces. And very often, the deadliest is the one you never see coming.

A MATTER OF JUSTICE
A Grey Justice Novel
Book Four

Their past is complicated, their future is deadly

She came from nothing and was no one until an evil man formed her into the perfect weapon, a beautiful creature of destruction. Capturing her prey held few challenges, until her target and her heart collided, and then the world came down around her. Irelyn Raine has worked hard to bury her past, but escape isn't always possible, especially when the one man she trusts above all others throws her back into the hell she swore she'd never revisit. Now Irelyn has no choice but to face down her demons.

Grey Justice lives by a standard few would approve or understand. Gaining justice for victims can be a messy business, and the outcome isn't always pretty. One woman knows all his secrets--the one woman who could break him. Irelyn Raine is his weakness and his strength, his shame and his redemption.

Someone else knows all their secrets, all their sins, and he'll use everything within his power to destroy what they've built together.

Surviving alone isn't possible, but can they find their way back to each other in time? Or will one of them be left behind? This time, forever?

No one escapes justice.

Made in the USA
Columbia, SC
04 June 2019